THE AUGUR'S VIEW

A
"New Earth Chronicles"
Novel by

VICTORIA LEHRER

THE AUGUR'S VIEW
New Earth Chronicles – Book 1
Copyright © 2019 by Victoria Lehrer
Cover Art Copyright © 2019 by Richard Tran

FIRST EDITION SOFTCOVER
ISBN: 1622533704
ISBN-13: 978-1-62253-370-1

Editor: Becky Stephens
Interior Designer: Lane Diamond

EVOLVED PUBLISHING™

www.EvolvedPub.com
Evolved Publishing LLC
Butler, Wisconsin, USA

Printed in Book Antiqua font.

BOOKS BY
VICTORIA LEHRER

DEDICATION

For fellow travelers seeking the heart of the labyrinth.

Doors

I

As Eena plotted her escape from Township 26, she never imagined departing in a plane with a mystery pilot for an unknown reason to an unidentified location.

The first citizen to be airborne since the Solar Flash of 2034, the twenty-five-year-old's gut screamed this flight was not to fulfill dreams of freedom. Nor did landing at a ghostly airport amid surreal runways of haphazardly parked jets ease the tension in her belly. A man in uniform told her they were in Transtopia Metro, formerly Colorado Springs. He escorted her to an overhauled car, and they sped away, swerving around potholes until they skidded to a stop at the hospital in Fort Carson, Colorado.

The stale air of an old building assaulted Eena's nostrils as she descended three flights of stairs, entered a long, narrow hall, and hesitated at the open door on the right. A man at a desk looked up from his clipboard to greet her by name and introduce himself as Doctor Olsen.

In the low-ceilinged room, the fluorescent lights buzzed and crackled a warning that she, a seeker of fellow insurgents, had landed in the lair of the controllers.

Head tilted, the doctor leaned back in his chair as though sizing her up beneath half lowered lids. Then he shifted forward and announced with the exuberance of a salesman, "You're about to learn that today is your lucky day."

At a loss, she stared blankly into gray eyes that matched the walls.

The official stood up. "But first a tour. Come with me."

Past a succession of closed doors, the doctor's shoes echoed an irregular staccato until, at a door labeled GESTATION CHAMBER, he paused to open it with an expectant flair. "Prepare yourself for the technology of the future."

A sense of unease clenched her gut as Eena entered the dimly lit room where recessed florescence cast a blue glow on transparent tubes that lined the walls. The liquid in each glass womb buoyed a baby attached to an artificial umbilical cord, a conveyance from an automated source of metered sustenance. At the far end of the room amid the murmur of soft beeps, a clinician with a clipboard and an air of detached efficiency checked monitors and gauges.

"Behold the future workforce," Olsen said as though a drumroll should accompany his introduction, "pride of the Social Engineering Initiative."

The subterranean realm enmeshed the visitors in gloom while Doctor Olsen prattled on about in vitro fertilization procedures, and red lights blinked the pulse of infant hearts beating in indifferent voids.

Reeling from the impact of this violation of the biological ordering of life, Eena leaned against the wall. A chilling warmth curved into her spine, and she jerked forward, recoiling from contact with the container that held a floating infant.

Apparently enamored with his clinical underworld, Doctor Olsen remained oblivious to Eena's emotional state and continued to lecture to an audience of one who heard only unintelligible babble.

He smiled at the conclusion of his dissertation. "Clones," he said and, with a dramatic sweep of his arm, paused as though to let her absorb the implications of the surrounding wealth of potential.

A baby, orphaned from the soothing beat of his mother's heart, sought comfort as he sucked a tiny thumb.

"*Your* future workforce, if you assume the mantle of your heritage — at least, on your father's side."

Eena struggled to withdraw her attention from the hypnotic hold of amniotic waters that answered every infant need except a mother's devotion. Fighting back the assault of dizziness, she looked around for a chair. "I need to sit."

She swayed. With a tight grip on her arm, Doctor Olsen hurried her away from the glass containers for the warehousing of cloned workers. The doctor's shoes *click-clacked* past the dun-colored doors, and they returned to the room where the nightmare had begun.

When Eena's head cleared, she sat across from the official and looked him straight in the eyes. "Please speak to me directly. You've alluded to 'my *lucky* day' and '*my* workforce.' No more hints. Why am I here?"

Doctor. Olsen's eyes flickered slightly as though impacted by the force of her impatience. He picked up a narrow book and slid it to her. "This is your genealogy on your father's side."

As Eena focused on the fifty-page chart of the family tree, he spoke another riddle. "Your father was what's known as 'a royal blood'—a direct descendent of Anu—ancestor of the puppeteers who have pulled the strings behind the human stage for thousands of years."

With those words, the dreamy sense of undisclosed truth that had dogged Eena's youth snapped her to wakefulness. Her parents, now buried beneath the rubble left by a devastating tornado, had paraded vague, disparate images from her European lineage, bequeathing speculation as her only heritage from her father's side.

Yet, the Hopi/Dine' roots that endowed her mother with doe-eyed beauty and a placid disposition had woven living connections into her psyche. Cords pulsed a vibrant continuum as her mother midwifed countless births, placing each newborn on the mother's breast close to her soothing heartbeat.

The evader was Eena's tall distinguished father, a naturopathic physician of penetrating intelligence, who alluded to his ancestry with an offhand shrug. Now, as though again to cheat her yearning to know the truth, a chart compelled her gaze along a remote succession of titles and names. Unlike Hopi/Dine' stories that quickened the pulse with tales of heroic feats, the inked genealogy entombed the echoes of the past in unresponsive silence.

The doctor's droned words pummeled her ears while her eyes traced the schematic, confirming generations descended from a single ancestor: Anu.

"What about the rest of humanity? Are we—they—not the children of Anu?"

"Ah, the worker race. The remnant of a catastrophic flood, with switched off DNA."

"DNA?"

"Yes, genetically modified by the progenitors."

"The progenitors?"

"Anu's cohorts, the progenitors, engineered a docile class of sturdy toilers, worshipful of royal hierarchies and willing to fight for them."

"I don't see the connection to inactive DNA."

"Genetic keys responsible for independence, assertiveness, rebelliousness—traits like that."

"Hmm, I think I'm getting it."

"Problem is the coronal mass ejections and concurrent Earth changes have given the royal bloods some major headaches."

Eena looked evenly at Doctor Olsen. "Other than blown transformers, fried engines and destroyed surveillance satellites?"

"Since Solar Flash, geneticists have made a startling discovery."

"That being...."

"A reversal of the blocked genetic traits in captured insurgents, runners and out-of-the-box thinkers. My understanding is that a charged plasma field entering our solar system caused both Solar Flash and a magnetic reversal of the deactivated DNA."

Eena nodded slowly. "You're saying the plasma stream triggered a DNA switch-on of insurgent traits in certain worker-bred people." Hope tweaked a sudden realization. *I'm going to find these rebels. They are our allies.*

Doctor Olsen whirled a pen between thumbs and forefingers. "Which brings us back to you, a mixture of royal blood and worker. There are many like yourself, children of defectors from the pure bloodline. But, after generations of intermarriage, their blood is more diluted than yours. To find a fifty-percenter is very rare, mostly because defections from the ruling class are rare."

Eena could be doggedly persistent. "So, how does this revelation make me 'lucky'?"

"You will never enjoy the prerogative of the ruling ten thousandth of a percent to set the course of human evolution. However, you are being offered an official role in the scientific design and ordering of the general population."

Eena stared at him, her brain offering its own analogy. "You mean like a beehive."

He looked startled as though such allusions to the natural ordering of life were far removed from his consciousness.

"You know, drones, nurses, scouts, guards, the queen—every insect in the hive doing its repetitive job instinctively and without question."

He whirled the pen to a vertical position and tapped the end on the desk. "Yes, like that. The landlords are offering you a choice—either to spend your life as a drone or to serve as the queen's attendant, so to speak."

Eena imagined herself feeding the queen bee royal jelly. Unable to penetrate the soulless eyes across the desk, she examined the tightly intertwined fingers on her lap.

"However, if you accept this honor, you will have to swear an oath of loyalty to your royal bloodline and its right to rule."

"I'm curious about my authority over runners from townships and insurgents against the Union of the Americas."

The doctor's next words sliced with a clean edge. "Eliminate them. Period. No exceptions."

Eena scanned the jutting jaw past clamped lips to cold slate eyes.

Her host glared ominously. "You will be watched."

She turned a page as though intently studying the family tree. "How long do I have to decide?" Concealing emotions that broiled behind an impassive face, Eena watched the doctor's raised eyebrows register surprise—as if it were inconceivable she would choose to be any kind of worker other than a privileged official.

"One week. If you decide to accept this honor, your rigorous personality purification processes will begin."

She nodded placidly while revulsion for the probable nature of "rigorous personality purification processes" churned her stomach.

Doctor Olsen leaned back in his chair to look at her over the pen twirling between his thumbs and index fingers. "I must warn you. You will not want to betray your benefactors with the slightest bending of the SEI policies."

"SEI?"

"Social Engineering Initiative."

"I understand." Eena closed the record of her lineage.

The doctor's lips contrived a smile. He placed the pen in the black mesh metal holder, retrieved the book and brusquely tidied his desk. "Is there anything else I can help you with?"

Eena cocked her head, her eyes focused on the red binders lining the shelf behind Doctor Olsen. "So, what happens to those babies when they outgrow the containers?"

"Nurseries, of course, where they'll be raised according to the strict guidelines of the SEI. The coming generation of workers will be *our* design from test tube to gestation tank to first through tenth developmental stage management facilities. None of these fortunate children will be subjected to the whims, outbursts, indecision, coddling—generally faulty modeling of biological parents. Instead, scientific protocols will steer their growth to an appropriate slot in the corporate workforce. When the grid is restored, we will resume the Enhanced Human Phase of the SEI."

"Enhanced Human?"

"Bionic humans with chip enhancements for ongoing and instant responsiveness to directives from the central A.I."

This assertion jolted Eena from appalled to perplexed.

Doctor Olsen seemed to enjoy her confusion. "Also known as 'The Black Sun,' placed in space countless ages ago by a race of sentient robots."

Eena leveled her return gaze as this information meteor cratered her brain.

"I've presented you a brief introduction to this." He pointed to the row of two-inch blood red volumes, books one through eight. "The Manual for Social Engineering Objectives and Protocols." As he read aloud the title, consummate zeal sounded each word.

A silent void engulfed Eena as the deafening *whoosh* of tiny hearts pulsed humanity's doomed future. She struggled to hold her shoulders erect.

Eena stood, lifted her chin, and nodded that the meeting was concluded. As she turned toward the driver seated in the hall, she felt like sprinting from this realm of gloom, but forced herself to walk with stoic resolve through the door.

Imperial Governor Charles Scholtz awaited his next appointment behind imposing carved teak doors. His office resided on the tenth floor of a still-standing tower bordering the scene of charred rubble—all that remained of the northern two-thirds of Transtopia Metro, the former Colorado Springs. A fifty-two-year-old of impeccable royal lineage, he resented the power shrink caused by Solar Flash. He resented being stripped of unbridled manipulation of those known as underlings, workers and eaters. He resented the severed connection with his god, the Black Sun.

Following the population-leveling effects of Solar Flash, remnants of the powerful Landlords of the World, such as himself, had settled in the midst of the underlings. But from this height he could look down on the workers crawling like ants along the sidewalk below. While he was exiled from his secluded mansions and denied access to the sky watch satellite, that elevated point of view helped keep things in perspective.

The governor's superior positioning enabled him to endure tiresome, but necessary, meetings with SEI officials. Awaiting his next encounter with annoyance, he looked at the refurbished electronic clock. While contact with social engineering scientists that groveled for his favor was an irritant, he did want to know about Doctor Olsen's meeting with the half-breed. As much as he disliked acknowledging a defector's offspring, she could prove useful.

Accustomed to godlike powers prior to Solar Flash, Scholtz and fellow progeny of Anu had siphoned the revenues of corporate appendages from the sale of arms, pharmaceuticals and petroleum. Meanwhile, humanity, the bionic workforce-in-the-making, breathed nano-particles rained from aircraft trails that cobwebbed the skies.

The White Sun's temper tantrum interrupted that glorious reign. But within a decade, by means of a restored grid and the rigorously re-implemented Social Engineering Initiative, the royal lineage of Anu would rise again.

He turned to the wall map of Sector 10. A red circle targeted the vast forested portion bordered on the south and west sides by six townships plus Techno City, and on the east by Transtopia Metro. He needed the labor of every underling survivor to restore the hierarchy of dominance as soon as possible. Yet, he suspected an absentee workforce of hundreds, whose skills were essential to reconstruction, to be secreted in those mountains. And he knew that runners from the townships had escaped to that rugged terrain along the Continental Divide.

He sighed in response to a tap at the door. "Yes?"

"Doctor Olsen is here."

Not disposed to pleasantries, Imperial Governor Charles Scholtz stared at the approaching scientist and nodded for him to sit.

Olsen swallowed nervously. "Eena Burgemeister escaped, taking five runners with her."

Outrage swallowed Scholtz's initial disbelief. An insolent half-blood, not only rejecting his generosity, but also collecting runners.

Leveling a hard stare at the man opposite him, he spoke with controlled fury. "We will find them." He scanned the forest enclosed in red on the map as though their whereabouts would jump out at him until the angry jab of his finger tore a hole in the heart of the mountain forests.

A gentle gust of pine-scented air feathered Eena's cheek as she recalled the suffocating blow—the stark presentation of wall-to-wall containers of infants—that propelled her escape from Township 26 to Three Mountains Community. Following the forest trail atop Quartz Mountain, she shook off the memory of the visit to Fort Carson. Nonetheless, in the early morning freshness the silken strands of a dew-laden web warned that the control network would soon spider to Three Mountains. In a few years, the cords woven by surveillance satellites, the censored World Wide Web and sky-born, population-subduing nanites would again ensnare the planet. Inevitably, the claws that wound the surrounding townships in strands of deception would bind the escapees in this mountain haven, enabling the spinners of the web to devour the runners' creative juices.

Eena's feet, moccasined in Matoskah's gift, felt the strong roots that secured earth and trees; yet, each step heralded humanity's precarious future. Of course, it was foolish for a woman in possession of a single pistol to strategize—okay, fantasize—how Three Mountains, a tiny, unarmed community of DNA-triggered runners, could depose a heavily weaponized regime. Yet she did. *Mine is the only gun. But before this saga ends, we will possess an arsenal.* A warbler's trill echoed her intent.

Eena had taken the problem to the old medicine man, who, in his familiar, enigmatic way, silently pushed together a little pile of grass and held an ignited stick beside it. What did that have to do with her impassioned query? No more was forthcoming. They'd have to continue that conversation—such as it was—another time.

A herd of deer crossed the trail ahead as she recalled the words of Doctor Olsen: "Through the SEI, the landlords are breeding a docile herd and culling the DNA-triggered insurgents." She wondered if she was so rebellious because of genes switched on by charged fields. Or was it the bloodline she shared with those she most detested?

Curiously, the lead pair of deer turned a sharp right at a tree beside the trail. Watching the next three execute the exact same swerve, she smiled inwardly. She and the landlords did have one desire in common:

both wanted to find these insurgents. *Freedom seekers. Divided, we're conquered; united — perhaps still conquered. But, who knows, maybe our rebellious spinnerets will weave our own web of power.*

Not one of the deer continued *behind* the tree to follow the herd's path. As Eena puzzled over the deer's odd behavior, her eyes followed a vine that wound its way straight up the trunk. Intertwined vines about thirty feet high formed a wide, symmetrical archway between two trees. The midsection of the arch grew as if extending over something solid. But no support was there, causing her to pause and ruminate over nature's remarkable feat. Knowing it's silly for a grown woman to respond to a childlike impulse, in which any opening is an invitation, she stepped through the vine bower — and into another world.

The Portal

2

Eena searched frantically for the familiar pines of Quartz Mountain as huge red-brown trunks closed ranks around her. Though the temperature was still cool, increased humidity caressed her skin. Cloud wisps mingled with a hazy mixture of terracotta reds amidst an array of muted greens as her gaze clarified a fantastic terrain. The trunk of the closest sequoia was so enormous, she imagined herself the size of the fairytale character, Thumbelina and speculated it would take close to twenty-five people with arms outstretched, fingers touching, to reach around its massive girth. She tilted her head back, her eyes following the staggering height of the giant conifer to the green foliage that, obscured by cloudbanks, capped the reddish bark.

Closer to her face a pale green butterfly, a swallowtail with brilliant blue eyes on its wings, flirted with her gaze. Entranced, Eena followed the enormous creature. The size of two fists, it fluttered and floated into a lush meadow for a rendezvous with the bright pink flowers of a hydrangea bush. Surrounding the soft radiance of the clearing, majestic sequoias reigned in stately splendor and barred the encroachment of shadowed forest beyond.

The only similarity between the portal-connected worlds was that in both Eena stood on a mountain slope, this incline being opposite the Quartz Mountain side. Feeling pulled farther into the exotic realm, she looked behind to locate the vine archway. But it wasn't there. As she searched for the arc of vines and alarm escalated to panic, Eena shifted her gaze from tree to tree until an escarpment, a background wall of solid rock jutting from the mountainside, commandeered her focus. Inwardly protesting the presence of the stone face at her point of entry, she peered until her gaze found the perfect symmetry of an arc of inlaid stones about thirty feet from the ground. The stone border continued straight to the ground on either side, right where the trees hosting the vines would be at the Quartz Mountain entrance.

Extending her arms forward, palms facing out, in case she was walking into a wall of solid granite, Eena retraced her steps through the portal and back again. Now confident of return access, she smiled with childish delight and resumed exploration of her newly discovered world.

Gurgling notes of water coursing over stone drew her to a nearby stream cascading down the mountainside. Tumbling over boulders and through gullies carved in remote ages, the crystalline flow guided Eena's descent through a primeval landscape of gargantuan proportions.

A half hour later, she arrived in a broad valley where the stream emptied into a river meandering through lush plains and waves of grass that rippled around trees. The sight of large birds ensconced in clusters stopped her in her tracks, and she slowly turned three hundred-sixty degrees beneath an expansive sky trafficked with the birds' takeoffs, flights and landings. Sunlight glinted on aquamarine plumage as flocks soared down to become patches of blue green moving in the pale green of the tall grass.

Excitement croaked her voice. "The birds—they're everywhere." When she realized those weren't flocks of large birds, astonishment gripped her. They were enormous, and she, proportionally miniature, like an inhabitant of Lilliput in *Gulliver's Travels*.

Something huge blocked Eena's view, and she almost lost her balance as she adjusted her focus to see a person looking down at her from the back of one of the creatures. Rider and bird spiraled downward, arcing to a landing a few feet away. As claws reached for Earth and powerful wings displaced the air with a resounding *phoom*, Eena brushed aside the curly black tendrils that swept across her view.

The mounted bird landed with wings momentarily extended, each easily a six-foot expanse from the torso. As the iridescent blue-green feathers folded along the coppery tinged underside, her gaze followed the powerful neck up to a small splash of copper behind the turquoise mandible. Crowning the head, a tall crest of pale, narrow feathers extended with diminishing length along the neck.

Eena stared in bemusement as the bird pilot slid down the back of her mount and stepped away at the base of the tail. Pulling an exotic fruit from a small pouch, she approached the head of the creature to feed him with one hand and stroke him with the other. With a resonance that rumbled from his throat to become a melodic coo, the bird arched into her touch and lowered his crown as if for a pleasant and familiar ritual. She murmured softly and pressed her cheek against one bony jaw as her free hand scratched the other.

A friendly smile lit the Polynesian features and crinkled tiny crows feet as her eyes turned toward Eena. "I'm Leiani." Spoken as though giving her name would allay Eena's confusion.

"Eena." After a brief pause, she asked, "The bird?"

"This is Diso, my nickname for him because he resembles a bird of paradise."

As Eena's gaze shifted back to Diso, she nodded, brimming with questions, not knowing what to ask first.

Leiani seemed to understand the visitor's speechless state. "My first trip here was an overwhelming experience as well."

Eena smiled her appreciation. "You're from the other side of the portal?"

After a final scratch, Diso moved away as Leiani answered. "Yes, my father first brought me here about twelve years ago."

"Your father?"

"He's from here, although I don't know if he's still alive in this world."

"*This* world?"

"The Land of Mu—also known as the Motherland of Earth's ancient civilizations: Peru, Egypt, India, to name a few."

As a voracious reader of alternative histories, referred to as "pseudo-science" by mainstream sources, Eena nodded.

Leiani continued with a matter-of-fact tone. "According to some sources, the last sinking of Mu was about 40,000 years ago."

"So the portal connects a different time as well as place." Eena's eyes turned toward the enormous bird devouring exotic fruit beside a tree.

"My father was the first bird pilot in Mu."

By now Eena was sufficiently grounded to be intrigued. "He trained them?" She noticed her companion wore on her upper arm a copper band etched with the vertical shape of a bird, head sideways, wings extended.

Leiani smiled again. "Come. You can listen to him in his own words."

Crossing the stream that had led Eena to the valley, the women followed the river toward a circle of tall rectangular stones — monoliths looming about forty feet above the ground in a circle close to fifty feet in diameter.

"This is similar to Stonehenge in England," Eena mused.

"Yes. It's also a sun calendar." Leiani led the way to the center of the circle. "The arrangement of the stones tracks seasonal events such as the solstices and equinoxes."

Eena's guide gestured toward stone benches around the center of the complex. "Have a seat."

Eena sat down as Leiani stepped toward two concentric circles of stones inlaid flat in the ground around a central stone platform. Strange etchings embellished the granite.

"The glyphs relate the story of the rise of the bird-riding culture in Mu. If you look closely, you'll see dots inconspicuously etched below the symbols. Pressed in sequence, they activate a code."

Leiani stepped on consecutive rectangles with one, two, then three dots, setting off a buzzing sound and a colorful spray of lights atop the platform. She hurried to sit next to Eena as the three-dimensional image of a man shimmered into view.

"It's a hologram," she whispered. "The speaker, my father, identifies himself simply as Birdman."

The figure standing with humble dignity appeared to be in his seventies. A copper armlet, etched with the symbol of an open-winged bird, encircled his forearm. The man's white cloth kilt was adorned with an overlay of long coppery feathers and trimmed with aquamarine plumage below the waist. Downy teal feathers covered a skullcap fitted over straight black hair cut chin length, and brown eyes set in Polynesian features faced the audience.

Static interfered with the beginning of the narration, but cleared up in time for the listeners to hear: "...the story of how I came to be called 'Birdman'."

Intrigued, Eena listened to Birdman describe how, from childhood through adolescence, he wooed the giant sky travelers. The latter stage of his narrative riveted her attention:

> By the time I turned fifteen, I began to envision the possibility of riding a young adult without interfering with the nesting cycle. Through the years of winning the sky travelers'

trust, I learned that, although fully grown at one year, they sexually mature at six years. During that intervening phase, they form flocks of adolescents, during which time piloting one would not interrupt courtship and nesting.

In order to get close to a particular chick, I built a sturdy ladder and leaned it against the branch that held the nest. For several weeks, I accustomed the parent birds to my presence on ever-higher rungs until I finally sat on the branch at eye level with the birds. I must admit this was a rather dangerous feat to attempt. Having received more than one bloody puncture wound to an arm or leg, I recommend great caution if you attempt this strategy. The only way I learned to spare myself those punishing jabs was to come prepared with peace offerings of star fruit, mango or guava.

Birdman continued to describe the bonding process during which he named the chick "Skylar." Eena paid close attention to the next segment containing information that sounded essential for anyone else wanting to pilot a sky traveler:

Skylar grew to be a fledgling accustomed to my voice and touch. As the yearling became a strong, short distance flyer, I noticed quite by accident that when I mentally called him, he came! I continued to perfect our telepathic communication even while planning the next big step — to fly with him. Day by day, I gained the full trust of the sky traveler, until at the age of one year he had grown to be a full-sized adult.

Gradually, I prepared Skylar to accept my weight as a mounted passenger by leaning into and on him. Then one day, standing at his tail section, I laid my entire body over Skylar's back. Startled, the bird mobilized into flight. I wrapped my arms around his neck and hung on for dear life. When Skylar finally landed, I immediately slid to the ground and approached his head for friendly reassurance. He had begun to relish a good scratch on the bony crest above his beak.

Soon Skylar came to accept it as natural that I should climb aboard to fly with him. I became adept at guiding him with light touches. The discovery of a psychic rapport between us led to guidance primarily by means of telepathy. Thus began my system of bonding with the birds and training them to allow riders.

I had not been to your world at that time, nor considered the possibility of piloting the birds through the portal.

The narrator continued for a few minutes more, describing in more detail the protocols he developed. The hologram shimmered out of view, startling Eena back into the present while the phrase "piloting the birds through the portal" fluttered like a swallowtail before her mind's eye.

"I noticed you stepped on three stones with dots, but there are actually six."

Leiani brushed away tears. "The second set activates another message. Altogether, it's rather a lot to take in on a first visit."

"So, is your father with you now in this world, in Mu?"

"No, I'm alone. The story of his life in America and how I came to live here is in a second message, which we can view another day."

Eena touched Leiani's arm. "On the other side of the portal and down the mountain are fellow runners from townships. You're welcome at Three Mountains Community."

Leiani beamed her joy, her eyes wide open, with one hand over her heart.

Drawn ever deeper into this fantasy world, Eena had a request, relayed in the tentative but eager voice of a child. "May I touch Diso?"

Wordlessly, Leiani slipped her arm through Eena's as though she were a long-lost sister and led her to the browsing bird.

"I'm not altogether sure of Diso's reaction, since I'm the only human he has ever known."

With Leiani positioned between the beak and Eena's extended arm, the visitor ran her fingers along the soft feathers of the neck. The bird's shiver of pleasure sent a responsive thrill through her fingertips, and she fluttered them over the raised hump of the forewing, her touch grazing the length of the wing.

Suddenly, the huge bird shifted position and his neck shot up, the head held high and watchful, the beak poised to strike. Eena jerked away her hand.

Reaching up to scratch Diso behind the jaw, Leiani spoke softly. "Augurs don't like their wings to be touched."

As the head descended to continue dismembering a mango, relief flooded Eena. "Augurs?"

"Yes, my father's name for the sky travelers."

"Where do they nest?"

"In those cypress trees lining the river. Come."

Glad to accept Leiani's invitation, Eena gazed at the augurs circling the cloudless sky above the savannah and landing in the trees. In this land of gigantic fauna and flora, she wasn't surprised that the massive trunks of the cypress trees rivaled, even surpassed, the girth of the redwoods. The trunk of the cypress just ahead of them was so huge Eena imagined a cozy room hollowed from its interior. The pair stepped over massive footholds securing the grassy shores and beneath lateral branching that formed graceful inverted skirts.

Immersed in a sea of *rumble-coo* bird communications, Eena became aware of a pulsing sensation and placed a hand over her chest in response to the vibration. The sonic drumming was so pleasant, comforting even, she gave Leiani a questioning look.

Her companion smiled. "The birds emit ultrasonic sounds beneath our hearing." Leiani halted beside her. "Look closely at the trees just ahead."

Eena peered into the dense foliage until she became aware of a tangled mass of large sticks and grass resting atop the thick branches near the base of the closest tree.

"A nest! Easily triple the size of large eagles' nests."

Leiani smiled. "And they last for many years. The birds mate for life and, unless a particularly strong storm destroys their nest, need to make only minor repairs for the twenty-five years or so they share it."

Eena touched her arm, and they paused. A fledgling soared to the ground and, in response to the resonant rumble-coo of the parent's encouragement, beat his wings furiously for the short flight back to the nest.

Though a sense of wonder in this world buoyed Eena, concerns for the one on the other side of the portal weighted her mood. A vague glimmer connected piloting augurs with proactively facing the challenges of a post-apocalyptic Earth, and the power of an inborn sense of purpose, directed her next demand. "Help me bond with an augur."

The
Runner

3

Before the horrific series of events shattered Gavin Michael's world, life in Bloomfield, New Mexico, was okay. Yes, the teen resented the dull confinement of high school seven hours a day, but since he never did homework, after school wasn't a problem. He had electronic games, TV, and the freedom to skateboard across town or explore the desert with Mackie on shared adventures—riding for miles on trail bikes, camping out far from home, and searching for buried treasure.

That was before Solar Flash blasted the grid in 2034, and with a dead engine, the plane crashed into a nearby apartment building, signaling the death of an era. Terrified, Gavin felt the shockwaves and watched smoke billow overhead. In the surrounding neighborhood, stillness prevailed—as though at the push of a pause button.

Splintering the fragile silence, which was eerily bereft of the shrill screech of sirens, his father yelled, "In the car!"

After Gavin and his parents piled in, he felt the jolt of a second shock when the ignition wouldn't turn over. Then, an hour later, the toilet wouldn't flush. And soon after that his mother cried because no water flowed from the kitchen faucet.

Life became a series of bizarre cessations of normalcy—the streets strewn with permanently stalled vehicles, no electricity or running water anywhere.

The following day he and his mother gazed at the walls violated by the jet's impact, jagged edges of stone engulfed in heaped rubble. "It's happened." They watched police and firemen scramble over piles of brick and concrete. "An EMP."

Gavin shot his mother a look. "A what?"

"An electromagnetic pulse from a solar flare. NASA released articles about this threat to the grid, to all electronics during recent years. Yet, there was no warning in last week's news."

That explained the killed engines, if not the Earth changes. A month later a third of the citizens of Bloomfield—those not in the path of horrific winds—were the lucky survivors.

The period of coronal mass ejections, plus escalated changes to Earth and living DNA, became known collectively as Solar Flash.

At first it felt like camping out when Gavin and his parents boiled water from the San Juan River over a wood fire and ate trout, crawdads, beans and pasta. Sharing the handful of still-standing structures, the survivors of the pre-Solar Flash world managed to hold out because they lived near the river.

After Gavin turned sixteen, when the army cargo trucks rolled in, he cheered exuberantly along with the motley gathering. They soon learned that the army had waited out Solar Flash half of a mile underground with heavy-duty trucks and supplies for a re-boot of civilization. But they weren't alone. There were whispers among the ranks that the powerful ruling families of the world had crawled topside to resume absolute control. The post-apocalyptic name given by dissenters to the now visible puppet masters was *landlords*.

The military fed the people before the officially-designated town father, Hugo Evans, arrived with three Social Engineering Initiative representatives to establish their headquarters.

Gavin noticed an unfamiliar emblem on uniform patches and vehicles. "The Union of the Americas? What's that about?" He traced his finger over the circle that enclosed two continents on the side of the jeep.

Bitter resignation contorted his father's face. "It's the final nail on the coffin of the U.S. Constitution."

Using the supplies stored in a Quonset hut near the remains of Bloomfield, the citizens of soon-to-be Township 23 worked alongside the UA military to restore electricity and running water before they plumbed, wired and framed in the housing units. Meanwhile, truckloads of people arrived to build and fill more units.

When the walls were up, Gavin stood next to his dad observing electricians install cameras on buildings facing the desert. "For protection?"

"For surveillance."

Gavin knew bands of armed rovers were a threat to towns. "To watch for rovers?"

"To watch us."

That was when Gavin realized the "citizens" were actually prisoners.

Concurrent with the construction, the UA confiscated all weapons while mechanics rebuilt the engines for six retriever vehicles to patrol the highways and ensure all citizens remained to enjoy the benefits of the scientifically managed and zealously enforced society.

Months later, when the hopeful families had finished roofing their future housing, the town father and his social engineering team faced two thousand people to share glowing plans for the scientific implementation of the perfect society. "You are among the fortunate citizens of Sector 10 of the Union of the Americas of the World Federation to take part in this futuristic experiment." Hugo Evans beamed.

At seventeen Gavin knew those were code words for "futuristic totally controlled lives." He felt caged by the security cameras staring into the desert. "Mom, I'm dying in this place. We're like rats in a maze."

"Go get Mackie." Her enigmatic smile said she had a plan.

At first, his best friend, older and more cautious, refused. "No way."

Gavin was relentless, and Mackie finally caved. As Gavin's mother pretended to shake out a blanket to hide them from the eye of the camera, they escaped to freedom literally undercover. The forbidden treks to the ruins of farmsteads bordering the east end of the township were glorious times.

They ended when Mackie trained to become a retriever—to nab escapees like them.

Two years later, nineteen-year-old Gavin sat across the desk from the SEI official as the detached monotone sentenced his yearnings to death. "As specified by your profile and the needs of the township, your Core Track Degree has prepared you to become an inspector of facilities."

His lifelong job would be to ascertain that businesses and institutions followed every tiny, invasive guideline with machine-like precision. He balked at the instructor-guided practicum in which he was to participate in harassing a young doctor in his clinic.

"I can't do this," he yelled, throwing down his clipboard and pen and ripping off the disgusting gray smock.

Severe punishment was inevitable. The SEI doubled the compulsory "citizen volunteer hours" for cleaning up the rubble from the plane crash and tornado. Beyond the punitive labor heaped on his parents along with their recalcitrant son, his father's cold fury, and, even worse, the dull weariness of his mother's compassionate half-smile, buried his life in brick and mortar misery.

The night of the April full moon, as Gavin stood under the surveillance camera and stared across the desert, the bright moonlight highlighted the silvery ridge of distant mountains. It was as though the reflected light were a beacon, shining across a sea of drowning dreams. The far-off summits represented adventure and happiness—freedom from aspirations sinking beneath waves of despair in that soul-devouring township. While he gazed at the heights, filaments of never-anticipated hope reached into his heart and, with an insistent tug, propelled a never-expected journey.

Early May was a good time to leave. Surprising his mother with a prolonged goodnight hug, Gavin whispered he loved her. As soon as his parents were asleep, he pulled his backpack, filled mostly with Ration Allocated Transitional Sustenance (RATS) bars, from under his bed. The sleeping bag strapped to his pack and the jacket tied to his waist would be bed and pillow. His dad's old army canteen attached to a belt loop, two stainless steel water bottles tied to straps slung over his shoulders, plus the water in his pack would have to suffice. With his heirloom Swiss army knife secured in the zippered pocket on his pants leg, he slipped out the door and crawled past the view of the surveillance camera.

Strategically, he chose to escape on the night of the almost full moon, so he would have at least three nights of bright moonlight. After three nights, both his guiding light and his water would rapidly diminish.

Having no compass and a limited supply of water and food, Gavin feared losing sight of the distant peaks and becoming disoriented in the twists and turns of desert ravines and gullies. He followed Highway 550 because it led directly toward his destination towering as though inaccessible to the landlords' control system. But it was harrowing to watch his step and keep the highway in view while avoiding detection by patrolling retrievers.

Mercilessly, he pushed himself and alternated walking and running until the moon, behind at the outset, taunted him at its zenith as though winning a race. But his lungs and thighs begged for rest. While he slumped beside a bristle bush to drink from the canteen and reflect on his life, the surreal present oppressed memories of a happy past.

The hum of a car engine alerted him to approaching danger as the searchlight from a retriever vehicle probed the sparse sprinkle of sage and dry grass. Gavin lunged to the ground a split second before the powerful beam swept the desert floor. Luckily, the probe passed over him, ahead of the swirl of dust that arose from the impact of his dive.

A lizard, startled by the intrusive thud, darted from its hiding place, paused as if to get a grip and scrambled over his outstretched hand. He breathed deeply of the sage-scented air to slow his heart's pounding, but as he exhaled, the bravado that initiated his escape drained away, leaving a void of hollow anxiety. *Almost got me.*

Shining ahead, the bright moon cast long bristle bush shadows, and a cool breeze nudged him to stand up and face the peaks—closer now than they had been that poignant night in April. As he filled his lungs with dry desert air, a wash of renewed courage poured in. So, given the choice to return to the awful familiar or continue into the fearful unknown, his gaze sought the seductive glow of the silver-tinged heights. His torso thrust outward like an upright lizard, Gavin darted fifty yards or so, paused to gasp for air, peered at the highway behind, and dashed ahead.

A densely branched cedar blocked the moon's glow when a false sense of security lulled him to carelessness. Too late, he realized that he was visible prey for the predatory searchlight of a second retriever vehicle. With a panicked burst of speed, he sprinted forward as the car braked to a stop, and the door on the driver's side opened. The chase was cut short as Gavin stumbled on a root, his pursuer tackling him. He hit the ground facedown, his nose painfully absorbing the impact of the fall. As the retriever handcuffed his hands behind his back, a sense of hopelessness engulfed him. He knew that retrievers generally worked in pairs to make doubly sure that captured runners would be returned to Township 23.

The retriever rolled Gavin on his back. As his captor searched his pockets, the youth squinted in the harsh glare of a flashlight. When he turned his head to avoid the blinding beam, ooze from his left nostril ran down the cheek pressed into still-warm sand, and he wished he had a free hand to wriggle his nose and ascertain if the shooting pains meant it was broken.

After locating the pocketknife, the retriever flipped it in the air as he stood triumphantly over his victim. Then he froze. "Gavin?"

Startled out of hyperawareness of his bloody nose, Gavin recognized a familiar voice behind the blinding glare of the flashlight. "Would you get that thing out of my eyes?"

"Oh, sure. Sorry!"

As the holder of the flashlight shifted the direction of the beam, Gavin caught a glimpse of his face. "Mackie, is that you?" The sight of his best friend cascaded a rush of memories.

Leaning down to clasp his captive's forearm and help him to his feet, Mackie chided his friend, "Hey, man, what d'ya think you're doing?"

The crowding of too many possible responses left Gavin speechless.

A flicker of shared nostalgia softened Mackie's glare. "Don't you know they're gonna make an example of you? And it's *not* gonna to be fun."

As the specter of a doomed future leered, Gavin looked away, and then probed Mackie's eyes. Urgency spewed a tumble of words. "I had to get away. Behind all the bull, that place is nothing but a prison—prison school, prison jobs, prison town."

Stepping behind Gavin, Mackie grasped his wrists to unlock the handcuffs.

Wriggling his still-intact nose, Gavin concluded his rant. "I'd just as soon you shoot me and get it over with. That'd be better than dying a slow death for the rest of my life."

Mackie was obdurate. "Man, that's just the way it is. I found a job where I can at least drive out of town several times a week."

As Gavin wiped his bloody cheek with his sleeve, he chose not to speak aloud his mental response. *Yeah, and look why you're doing it.*

The moonlight shadowed lines of anguish on Mackie's features as the friends faced one another.

"Come with me." To convey the intensity of his plea, Gavin rested his hand on his friend's shoulder. "Let's escape to freedom like we did as kids—but this time permanently, never to return!"

Pulling away from the charged touch, Mackie's expression hardened. "Are you kidding? They won't let anyone escape. No one. It's too big a risk."

"Not for me." Gavin's forcefulness seared Mackie's return gaze.

Mackie looked shaken, as though struggling to keep his expression tough. "Come on, Gavin, let's get this over with." He grabbed the runner's forearm.

Gavin jerked his arm from Mackie's grasp. "How come you don't have a partner? I thought you predators always stalked your prey in pairs."

Mackie flinched—a sign the verbal barb penetrated his emotional armor. "He got sick. There was no one else."

An awkward pause filled the space between the childhood companions before Mackie spoke again. "You know you shouldn't have run away."

"What I *know* is I'm *not* going back."

The friends remained locked in a silent, psychological tug-of-war as Gavin's future hung in the balance for two long minutes that felt like an eternity.

A barely audible sigh escaped Mackie's lips. "If you get caught, you never saw me. Understand?"

Limp with relief, Gavin shot his friend a crooked smile. "You know me better than that."

The retriever gripped the handcuffs in one hand and returned the pocketknife with the other. Gavin grabbed his liberator, and they shared a desperate bear hug.

"Now get out of my sight," Mackie ordered gruffly. He grasped his friend's arm and roughly pushed him away.

"You won't regret this." Backing up, Gavin watched Mackie brush the moisture from his eyes—as though a secret part of him wanted to join this latest adventure—even as he turned, and his legs carried him toward the waiting car.

As Mackie sped away, the god-awful instrument of doom scanning the highway for runners, a silent farewell, tinged with regret for something lost, followed.

Gavin pressed on, his attention riveted on forward progress as scrubby cedars signaled increasing elevation. Until well past midnight, only the distant yowls of a coyote pack and the determined thuds of his shoes challenged the lonely silence. When declining moonlight threatened to abandon his solitary ascent, and the eerie howls and high-pitched yips grew louder, irrational fear of the noisy cacophony coupled with his anxious retriever vigil. He quickened his pace, stumbling and lurching until a faint glow escaped the eastern horizon. In the early dawn it seemed as though the coyotes encircled him, incessantly yowling their whereabouts to fellow pack members, until excited yips nipped at his heels, barking the predators' jubilance to bring down their hapless prey, and Gavin's heart pounded his terror.

Augurs

4

Eena was eager to see her future bond-mate as she followed Leiani into the cypress grove a second time. "Is the chick I'm to bond with around here?"

"We're close. I'll go first. Stay beside me and be as quiet as possible."

After a few more steps Eena followed Leiani up a ladder leaning against a branch that held a nest with an augur inside. At first only the body and wings of the parent appeared to fill the nest. The mother half opened and then closed the eye that was nearest them, obviously unperturbed by Leiani's presence. She pulled a small pouch from her pocket, poured pine nuts into her palm, and extended her hand. Again, the eye half opened, closed, then opened wide at the sight of the offering-filled palm. When the mother shifted to reach for the nuts, her extended wing folded, exposing her chick curled in a little ball. Awakened by the withdrawal of the warm, dark enclosure, it popped its oversized eyes open, stretched its long, thin featherless neck and then flapped its tiny wings. With patchy tan and gray plumage protruding from soft white down, the chick was very much an augur version of the "ugly duckling." When it poked its head over the rim of the nest, Eena's whole being reached out to the baby creature, enfolding it in protective tenderness. She longed to touch the tiny beak, but anticipating painful reprisal from the much larger one, resisted the urge.

Mimicking its mother's actions, the chick flapped its wings and hopped to the rim of the nest, teetering as it reached toward Leiani's hand.

Eena gasped as, with a swipe of her neck, the mother pushed her baby back inside the nest. Alerted to danger, ignoring the remaining pine nuts, she raised her head and eyed Eena as though she were somehow responsible for the near mishap.

In response to Leiani's slight movement, Eena backed to a lower rung, and they descended the ladder together.

Eager to begin, Eena fired questions at Leiani. "How do I start? How do I get past the mother?"

"First, with patience. Then, by coming here every day for the next eight months."

Eena sighed. "Beginning tomorrow?"

A hint of mirth brightened Leiani's expression as she nodded assent. "For now, would you like to hear part two of my father's narration?"

Glad for something to distract her from her impatience to connect with the chick, Eena nodded. After retracing their steps to the circle of stones, she sat on the stone bench while Leiani triggered the code to resurrect her father's image and refresh the lyrical cadence of his voice.

> *I have given this species the zoological classification Avis gigantus and the common name augur, associating them with an ancient divination system in which flocks of birds augur or presage the future. It has pleased me no end that this system of flight has become a valuable form of transportation for my people.*
>
> *You, who are listening to this narrative, may be wondering how it is that we have developed holograph emitters while relying on birds for transportation. On several occasions after I reached my mid-twenties, I passed through the very same portal that you have crossed. Of course, I was seeking to explore in the opposite direction.*
>
> *Eventually, I remained in your world, a future space/time to me, for several years. During that time, I learned your language, married, had a child, and studied at a major university to become a scientist. Several years into research and development of both free energy devices and holograph emitters, I learned of scientific speculation concerning an imminent solar eruption that might temporarily set your society back to horse and buggy days.*
>
> *The interior nudge to return home through the portal wasn't cowardice. The imminent changes reminded me that my own people needed my help, as Mu had been in the midst of catastrophic shakings and sinkings.*

Although it's generally best to leave artifacts in their originating space/time, I carried this crystal holograph emitter through the portal from your world to my home here in the Land of Mu. It's a free energy prototype, a closely guarded secret in your time, which should run indefinitely.

In gratitude for the time spent in your future reality, I now use this emitter for a return favor to your space/time. The augurs have benefitted our society greatly, and it may be that for a while, this form of transportation will help you. If someone follows my protocols for bonding with the chicks, it should be easy to pilot the adult birds through the portal. Should it be that the life-changing events have happened, may Avis gigantus be of assistance to you during your society's years of recovery from initial setbacks.

In conclusion, I must share with you that a series of catastrophic shifts have greatly diminished my own continent. Because of recent rumblings, my people are preparing to evacuate our rapidly sinking village and sail away to stable shores. When you arrive, you will very likely stand on the last vestiges of what researchers from your time will call 'The Lost Continent of Mu.' Take care, for a final submergence may be imminent.

After Birdman's voice died away, the women sat quietly, each lost in her own thoughts.

Eena broke the silence with a question. "So, did he sail away with the villagers?"

"Yes. Although the houses are still mostly above water." As they walked away from the stone calendar, Leiani added, "When my father decided to leave America, my mother refused to go with him. They had many arguments, which were a torment for me. When I turned twenty-two, Dad simply disappeared—I was inconsolable for days. A couple of years later the solar EMPs struck; the following year, Mom and I were hauled to a township. After she became ill and died, I escaped that awful existence to return here."

As the pair crossed the stepping-stones over the creek that Eena had followed down the mountain, Eena's eyes sought Leiani's. "To freedom, but all alone." She beamed at Leiani. "Come with me to Three Mountains. You can stay in my cabin for a few nights."

"Give me a few minutes." Leiani sprinted toward the grove of cypresses to return wearing a backpack, her face glowing.

Deep in thought, Eena stared across the plains toward the spectacular sunset of gold-tinged magenta. "Your father is right. We *do* have a use for the augurs."

For several seconds they listened to the melodic play of wind on grass.

The tightness in Eena's voice shattered the meditative calm. "Retrievers from the townships patrol the highways, driving the only operational cars."

Sadness tinged Leiani's response. "Looking for runaways such as ourselves."

Eena nodded. "Also, armed gangs known as rovers now roam the countryside."

A glimmer of comprehension lit Leiani's eyes. "So, from the sky you can watch for both threats and new arrivals."

"I'm sure you see how important the augurs can be."

"Definitely."

"Will you help me build a team of augur pilots to patrol Three Mountains?"

The shine in Leiani's eyes communicated her willingness.

Eena's voice softened. "The moment I looked at the chick, his name popped into my mind."

Leiani's eyes widened.

"Cesla."

Exhilaration hastened Eena's stride across the savannah. As Cesla approached, the play of greens and blues in his plumage gleamed in the sunlight. Guided by Leiani's instructions, she had faithfully companioned Cesla as the four-month-old grew to fledgling and then full-grown traveler of the skies. Attending the young augur, she marveled at the deepening connection that was something more than one shares with a favorite pet. Cesla could fasten one eye on his bond-mate and evoke a sense of communion that flowed beneath words. Likewise, the augur responded seamlessly to Eena's psychic calls, gradually made from farther away, as though distance weren't a factor.

As he ate tomatillos from one hand and arched into a head scratch from the other, she sent an image, the culmination of months of bonding, to Cesla. "Today's our first flight."

Their familiar ritual of feeding, stroking and scratching resumed for the usual amount of time, until Eena walked behind the augur to straddle the tail. Trepidation and excitement vied as she took a deep breath, and a responsive shiver ruffled the waiting stillness of her bond-mate. She lowered her body over his back, reached her arms around his neck, and bent her knees, drawing her shins upward to the base of the wings.

For several seconds motionless expectation prevailed.

"*Cesla, take flight.*" Clarity and strength resounded in the psychic command.

The familiar *phoom* drummed the power of the great wings, and Eena felt herself lifted above the Earth. Pressing her cheek against his strong neck, she looked down as the cypress-lined river and then the sea of grass receded. They flew a wide swath rising halfway up the mountain, then down past the stone circle toward a collection of round buildings. Bright blue, orange, magenta and yellow paint peeling from adobe walls and gaps in the rooftops of bundled hay bespoke neglect. Just beyond, the voracious ocean devoured the shore around the visible top half of buildings while, farther inland, tongues of water lapped the foundations of homes.

Eena remained acquiescent to Cesla's guidance system as they looped a return, following the river into the society of Giant Sky Travelers nesting, flying and feeding. For the pilot, this first flight was the glorious fulfillment of eight months of honing the augur/human relationship and perfecting their telepathic exchange.

In the final arc of their flight, Eena spied Jarrod, a tall, dark-haired youth bounding across the savannah toward the cypress groves for a two-hour bonding session with the fledgling, Espirit. Somewhere among the cypress trees, Chuck and Lori, excited about bonding with and piloting an augur, were at various stages in the process under the thoughtful guidance of Leiani. The team of four patrollers would be complete and operational by this time the following year. Meanwhile, Leiani was bonding with six other birds that would become aerial pack animals to transport goods and supplies.

The next day Eena and Cesla's second flight crossed the boundary to a destination never before reached by an augur. The airborne pair rose over the redwood mountain and followed the upward slope toward the stone archway. Eena pictured a slight swoop down and through the portal before she and Cesla flew under the arc and over the pines of Quartz Mountain.

The first season that four patrollers flew the skies around Three Mountains Community was exhilarating. Given just a little more experience and coordination with one another, Eena and Jarrod, the most adventurous of the patrollers, could fly missions to seek and make contact with other settlements of runners gathered in the mountains.

"I know my girlfriend, Laura, is miserable in the township. I have to bring her here," Jarrod had said, causing alarm bells to ring in Eena's head. But there was no stopping him from returning to retrieve her.

For the next few weeks, Eena's flights were mainly patrols to watch for Jarrod's return, her concern and sense of loss growing with the passage of days.

As the sun presented a sliver of white light, the coyote voices that had excited Gavin's imagination and evoked terror through the night grew silent. Cedars, shoulder height at first light, now reached overhead, anchoring the pebbled foothills of the Rocky Mountains. After gulping a bottle of water, Gavin crawled under the sheltering branches of an ancient evergreen. Grateful for the shade, he untied his jacket from his waist, folded it under his head, and fell into a predator-riddled dreamscape.

In his dream, he stood exposed in the sweltering desert, panic-stricken as a circle of snarling coyotes milled around him, and hot-breathed pants seared his face, brown eyes glinting shards of reflected sunlight. Cold fear clutched his heart with a viselike grip. Should he run? No, they could easily outrun him. He scanned the ground for a stick, anything for self-defense, as the ring of predators closed in on the surrounding sand, pebbles and twigs. Reaching into his pants leg pocket, he pulled out his scout knife and lunged menacingly with his laughable weapon.

Backing into the dubious protection of a knee-high bush, a movement in the sky caught his eye. As bright turquoise swallowed the lavender glow of the horizon, an eagle flew toward him. Momentary timelessness fixated his entire focus on the raptor, and the compelling image lifted his consciousness above his dire dilemma, as though he soared on the wings of sky-born reprieve. Then, as suddenly as it appeared, the vision arced out of sight, and the dreamer felt his feet on solid ground. His legs pressed into the meager limbs of salt brush as the encircling coyotes melded into one. And the one faced him with the fixed gaze that had first alarmed him.

Oddly, something protruded from the animal's mouth. Understanding it was for him to take, the dreamer reached for what appeared to be a playing card. Grasping the proffered card, he held it up to examine it more closely, surprised there were neither numbers, nor aces, clubs, spades or hearts. A young man, the sole subject of the image, carried an old-fashioned knapsack tied to a stick over his shoulder. His eyes sparkled with anticipation as a youthful smile lit his face. Yet, the card portrayed the youth's adventure beginning near the edge of a cliff, from which he bounded forward with naive optimism, oblivious of stepping from solid ground into thin air.

The coyote had vanished when a resonant voice, seeming to come from the arboreal guardian, shook Gavin to momentary wakefulness. "Merge with me and rest, young fool. Wispy dreams sustain your journey, which nonetheless, has begun." The soft mauve colors of sunrise gradually yielded to aquamarine blue as Gavin slept on, free of coyote invaders.

Mid-afternoon, the third day of his trek, Gavin awoke in a confused daze. Expecting the card to be clasped in his hand, he opened his fist to release only a few grains of sand. He shook his head to dislodge clinging impressions from the strange dreamscape—as if to return the astral card to the dream world and face the challenges of the real one. Puzzlement scrunched Gavin's brow until he recalled a visit to a Tarot reader in his building unit.

Pungent incense pervaded the dimly lit room as a reader of Tarot cards explained the meaning of a few of them. "They depict both the events of life and the roles people play in the dramas."

She turned the card bearing the image of the youth with the knapsack face up. "This first card, representing the starting place for human experience, features the character known as either the fool or the adventurer, according to one's perspective."

She tapped the card with her long, painted fingernail. "The youth ventures into the world, enthusiastic to discover the possibilities ahead, oblivious of the challenges that will sculpt a wise old man from a young and foolish one."

The tarot reader's bracelets jangled as she re-assembled the deck to dangle the fool's card between two fingers, the remaining cards stacked beneath the palm of the other hand. She smiled into his eyes. "Taken altogether — the accumulated experience for the transformation of the fool's journey into the hero's epic."

As if satisfied by Gavin's scrutiny, the dream world finally freed him to focus on the needs of his hungry body with a meager breakfast while he shrugged off the meaning of the tarot card as though dispersing fluff beyond the horizon of his dreams.

The Bridge

5

Doctor Ayako and Police Marshal Greer, their lips pursed in tense, professional seriousness, responded to Governor Scholtz's probing questions.

Marshal Greer sat erect in his chair, his deep voice booming. "We have captured seven runners from Townships 21 through 26 in the past six months."

Scholtz turned to Doctor Ayako. "And the results of the DNA tests?"

"Switched on in every one."

This was unsettling news. Charles Scholtz was accustomed to manufacturing fear, not being the recipient. Thank the gods they had confiscated all weapons prior to and after Solar Flash.

"Were the runners eliminated?"

"Yes."

"Other than Eena and her group, have any runners evaded retrievers?"

Marshal Greer hesitated, as though reluctant to offer the next information. "Only one. His location is unknown."

With an ear-splitting fist pound on his desk, the landlord spewed profanities before issuing a dire warning to the retriever force that there better not be any more escapees to those mountains.

The whole DNA/runner issue was infuriating. It was as though the universe were conspiring for his demise and of his kind. But this was his endowment, his planet, the progenitors' system of suns, the Black Sun, his anti-photonic god's quadrant of the galaxy.

At dawn Gavin left Highway 550, to head directly toward the compelling peaks. Forgoing sleep, he finished off the water in his canteen and continued northeast in full daylight. Abandoned farms populated with feral chickens depressed his spirits, and he veered away from a distant pack of wild dogs before crossing Highway 160 to head north through the foothills of the Rocky Mountains.

You must be insane, he chided himself. *No highway to follow. No signs of people anywhere – the sun, your only compass to an unknown destination. You're going to become hopelessly lost in the mountains of Colorado – and probably die.*

Out of food and water, exhausted from twenty-four hours without sleep, Gavin pressed on. By late afternoon, desperately thirsty, his stomach rumbling, he reached a highway that flanked the southern edge of mountainous terrain. He paused to catch his breath as an eagle, its wings shining golden brown in the receding light, circled overhead three times, then soared northward over the mountain. As though in response to a subtle nudge, the youth looked furtively west and east and sprinted across the highway.

At the base of a pine-covered mountain, Gavin found his way blocked by a tangle of prickly vines and shrubs. Sharp thorns tore at his clothes and pricked his skin as he hurriedly sliced the roped vines while scanning the highway until scratched and bleeding, he broke through the barrier and scrambled upward over a spongy cushion of last year's pine needles.

Screened by a dense growth of pines, he relaxed and noticed a road about fifty yards away, which was hidden from view of the highway. His eyes followed the narrow ribbon of asphalt backward to a tangle of vines and shrubs that overgrew piled brush, branches and logs. It appeared as though the entrance had been deliberately covered, rendering it invisible to passing motorists. His heart quivered in anticipation. It must have led from the highway to somewhere with people.

Just beyond the first bend in the mountainside, a tiny stream from a stone outcropping gurgled the promise of merciful relief to Gavin's cracked lips and parched tongue. He fell to his stomach and opened his mouth so that the cold trickle wet his lips, rolled over his tongue and refreshed his throat. His thirst quenched, he splashed water on his bleeding arms and drenched his whole head in the refreshing coolness. Soothed by nature's gurgling lullaby, the bone weary runner lay his head on his arm and succumbed to the most restful sleep since his trek began.

When Gavin awoke early afternoon and replenished his water supply at the spring, the happy realization dawned that his continuing trek would be hidden from the patrollers' view. He set off with a spring in his step, but after the asphalt yielded to dirt around a second flank of the mountain, the ascending and descending twists and turns marked switchbacks between hope and despair of ever again seeing another human being.

Eena pushed her fingers through the soft, layered feathers of Cesla's neck, burrowing through the blue-green outer layer to snuggle her fingertips in the warm down. Curly black strands of hair escaped the scarf restraint to blow in front of her eyes as she pressed her cheek against the soft feathers covering the muscular neck. Flight provided a meditative reprieve, her way of putting problems into perspective, as she scanned the vibrant greens that clothed the jagged crags of the Rocky Mountains.

The human and bird communication, the outgrowth of their bonding, was literally wordless; the psychic conveyance so elegant that response was instantaneous. Eena's feathered attire was designed to be indistinguishable from her mount's plumage, but their connection extended beyond appearances. Soaring over Thunderbird, Blue Lake, and Quartz peaks, the rider's shins absorbed the rhythmic pulse of the powerful wings, and they soared as one being. She couldn't imagine a better job than patrolling Three Mountains from the vantage point of a fourteen thousand-foot elevation.

Sensing the augur was tired, Eena mentally suggested a return to the portal. The augur's response was a left bank that synced with the wordless impression of the bird's savannah habitat in the Land of Mu.

The recent double patrols, due to the loss of Jarrod, had stretched Cesla's flight time to the max. Eena scanned the terrain carefully, as she had for a month, hoping to see the youth hiking a return trek to the community. But her search was to no avail, and once again the seeping resignation that had concluded each fruitless patrol oppressed her spirits. Jarrod was lost to the community—his augur, Espirit, riderless. Instead of gallantly bringing his girlfriend to the secret haven nestled in the mountains, the patroller must have been re-assimilated into Township 21—or worse. She shuddered, knowing how he would have been made to suffer for daring to escape the controllers and elude retrievers.

Eena had another concern. Three Mountains Community needed to find any and all possible allies, hidden like themselves beyond the landlords' current reach. Soon, the patrols should extend in ever widening sweeps across the mountains. She figured that in the absence of arms, there was power in a unified thrust.

They needed a new patroller of Jarrod's ilk to fill the vacancy, which meant bonding with Espirit—but who?

Riding an air current over Lemon Reservoir, Cesla soared toward Promise Pass, the usual prelude to returning to Quartz Mountain. Approaching the point of the westward arc, a movement on the mountain face bordering the east side of the pass caught Eena's eyes. Could that be Jarrod? After excursions to surrounding farms, he had always returned to the community by way of the reservoir and pass. Why would he follow a path halfway up the mountain on the far side, the route leading to the rickety bridge that spanned the river where the pass narrowed? No one dared cross that bridge anymore.

Eena reached for her binoculars. The blond youth was definitely not Jarrod. Must be another runner. Although she wanted to help him, her immediate concern was returning the exhausted augur to his own time and terrain; she turned Cesla toward the peak of Quartz Mountain and to his sub-tropical home on the far side of the portal.

She hoped Grandfather's raptor honing system was working on behalf of the traveler.

Trudging along the dirt road, Gavin followed switchbacks up, and then down, until midday, where it degraded to a rocky trail, washouts and exposed rocks warning that he was on a dead-end trek. Hunger dogged his steps by late afternoon when he reached a wooden bridge. His gaze swiveled between the rocky trail and the rickety expanse with missing slats. Forty feet of wood and rope stretched precariously over an alarming abyss.

A sickening feeling churned Gavin's stomach as he stepped onto the first slat. In the depths of the canyon, a sinuous ribbon of cobalt blue snaked a warning, and he hastily retreated to solid ground. But he no sooner stepped on the mountain path than a movement in the air caught his attention. Shading his eyes, he squinted skyward. A large raptor, like the one Gavin had seen at the highway and dreamed of a couple of days ago, approached to fly directly above the bridge. It sketched three complete circles in the sky before disappearing due west, precisely in the direction toward which the risky conveyance extended. Was that a man-made structure jutting from the cliff face ahead? His heart skipped a beat as if in response to a personal call.

"What's with you, bird?" he wondered aloud. "If I end up in the middle of nowhere, with no signs of civilization and no way to survive, I'm going to blame you."

Amused at himself for chastising a bird, he peered at the precarious means of passage from this mountain to the next. When he realized something in him had made the decision to cross the life-threatening structure, he sighed. His apprehension tinged with dry humor, and he inwardly chided himself. *You must be kidding. Across this broken down excuse for a bridge?*

Firmly, he clasped the handrail that had been cut from an aspen sapling. The entire length of overlapping saplings, nailed together and secured with bands of thick rope, were securely fastened, and it appeared as though repairs had been done just prior to Solar Flash. The slats he would be walking on were a different matter. Jagged edges where rotted wood had split apart and gaping holes where whole slats had fallen the fifty-plus feet to the stream shouted a warning to hold tight to the rails and watch his step. He peered into the depths, knowing that a single misstep could mean plummeting to certain death. Nonetheless, a voice deep inside was insistent. *This way.*

Gingerly, Gavin tested the first slat. It held, and he proceeded to the next. As he tentatively continued one cautious step at a time, creaks and groans announced each footfall. The bridge swayed sickeningly, but he wrapped his fingers around the sapling rails with an iron grip. His progress was slow as he carefully tested each slat and either stepped on it or bypassed it. As he neared the opposite end of the bridge, confidence in reaching the last steps eased the tension in his belly.

He peered ahead at the structure he'd seen, a sod-covered awning, extending from the rocky face of the mountain. Oddly out of place, yellow and lavender columbines skirted the supporting posts and lent cheery softness to the stalwart gray of granite walls.

As Gavin tried to make sense of an awning with no building attached, he unconsciously took the next step, and with a loud *crack* the slat beneath his right foot gave way. As he fell through, he lost his grip on the rails, frantically grabbed the sides of the walkway, and landed with his lower torso and legs hanging below the bridge. Wedged on the slat behind, his backpack lent unreliable support as he held on—literally for dear life.

The bridge amplified the slightest movement with an exaggerated sway, surging fear to Gavin's extremities. His heart pounding, the youth clutched the sides in frozen animation. He was mesmerized by the gaping hole and fearful of evoking chaos in an attempt to lift his dangling body over the next slat. Directly below, jagged edges of tumbled rocks jutted menacingly along the twisted course of the river. As nausea wrung his stomach, he wondered how many bounces it would take to die.

Well, he mused with wry anguish, *I guess it's to be a rapid death, rather than the slow one I left behind.*

The escapee from Township 23 felt betrayed by something unknown beckoning from some improbable future. Evil, the trickster that enticed him to choose this treacherous route to some delusional destiny!

As Gavin gazed down at his feet hanging over white sprays of tumbling water, the image of the eagle inserted itself into his consciousness and descended toward the bridge.

"Grab my arm."

A feminine yet strong hand extended in front of his confused sight to firmly clasp his forearm. But sheer terror refused to unlock the fingers that gripped the sides of the suspended walkway.

"My weight will help steady the bridge. Quickly. Don't think. Just grab hold."

He risked the terrifying instant to release the bridge and secure the mutual arm lock. When the bridge reacted with precarious rocking, a tremor of alarm electrified his heart.

"Help me help you," commanded the husky feminine voice.

Leveraging his left arm, Gavin raised his torso as, with remarkable strength, the suntanned arm pulled him up and forward.

The young woman backed up to pull him to a prone position on the intact slats. As a jagged edge resisted flesh, a searing pain shot through his left thigh.

"Now, crawl forward on your belly." She repositioned her body and tightened her clasp on his forearm.

Bracing his left elbow, Gavin inched forward until his thighs were atop the bridge. He raised his trunk as if to pull his body upward.

A crisp command stopped him. "Wait! You're almost to land."

He scooted on his belly until his free hand touched the final slat of the bridge, and his whole body length was horizontal.

Exhausted relief flooded his being, and after momentarily resting his head on his arms, he lifted his gaze to meet gold-flecked green eyes that briefly smiled into his. An olive green bandana subdued the curly black hair that framed the rosy tan complexion, and leather straps crisscrossed her midsection, holding a bow and quiver of arrows — altogether giving an impression of strength and femininity that comingled in a no-nonsense presence.

"Just a little farther."

After Gavin pulled his chest to solid ground, she helped him raise himself up. When his left hand clutched the edge of the aspen rail, she gently loosed his right hand to do the same. Wincing in pain, he stood on the welcome earth.

When he grimaced, favoring his left leg, Gavin's benefactor slipped his left arm over her shoulder. "Let's go," was all she said until after several steps, she added, "I'm Eena."

"Thanks, Eena. I'm Gavin." His impression was that his companion, exuding robust beauty, was in her mid-twenties.

Eena's stout body easily supported his lanky frame as he hobbled with jerky steps to avoid stabs of pain, and they followed a steep narrow path toward the sod-covered awning that had earlier fixated his gaze.

Gavin noted that lining the path were gleaming white crystals. "Quartz?"

"Yes. This mountain is filled with veins of quartz. It gives this area... rather unusual properties."

A few steps after Eena's comment, her hesitation and slight emphasis on the word "unusual" echoed in Gavin's brain. A shock of blond hair partially obscured his questioning glance, but no answer was forthcoming, nor was it written on her inscrutable face.

Three chickens, seeming out of place, crossed the path, and to the right on a clearing open to the sky, perched an equally incongruous round glass house with a domed ceiling.

Eena acknowledged Gavin's unspoken question. "The greenhouse."

Just ahead, the sage and grass growing on the post-supported overhang gave the appearance of an extension of the mountain, but as they came closer, Gavin peered underneath and toward the back of the awning. Compounding his sense of otherworldliness, a hobbit-like entrance with a wall of diagonal pine planks, a large hexagonal window, and a door with a massive cast iron handle, sealed the front of a cave.

Eena signaled for Gavin to take the handle and pull open the door. Then she slipped his other arm over her head, and while she held the door, he clasped the door jam for support and hopped through.

The
Cave

6

Despite being a cave, a soft glow mysteriously lit the room from everywhere and nowhere to augment the limited amount of light filtering through the front window. The scents of fragrant dried herbs hanging from wooden rafters at the rear of the cave permeated the space. A long stone ledge two feet above the floor and covered with a blue mat extended along one wall, supporting a pillow at one end and a neatly folded blanket of pale blue wool at the other. Along the opposite side, a pair of chairs flanked a small table that held a large rose quartz crystal. Beside an opening at the back of the room sat a tall stool and even higher table holding an array of small amber bottles.

Gavin estimated that the cave room was about twenty feet by twenty feet and with amazement admired the smooth, perfectly symmetrical arch that formed the walls and ceiling. Veins of white and pink quartz, extending from top to bottom, reflected the pervasive glow of the room. Even the earthen floor appeared to have been smoothed and polished to a translucent sheen.

The most striking sight of all was the appearance through the rear opening of a tall, slender young woman with shoulder length silvery blonde hair. Her pale skin, resembling smooth alabaster, was tinted with a slight lavender hue, and high cheekbones formed prominent ridges above her delicate jawbone, nose and lips. Exceptionally large gray-blue eyes, with a slight upward tilt at the outside corners, lent an Asian cast to her exotic loveliness. For a moment, Gavin gazed in astonishment because her appearance was unlike anyone he had ever seen.

His awareness shifted to Eena's barely concealed mirth as she introduced the newcomer.

"This is Anaya, the local healer."

Anaya's gentle smile belied her careful and detailed assessment of the patient. Requesting that Gavin remove his pants, she held up the wool blanket to screen him.

Moments later, as she applied soothing oils to his bruises, the healing scents of basil and marjoram wafted through the cave room. Gavin sighed and closed his eyes, smiling blissfully to be recipient of the ministrations of a beautiful woman—a remarkable turn of fortune from the specter of loneliness and even death that loomed just hours before.

After carefully massaging in the oils, Anaya replaced the caps on the bottles. "The warmth is penetrating the bruised muscles and flesh." She paused before adding playfully, "Soon to decorate your thigh with purple, magenta and yellow."

While the therapeutic oils brought relief, Gavin's stomach audibly signaled distress. Anaya disappeared through the opening at the rear of the cave to return with a plate filled with jerky, cornbread, peas, carrots and sliced apples sprinkled with cinnamon.

"From our smokehouse, a neighbor, the green house, and an orchard in the valley," she replied to his questioning look.

Seated next to the table that hosted the crystal, Eena had observed the woman's tender assistance, smiling inwardly at Gavin's bemused surrender to Anaya's sensitive touch and gently probing fingers.

As Gavin devoured the meal, Eena recalled the events that triggered her own trek to Three Mountains. Surrounded by jet airliners resting in forlorn abandonment at the gates of Transtopia Metro Airport, she had reboarded the Cessna. According to the pilot, the small jet was one of two recently overhauled post-Solar Flash. During the flight she had stared at ravaged forests and mentally sloughed-off emotional goo from the permanently embedded images of floating babies. The offer of raised status, albeit increased danger, danced a razor's edge in her musings as the plane landed in the field beside Township 26.

Her apartment had become a magnet for misfits—young adults simply unable to conform to a system that was irrelevant to their passionate interests, cold to their unique talents. Five, in particular, approaching or just past twenty, were carriers of a new vision. The group included Marva, who cultivated an organic garden during her off hours for the people in her housing unit, to offset the processed, preserved stuff, including the RATS bars they consumed daily; Jeffry, who sketched drawings of futuristic architecture, and whose three-dimensional intelligence enabled him to repair just about anything mechanical; Ansil, who wrote lyrical poetry and compelling prose about a new society; Leslie, whose room was a lab inspired by the genius Nikola Tesla, and who experimented with prototypes for a free energy device; and lastly, Caellum, the oldest, who spoke of rebellion and leading a *coup de grace* against the controllers.

Drawn together by irrepressible intelligence that was out of sync with an unquestioning society, the youths met at Eena's apartment a couple of times a month, seeking camaraderie and stimulating discussion.

Endowed with a strategic intellect that commanded respect, Eena knew she could have survived, even reached the upper tiers of social stratification in the township. But the inward yearning for a more humane society persisted. However, though she shared Caellum's rebellious nature, she knew the futility of bravado in the face of the entrenched wielders of power.

"He's asleep." Anaya's voice startled Eena from her recollections.

The healer exited momentarily to return with a sleeping bag and pillow.

Eena nodded, grateful to stay the night. "Against all odds, another one has found his way here," she whispered.

Radiant from assisting the patient, Anaya smiled. Then she tidied up her apothecary of oils and herbs and dimmed the light with a wave of her hand before retiring to her sleeping quarters deep in the cave system.

Eena glanced toward Gavin and made a mental note to take him through the portal as soon as his leg was sufficiently healed. She wanted to introduce him to the augurs.

In the softened light of the cave apothecary, Eena burrowed into the warm sleeping bag, recalling the dream that propelled her to leave Township 26 her first night back from Fort Carson.

Through the open patio door of her second floor apartment, an insistent wind whistled, folding and twisting the sheers like weary dancers. As she tossed and turned, restless sleep interwove a confusion of images. A particularly strong gust rattled the glass, inserting an unexpected guest into her anxiety-riddled dream.

In the dream, she stood facing the balcony, her gaze riveted by the light of the full moon, as a dark speck grew to become a golden eagle that alighted on the patio floor. The creature tossed a shiny object from his beak that landed with a metallic clank.

Its luminous black beady eyes peered into hers. "Grandfather calls you."

"Grandfather?" In confusion, she thought of her mother's father who had died prior to Solar Flash.

"Come with me."

"Come with you? That's impossible. You can fly; I can't." In the dream, Eena backed up.

The bird eyed her with a piercing gaze. "If you fly with me, you will find refuge and bring others to safety."

Unable to fathom the absurd directive from this raptor, she held the flapping curtain still as he retreated toward the balcony, spread his wings, and flew away.

Bereft in the lonely silence, wracked by the shrill whine of the wind, she stared at the speck until it disappeared in the night sky. Tears for a lost opportunity spilled from her eyes. The edge of the curtain stroked her skin as the night's breath stoked the fires of a new intensity. The desert, which had loomed as a formidable impasse, shifted into a navigable way to the distant mountains.

Again, the outline of a bird grew until it filled the dreamscape beyond the balcony. Eena stumbled away from the opening, her heart pounding with anticipation.

A vulture, even more imposing than the eagle, jumped to the floor, walked past the curtains, and leered at her.

"Don't waste your time on such absurdity," he sneered, obviously referring to the plans brewing in her brain.

"Some of us must have our freedom," she retorted.

"If you head out across that desert, you'll drop dead from sunstroke and dehydration." The bird contrived an awful grin. "And guess who will be picking your bones?" Cynical laughter crackled from his skinny red throat.

Angrily, she demanded the scavenger leave. At that moment, her eyes fell on the shiny object on the floor. Suddenly, it seemed important—familiar somehow. As she dove for it, the vulture lunged, his beak bloodying her hand.

Eena shouted and drew back in pain, her shoulder knocking the bird away. Frantically, he flapped his wings to regain his balance, giving her the seconds she needed to throw her body over the silver disk. Her back to the vulture, her trunk serving as a shield, she held it in the palm of her hand.

With a start of joy, she recognized the pendant as an amulet of protection that had been in her family's possession for generations. Etched on the silver was a labyrinth, symbolizing the journey of man, and in the center stood a tiny stick figure.

The bird at her back shifted side to side, insistently stretching his neck over Eena's shoulders to attempt to snatch the medallion. Beneath her hunched torso the metallic surface yielded a flash of light—a three-inch hologram of a man clothed in buckskin, his coppery flesh burnished by the sun. Leather moccasins clothed his feet, and a red headband crowned his silver-streaked black hair. She noticed a slight movement and looked closer to see that the tiny man was beckoning.

The vulture lunged again, but Eena, knowing what she must do, was too fast for him. Clamping her teeth on the prized amulet, she turned toward the patio door, again knocking the bird out of her way. Feathers rustling, he reeled and collided with the floor and walls. She felt an upwelling of hope, for just ahead, the eagle circled in the sky, and in response to her inward call, arced toward her.

"Fly with me."

Transforming into an eagle, she spread her huge wings and lifted off the floor and beyond the patio.

In an instant, she felt herself soaring beside the raptor over the rooftops of the township, then over the desert toward the mountains that rose above the eastern horizon. The eagles flew side by side over rugged forested terrain to approach a triangle of peaks, spires of quiet majesty above the wispy clouds that clung to the mountainsides.

They navigated the frigid air currents and descended toward a man that stood with still dignity beside a cobalt blue lake sparkling near the summit of a mountain.

Standing on human legs planted on solid ground, Eena faced the reality behind the hologram. The sun glinted on the silver pendant that hung on the elder's chest, a larger replica of the one now in her hand.

The tall medicine man, lines of courage and endurance etched on a pale ocher countenance, nodded with welcoming eyes.

With a heartfelt sigh of affinity, she stepped forward.

"Grandfather!"

No sooner did Eena address the venerable elder than the dream world evaporated, and her eyes flew open, the sound of her voice probing the eerie silence. In the moments it took to realize she had just awakened from a vivid dream, firm resolve set in. From her bed she stared out her window at the morning sky, the curtains now resting in still surrender. She was going to leave Township 26. Somewhere in the mountains a new beginning awaited her and whoever wanted to come along. Her first step in preparations was to dig to the bottom of a wooden chest in the back of her closet to retrieve the pendant.

Listening to the slow, deep breaths of the runner, Eena smiled, fluffed the pillow under her head, and closed her eyes, the pendant resting close to her heart.

There was only a dim hint of morning light in the cave room when she woke up. She glanced over at Gavin, who was still in deep slumber, as she scooted out of her sleeping bag. Hoping the community had gained a badly needed auger pilot to replace Jarrod, she grabbed a red-checkered wool jacket from a wall hook and walked outside to start the fire.

Soon, using a hefty potholder, she picked up the pot of boiling water and filled her mug. As a nearby bird announced the first faint rays of sunlight, she sat on a stump and sipped the pungent sage tea before preparing breakfast.

The warm oils that Anaya re-applied soothed the throbbing, rainbow-colored flesh on Gavin's thigh. Carefully shifting his leg, he pulled on his pants with exhaustive effort. Wincing, he tried to stand on both legs, but the pain forced him back down.

Anaya approached with a twisted walking stick in hand. "You may need this." She smiled, handing him the artfully carved cane.

Gavin grimaced as he grasped the smooth knob at the end of the stick. Like every object in this room, it was a thing of beauty as well as utility. His expression registered admiration for the smooth undulating surface from handhold to point.

"Cedar?"

Anaya nodded.

Gavin gladly leaned on the cane as he stood.

"Much better." He grinned.

"Breakfast anyone?" As Eena poked her head through the door, enticing smells wafted in from omelets cooking on the grill.

Anaya helped Gavin put on his jacket before taking a brown wool shawl from a hook for herself.

The crackling blaze in the fire pit offered inviting warmth to ward off the early morning chill as Eena dished omelets laced with tomatoes, spinach and basil onto their plates. The three devoured the breakfast and sipped steaming tea while the women listened intently to Gavin's tale of escape, capture and release.

He shook his head in disbelief. "How is it, that faced with a number of choices, I followed the dirt road that led me to the bridge and to you?"

The girls exchanged enigmatic looks.

"We also have stories to share."

Gavin gazed steadily at his rescuer. "Eena, I would like to hear how you came here."

She pulled back her unruly mass of curly hair and secured it in a clasp, a few errant tendrils still framing her face. Her story began with the night she and the five youths fled the township.

"Wanting a gun for protection and to hunt small game, I concocted a scheme to obtain one. The evening of our escape, I stood on my balcony and flagged down an officer patrolling on foot. With an alarmed cry, I motioned him to come to my efficiency apartment. Hurrying to the back of the room, I posed as though I were leaning over something. As he rushed forward through the open door, my fellow escapees, who were hiding against the front wall, jumped, bound, and gagged him. Soon, I held the pistol as well as a supply of bullets.

"We crept away expecting to hear 'halt' from a policeman at every step. Somehow, we managed to evade surveillance cameras and patrolling retrievers and headed southeast across the desert. During the day the July heat was unbearable. By the fourth day, our lips were cracked and bleeding. We'd finished off those abhorrent RATS bars, yet I didn't want to waste any bullets to hunt game. As we trickled the last drops of water over our tongues, vultures circled overhead.

"My fellow runners dropped to the sand heaving and gasping. I was beginning to wonder if we'd make it when I heard the cry of an eagle. Oddly, it felt like a call. I climbed a jumbled pile of boulders to peer ahead. About forty paces away was a tiny stream. Eureka!

"Anyway, we scavenged through the ghost town of Durango, then followed the Animus River. As strange as it sounds, a reappearing eagle guided us through the mountains to the green valley below.

"There was Anaya with a handful of people you have yet to meet. I was especially happy to meet the old Native American medicine man named Matoskah whom I had seen in a dream. We call him Grandfather."

Anaya gestured gracefully with her slender hands. "Matoskah was instrumental in each of us reaching this wonderful, magical mountain."

"I found my own way," Gavin responded stubbornly. "And I'm glad to have left my old life behind to enjoy a new one."

He felt the penetrating impact of Eena's gaze. "But we haven't left it behind. Very soon, by land or air, the awfulness we escaped will reach this little haven."

Nathan Abelt donned a suit and tie for the first time since Solar Flash. He could hardly believe he had been called to meet with Imperial Governor George Scholtz, but assumed it had to do with a piloting job assignment. Lydia lovingly straightened his tie and held the sticky fingers of the twins away as he kissed her cheek and hurried to the waiting car. When he arrived at the tower, he was amazed to ride a working elevator to the tenth floor where a smiling receptionist invited him to sit. About an hour later a man exited impressive doors, and he was summoned.

After motioning for Nathan to sit across the mahogany desk from him, the governor's demeanor was to the point.

"Nathan, we appreciate your reliability as a pilot. We'll need your expertise soon to transport a teacher across the Rocky Mountains to Township 24. But that's not the topic of today's discussion."

Nathan waited in suspense, unable to fathom another reason for the meeting. He only knew that he was glad to be of service to the Union of the Americas government.

The governor looked him in the eye. "A growing number of insurgents threatens our recovery efforts."

Nathan's eyes widened.

Scholtz put up his hand. "I agree. It's alarming. We believe the campus of the University of Transtopia may be the point of origin of several troublemakers."

"Kids! They don't know how good they've got it."

Scholtz grimaced. "Apply your background in military espionage as a government informant. Find them, take pictures, get names, and listen to their conversations."

Honored to have been approached, Nathan could hardly wait to begin.

"And one more thing." The imperial governor glanced toward the punctured map. "There may be strongholds of runners from townships in the mountains. A few weeks from now when you fly the teacher, we'll ask you to be on the lookout for settlements and note corresponding coordinates, especially along the Continental Divide."

The
Downpour

7

Eena's one-room cabin was tucked deep in the woods downhill from Anaya's cave and the patroller bunkhouse. At the first glimmer of daylight she lit the oil lamp, considering what she would wear for Chas. When the two pans of water heating on the woodstove stove rumbled to a boil, she poured it into the small aluminum trough that was her bathtub. Thinking it doesn't take luxury to luxuriate, she mixed cooler water into the hot and eased her body in, then smiled at her private joke and lowered her head to immerse her hair in the hot bathwater.

It had been over a week since she had seen Chas and, while she had important strategic plans to discuss with him, her feminine aspect wanted to bring along her most alluring wiles. A half hour later, in the light of the morning sun, she freed her hair from the towel. Parting it on one side, she brushed it into shining waves until she could run her fingers smoothly through the silky strands. She carefully selected each article of clothing from her limited wardrobe. The white blouse, chosen for the scoop neck to showcase the smooth, tanned skin of her throat and shoulders, slid over her arms with cottony coolness; the peach-colored linen skirt, which flowed softly over her hips, flared gracefully at the ankles and made rustling sounds as she walked; the wide tan belt, secured around her waist, accentuated her hourglass curves. The earrings, slender one-inch silver hoops, completed the impression of seductive softness to complement Chas's tall, lean strength.

Wishing she had a full-length mirror to appreciate the effect, she completed her enticing ensemble by lacing on dusty, rugged hiking boots with scuffed-up toes which, to accommodate thick wool socks in the winter, were a size too big.

A pair of moccasins with delicate orange and blue beadwork on the toes — the only pair of shoes that weren't for hiking and mountaineering — joined a change of clothes in her pack. Headed toward the trail to the village — her term for the community of around one hundred and fifty people in the valley — she met up with Gavin.

"Eena," he called, his eyes wide.

Accustomed to turning heads, she registered his surprise. "Well, I don't always dress like a wild mountain woman."

With a rearranged expression, he cocked his head. "For what it's worth, you look stunning." Then, turning to continue his walk, he added, "It's all in the boots."

She grinned and continued down the slope, sure-footed in the incongruous footwear. The half-hour hike provided valuable time to collect her thoughts. Whether airborne or earthbound, an ever-present tension tumbled thoughts about the post-Solar Flash years of opportunity. She recalled pre-Solar Flash articles asserting that once the grid was down, about a decade would be required for restoration. Three years had already passed.

Although she knew the sovereignty movement would need to spread to the whole continent — no, the entire world — her immediate focus encompassed the six townships of Sector 10. If humanity were to gain a foothold in its own governance, this was an opportune, but limited, stretch of years that would end and perhaps never return.

She navigated a particularly steep bend in the path with increased caution.

In the precarious balance of power — citizens minus guns for a rebellion, and rulers minus the grid for surveillance and mind-control — the landlords and their minions ruled the townships, but the citizens far outnumbered them. Another boon was that shared duty as re-construction project engineers limited the military's ability to be an armed presence in established townships. Wishing for a stash of weapons in the community rather than her single gun and for citizens in the townships to arm themselves was a waste of time.

The trusty soles gripped the ground until the next bend, and her confidence in negotiating both the trail and the challenge she pondered resumed. She had to think strategically. She recalled the time she had taken the problem to Grandfather's brush pile and fire starter enactment and how the dry tinder burst into flame.

Okay, so Three Mountains' challenge was to ignite a resistance movement in the townships. Which brought her to the next bend in her musings. The greatest obstruction wasn't the controlling hierarchy; it was the complacency and gullibility of the people. They had been through a lot and now just wanted to be taken care of and to believe the bombardment of propaganda that encouraged their dependency. At the moment, her frustration with Grandfather's hint rivaled her despair over the duped citizens. Lighting their fire wasn't enough. They needed weapons in their hands to feel their power.

The trail followed an ever-widening stream until it reached the base of the mountain where the forest opened to a crystal clear river flowing through a green expanse of grass and wild flowers. In the distance, someone crossed the bridge while voices, ax blows, and hammering echoed through the valley. When the smell of rain teased her nostrils, she looked up to see darkening clouds in the west and was glad she'd reach Chas before the downpour. So as not to dirty her skirt, she carefully brushed dust and debris from a rock before she sat on it and unzipped her pack to exchange the hiking boots for the doeskin moccasins. Chas's cabin, located at the edge of the valley, faced her across a narrow bridge over Destiny River, and as she approached, there he stood waiting at the door, his eyes shining the love that hers surely reflected.

While Eena greeted Chas, Anaya filled two packs and two bags with produce from the garden including tomatoes, cucumbers, onions, squash and potatoes, along with smoked venison and rabbit, compliments of the patroller/hunters. On top of each she had carefully cushioned baskets of eggs.

With the packs and bags propped on the ground beside her, Anaya spoke to Gavin as he approached with the bucket of ash. "Does your leg feel healed enough to carry a load down the mountain with me?"

"Yes!" Glad to escape more chores and to further explore his new home, he placed the emptied bucket by the compost pile.

"We're heading toward Three Mountains Community," she said as they hoisted the packs on their backs. She also strapped a bag of produce over her shoulder and one over Gavin's.

Following the path from her cave home, which Gavin referred to as the hobbit house, they soon came to a stream. Anaya led the way. "This stream flows into a valley protected by Quartz, Thunderbird and Blue Lake Mountains. Our one-mile hike down Quartz Mountain will take us to Three Mountains Community, where the valley widens at a bend in Destiny River."

When they approached a grassy knoll filled with the sounds and sights of people coming and going, Anaya announced, "The Community!" With brief glances, the people accepted Gavin's presence as a probable runner like themselves. Half a dozen cows grazed contentedly with a couple of horses in a section of tall grass while a couple of men with old-fashioned scythes mowed an area nearby.

"Hay for the livestock during the winter," Anaya explained.

Friendly shouts and the clank of tools resounded with slight echoes as a group built a structure that appeared to be a new dwelling.

The arrivals passed three people working in a large garden. Someone emerged from a nearby greenhouse — much larger than the one by Anaya's cave house. With a friendly wave in response to a greeting, Anaya said, "Green houses are vital in the mountains because of the short growing season."

Gavin noted it was one of three such structures in the valley, each located next to a quarter-acre fenced-in garden.

Anaya indicated the split-log fencing with chicken wire stretched along the lower four feet. "Without fences, the deer, livestock, and rabbits would eat all the produce."

People greeted Anaya as the pair approached a large centrally located structure with an equally large covered area outdoors. The most remarkable feature was the sod roof, which appeared to rise out of a manmade mound of earth as if for the purpose of camouflage. The exposed roofline, supported by large pine poles, had rounded edges that undulated in an irregular pattern, rather than the expected straight edges.

Anaya gestured toward the structure. "The pavilion."

Children's laughter sounded nearby and Gavin noticed a group jumping rope near the trees. A man and woman strolled across the grass, headed for the central wooden bridge that spanned the river.

Gavin wondered where the people lived until he spied their cabins hidden among the tall pines on either side of the river. But rather than being in a single-story row, they were stacked in an alternating upper and lower pattern that created open breezeways at ground level. Most of these were fenced in, apparently serving as enclosures for livestock. Gavin estimated there were around fifty family dwellings in all, plus a couple that appeared to be bunkhouses.

As the pair approached the far end of the valley, Gavin noticed the darkening clouds overhead.

"Rain," he said. Raised in the desert, he spoke as though announcing a celebration.

Ahead of them a conspicuous solar array loomed in front of a sprawling building. Unlike the other structures that were either hidden or camouflaged, the solar panels faced the blue sky, startling evidence of late 20th century technology in this early 19th century village.

A large clap of thunder delivered huge plops of moisture as a man, whom Gavin judged to be in his early twenties, opened a nearby door and ushered them in. After introductions, Steve gratefully accepted Anaya's offering of two dozen eggs, a two-pound pouch of smoked strips of rabbit and venison, as well as the produce from the garden. After expressing his gratitude, Steve excused himself and headed back to his lab.

Anaya led Gavin to the next room, where a woman about his age, her shiny brown hair pulled back in a ponytail, looked up from peering at a device on a table. A faded sweatshirt and worn jeans belied her slender prettiness. She smiled at Gavin, winged brows arched over the rims of her glasses, and he became immersed in the depths of her dark brown eyes.

As the nearly palpable energy exchange passed between Leslie and Gavin, Anaya looked from one to the other. She smiled. "Gavin would probably like to hear about the devices you're designing."

Leslie's expression was animated as she gestured toward a small assembly of wire and other components, calling it a "free energy device." A copper coil within a coil was attached to a motor, which hummed along on the table.

The music in Leslie's voice captivated Gavin as though she were describing the recipe for a delicious soup rather than dry bones science. "You see how this motor continues to turn this wheel?"

His eyes tracing the contours of her full lips, he nodded.

As much as looking at Leslie and listening to her entranced Gavin, she had lost him at the words "free energy."

"Notice this device is not plugged into anything. There's no battery attached."

Gavin gazed at the seemingly crude contraption with new respect. "How is that possible?"

"It draws power from the electro-magnetic fields of Earth's atmosphere."

Gavin's eyes widened as he looked at Leslie and back toward the device.

"Without going into much explanation, these copper coils, this capacitor, and this transistor create an electrical feedback loop."

"Feedback loop?"

"Yes, which means that once it gets going, it's never necessary to plug it in to a power source."

"You mean the motor keeps running indefinitely? A perpetual motion machine?"

"Theoretically. Hence the term 'free energy.' This prototype has continued nonstop for four months. Eventually, a larger one may power this entire lab. Beyond that, similar devices may fuel this whole settlement—the world."

On the window behind Leslie, only lingering drops remained of the rivulets of rain that had coursed the panes earlier. Anaya signaled that she and Gavin needed to make other stops, but wishing for another hour—an eternity—to gaze at Leslie, he was as reluctant to relinquish this encounter as he had been anxious to venture down the mountain. Every morose, skeptical tendency in his nature reveled in Leslie's cheerful demeanor, the open friendliness of her glances. After he and Anaya thanked Leslie and walked through the doorway, Gavin turned with a last look to wave goodbye. He hoped to see more of those expressive brown eyes.

Eena knew Chas, a man of few words, wouldn't compliment how she looked today. But it was his solid quiet strength that attracted her in the first place, along with his grounded connection to his farm. He could hold a clod of dirt in his hand and convey the sense of sharing a treasure trove of jewels; likewise, when he ran his hand along the flanks of his mare, one would think she had been gifted by royalty; and seated on the porch among his hens, which he referred to as "the girls," he often held Chelsey, the one with a deformed claw, the one with a name, as though she were his lap dog. As Eena approached, the sow and piglets rooted among the wildflowers, the hens scurried out of her way, and the mare lay in the shade of the lean-to.

"Is today the day?" she asked.

"Yes, she's foaling. But it's taking too long. After breakfast I need to get back to her."

They were attracted to one another precisely because they were opposites. This was his world, while her domain was *the* world. He was still water to the cyclones of change in hers. She felt calmer when she poured out her concerns to his quiet receptivity.

Today, Eena needed the mirroring of his reflective depths, but first she stood on her toes to melt into Chas's strong embrace. He greeted her with an almost ready breakfast and insisted she sit, sip carefully hoarded chicory coffee, and talk to him while he scrambled eggs.

"Chas, we have to resume daily patrols." Urgency punctuated her words.

"You mean flying the augurs?"

"Yes, but we desperately need a fourth patroller."

"The new guy?"

"I hope."

Silence. "It's likely within three or four years planes will be operational again."

Several scrapes of the spatula against the pan ended the scrambling and he transferred the eggs to their plates. The aroma of caramelized onions in the home fries teased Eena's nostrils.

"We're sitting ducks if a plane flies over Three Mountains."

Chas's blue eyes in angular Japanese features stared directly into hers as he placed the plates on the table and sat across from her.

Eena picked up her fork. "We have to make plans."

"Such as?"

"There must be other settlements in these mountains. We need to find them."

"To accomplish what?"

"Make allies. Maybe some have weapons." She shook the saltshaker as she smiled "thank you" for breakfast. "Then connections with the townships."

"Dangerous thinking. What do you hope to accomplish?"

"Maybe nothing. Most survivors are cowed by the lies and grateful for the tyranny."

Chas nodded and gestured with his fork for her to continue.

"To reach already activated insurgents."

"And then what?"

"Help them band together."

"To?"

"That's where I get stuck. Without guns, a plan for a government takeover is only a pipe dream. The military has mostly withdrawn, but the minions serve the state, and the police have weapons to effectively squelch a coup."

Chas looked at her steadily. "The minions, troops and police are human too, some with the same yearnings for sovereignty and equality."

His reply startled her almost as much as the clap of thunder followed by a downpour.

Bumping the table, Chas stood up. "The pigs will run into the forest for shelter. I have to pen them."

Eena followed him through the door. Immediately drenched, they hurried toward the already on-the-move sow and half-grown piglets. As Chas turned the sow toward the pen, four piglets followed. The fifth veered off in the opposite direction. Eena dove for that one. Wet, slippery and panicked, it struggled to wriggle out of her grasp while full bellied in the mud and rain-soaked grass, she held tight until it was transferred to Chas's arms.

After the sow and piglets were secured, Eena and Chas stood side by side on the porch surveying the downpour. When he smiled at her, she was miserably aware of her bare feet, mud-soaked blouse and skirt, one missing earring, and rain flattened hair.

He slipped his arm around her waist. "You look beautiful," he said, and his eyes said he meant it.

The
Invitation

8

Eena approached with that purposeful attitude Gavin had come to associate with her, and as he recalled her penetrating gaze and the power in her husky voice each time she warned of inevitable discovery by the controllers, he shuddered. As he walked limp-free among the softly clucking chickens, the adventure-seeker vehemently rejected the threat of eventual invasion of this safe, secluded world—of his life morphing into a purpose beyond mere escape.

Eena's green eyes flashed as, with a friendly toss of her head, she headed down a trail he hadn't noticed before. "I have something to show you."

Eager to discover a new aspect of Three Mountains, Gavin gladly followed Eena toward the mysterious destination. As they walked, the cool surface of a quartz rock pressed against his palm, and he ran his thumb across a faceted edge.

Eena gingerly moved a thorny vine to the side. "I suppose you've heard of quartz being used to power electrical devices."

Gavin nodded.

She continued along a well-worn path that appeared to be almost solid crystal. "A whole mountain of it is like a very powerful generator." She glanced back at Gavin. "We're about to step through a portal that may be the result of activation of this power source by the solar eruptions."

Hurrying to catch up with Eena, Gavin reached out his arm to halt her progress. "You mean like a stargate?"

"Not exactly. A door to another space and time here on Earth. You won't see an opening. Just follow me."

Astonished, Gavin froze as Eena disappeared ahead of him. Curiosity grappled with instinctual hesitation, before he shoved aside all rationality and stepped exactly where Eena had gone.

A wispy mist veiled the reddish hues of the nearest tree trunk, which assaulted his gaze with its massive girth, its crown resting somewhere beyond the clouds. He was struck dumb by the mind-boggling proportions of life in this land as awe vied with the jammed cogwheels of his brain.

"To the best of my knowledge we are in a forest of giant sequoia." Eena clasped his forearm. "Now stand very still."

Within moments a swooshing sound enveloped the visitors, followed by a rush of air and an enormous blur of iridescent blue-green that commandeered Gavin's view.

Instinctively, he stepped backward with a sharp intake of air. "What the...." He blinked to bring his eyes into focus.

Eena stepped forward to ruffle the soft tufts along the bird's neck. "This is Cesla," she said matter-of-factly, as if this would allay Gavin's confusion.

"He looks like a cross between an archaeopteryx and a modern bird on steroids!" Unconsciously, Gavin took another step back.

Laughing, Eena nodded. "I really don't know anything about his genetic ancestry. In our time the bones of these birds are probably part of the limestone on the floor of the Pacific Ocean around Micronesia."

At a loss for words, Gavin vacillated between amazement and incredulity.

Eena retrieved a small cloth sack at the base of the nearest sequoia and pulled out a star fruit, while Cesla reached around to preen his feathers.

Startled by the sudden movement and alarmed by the pointed, lethal-looking beak, Gavin moved back another step. In his mind's eye a series of horrifying frames presented a lunging beak that pierced his flesh. With his body poised to run, his heart began to race. Waves of revulsion moistened his palms as he forced his feet to hold their ground because he didn't want to appear cowardly.

Cesla wiped his beak vigorously under the wing base, and then carefully stroked the feathers on his wing one by one from base to tip.

Seeming oblivious to Gavin's interior dilemma, Eena smiled as Cesla oiled and cleaned his feathers. "Behold a specimen of *Avis gigantus*. Impressive, isn't he? Cesla and his kind are called augurs, meaning, and I quote the one who named them, "'Their help heralds a better world for humanity.'"

Descending into complete overload, Gavin estimated this monstrous representative of avis must be twelve feet long from the point of his beak to the tip of his tail. The wingspan appeared to be at least that.

"We're bonded," Eena said as the bird, his preening session completed, pecked at the fruit in her outstretched hand.

"Bonded?" Gavin wiped his hands on his pants legs, calmness returning as he retreated into emotional distance from the scene.

"I've been part of Cesla's life since he was a four-month-old chick." Eena paused as this sank in.

Gavin struggled to absorb this unbelievable scenario, growing stranger by the minute. "So, he's sort of like your pet?"

Without answering, Eena circled to Cesla's tail feathers. The augur remained perfectly still as she straddled the base of his tail and leaned forward to rest stomach-down, knees bent on either side at the base of his wings. As Eena lay in a prone position, arms around his neck, the augur moved toward the clearing without any outward sign of communication.

From several feet away Gavin felt the rush of air and heard the flap of the powerful wings as the huge bird lifted into the air.

Eena waved a friendly salute as she soared upward. Cesla circled overhead, the rider's face beaming over her mount's wing. When they flew out of sight, Gavin squinted into the sunlight, searching the sequoia canopy for a glimpse of Eena and the augur. They reappeared and swooped down to the grassy knoll.

"So, what do you think?" Eena grinned broadly as she backed off her mount.

Gavin shook his head slightly. "This is like a crazy dream—one so real, it's hard to wake up to the actual world."

Eena laughed. "This is no dream, and you ain't seen nothin' yet!"

She looked at the bird, flecks of love lighting her eyes. "Cesla and three others like him are the village eyes."

"There are more like this one?"

Eena seated herself at the base of the tree and motioned for Gavin to sit next to her. "I think you need more background information."

The giant bird moved off toward a stand of guava trees to forage for fallen fruits in the open meadow. At this point, more numb than amazed, Gavin watched as, within minutes, three other giant birds flew down. It was reminiscent of watching flocks descend to the yard of his childhood home, except that now he was in a world of winged creatures that Eena referred to as *Avis gigantus.*

Gavin turned toward Eena, the brain cogs now unstuck, shooting questions in rapid-fire exuberance. "Where in space and time is this place? How did you ever find out about the portal and this land? How did you learn to tame Cesla, let alone ride him?"

"Whoa!" Eena held up her hand in a friendly 'halt' gesture to break into the barrage of questions. "First, I discovered the portal by accident, while exploring Quartz Mountain. Second, I have a story to tell you that goes back possibly more than 40,000 years."

"Cave man days?"

"According to ancient writings all over the world, a continent and its thriving civilization sank into the Pacific Ocean."

Gavin's expression was blank. Textbooks had referenced neither the civilization nor the continent.

"Today, only remnants remain as islands."

Gavin processed this information as Eena peeled a mango with a pocketknife and offered him a slice. They devoured the juicy sweetness before Eena continued. "According to James Churchward, ancient texts—including the Lhasa Records, Easter Island Tablets, Greek Record, Troano Manuscript, and many others—refer to a sunken continent called The Motherland or Mu."

Serious doubt punctuated his response. "What supposedly happened to it?"

"Apparently, a great shaking and shifting of the Earth occurred. The texts describe volcanoes erupting violently as portions of the continent sank. Cataclysms separated by thousands of years led to the final sinking."

Gavin broke in, skepticism written on his face. "According this fantasy, where in the Pacific was this continent located?"

"Good question," Eena replied. "Mu was said to be huge, its remnants stretching from Easter Island and the Hawaiian Islands to the archipelago of Micronesia.

Eena paused so as not to disturb a blue morpho butterfly that had landed on the bark near her head.

As this account of the past sank into Gavin's consciousness, he wavered between disbelief and credulity. "Solid evidence verifies the truth."

Eena grinned as she stood up to continue down the mountain. "Is standing on solid ground sufficient verification?"

As Gavin wordlessly followed Eena, she smiled. "There's more to see."

Gavin looked up at her beneath raised eyebrows. "More?"

"Yes, at the base of this mountain."

Their eyes fastened on the ground, the pair followed a stream and navigated a path through thickets, trees and boulders. Musical tones orchestrated by the play of water over stone percussion instruments accompanied their descent.

When the red woods opened to a vast savannah hosting a cobalt blue river, Gavin gasped his surprise to see giant replicas of Cesla coming and going between sky and plains. The birds soared from dense green canopies to become splashes of shimmering aquamarine in the tall grass or rise with powerful wings to disappear in the azure expanse beyond.

A woman emerged from the shadowed realm of the trees. Her straight dark hair hung just below her shoulders, and she wore a plaid cotton blouse tucked into khaki pants. With a friendly wave, she bounded forward, strength and energy in her stride.

"Eena!"

The friends greeted one another with a warm hug.

Eena released her friend and turned toward Gavin. "Leiani, meet Gavin."

After lighthearted greetings, Eena turned to Leiani. "Would you mind bringing Gavin into your tree world?"

Leiani led them nearer the clusters of cypress. "Look closely at the lower branches just ahead."

Gavin peered into the dense canopy until he became aware of a tangled mass of wood and grass resting in the crotch of the closest tree where thick branches extended from the main trunk.

"A nest!" He turned to Leiani in amazement. "The birds nest in these trees."

Leiani laughed. "They have to nest somewhere."

Gavin gave a low whistle.

Quietly, the three watched in silent wonder for several minutes as adult birds busily flew to the grass, foraged fallen fruits from the scattered trees, and returned to nests to feed hungry clamoring chicks.

"Would you like to see *my* home?" A hint of humor lit Leiani's smile.

Gavin nodded, responsive to the Polynesian woman's open friendliness. He and Eena fell into step behind her as she made her way through the cypress forest.

When they stopped in front of a cypress tree, Gavin looked around, puzzled not to see an inviting log home nestled among the trees.

Leiani laughed. "You have to look up. Here." She directed his eyes to a nest, more regular, less messy than those he'd seen, but still a nest.

Nonplussed, Gavin's gaze shifted from Leiani to the stacked sticks balanced on two limbs of a cypress.

"This nest home, which my dad and I built, is a good solution because it's higher than river floods and endures for many years. Per Dad's instructions, I observed as the augurs constructed the sides of their nests in a roughly spiraling stick polygon. After securing the floor, we built this one the same way.

"To keep out the rain, we drew up plans for that hanging teepee you see attached to the limb directly above the nest. We attached sections of waterproof tarp to bamboo poles to fashion a cone shape. The six rope loops formed from rope woven through the nest wall secures the overhead shelter.

"Would you like to see inside?"

Gavin followed Leiani up the ladder to step inside and sit side by side on a bed extending the diameter of the nest.

"Mimicking the way the augurs made the interiors soft and cozy for their offspring, I fashioned a mattress of pillow cases stuffed with bits of down and the cottony interiors of cattails. When I laid these and my sleeping bag over two planks, my bed was complete. What do you think?"

Gavin had reached the matter-of-fact stage of comprehension. "Comfortable." He looked around to either side of the bed to see clothing and sundries on one side and food, cooking utensils and tools on the other. A bow and quiver of arrows and medical supplies were stashed under the bed.

"This *is* impressive," he remarked.

It had been an interesting day, but Gavin was growing tired, not sure he could take any more of making the unbelievable believable. He stood up, and the women rose with him.

As they climbed down the ladder, Eena said the dreaded words. "We have one more thing to show you."

When they emerged from the trees, he saw her glance at Leiani. Moments later an augur landed, its plumage less colorful than Cesla's.

"Meet Espirit."

While certain he did *not* want to meet an augur, he detected the hopeful cheeriness in Eena's voice. "Espirit no longer has a bond-mate."

Gavin raised his eyebrows in an unspoken question.

"Jarrod, the patroller who piloted this female, returned to Township 21, and we haven't seen him since."

Pure shock charged Gavin's retort. "Why would he return to a township?"

Eena's reply was sharp-edged. "To help his girlfriend escape."

Gavin felt genuine regret for Jarrod. "Oh, so they got him. Too bad."

Eena continued. "We believe Espirit's bond is transferrable to a new patroller."

Gavin remained silent. *Hope you find someone. For sure it won't be me.*

Leiani caressed the bird during the awkward moment of Gavin's silent refusal.

"I've enjoyed meeting you, Leiani," he said to put closure on the topic and the visit.

After the women hugged goodbye, Gavin and Eena retraced their steps across the valley to follow the stream up the dormant volcano toward the portal. Gavin's leg began to ache, but, distracted by a flood of recollections, he hardly noticed. He was glad Eena remained quiet, apparently respectful of his need to process the new information and amazing sights of Mu.

Halfway up the mountain, Eena gave Gavin a sidelong look. "Interested in becoming the pilot of an already trained augur?"

Gavin looked straight up the mountain, calculating the number of steps to relief from both the leg pain and Eena's persistence. "Nope." He hoped his reply nailed the lid on the topic of piloting an augur.

The
Journey

9

Anaya filled two backpacks with bottles of oils and tinctures, and bundles of freshly dried herbs from the greenhouse. She had expanded Matoskah's knowledge of herbs and healing oils from those that strictly grew around the four corners area to powerful varieties from around the world. Together, she and the medicine man filled packets yearly so that the families would be well stocked for the winter; that being the time when people most needed some of the herbs like sage, echinacea, and goldenseal. Today they'd be making the squirrel skin pouches with Grandfather.

Her intent was to combine a trip to the community with an opportunity to prepare the pouches with the venerable elder. Eager to see Leslie, Gavin was glad to accompany her.

Greeting them at the door, Steve placed the bag on the counter in a small kitchenette area to one side of the main living area, which housed an old sofa and matching chair and three TV trays. In the bunkroom to the left, a crumpled sleeping bag lay on one of four bunks, and socks, underwear, shirts and pants spilled out of a canvas bag in the corner, matching the host's unruly hair and disheveled appearance.

Anaya smiled at the scientist. "Steve, do you mind showing Gavin around the lab?"

He nodded and gestured toward Gavin, who was disappointed, wanting to connect with Leslie. In the three lab rooms where Steve and three other scientists worked, tables and wall space were covered with electronic equipment, some of which Gavin didn't recognize. Now, at least, he had an inkling of the purpose for the large solar array.

In a middle lab, two men who appeared to be in their late twenties turned from computer screens, and Steve introduced them as Rigel and Ryan.

In the third room, Gavin greeted Eena, Chas and Leslie, who were there for a meeting with Steve. After greetings and a special smile for the petite, brown-eyed scientist, he headed for a chair beside her, and a large apparatus in the center of the room drew his attention.

Steve looked at Anaya for confirmation that it was all right to speak openly. "It's a projector."

Gavin gave the scientist a sidelong look. "So, are we going to have Saturday movie night here?"

"This is not exactly that type of projector. It's a holographic 3D projector."

Unfamiliar with the term, Gavin stared at the device.

"This immersive three-dimensional projection system can produce a life-size illusion, a three-dimensional hologram within a live setting."

"You mean like a hologram of a person appearing right in this room?"

"Sort of, but 3-D holographics can also appear to replace what's really around you."

"Like the holodeck on Star Trek!"

Steve grinned and nodded. "Yes, very similar."

Eena broke into the dialogue with her customary one-pointed seriousness. On a wall map she pointed out the locations of Transtopia Metro and Durango with Three Mountains in between. "Transtopia, the seat of government for Sector 10 already has two operational planes. These are flown to other sector capitals, townships and Techno City. As soon as Durango is settled, planes may be flying directly over Three Mountains." She paused to let this sink in.

Rigel spoke up. "We are working to create a holographic forest to hide Three Mountains from aircraft."

In Gavin's head, the first almost audible *click* resounded the importance of protecting Three Mountains from detection. While he was increasingly distracted by impatience to hang out with Leslie alone, the discussion continued with plans for a "shopping expedition" to Durango to obtain additional badly needed electronics equipment. The mission would require the well-planned orchestration of patrollers and augurs.

The sounds of the burgeoning village echoed below as Anaya and Gavin, carrying packs of herbs and bottles of tinctures, followed a deer trail along the pine-scented slope of Thunderbird Mountain. The sun was at its zenith when they reached a clearing that had been leveled by geological forces. A third of the way up the mountain, this grassy area hosted an even more unlikely form of housing than the cabins—a teepee.

"It is thanks to the man we are about to visit that most of the people we saw today have gathered here," Anaya mused. Tears moistened her eyes as she spoke.

Gavin thought she must mean people other than him because no one, except Eena, had anything to do with his arrival at Three Mountains Community.

First, the teepee came into view, then the gray-streaked black hair of a man seated on the ground before the glowing embers of a morning fire. Streaming sunlight glinted off the broad shoulders and straight back of the elder as he tanned a deer hide. Suddenly, Gavin realized this was the oldest person he had seen in a settlement of youths and young adults.

Anaya spoke softly in Gavin's ear. "His name is Matoskah, which is Lakota for 'White Bear.' But most call him Grandfather."

After acknowledging Gavin with a friendly nod, Grandfather glanced appreciatively at the packs and then at Anaya. "Good."

They prepared a meal of Grandfather's freshly caught fish with carrots and onions from Anaya's garden, then sat around the fire companionably while they ate and talked.

Anaya told Matoskah that Gavin had met Leslie.

"Ah, that girl's got a real sense of mission." His eyes caught Gavin's. "You can have that too if you undergo the proper training."

Gavin felt a powerful response to the thought of sharing a mission—anything—with Leslie. "Training? Absolutely!"

Matoskah prodded exuberant sparks from the fire.

"So, Grandfather, how do I get started?"

The medicine man, who seldom answered quickly, grabbed a tarp and threw it on the ground just outside the circle of logs around the campfire. Anaya handed Gavin a knife and showed him how to prepare a squirrel skin to become a pouch.

"Would you like to hear a tale of courage told to me by my father?" The older man sat down cross-legged to work.

Gavin nodded.

Once they were all seated, their hands busy with squirrel skins, Grandfather told his story.

"Many years ago at a clan gathering, a young warrior named *Wahkoowah* — that's Lakota for 'Charging Bear' — met a young girl named *Potawatomi*, whose name means 'Dawn.' She was the only girl out of all those he had ever met whom he wanted to marry. At the time, he was too young to ask for her hand in marriage, but two years later he was old enough. However, just getting to the young woman's camp presented several challenges."

Poised to hear a good story about the tribulations a courageous young suitor would overcome against all odds in his quest to reach his beloved, Gavin cut a skin into a circle.

"But so that you won't have to listen in suspense," Grandfather said, "I'll just go ahead and tell you the end. After a long journey with many difficult trials, the young warrior reached *Potawatomi's* tribe with his bride gift of seven horses and asked to marry the girl."

Knife poised in midair, voice up an octave, Gavin protested. "But that's not a story, Grandfather. You skipped over all the exciting parts." With the awkwardness of a beginner, he used the knifepoint to poke holes in the leather.

"You mean the hardships Charging Bear had to go through to succeed in his quest?"

"Yes, yes." Gavin spoke with a *please get on with it* tone. Seeing Anaya thread thin strips of leather through the holes of a pouch, he did the same.

Grandfather continued. "The youth left with a bearskin, snowshoes, a bow and quiver of arrows and a hunting knife. He wanted to reach *Potawatomi* and ask for her hand by springtime. So he left in late winter just before the spring thaw.

"Then the most terrible blizzard of the season came with a vengeance. The fiercely blowing wind was so frigid *Wahkoowah* had to wrap the bearskin around himself. So much snow fell so fast, that even with snowshoes, the brave warrior soon could not take another step. Besides, he couldn't see two steps ahead of him. Suddenly, he heard a loud *crack* when the strong wind blew down a huge old tree. The falling tree narrowly missed the warrior."

Grandfather paused.

Gavin waited for a couple of minutes that seemed like an eternity, hoping the storyteller was about to continue the story. However, since nothing was forthcoming he impatiently nudged the story on. "So... how *did* he survive the blizzard?"

Grandfather shrugged. "I'm not exactly sure. Anyway, Charging Bear made it through."

Grandfather and Anaya continued preparing the pouches. But Gavin sat motionless, grappling with the missing plot points.

The elder continued his narration. "After surviving the blizzard, the suitor continued his quest down the mountainside. Charging Bear was walking along a ridge when he realized a bear was following him. He began to run and tripped over a rock. Then he watched his quiver of arrows fall into the canyon below. The bear had begun to run and came so close, the frightened boy could hear its panting. The warrior saw a sturdy tree growing sideways at the edge of the cliff as he felt the bear's hot breath on his neck."

He paused again.

Gavin looked expectantly at the old man's stoic face.

Grandfather sighed. "I honestly don't know how he got out of that fix."

"Aw, come on, Grandfather. You're leaving out the exciting dramas."

His face impassive, Grandfather continued his story. "Anyhow, Charging Bear did escape the bear. Soon he came to the plains where buffalo were grazing. Then he came to a raging river. The force of the rushing water was so powerful it carried large tree branches. The warrior watched a buck struggle to reach the shore. But the swift currents repeatedly pulled the magnificent animal back in."

This time, when Grandfather's voice stopped, Gavin didn't try to hide his disgust. "You're not going to tell me any of the good parts of the story, are you, Grandfather?"

Grandfather's reply was quiet and measured. "We have to live the 'good parts' for ourselves."

"You mean the challenges?"

Grandfather looked directly at Gavin. "That's the way we figure out how to overcome them."

"So, how *do* I undergo the proper training?"

"You have to speak to Eena about that."

Gavin groaned. This was Grandfather's sly way of teaching him a lesson. "The augurs. I have to overcome my fear of birds."

Grandfather shook his head. "I'm not telling you that. You decide whether each obstacle is a step toward your goal."

As Anaya and Grandfather prepared squirrel skin pouches for herbs, Gavin sat motionless, resisting the pull of an undefined quest.

Gavin needed a place to live, so Eena led him to a cabin near her own deep in the woods. "This is the bunk house of the patrollers. You can stay here until you decide how you are going to contribute to the community."

Feeling irked by the ever-surfacing pressure he felt coming from Eena, Gavin surveyed the bunkhouse. Behind the three cots that lined the walls was a small room at the back with a composting toilet and large washtub with a plastic curtain drawn around it. On a high ledge sat a five-gallon container for water with flexible rubber tubing attached to the lip and a sprayer nozzle attached to the end.

Eena gestured toward the makeshift ensemble. "For an occasional shower," she said.

Four feet of counter space with a basin in the center served as a kitchen of sorts. On the counter sat a five-gallon bucket requiring a daily haul from the nearby stream. Along one corner of the cabin, a black stovepipe extended through the ceiling from a cast iron stove with a hot plate for cooking. On the floor next to it was a pile of wood that, by winter, would need frequent replenishing from the outside woodpile that, thanks to daily chopping and log splitting, grew daily. A bow and quiver of arrows hung from a hook on the wall in the far corner of the room.

At that moment two youths about Gavin's age appeared at the entrance with noisy stomping and greetings. Like Eena, they carried bows and wore quivers of arrows. She introduced Gavin as a new resident and them as fellow patrollers.

Lori was eighteen, short and slightly plump, her dark blonde hair cut just below the chin.

Chuck was strongly built, about Gavin's age, medium height with wide shoulders.

Freshly killed rabbits and squirrels hung at the youths' waists.

Chuck grabbed Gavin's shoulder. "Great! Now there are three of us to skin and prepare the meat and pelts. We have a lot to accomplish before sunset."

The rest of Gavin's day was spent unadventurously skinning rabbits and squirrels. After hanging up the pelts, they cut the meat into thin strips and placed them in the smokehouse to dry.

The dried meat would be placed in jars and stored along with the preserved fruits and vegetables in the pantry. The entire community was feverishly stocking their winter storage.

The tug of Chuck and Lori's sense of mission was subtle, but palpable, and Gavin became connected to his new roommates. He felt a tinge of wistfulness when they headed through the portal to call their augurs or into the forest armed with bows and arrows. One day, he asked about the set that hung unused in the cabin.

"It belonged to Jarrod, the fourth patroller," Lori explained.

Chuck cocked his head to look sideways at Gavin. "Want archery lessons?"

After a couple of weeks of practice, he joined the pair as they tracked sufficient game to fill the smokehouse. But each time they disappeared through the portal with a powerful *whoosh* of wings, Gavin imagined a phantom version of himself flying with them, while with wistful longing he stood just this side of the entrance to the ancient home of the augurs.

Decisions

Since Eena began patrolling, Three Mountains Community had seemed safe from detection. The primary east–west military route was Highway 160 at the closest point fifteen miles south of the Three Mountains perimeter. She'd never seen any vehicles cruising Highway 240, the closest east–west route, two miles to the south, which reinforced a feeling of security—until today. She peered at a jeep that wasn't cruising. It was creeping. Binoculars trained on the jeep of four men, she flew Cesla low, screened by pines. They approached from the direction of Durango, which didn't bode well.

The driver slowly approached northbound Highway 243, the road to Lemon Reservoir, which bordered a trailhead leading to Three Mountains. The jeep stopped at the well-camouflaged barricade built two years before to hide the dirt road to the reservoir. As Eena circled anxiously, the driver jumped out, approached the barricade, and scrambled to the top as though expecting to see the road on the opposite side. Apparently encouraged by the sight, he returned to the vehicle and simply bypassed the barricade by driving up and over the base of the mountain at a forty-five-degree angle, then down to the road, continuing to the dam. Stopping again, the four men piled out of the car to study the map laid on the hood. After the driver pointed in the direction of Quartz Mountain, they jumped back into the jeep.

Are they looking for us? A chill coursed the length of Eena's spine.

Momentarily, she lost sight of the troops as she flew Cesla to the opposite side of the peak to land on Quartz Mountain. From there, screened by pines, she could see north of the reservoir, where the river ran through the ravine named Promise Path and, above it, the bridge that Gavin had crossed about a half mile ahead of the soldiers.

No jeep. She breathed a sigh of relief. Maybe they had turned around. Well-screened, she continued to watch in case they reappeared—which they did. The jeep bounced along, the road increasingly rough and rocky.

Like Blue Lake and Thunderbird Mountains, Quartz Mountain, a 14,000-foot mountain, was among the tallest in Colorado. Were they simply admiring it? Or did they know something? Had Jarrod been forced to give away their location?

The trail between mountains that the community used to come and go was about 100 yards beyond the patrollers, the rocky terrain impassable, even for a jeep. The men got out, milled around, and approached the base of the mountain before disappearing from view. Could they have noticed the stream that bordered the trail? If so, and if they followed it, in about an hour they would reach the valley—and the community.

No, that mustn't happen. She considered her options. They were four armed men. Get her gun, the only one in the community? The patrollers had archery sets. Distract the soldiers? How? Warn the community? Then what?

Cesla was growing restless, probably hungry, extending her wings and standing on one claw and then the other.

Eena calculated the time involved in flying Cesla back to the portal. To retrieve her gun and return by foot to the entrance to the valley trailhead would take too long. By then they'd have entered the valley.

A shriek from Cesla and the augur's distressed wing-flapping forced a decision. She gave the psychic command: *Leave me. Fly home through the portal.*

With her great wings spread, the augur took four steps, her claws digging into the earth, before lifting off. As Eena watched the bird arc over Lemon Reservoir, the sound of a gunshot surged instant regret. A long iridescent feather torn from the wing floated past her gaze, which shifted anxiously back to Cesla, but the augur continued to fly, disappearing from sight.

With a surge of relief, Eena grabbed her binoculars. The soldiers were once again in plain view, having run to the more open area to view the augur. The soldier with the gun was laughing. Another pushed him, his face contorted in anger. The soldier on his opposite side shook his head in disbelief while the fourth ran forward, his eyes fixed on the falling feather, which floated in rhythmic waves to the shore. Eena willed the feather away from its inevitable destination until, shaking his head, the soldier retrieved the four-foot long feather and carried it back to his companions.

After a few minutes of speculation and head scratching while scanning the sky, the soldiers jumped into the jeep and drove away, taking their souvenir with them.

The episode haunted her. The military was too close to Three Mountains. What did they know? What did they want? Would they return to look for more giant birds? As vocal as Eena had been about humanity's complacency, the arrival of the military shook her into hyper-awareness of imminent danger to Three Mountains.

Slowly, she turned, completing a full circle. The rugged islands of stone jutting from a tumultuous sea of green floated a sense of urgency to her consciousness. The augur pilots must seek contact with other settlements hidden in the mountains immediately. Surely there were other enclaves of people, either missed by the post-Solar Flash military sweeps or populated by runners, with whom Three Mountains could connect and form alliances. True, without weapons, they would be no match for armed advances. But, if nothing else, alerted people could scramble into the forest, perhaps even to hidden retreats, or trek to alliance strongholds.

She needed to share these scouting missions with a special partner. Chuck and Lori were good at what they did: hunting and patrolling. Jarrod would have been ideal, but she had given up all hope of his return. Caellum's determination to bring down the power hierarchy matched her own. His independence would be valuable in a township. Gavin. As much as he protested any commitment beyond an extended vacation, it had taken considerable boldness for the nineteen-year-old to escape the township alone. If Gavin would finally bond with Espirit, she would ask him to accompany her on scouting missions.

Anaya invited Gavin to return to Grandfather's to fill pouches with herbs and bottles with oils. Eager to see Leslie, Gavin was glad to accompany her.

As though he knew they were coming, Grandfather waited for them, the bags of squirrel skins and bottles on the tarp.

This time, Grandfather's prolonged silence felt like an unspoken invitation. Finally, Gavin could keep quiet no longer concerning his first augur contact. "A feeling of revulsion overcame me when I looked at that huge bird." He opened up to Grandfather, telling him the augurs reminded him of the Saturday night when he sat on the sofa next to his dad watching the movie *The Birds*, produced and directed by Alfred Hitchcock. At seven years old, the sight of the attacking gulls had terrified him so much that for a year after witnessing those scenes, he had nightmares filled with blood, terror and the assaults of birds.

Grandfather nodded. "Too bad. Your father didn't understand that such images damage the spirit of a little boy."

"When I'm near an augur, that's all I see—the image of stabbing blows from those huge, sharp beaks. Besides, I came to escape the controllers, not confront them."

For another half hour as they filled pouches, Grandfather's slight nods of understanding loosened interior bonds of imagined terror.

Finally, nudged to readiness for flight, Gavin spoke. "I'm ready to begin my mission."

He stood up. *And I'm ready to see Leslie now.* "Thank you, Grandfather."

"At least you won't have a huge, angry bear breathing down your back."

The cryptic response was to both the voiced and unvoiced intentions.

Gavin opened the bunkhouse door for Eena.

She smiled as he put on his socks and shoes. "This will be an experiment," she said, "to see if Espirit transfers the bonded relationship to you."

Despite his decision, Gavin struggled to imagine being bonded to a bird.

"If you're going to be a good rider, you will have to develop your imagination."

"What does imagination have to do with riding a big turquoise bird?"

"It provides a form of communication through pictures. If you want Espirit to bank left, you picture banking left. Once you and the bird are bonded, this picture communication becomes as natural as breathing."

Gavin followed her through the door. "I don't understand."

"Mental communication is instantaneous. The bird reacts with more fluidity when the two of you are connected mind and spirit. This can mean the difference between life or death in a crisis."

This got Gavin's undivided attention. "What kind of crisis?"

"One where we get spotted by the wrong people—people posing a threat to the community."

They paused momentarily on the path and lowered their voices as a small herd of deer crossed the trail ahead, oblivious of the hidden watchers.

Gavin could tell Eena was gauging his reaction as he faced this possibility. "Our task is twofold: to scan the perimeter of Three Mountains for the approach of unwelcome intruders." She resumed walking. "And second, to expand our range of flight to seek and find like-minded communities in the mountains."

Her words provoked Gavin's realization that the world he wanted to explore was one of strategic alliances and imminent invasions.

"I hope you are beginning to understand how important the patrollers are," Eena called back just before she disappeared through the portal.

Gavin followed her into the subtropical paradise where he must face his fear.

Eena's voice intruded on Gavin's wry musings. "Now, we look for fruits to feed the augurs. Tossing him a pouch to tie around his waist, she led him to various fruit trees that grew in clearings among the sequoias, sharing the names for the star fruit, the dark cherry-like fruits called *grumichamas*, and *tamarillos*, known as tree tomatoes. Eena opened the large green pinecones of the giant conifers with a pocketknife to extract the pine nuts. When the pouches at their waists were filled with fruits, she placed some pine nuts and tamarillos in their palms and held up her finger for silence. A few seconds later Espirit spiraled downward, huge claws spread to meet the earth.

"Normally, augurs have only one bond-mate. But Leiani helped me become a secondary bond-mate to this one." Eena approached the bird and reached for her head. "Espirit likes to have her head and throat scratched," she said, signaling for Gavin to come closer. "First, hold out your hand, palm up, to offer her the food."

Gavin stood frozen to the spot, unable to move his arm.

Eena's green eyes probed his. "You can do this."

Gavin breathed deeply to slow the pounding of his heart. The image of the large pointed beak coming toward his hand conjured the memory of slashing beaks.

"She won't hurt you." Eena's voice was soft and gentle. "Do keep your hand flat."

Gavin timidly moved his arm to offer the pine nuts to the bird. Eena cradled his hand in her own and slowly brought it under the bird's beak.

When the pointed tip approached his palm, Gavin's hand jerked away involuntarily. The nuts spilled on the ground.

Apparently, having anticipated this possibility, Eena fed the bird the pine nuts she had in her own palm while she quietly directed Gavin. "Pick up the nuts from the ground, and let's try again."

This time, the youth steeled himself not to flinch as the beak approached his hand.

Pleased wonder flowed through Gavin as the bird pecked at the food, the tip of her beak lightly brushing his palm. Each time Espirit pecked, she raised her head to gulp down the nut. Each time she lowered her head, Gavin grew more relaxed.

Gavin and Eena returned through the portal several times until Espirit and her future rider began to enjoy each other's company. As the bonding progressed, Eena coached Gavin in communication through combined feelings and images.

Gavin was amazed that the bird often fluffed with pleasure prior to his touch, confirming the physiological response to his intent.

Finally, the day came to call the augur from the treetops.

Brow furrowed and eyes scrunched, he tried with no result.

"Relax. Just call her like you would a friend from across the road."

Gavin took a deep breath. He pictured Espirit, felt the familiarity of their bond, and pictured her flying down to the ground.

During the intervening seconds, he assumed he had failed again until the giant wings shadowed the ground, and he felt the familiar rush of air at her approach. A happy feeling he hadn't anticipated permeated his being. The augur had landed in response to his call. But the surge of happiness yielded to a fresh round of aversion.

Eena looked directly at Gavin, startling him with her next words. "No one else in the community is as right for this mission as you."

Eena, dressed in the feathered garment, called Cesla from foraging in the meadow, and walked to the rear of the augur, leaving Gavin alone with his interior battle. From his irascible perspective, Gavin thought Eena looked ridiculous dressed in the shapeless feathered garment. He stood sullenly thinking that bird training was far removed from his dream of exploring the three mountains and beyond. He had not even set foot on Blue Lake Mountain. Gavin flashed back to Grandfather's words. "You decide whether each obstacle that presents itself to you is a significant step toward reaching your goal," he had said. *Riding one of these birds isn't really connected to my goals,* he thought peevishly.

Applying his freshly proven power to assert his wishes to Espirit a second time, he mentally commanded, *"Go. Fly free, and I will walk free."*

He watched from an emotional distance as Espirit flapped her powerful wings and slowly rose in an ascending spiral.

He began to fold up the gear that was for Espirit's rider and stuff it into the duffel bag. He had decided to leave this strange tropical land and never return.

He ducked as Cesla and Eena flew over his head to disappear through the portal.

Impulsively, Gavin ran under the stone arch and on the opposite side looked up to see the bird soar in a circle above him. The flight over the tree canopy was low enough that he could see Eena beaming her joy over the augur's wing.

It dawned on him for the first time that, for Eena, bird piloting wasn't just a job. She was enjoying herself. She looked like a person having the adventure of a lifetime. The sight blasted the final vestiges of the internal barrier to his chance to fly, not climb, to the summit of the next mountain. He recalled Grandfather's story. *Potawatomi's challenge was a bear; mine's only a bird. Surely I can do this,* he reflected wryly.

Frantically waving his arms, he signaled Eena to return. As she and the bird circled back through the portal, he ran back to hastily don his patroller uniform. Taking a deep breath, with Eena standing by, he called Espirit. As he watched the distant speck grow larger, an undeniable thrill of pleasure—maybe it was power—swelled in his heart.

With wings extended, seeming to encompass the entire sky, the augur's claws reached for Earth. Once landed, Espirit slowly, ceremoniously folded her wings and lifted her head, as though requiring the human, who so easily dismissed and recalled her, to appreciate her full stature. The regal pose lifted the beak he had so dreaded, beyond reach, as though to signify that to win her acceptance was no small thing.

Gavin grabbed a star fruit from the pouch and held out his hand in a truce offering. Espirit deliberately lowered her head to Gavin's extended hand that signified reversal of the former withdrawal. As Espirit delicately dismembered the skin and pulp and extended her neck to swallow, Gavin ran his fingers over her jaw with the other hand, passing over the edge of the jawbone to feel the powerful neck flex in response to a series of gulps. When Espirit lowered her head once more, he surprised himself by touching the tip of his index finger to the smooth, hard keratin of her beak. He traced the curved surface to the point that had so intimidated him while the motionless bird accommodated a milestone in their bonding.

Patiently, Eena supervised as Gavin fumbled through his first attempt to don the feathered suit.

She reached into his bag and tossed him a small hand-held device.

"A radio?" he asked with raised eyebrows.

"Yes, so you can communicate with other patrollers. Also, in case we need to radio important information, perhaps of an intruder, to the people in the community. Here, strap on these binoculars."

Eena mounted Cesla and waited.

Gavin's heart pounded in full trust of the augur, if not himself. He lay on Espirit's back, folded his legs over the surprisingly accommodating torso and wrapped his arms around the muscular neck. With the eagerly conveyed image of rising above the earth, the powerful wings lifted and extended. The bird stepped forward and the wings, like giant oars, propelled bird and rider upward through the ocean of air. Surprise and elation vied for supremacy as the earth receded below him.

"This first trip, we'll fly together," Eena called back before disappearing through the portal.

When Espirit arced above the meadow, he felt the power of the wings that held them aloft, captain and living vessel churning waves of air.

Astounded to be enjoying the most exhilarating experience of his life, Gavin wondered why he hadn't jumped at the chance to become a patroller. Among the barrage of emotions, the tingling sense of meaningful engagement with life added color and texture to his dreams of adventure as Gavin guided Espirit through the portal to fly his first patrol mission.

The Mission

Eena chuckled at Gavin's mixed chagrin and awe as he ruminated aloud about his encounters with Matoskah, who seemed to take perverse pleasure in shattering statements dropped like small bombs. Enjoying this new side of Gavin—his enthusiasm for seeking groups like theirs in the mountains—she glanced at him. He was mounted to fly their third scouting expedition, binoculars strapped on. With a slight nod, she signaled Cesla and, with the exhilaration that came with liftoff, led the way through the portal.

A half hour later, when they saw a convoy crawling along Highway 50, Eena regretted her decision to leave her gun behind. She had anticipated it might make people nervous, or worse, be taken from her in a confrontation.

Gavin peered through his binoculars. "Wonder where they're headed."

Eena put hers down. "Let's follow the highway."

After another half hour she thought they needed to land the augurs for a rest when she saw the ruins.

"Looks like another town destroyed during Solar Flash." In a one-mile long swath of devastated forest and leveled buildings, it looked like a bomb had hit the place.

As Eena's eyes scanned the perimeter, she saw a nearby settlement. "The survivors simply moved into the forest."

They circled a village similar to Three Mountains, but double the size. Two miles from the old town, log homes surrounded a lake ensconced in hilly, forested terrain.

Not wanting the sight of giant birds to alarm the people, they looked for a clearing close by and circled for a landing.

Eena knew Gavin wanted to accompany her, but she worried about attacks on the augurs from large predators. She looked at him apologetically.

He shrugged. "I'll stay with the birds. You go."

Stepping out of her augur garb, she tucked the radio into her pocket. "Keep your radio turned on," she said and walked toward the town.

The first to notice Eena was a man harvesting lettuce from a garden. He stared as though it took a moment to register she was not from the settlement.

Approaching with a friendly smile, she met the man who introduced himself as George Wilson, the mayor. Others began to gather.

After more introductions and small talk, she faced the mayor. "I have important information for you."

Mayor Wilson, who had governed the town before Solar Flash changes, stood on a stump and called more people to the gathering. "We have a visitor who wants to speak to us."

One by one people ceased their labors, put down fishing poles, and emerged from cabins until a large crowd assembled by the stump with children whooping and running on the outskirts. The mayor put up his hands and waved them over his head to signal the people to be quiet before he introduced Eena. "Please give Eena your full and respectful attention."

He stepped down and offered his hand to Eena, who politely ignored it as she replaced him on the stump. She took a deep breath and dove in with the startling news.

"A military convoy is headed this way," she began. Observing the reactions, she noted a mixture of consternation and happy relief. She waited for the buzz to die down. "They're about an hour away."

This time, a more tumultuous series of gasps and exclamations followed her announcement.

Someone from the crowd called out, "Are you warning us or informing us?"

The crowd quieted again as she held up her hand. "That depends on your perspective. Please hear me out. I'm from a township that welcomed a military convoy. They saved us from barely surviving. However, it wasn't the good old U.S. Army coming to help us. It was the Union of the Americas."

A disbelieving uproar ensued.

Again Eena raised her hand. "I must make this story short. So listen carefully. You have to make a decision that will dramatically change your life for better or for worse. And you have to do so quickly."

Except for the peripheral shouts of children, silence greeted her pause. "A totalitarian regime is now fully in control on this continent. If you remain in this camp, the army, a hand-picked town father, and a construction crew will help you rebuild infrastructure."

"What can be bad about that?" The disgust barbed the woman's voice.

"Then they will imprison you in it."

Anger broke out in the confused audience. Several hurled profanities at Eena as though she were the entity attempting the hostile takeover.

The mayor held back a surge that could have knocked the stump over and her with it.

"What makes you think you know so much?" a man yelled, shaking his fist.

Eena's unflappable demeanor belied her pounding heart. "Almost everyone in my community is an escapee, a runner from a township — like the one you'll find yourself in if you stay."

Her heart vied with impatience as, in confused dismay and panic, the people argued loudly. Knowing how desperately the majority wanted the convoy to be good guys offering aid, she waited for several minutes until the mayor, with a dark scowl on his face, motioned her to step down.

Before acceding the stump to him she raised an arm for her final words. "I will wait fifteen minutes at the edge of your village. You have the choice to leave freely with me now or attempt a dangerous escape later." She paused, the mayor motioning her down, the crowd closing in again. "And risk execution with retrievers running you down," she shouted over the chaos as she turned to leave.

Mayor Wilson practically pushed her off the improvised speaking platform. He mounted it and stood raising and lowering his hands with a calming motion to quiet the survivors of his town. A hush fell over the agitated group as Eena walked away and the people attended his soothing words.

"Listen, there is *nothing* to worry about. You have been through too much to be subjected to fear mongering."

Sharp hits and pings pummeled Eena's back as people threw rocks, sticks and pinecones at the retreating bringer of doom. As she hurried to the far side of the lake, she heard the mayor's benign promises to protect them and assurances of guaranteed rights. At the edge of the forest on far shore, she saw Gavin approaching.

"Go back," she hissed. "Move the augurs deeper in the forest."

He hesitated, as though wanting to stand his ground to protect her, before he turned on his heels.

Eena moved further into the veil of trees as she waited. She saw the mayor raise his fist and shake it, and heard rousing applause before the people began to disperse. After several minutes, sufficient time for people to gather clothing and toiletries, no one came. Disheartened, she turned, leaving them to their fate.

As she stepped away, a slight movement in the forest drew her attention. A man, woman, and three children approached.

"The mayor warned us not to try to leave," the woman explained in answer to Eena's questioning gaze.

Over several minutes two more families and two couples quietly emerged from the screen of trees. The group waited in a whispering huddle, but no more came.

With a silent hand signal Eena led them deeper into the forest before she stopped to prepare the listeners for the next surprise.

"My partner and I have reached you by means of a rather unusual form of transportation." As they waited quietly and expectantly, she was sure that whatever each was imagining was far from what they were about to see. "There's no time to explain now. But we rode here on giant birds."

Those gathered simply gazed at her, without comprehension.

"Please keep a respectful distance. They're not used to so many people at once."

Turning to lead them, she couldn't resist a private smile.

"Wait," someone called out.

She turned to see a male youth emerge from the shadows.

"We're headed toward a couple of big birds," a woman explained, provoking a ripple of uneasy chuckles.

Watchful for Eena's approach, Gavin had relocated the augurs in a clearing sufficient for takeoff. When the huge creatures came into view, the people were more than glad to keep a respectful distance.

Holding Espirit and Cesla, Gavin waved and calmed the augurs while Eena headed straight for Cesla.

Feeling this a safe distance from the village to address the gathering, Gavin spoke. "We didn't expect to be taking people with us today."

"We were seeking communities like yours to open communication between us," Eena said.

The people remained quiet as Gavin picked up the thread. "The convoy surprised us."

A man stepped forward. "So what now? We've left our homes and can't return."

Eena and Gavin quietly conferred before Eena spoke. "I'm going to get more augurs to transport you to our village."

Apprehension rippled through the assemblage.

Quickly, Gavin spoke to their fears. "There's no danger. It's really a fun ride." He turned to Eena. "While you go, I'll introduce them one at a time to Espirit."

"I'd rather walk," insisted a woman.

"That's an option," agreed Eena. "But it's a four- or five-day trek."

"I'm really frightened of those birds—for my children as well as myself."

Gavin's face registered compassion as he nodded.

Before a spellbound crowd, Eena donned her augur-feathered garb and mounted her bird. When she was prone on Cesla's back, her arms around his neck, the augur lifted into the sky over the heads of the enthralled audience, and receded into a speck before disappearing.

Gavin called on the most recent arrival to approach Espirit, and for the next hour all but a handful came forward to stroke the bird as Gavin held tightly to her bridle. According to his calculations, the sixteen people—eleven adults, and five children—would require two trips, loading children with adults on five of the six pack augurs.

Afternoon shadows were growing by the time Eena's voice came on the radio.

"Had to rest Cesla. Over."

"Understood. Over."

"Everything okay? Over."

"Ready and waiting. Over."

The response was a series of crackles.

"Eena, you there? Over."

Nothing.

People were struggling to keep the children's voices lowered, half smothering the cries of restless toddlers while nervousness about being discovered escalated with the added worry of lost radio contact.

When the flock of huge birds flew into view, a communal sigh of relief indicated taut nerves unwinding. Unlike the wary adults, the children, having been introduced to Espirit, were beside themselves with excitement, yelling, "The birds are here."

Led by Cesla, with the resounding *phooms* of huge wings, the six pack augurs landed one at a time with barely enough space in the meadow. Anxious about being seen by the townspeople, Eena had entered from the far side of town.

Gavin walked up to help with the augurs. "What happened?"

"My radio's out."

"Not a good time to be out of contact."

"I can't fly Cesla anymore today. You'll have to fly the first group to Three Mountains and return in the morning. And bring me a battery for my radio."

After the augurs were fed and rested for a half hour, she leveled her no-nonsense, no-time-to-waste voice at the people. "It'll take two trips to get all of you to Three Mountains." Quietly, she addressed Gavin. "I've brought food and sleeping bags for those of us who remain behind."

She and Gavin paired each of the children with a woman for safety and their combined weight. Then they loaded nervous passengers on five augurs plus the youth on the sixth. Tears watered the cheeks of a still-frightened woman, but she allowed herself to be half-shoved onto an augur, covering her toddler with her body. Sending wives and children first, the anxious husbands on the ground watched the augurs take flight.

That evening after the birds had disappeared from view, and Eena and the men had eaten and crawled into sleeping bags, the soldiers appeared.

The Interrogation

12

Captain Donahue, a man in his mid-thirties, assumed a condescending air as though scolding naughty children. Mug in hand, he stood facing the prisoners who were seated in a row of folding chairs.

"Let me get this straight. You men were removing your families *from* the protection and assistance of the UA military?"

The five men sat in various postures allowed by handcuffed hands, their expressions ranging from glum to defiant to hostile.

The officer turned to Eena. "And you? The instigator? Upsetting the people of a camp on the verge of receiving government aid?"

Eena stared at him, struggling to mask the inwardly broiling concerns as she wondered where they had taken Cesla. *Cesla, I know you're frightened. I'm so sorry.* If only she could warn Gavin. *Gavin, take care. No way out of this one.* She maintained an impassive expression, determined not to reveal the sinking feeling in her heart.

"A pretentious Joan of Arc lying to these people?"

And you, a foolishly deluded puppet.

After ordering the men to be removed from the tent, the captain brought his chair to sit directly in front of Eena. He arranged his freshly shaved features in a mocking smile.

"Okay. It's just you and me. Time to come clean."

Dread fueled her racing thoughts. *He's going to ask about Cesla.*

"So... Big Bird. I'm intrigued."

Eena shrugged. "Some kind of weird mutant."

He assumed the overly patient attitude of a big brother, signaling with one hand. "More. Out with it."

Eena stared at him. *You think I'm going to make this easy for you?*
"Mutant?"

"As you probably know, the solar flares messed with DNA."
Certain he didn't know, she watched a startled look momentarily
rearranged his superior smirk.

Captain Donahue got up to refill his mug. "Tea?"

She shook her head. As he picked up the metal pot heating over the
low flame of a camp stove, she anticipated his next strategy for forced
entry into her locked brain.

"And the women and children?"

"Escaped, obviously."

"You need to tell me where they're headed."

"Through the forest."

A threatening look cracked the friendly veneer. "Before this night's
over, you're going to tell me *where*."

If I volunteer a direction too fast he'll know I'm lying. "I'm sure you
know where settlements are in the area."

The slight flicker of his eyes revealed he didn't. "What you're going
to tell me, is why just women and children?"

The direction of the interrogation gave Eena an unanticipated tack.
"Wait three days and see." She watched him calculating. *Probably
picturing the arrival of unarmed men against the UA military.*

A huge grin relaxed Captain Donahue's features. "So, a bunch of
mountain men are going to surround the UA military?" He burst out
laughing.

Eena stared at him, deliberately raising her chin in defiance to give
the impression he was ridiculing the truth.

After his hearty laughter lost its punch, he traced the rim of his cup
with his forefinger. "I have a hunch you're attached to that mutant bird."

This was the first crack in her wall of deflection. She was sure her
face gave away the interior jolt.

"He'd make a month's worth of chicken dinners for the town and
my men."

Now was the time to mislead. "Okay. The settlement's about thirty
miles northeast of here."

The captain tilted back his head and looked at her through half-
closed eyes.

He's considering whether or not I'm lying. "What've you done with
Cesla?"

"Cesla? Big Bird?"

Eena acknowledged with a stare.

"Tied up in the center of the town."

His words sliced through her heart. *This is all my fault.*

"Tears? Now we have tears? Now, after all the trouble you've caused?"

Her distress seemed to anger him. His features darkened.

"You deserve a good paddling, little girl."

"And you, you're playing soldier so you can torment innocent people."

He moved his face to just inches from hers. "Just bad little troublemakers like you."

"Remember the oath you swore to defend and protect the people?"

"Exactly."

"United States citizens, free to come and go as we please."

"Free as long as you obey the laws."

"Of a constitutional government, *of*, *for*, and *by* the people."

"The UA government."

"The one holding the people of Sector 10 hostage."

"The government giving aid."

"The *aid* they're *not* free to forgo."

"This is about *you*. About *you* inciting rebellion against the government."

"Not my government... or yours, if you're honest."

Shaking with fury, his free hand in a clenched fist, the interrogator loomed over her. "Sergeant, take this woman to the other tent."

Assuming the captain's attitude, the soldier roughly grabbed Eena's arm. She stumbled, and then assembling all the dignity she could muster, walked with him into the tent where the handcuffed men lay in the dirt and he pushed her to the ground.

It was a long and sleepless night, but with one big consolation. Her radio was broken.

Leiani's warning of large nocturnal predators discouraged Gavin from spending the night in Mu. At first light, radio battery in a pocket, he approached Leiani standing with bags stuffed with fruit. She called the pack augurs, knowing they'd follow Espirit, thanks to the flocking instinct. When Gavin arrived, they loaded the birds with their food supply, and Espirit, with Gavin mounted, led the flock through the portal. When he was sure he was within a twenty-mile range, he radioed Eena, just in case her radio was working.

No response.

"Eena, you there? Over." Uneasiness gripped Gavin.

Five minutes later, followed by the six pack augurs, he flew Espirit over the meadow. Nothing but disheveled sleeping bags. Alarm spurred him to action. Landing not far from the embers of last night's fire, Gavin tethered Espirit to a tree and the pack augurs to her. He fed the birds and emptied the burlap bag of the remaining fruit into a separate pile for later. After stacking the scattered sleeping bags and restarting the fire, he found a hefty branch. When he had wrapped and secured the burlap around the tip, he placed his makeshift firebrand beside the fire. Just in case he needed it. Conflicting concerns about both the augurs and probable captives weighed on him as he headed toward the periphery of the village.

Avoiding the dirt road where two jeeps and three cargo trucks were parked, Gavin circled one way and then the other behind the dwellings around the lake. He observed both soldiers' and villagers' patterns of behavior while scanning for Eena and the five men. Each time he circled, he checked on the augurs.

After several hours and not a single glimpse of the hostages, he knew that most of the soldiers were armed and that Cesla was tied up on display in the center of the town. It took considerable restraint not to stride toward the augur, slice the tether that bound him, and fly him away. Painfully, he noted an overturned bowl of water that went completely unnoticed, yet the bird's distressed movements received little sympathy as people walked past, conferring or stopping to laugh and make jokes about "Big Bird."

Handcuffed and tied to a chair along with the men in a row of chairs, Eena faced the window on the opposite side of the large one-room building that served as the mayor's office. Mayor Wilson's desk was to her right, the front door to her left where at a table nearby sat a soldier. Tall, with graying sandy hair, his face was lightly freckled with crinkle lines forming at his eyes and parentheses beside his mouth. But it was his hands that drew her attention. Smooth, looking like they should belong to a youth, they moved with slow deliberateness, as though designed for fine-tuned precision. Behind him hung a white smock, a stethoscope, and a handcuff key on hooks.

At the moment, the mayor stood directly in front of Eena, shaking his finger at her. "God shall smite the wicked and cast them into everlasting hell."

He treated the men merely as sons who had gone astray, irresponsibly sending their wives and children into harm's way—the dire consequences of wickedness being reserved for Eena.

Hmm. Mayor turned preacher. She stared past him, distracted by the slight bang and clicking noises as a cardinal frantically flapped its wings in an attempt to fly through the window. *You definitely don't want in here,* she thought, addressing the bird instead of the caricature facing her.

His bible-thumping harangue, jumbling punishment for sinners and the alliance of God and the UA, came to its triumphant conclusion with the allusion to everlasting hell. Spent with his sermon of allegiance to righteousness and the magnificent comparison of the military to legions of angels come to save the elect, he moved to his desk as though gliding over water.

Desperately worried about Cesla, Eena gazed at the soldier. Her thoughts echoed Chas's words. *They're human too.* So, she reached out, seeking the man's eyes until he looked up.

"The bird tied up outside eats fruit."

He returned her gaze, his expression blank, then shifted his eyes toward his paper work. She sighed her despair and stared out the window toward the uninteresting wall of the neighboring cabin.

Several minutes later, without the slightest flicker of response to her request, the man stood up and walked out of the room. The captain returned not long after.

Eena glanced toward the vacated chair by the door. *That weasel. He tattled on me for wanting to feed my bird. Now I have to face this pompous buffoon again.*

"What's the story with the bird?"

"I told you. He's a mutant ninja bird." Her voice was like acid. She had to admit she took perverse pleasure in watching the captain's blood pressure rise.

He strode to the chair beside Mayor Wilson's desk, carried it toward Eena, and set it down with a resounding bang. The soldier sat with his legs straddling the back of the seat.

"You're going to tell the truth, or face the consequences."

Not wanting to be bit for hours by this flea, she assumed a serious, direct attitude. "Three years ago, Dr. Olsen at Fort Carson told me about the DNA changes."

"Fort Carson?"

Eena nodded. She could tell her answer surprised him.

"You expect me to believe you've been to Fort Carson since Solar Flash?

She shrugged and returned his stare.

"And?"

"Solar Flash."

Remaining silent, the captain flicked his wrist in a circular motion, indicating that she should keep talking.

"According to Dr. Olsen, The most powerful solar flares in over twenty-five thousand years—"

Derision curled his lip. "So?"

"Affected the DNA of all life on this planet."

"Bingo! Three years later—Big Bird!"

She cocked her head. "Got a better explanation?"

His lips turned down at the corners in fury. "You pull this bogus stuff from the air."

Eena had a sudden realization. *I can have fun with this.* "The DNA changes in people are causing the landlords real headaches."

"Landlords."

"The rulers. The ones that trounced on our freedoms."

"Fantasy."

"And here's equal fantasy. After taking me to the baby factory, Dr. Olsen told me about what's happening to humanity."

The captain cocked his head. "Stop talking in riddles. Baby factory?"

"Actually, the cloned work force of the future, growing in big tubes." Eena had to admit she liked this game, watching confusion derange the captain's arrogant stare.

The mayor spoke up. "You can't believe anything she says, Captain. Just one lie after another."

Her voice silky smooth, Eena continued. "The DNA activation is triggering a big resistance movement."

Captain Donahue stood up to his full stature as an officer in the Union of the Americas Army. His height lent power to his look of proud disdain. This was his kind of talk. "Let them — whoever *they* are — just try."

Her prideful feeling of having scored struggled against the dread of what might be coming next.

"As for you, guess what?" He paused, his gaze that of the victorious conqueror delivering the decisive assault. "You're going back to Fort Carson."

The counterblow hit its mark. She remembered being told that she would be watched.

"The interrogation squad at Fort Carson's gonna bring... you... down," he said as if firing carefully aimed bullets.

He must have forgotten about his determination to hear the details about the bird because he turned on his heels to leave, spit-shined shoes pounding his army-issue power on the wood floor.

When he opened the door, a glimpse of Cesla further deflated Eena's bravado, and suffocating despair engulfed her like a collapsed balloon.

A few minutes later she eyed the soldier as he returned to the table. He nodded nearly imperceptibly at her. *What did that mean?*

He returned to his paperwork and she to her contemplation of the fate that awaited her.

Chas had asked Eena to radio him when she returned after the first day. Instead, Gavin had returned with the first group and radioed that, by the afternoon of the next day, he and Eena would return with the second group. By the following evening, Chas was sure something had gone wrong. After sitting awake all night, he was out the door before dawn, using his flashlight to head up the mountain.

By the time Chas reached the portal, the top of the sun, curiously synced on both sides of the archway, had peeped over the horizon. Aided by the early morning light, he hiked as fast as he dared down the mountain in Mu. Propelled by fear for Eena, he strode across the savannah, sending augurs hopping and lifting their wings for jump flights out of his way. Not knowing the location of Leiani's nest home he shouted for her as soon as he reached the cypress grove. Within minutes a tall, slender figure emerged below the canopy.

Despite the haste that had brought him to her, he faced her in his steady, direct way. "Leiani, do you know where Eena is?"

"Gavin circled the location on the map at my nest." She turned and led Chas to the interior of her nest.

He scanned the map. "I need a compass and an augur."

She rummaged through her things to retrieve the compass. "Diso is the most likely augur. Let's see how he responds to you."

Chas approached Diso with the quiet, interior core that blended with the essence of any animal. Immediately responsive to Chas's voice and touch, Diso pressed his crown into his chest for more strokes, scratches and soothing words.

Leiani's voice flowed through the bonding. "I assume Eena explained to you about telepathic guidance."

Chas nodded. "Similar to the communication system I share with my farm animals." After a few minutes Chas looked at Leiani with an expression that said he was ready to leave.

Leiani knew the pack augurs, Cesla and Espirit would be thirsty and hungry by the time Chas arrived. "Wait. Help me gather fruit." They hurried to stands of fruit trees to fill a burlap bag. It was a meager offering, but Leiani worried that along with carrying Chas, even that was too much added weight for Diso. "These supply some of their need for water, but they'll need more. I believe you'll be near a lake."

Chas nodded as Leiani looped the bag's rope handle over his shoulder and around his waist.

Chas flashed her a brief smile. "Thank you."

He mounted the augur and, in response to his command, Diso lifted up and flew toward the portal.

The Rescue

13

By late afternoon Gavin was fairly certain Eena and the five men were being held in a square log building, which appeared to be the town headquarters. More than once he saw a high-ranking officer pass through the doorway and also noted an unarmed soldier that twice came into the woods and for several minutes stood silent and alone.

When Gavin returned to the augurs, he was met with a strange low-pitched snarl and the shrieks and rustling of the tethered augurs flapping their wings and jostling one another, their wings lifted in readiness to fly. Running in the midst of them, Gavin thrust the firebrand into the smoldering fire that he had kept going all day, grabbed his bow and arrows, and ran toward a struggling augur with a cougar on its back. A single piercing cry gurgled to silence as fangs sunk into his neck. Succumbing to the fanged stranglehold, the augur sank to the ground.

When Gavin shouted and waved the torch, the cougar faced him, screaming its fury with bared bloody fangs. Again, Gavin waved the firebrand menacingly, and the cat swiped its paw as though to knock it from his hands. Slowly he backed up, brandishing the torch as the enraged animal moved toward him. He thrust the burning branch toward the cat to force it back in order to buy a few seconds, dropped it, notched an arrow in the string and pulled. The cat leaped, and the arrow hit its mark.

After the cougar fell lifeless to the ground, grief and remorse for the augur's death slammed Gavin, for it seemed like a terrible betrayal to bring the creature to this foreign soil to be slaughtered. Vision blurred by tears, shoulders slumped, he looked from the cat to the augur and back again as he considered what to do next. It seemed imperative to move the camp away from the corpses, which would entice carnivores from every direction, so using the last light of dusk, he explored beyond the clearing until he found another open area fifty yards away. Yet even with this distance between his camp and the scene of the kills, he knew this night would not be spent sleeping.

Throughout the night, his face toward the menacing dark, Gavin listened to the snarls of wolves as they devoured the augur carcass. Assailed by grief, he paced a circle outside the clustered augurs. *This shouldn't have happened*, he thought over and over.

Periodically, he leaned against a tree and slipped into a brief half sleep, such that a mere crack of a branch, a grunt, or a distant howl startled him to wakefulness.

He'd never been so glad for the first rays of morning. Having a single fruit left for each augur, he fed the birds, ate a mango himself, and sat by the fire to rehearse tackling the unarmed soldier in the forest. As Gavin's build was lanky and medium height, concern about successfully bringing down the taller, huskier man and donning his uniform wormed his gut.

An hour after leaving Three Mountains, Chas spied the lake and town, navigating a wide swath around it to avoid being seen. When he reached the augur-filled clearing, he set down. After tethering Diso to a pack augur and running around to place fruit in front of the augers, he hurried through the forest until he spied Gavin. "Psst!"

Gavin whirled around, pulling an arrow from his quiver. "Jesus!" He heaved a deep breath as he lowered the bow and arrow.

They moved deeper into the forest before Gavin spoke again. "Glad you're here. I have a plan."

Chas nodded for him to continue.

"Sometimes, a particular soldier comes to the woods.

"Is he armed?"

"No. And all he does is stand there."

"Wait. He doesn't do anything? Smoke? Pee?"

"Nope. Just stands for about twenty minutes or so. I figure we can jump him, then tie and gag him, and take his uniform."

Chas seemed reflective. "Could the man be meditating?"

Gavin shrugged. "Yeah, I guess so."

Chas looked Gavin straight in the eye. "A man communing with nature is likely a man we can communicate with."

Gavin looked shocked. "What if he yells for help?"

"What if we try to reach the man behind the uniform before we take it from him?"

Gavin looked as though he thought Chas was crazy. "That's taking a big risk."

His expression impassive, Chas returned his gaze. "How about this: We carry out your plan, if necessary, after I try mine. You hide behind a tree. If a skirmish starts, attack. We'll bring him down together."

Gavin felt impatient. "Let's just do *something*."

Chas nodded. "I'll follow you."

They hid behind trees at the point the man usually entered the forest. Hours passed before the target sauntered into the woods.

To Gavin it seemed like an eternity before Chas approached the soldier with a friendly wave. For another unbearable stretch a low-voiced conversation ensued before they undressed and traded clothes. Chas became the man in the uniform.

After observing the exchange in stunned silence, Gavin emerged from behind the tree. Chas was obviously a better fit for the uniform than he would have been. "Good thing you came."

The soldier, now in civilian clothes, spoke, his eyes clear and direct. "The prisoners are in the mayor's office behind us."

Feeling suspicious, Gavin turned to Chas. "This could be a trap."

"I do have a return favor to ask." The soldier's eyes searched those of his companions.

No doubt. Gavin awaited the toss of the bargaining chip.

"Take me with you."

Chas's touch on Gavin's shoulder quieted his alarm. "It's okay. We can trust Doctor Sanchez."

The doctor turned toward Chas. "The commanding officer, Captain Donahue, who has his own tent, has been interrogating the prisoners. Go in and say 'Captain wants to see the prisoners.'"

Chas nodded. "Good plan."

"The mayor's office is my temporary clinic. The handcuff key hangs behind my table on the left front wall as you enter." Doctor Sanchez paused. "After you free the prisoners, I suggest you stand guard at the front corner while Eena and the men run around the building into the forest."

Chas suggested the next stage of the escape strategy. "After they have time to reach you and Gavin, I'll cut the line that holds Cesla, climb aboard, and fly away."

Gavin nodded agreement, although internally he remained skeptical of Chas's trust in Doctor Sanchez as Chas disappeared around the corner.

Wearing Doctor Sanchez's uniform and looking as though he belonged among the troops, Chas strode from the clearing into the village and entered the designated door. The prisoners sat in six chairs arranged back-to-back with a chain woven through the chair backs, the handcuffs attached to it.

Chas nodded briskly toward the mayor. "Mornin', sir. Captain wants to see the prisoners."

"Good riddance," Mayor Wilson grumbled with a dismissive wave.

Chas retrieved the key and proceeded to unlock the handcuffs.

"Let's go," he barked. The prisoners filed out, and he closed the door behind them. Looking into Eena's eyes, Chas jutted his chin and thumb toward the rear of the building. As he turned to face the town, blocking a clear view of the escapees, they ran around the building and into the forest.

He continued to stand as though he were on guard until another soldier approached. To avoid being questioned, Chas walked toward Cesla and hunkered down, pretending to right the water bowl. Then he loosed the tether and, with one swift, smooth motion, straddled her tail and lay on her back. He didn't have to communicate flight. They were already off the ground. The state of shock on the ground delayed the shots that rang out after bird and rider were out of range.

As Eena and the men hurried to the augurs, Gavin yelled, "Over here!" to further confuse the people in the town before he and the soldier dashed away to circle to the augurs from opposite directions and meet up in the clearing.

Glimpsing Eena's wide-eyed surprise, he signaled. "It's okay. Mount up." He practically shoved Doctor Sanchez onto Diso. "Sorry. No time to lose." He darted to Espirit.

In masse, led by Eena, the group rose into the air behind Cesla minutes before soldiers swarmed over the clearing.

Within an hour they arrived at Quartz Mountain and landed in a meadow near the portal. After dismounting, Gavin and Chas stood beside Doctor Sanchez as Eena approached.

"So, when you left that time...."

"I took a handful of apricots from the old town's orchard to the bird."

"Thank you," she said, her eyes teary.

She turned to Gavin. "You'll return the augurs?"

He nodded.

Eena shared a relieved embrace with Chas before she turned toward the new arrivals.

As the men followed Eena down the mountain to join their families, Gavin asked Chas a question he had been mulling over since the uniform swap. "So, if Sanchez was sympathetic toward us, why didn't he simply play the role of the soldier ordered to take the prisoners to Captain Donahue?"

Chas paused, as though considering his words carefully. "Anyone can play the soldier. Piloting an augur away from hostile territory—not so easy."

Drawn to Matoskah's to recount his heroic role in saving Eena, Gavin hiked to Thunderbird Mountain. Grandfather pieced together moccasins as he related his latest adventure.

Abruptly, the old man's gaze changed—his eyes unseeing as though directed inward.

From the slight movement of his palm, Gavin knew to sit in unobtrusive stillness.

"Now, I must direct my attention to another," Grandfather said abruptly, shattering the silence. "Danger stalks the young girl who will soon approach."

Gavin searched the medicine man's face. "Does she know this? I mean, that she's coming here?"

"No. She only knows that fear of oppressors drives her."

"But how is it that you know that about her?"

Silence reigned until Grandfather spoke softly. "It's been said, 'That which we seek also seeks us.'" His faraway look indicated that he had turned his eyes inward toward the vulnerable young girl.

An Approach 14

Compared to the pre-Solar Flash stores with colorful walls, conspicuous displays and artfully arranged counter space, the commissary where Cosi worked after school was a drab place to shop. It never occurred to her that, for the people who knew her, *she* was the main attraction. Not because she was a good salesperson, but because she listened to their woes.

During slow hours the store manager, who moved within earshot of the dramas, allowed these sessions if they weren't too prolonged — unless an official from the SEI walked in. In which case he hurried over, hissed at Cosi to get busy, and made a show of being buried in work himself.

Cosi wasn't one to rush in with advice when Janey Egger showed her the bruise where her husband had grabbed her, or arthritic Jack Rosen wiped his eyes as he relived fond memories of his deceased wife, or overweight Regina Litfeld complained of the cruel names a group of fellow teens had called her that day. The sixteen-year-old simply listened, not just politely, but with wholehearted attention as if their pain mattered — as though she shared their suffering.

Because the emotional tug of the misery prevailing in people's lives exhausted Cosi, she frequently sought solitary refuge in the desert. Careful to remain near the edge of the township so as not to excite a reaction from whoever watched the surveillance cameras for fleeing citizens, she sat with her back to the township as though to momentarily erase its existence from her world.

Then she communed. In this realm of cactus, brittlebush and sage, she was certain that an energy exchange transpired between the saguaro cactus and herself. As she sat in its shade, her sense of self expanded to include every creature that crawled, hopped and scurried on these sands—as though each rabbit, lizard and tarantula energetically comingled with one another and with her.

Here, where the sky opened its blue vastness to a world scented with pungent sage, a sense of living connections prevailed over and above her seething resentment of the watching, policing judgmental controllers. Hauling in policy violators like truckloads of RATS bars, they zealously unloaded pages of infractions onto charts and records stored in manila folders. Though only blocks away from the desert, the SEI lockdown was light-years removed from nature's solace.

Cosi despised her timidity in the face of overbearing authority. She hated that, when an official dressed her down for inefficiency, she lowered her lids over unwelcome tears, clenched her fists and trembled her sense of impotence. The words she dare not say rose like bile from her churning gut, when what she wanted was to rage at the people who so relished bullying, strip them of their power and force them to admit the shamefulness of their violations.

Yet, a part of her—the aspect that saw into people's hearts—knew they themselves must secretly cower in fear. They reminded her of the possum once cornered in her family's garage. Pressed against the wall in terror, the creature became all threatening mouth as it pulled back its lips, snarled and displayed frightful rows of razor sharp teeth.

Cosi's father had once held her close and, stroking her hair, told her that her given name Cosima meant harmony. "I sometimes wonder whether your compassionate spirituality comes from the name, or if your mother and I simply intuited the best name for you." His lips brushed her forehead as if offering his blessing for her special qualities. She thought the name to be often far from indicative of her true emotional state, especially after the loss of her father.

More recently, concern for her mother's illness had taken upper hand. In the months since her mother had been in the hospital, Cosi's fear had intensified until the day when her boyfriend, Johnny Holcomb, who was a nurse, walked into the commissary and headed straight for her. She knew from the expression on his face what was coming.

"Cosi, I...." was all he could utter before she dropped the stack of folded clothing and ran past him. Heaving gulps of air, she arrived at the doorway to her mother's room. Sterile linens on an empty bed awaited the next patient.

She dare not seek her mother's body. She needed to disappear.

Cosi had only been home about an hour, her face swollen from crying, when she opened the door to Johnny's familiar knock. Obviously agitated, he cared about her more than a little.

"Cosi, as soon as the paper processing gets to the Relocation Department of the SEI, they're gonna to take you to the Youth Home."

Both knew of the unspeakable abuses that took place there. They stared at one another, Cosi's abysmal future looming larger than either in the small room. They discussed a range of possibilities, but they were too young to marry, and he couldn't hide her in his parents' apartment. It would be searched. Nor would she be allowed to remain in this allocated unit.

At that moment, as insurmountable walls blocked every conceivable direction, a vague memory of a small farm in the western foothills of the Colorado Rockies glimmered through a tiny crack. The summits to the east had reflected the glory of burnished sunsets, and hosted sunrises of mauve and periwinkle blue. As the image quickened her pulse, an interior voice whispered, *Go right away*. Yet, paralyzing fear of the unknown rivaled dread of the Youth Home.

As Johnny paced the room, her announcement cut through the tumult of possible futures. "I'm leaving."

Shock registered on Johnny's face before he nodded. They both knew she had no other option. He looked at his watch. "I have to return to the hospital." His voice cracked.

She ran into his arms, their desperate embrace lasting as long as they dared. When he pulled away and paused at the door to stare into his love's reddened eyes, she choked down a final sob.

As though her parents were present and urging her behind a cloak of invisibility, the dreadful silence amplified a persistent nudge to an insistent push to flee. With the realization that she would not be attending her mother's funeral, grief threatened to overwhelm the girl again. But mercifully, a detached part of herself stuffed water, food, supplies and clothing into a backpack, attached a rolled up sleeping bag, and opened the door. Glancing a sorrowful farewell into her apartment, she stepped out onto the sidewalk.

The hood of a government vehicle appeared at the far edge of the complex, surging panic through her body.

Cosi hurried around the corner along the hidden side of the building to zigzag through the canyons of the four-story complex. At the narrow stretch between the housing units and the heavily patrolled

Highway 64, she hunkered down in a cluster of tumbleweed as a retriever cruised by. When the rear of his car disappeared, she darted across the pavement and into the desert, aware that security cameras tracked her escape.

Two days and thirty miles later, when she kneeled on the sand, exhausted and afraid, an eagle circled overhead, and a wordless message renewed her courage.

With a deep intake of breath and slow exhalation, Grandfather opened his eyes. He handed Gavin a fishing pole, and they fished for an hour before he spoke.

"She's only sixteen," he said softly. "And she's in grave danger."

A golden eagle swooped to a high limb of a dead tree trunk that had been secured in the ground. Seen at such close range the impressive eagle was jaw-dropping.

In the sunlit glare the old man squinted toward the bird. "Uncle, you have done well. We thank you."

As if in respectful salute, the eagle left the perch to circle once over Matoskah's head. With quiet awe, Gavin watched the magnificent raptor's ascending spiral to somewhere near the top of the cliff face that walled one side of Grandfather's camp.

Gavin faced the medicine man to ask the question that burned in his heart. "Grandfather, what's the deal with that eagle?"

There was a hint of mirth in Grandfather's eyes as he returned Gavin's quizzical gaze.

"What eagle?"

"The one that keeps flying to that perch you made."

"Mm-hmm."

"I think I saw one like him on my way here. More than once."

Grandfather poured tea into Gavin's mug.

Gavin knew Matoskah was evading his implied question. "Grandfather, is that eagle your pet?"

"No. He's a relative."

Gavin continued to stare at him, his expression expectant.

"He's also an assistant."

"Did you direct him to go somewhere three weeks ago?"

Grandfather nodded. "Yes."

He was not making this easy. The boy persisted. "He flew off to signal me to cross the bridge, didn't he?"

"Uh-huh."

"Did you send him to me?"

Grandfather's face remained expressionless. "What do you think?"

Gavin waited a moment and took a deep breath. "It appears that you sent him. But that implies that you knew I was coming."

"Uh-huh."

"Well, did you?"

A long pause preceded the reply. "The signs told me."

The elder's disclosure gave Gavin a jolt of happiness. But he wondered aloud, "Signs, Grandfather?"

"The sign can be anything—a deer appearing and melting back into the forest, a passing bear, or, as in your case, a butterfly struggling to emerge from its cocoon."

Gavin still had one pressing question. "But, Grandfather, I could have died falling from that bridge your eagle influenced me to cross."

Grandfather put down his pole. "He's not *my* eagle. And you *did* get careless. That was risky."

Gavin took a deep breath to control his exasperation. "What if I had fallen?"

Grandfather lifted the bucket of fish. "Then your backpack wouldn't have caught on the slat, and Eena wouldn't have helped you."

"So your eagle knew it was going to turn out okay?" Gavin leaned the poles against a tree and followed Matoskah to the fire.

"I don't own an eagle."

As Gavin glared at him, Grandfather hunkered down to prepare the fish. "*You* knew it."

As the sun sank below the western horizon on the third day of walking, Cosi approached a highway ahead, which, according to the map, was Highway 160.

Alert to the danger of patrolling retrievers, she paused. Yet the promise of freedom coaxed her forward—she had reached the point of no return, whatever the price.

Though the highway looked clear as she crossed, retrievers, approaching around a bend, glimpsed her fleeing figure. In the deepening dusk the silent forest of cedars had closed around her when the car screeched a halt.

Cosi ran—pursued by shouts and metallic jangling. Growling yips intensified her fear to terror. An attack dog? A gunshot blasted her ears, exciting wrathful snarls and snapping teeth. It didn't make sense. As she pushed through limbs of thickening stands of cedar, the enraged growls threatened at her back. Yet, the darkening sky and an overlapping profusion of cedar bows cloaked her escape. A second shot followed, then a whimper. Another shot, and then silence. Panicked, Cosi slid under the thickly layered boughs of the nearest cedar.

Under cover of darkness and heavily laden limbs, she glimpsed the circular glow from the retrievers' flashlights sweeping the ground. Footsteps, heralded by loud crunches on the gravely sand, approached her hiding place. Her heart thumping in her ears, Cosi quieted her breath and scrunched her body and gear as small as possible. After a half hour of dread that seemed to stretch into hours, the driver called off the search. The echoing grind of soles on gravel receded until she heard the engine start. Its hum diminished as the predatory vehicle sped away in search of other prey.

At this higher elevation the night air was chilly. So, after a few swigs of water, Cosi wearily unrolled her sleeping bag and burrowed inside.

The next morning an eagle circled and glided in the direction of a mountain pass just ahead. Without questioning her intuition, Cosi followed the raptor's lead. She came to a spring a half mile into the pass and stopped to drink and refill her water bottles. It was then that she heard whimpering. Following the direction of the sound, she approached a large boulder through the cover of pines. A wolf pup, which appeared to be about two months old, rubbed its nose with a forepaw as it hunched on its stomach before the entrance to a stone-encased den.

She knew the mother could appear at any time, but a feeling told her to remain quietly nearby. As the long morning shadows shortened and disappeared, her patient vigil became certainty that the mother would not be returning. She sensed she knew where the mother lay.

Backing up so as not to be noticed, Cosi unzipped a pouch in her pack to retrieve the dried meat. In one swift, graceful motion, she moved through the trees to sit on the ground visible to the pup. Startled, he yipped and whined, escaping into the den.

Having read that wolf mothers chew and regurgitate meat for their pups, she tore off a strip of jerky and proceeded to chew it. Then, placing the chewed mass on the ground, she waited. It took a while for the pup to re-emerge at the den opening and cautiously slink forward to gobble the food.

A couple of hours of snatching chewed meat and water led to asking for more with raised ears and insistent whines. When he began playfully attacking her ears and arms with needle-sharp teeth, the girl knew she had become his surrogate mother.

Under the bright morning sky Grandfather and Gavin cleaned their breakfast plates. A soft utterance confirmed the old man's thoughts weren't on his dishware.

"Did you say something?" Gavin asked.

The elder nodded. "Last night a wolf saved a young girl from capture by retrievers."

Gavin listened to this disclosure in stunned silence.

"The starving omega was expelled from her pack and growing weaker each day. Then the Great Mystery directed her to leave her pup. The dying wolf summoned her last reserves of strength and distracted the girl's pursuers before being shot."

Gavin's face reflected his interior shock.

The corners of Grandfather's eyes crinkled. "There's more to the story. The orphaned runner, for whom the dying wolf sacrificed her life, saved the life of her orphaned wolf pup."

The medicine man paused to let this sink in. "Moments ago, you heard me thank the Wolf Spirit and the Great Mystery that brings balance to all things."

The Shoppers

15

"Do you think you're ready to join Lori and Chuck on a shopping mission to Durango?" Eena looked at Gavin expectantly.

Doubt furrowed Gavin's brow as his eyes searched Eena's.

Apparently, Eena didn't share his concern. "I need to give you some background information. Word is three months after Solar Flash, the residents of Durango were evacuated under false pretenses. UA troops warned them of impending danger. Military convoys hauled away every last occupant, dispersing them to various sectors. The 'impending danger' never materialized. I've heard rumors that the UA government has designs on that city—that they're going to install themselves and their most loyal people there. With Durango only thirty miles away, this is of great concern to us.

"However, in the meantime, we're making use of supplies sitting there unused. As you know, all goods left on shelves in stores in vacated cities have been declared property of the new nation, to be dispersed as deemed necessary by the controlling landlords and their minions. We don't agree that the UA owns the goods any more than the right to control our lives.

"The shopping expeditions provide the community with badly needed electronic equipment, clothing, and tools." We know that this expedition could be our last, and it's urgent that we obtain the needed electronics for the projects in the lab."

"You mean like Leslie's free energy devices."

"Those and the hologram project could be essential to the survival of Three Mountains." She paused allowing Gavin time to process the information. "As for Durango, the military could arrive any day now with engineers and construction crews to begin re-establishing infrastructure for the controllers."

"And the role of the patrollers?" he asked.

"Your job will be to survey Highway 550 as the shoppers gather goods and pack them on birds and in wagons. You'll watch for one of the military convoys that occasionally travel that route. Meanwhile, I'll patrol Three Mountains."

Gavin fought down a tremor of apprehension. He honestly didn't know if he was up to the task. But he could feel Eena's eyes boring into him and knew that his reluctance to ride an augur had seemed cowardly to her.

Wishing to live down that image, his reply rang with false confidence. "Sure, I'll do it."

He wondered if he knew inside that he would succeed, as Grandfather said he had known that he would make it across the bridge.

Dale pulled out his radio.

"We're near Highway 550 at Durango. Over."

Ready for his call, Gavin, Lori and Chuck scanned the highway for several miles in either direction of the shoppers.

Lori held tight to Cielo's neck as she replied. "Highway all clear."

The shoppers and patrollers agreed to meet behind the Wal-Mart. After retrieving two metal 3' × 5' wagons stored in an empty building on the outskirts of the city, they crossed the highway pulling them to the parking lot where Wal-Mart, Fry's, and a small strip mall were located. Picking up their pace, the group on the ground watched the augurs fly overhead then descend behind the building.

The patrollers carried star fruit and mangoes, brought through the portal from Mu, to supply both moisture and nourishment for the birds. As they fed the augurs, the shoppers moved swiftly. Four shoppers, pulling the wagons, hurried around the building to the rear of the store. With powerful swings of a sledgehammer, the remaining two shattered the glass in the entrance door. They ran through the store to the loading dock located at the rear and pulled up the door. The waiting men rushed inside.

Gavin mounted Espirit to patrol the highway while Lori and Chuck remained with the augurs. Loosely tethering six birds to Cielo, they tied him to a post connected to the trash bin enclosure. They couldn't risk the flock suddenly taking flight. As the birds foraged on the fruit scattered on the pavement, Chuck checked the cargo packs worn by each, and began untying the nylon rope that bound the folded tarps sewn into lightweight frames.

Inside the building, the crew headed first to the household goods department where they removed blankets from the packaging. Each carried a couple of blankets as they scattered to assigned parts of the store to gather clothing, hardware, toys, groceries, sporting goods, camping gear, gardening tools, rope, hardware and bicycles.

Within half an hour, the first shopper appeared at the dock, dragging a blanket loaded with clothing. Moving swiftly, Chuck and the shopper hoisted the goods beside a bird. Within minutes, all the shoppers met at the dock dragging more blankets filled with supplies. A half hour later the birds were each loaded with around a hundred pounds tied inside the packages on their backs.

Lori radioed Gavin. "Birds packed. Over."

Gavin's eyes scanned the highway in either direction once more. "All clear."

Lori loosened Cielo's tether, and Chuck untied Vista and the remaining birds. Mounting Cielo, Lori took flight. Almost as one organism, the pack augurs flapped their wings and rose into the sky.

Gavin's voice barked over the radio. "Retriever three miles to southeast. Over."

"Not good. Over." Lori signaled for Cielo to gain altitude, and Chuck and the remaining birds in the V formation followed. On occasion, the retrievers had seen the large birds in the distance, probably assuming them to be some type of raptor or vulture. But none had ever seen a flock of them. They needed to cross the highway and be a couple of miles past it by the time the retriever vehicle passed by.

Remaining behind a screen of trees, Gavin kept his binoculars trained on the approaching vehicle as it swerved to the side of the road and stopped. The retriever and his partner stepped out of the car. Apparently unable to believe what he was seeing, the retriever blinked. Then he reached inside the car, and stood up again peering through binoculars, while his companion watched with unaided vision. Their eyes followed the formation of large birds for several seconds, until the flock disappeared from view beyond the foothills.

The partner asked a question and the driver scratched his head. The two men stood for several seconds dialoguing between shrugs and head-shaking before getting into the car and driving away.

Grinning as though at a private joke, Gavin waited for the vehicle to speed out of sight before he headed across Highway 550. Espirit needed food and rest. He landed behind the Wal-Mart and laid several fruits on the pavement. The shoppers emerged through the dock entrance to load three all-terrain bikes, air pumps, tire repair kits, extra bike tires, tool kits, shovels and rakes onto a wagon. Minutes later the crew put closure on the heist by shutting the dock door.

As planned, the shoppers sat down on the loading ramp to wait with Gavin. Refreshing themselves with bottled water, they sat on the concrete and munched on stale snacks.

Gavin took a swig of water. "Espirit needs to rest for half an hour."

As Gavin and the shoppers bantered about the incongruous participation of the augurs, Espirit pecked at the fruits until she was satisfied. Then, lulled by the human voices, her eyes closed for a nap. When the augur opened her eyes and ruffled her feathers, Gavin told the men to proceed to phase two of the shopping spree.

Gavin and Espirit took flight as the others pulled the wagons across the asphalt. Their next destination was the neighboring Fry's Electronics, where they had to fulfill the requests of the inventors. Last stop, at the behest of the musicians, would be the music store in the nearby strip mall to pick up a couple of instruments.

Repeating the Wal-Mart procedure, while two bashed in the glass of the front door, four shoppers parked the wagons at the loading dock located at the rear of the building. Within twenty minutes, they had retrieved boxes of cables, transistors, capacitors, wires, and myriad devices and tools along with unwieldy cables of all sizes.

From his elevated vantage point Gavin watched the shoppers haul the wagons to the strip mall between Highway 550 and Fry's. Fortunately, the south wall of the L-shaped mall offered a broad section of wall space to hide the wagons. A dress shop was closest to them with the music store two stores away.

As Espirit gained elevation, Gavin peered at the highway and was about to radio "all clear" when he saw moving specks. Feeling a jolt of alarm, he fumbled for his binoculars. From Hwy 160 four westbound military vehicles were approaching Highway 550.

The moment the shoppers parked the wagons, Gavin's voice came over the radio. "Convoy five miles ahead. Moving at about forty miles per hour."

A surge of panic electrified the team.

"We can't leave the wagons exposed." Urgency punctuated Marcus's warning.

Swiftly, two ran to the arm of the strip center that faced the highway. At the entrance was the dress shop's large plate glass window with three smaller windows on the side facing Wal-Mart. Fred bashed a side window, climbed in, and ran to open the double metal doors at the rear. They pushed the wagons inside and closed the doors.

The men secreted the two wagons plus two bikes behind clothing racks and accessory stands at the far corner flanked by windowless walls. Meanwhile, two shoppers chipped away the glass shards in the window frame, cleaned up the glass on the sidewalk, and arranged the window dressing to make it look as normal as possible, at least from a distance.

After carefully ascertaining that the wagons and bikes were completely hidden by clothing racks and accessory stands, the group hunkered down below the window ledge to peer across the parking lot. Tension mounted as they waited, having no weapons to defend themselves if they were attacked.

Manifesting the shoppers' worst fears, the convoy turned off the highway and pulled into the parking lot, headed toward Wal-Mart.

Gavin contacted the shoppers anxiously. "You guys all right? Over."

Marcus held the radio. "In hiding. Wagons and all. Over."

"Need to fly this bird to a resting place. Over."

"Understood. Over."

While the shoppers hid in the dress shop, Gavin rested and fed Espirit on a dirt road five miles east of the highway. As his thoughts returned to the puzzled retrievers and forwarded to the approaching convoy, he appreciated for the first time the precariousness of life in Three Mountains. His eyes turned skyward with the dawning realization that, when air traffic resumed, it could very well be their undoing.

Meyer Johnson read the mail from the education department, surprised to receive a mandate for a teacher transfer to a township. His source of transportation would be the single overhauled commuter plane in Transtopia Metro.

Wavy brown hair spilled over Meyer's forehead as he examined the assignment.

His roommate, Edward, was absorbed in a textbook at the desk beneath the window.

Meyer folded the paper as he looked up. "Hey, I'm being transferred!"

Edward looked up, eyebrows raised over his glasses. "Where to?"

Meyer gazed out the window. "Township 24, about sixty miles west of Durango." He'd be crossing the Continental Divide for the first time since childhood.

Edward groaned. "Ugh, one of those godforsaken townships." Working toward a Doctorate in Education Administration, at least prior to Solar Flash, Edward's ambitious trajectory was school principal, then superintendent of schools in Transtopia Metro.

His disdain rocked Meyer. "Why do you say that?"

Edward shook his head. "There's just no way those kids are going to meet the rigorous standards of the students here in the city."

A knock brought Meyer to the door.

"Hey, Meyer, you coming?"

Meyer grinned at the kids—one six years old, the other ten. "I'll be right there."

Meyer looked at Edward. "I appreciate your emphasis on standards. But they're stressful for kids."

To Edward the only worthy consideration of children was as students whose high scores would skyrocket his career in Transtopia Metro. The population of 100,000 in the governing capital was simply his stepping-stone to Minister of Education for the Western Region.

The older child, a tow-headed boy, had more immediate goals. "We're starting on the tree house today, right?"

Meyer picked up a duffel bag. "Can you two carry this? The hammers, nails, saws and a tape measure are inside."

The pair each held a portion of the handle as they walked out. "Hurry, would you, Meyer?"

"I just need a couple of minutes."

Edward commented on the stress issue. "Children today lack discipline." He planned to send a stringently disciplined, highly skilled labor force, including the best technocrats and scientists, into corporations. Already on the A-list of the Social Engineering Department, he had a sense of pride in his destiny. The graduates of Transtopia Metro were going to be highly regarded and sought after, his own reputation, impeccable.

Meyer stashed the folded letter in a drawer. "I police more than I teach."

"You have to be strict. Strong consequences for students. Hit the parents in the wallet where it counts."

Meyer sighed and gazed out the window at the children headed across the greenbelt. Now, since both parents were mandated to work full time, government-owned and operated child management and schooling facilities operated year-round six days per week from infancy through seventeen years old.

Edwards's final words intruded on his reflections. "With a spineless attitude you'll never succeed."

Meyer winced, knowing the truth in Edward's words. "I question the accuracy of the Career Determination Test. I'm not sure I *am* a school teacher."

He headed out the door to join the tree house crew collected on the twenty-acre naturescape just across the street from the housing units. It had become his Sunday routine to spend time in this expanse of cottonwood trees and grassy fields filled with trails to explore, and nooks and crannies for hideouts and households. Near the stream that flowed through the middle was a favorite cottonwood tree.

Glad for the return of spring, he approached the chaotic beginnings of tree house construction.

"Hey, let me saw."

"It's my turn."

"This is a stronger branch."

"Too crooked."

Quarrelsome expressions of exuberant intelligence obstructed the collaborative construction. They turned toward Meyer, yelling accusations at one another, until he quietly mediated to help them arrive at a consensus. This was his way of being with kids. The contrast between policing at an emotional distance and assisting self-initiated co-creations increased his dread of returning to the classroom — anywhere.

That afternoon Meyer waved goodbye to some and hugged others as he left to meet with Principal Martin.

"You're to ride in the single small plane in operation in the Metro." The principal beamed enthusiasm Meyer couldn't muster.

This commuter craft was the only local plane that had been completely overhauled since Solar Flash. Regional flights were rare and strategically planned, usually high officials flying to outlying sector capitals. But the imperial governor had decided it was expedient to transport Meyer by plane. Township 24 was located across the Continental Divide from Transtopia Metro, about sixty miles west of Durango.

The Apprentice

16

Following the lead jeep, the drivers positioned the convoy in a line parallel to the storefront and facing the strip mall. The tense observers in the dress shop watched four soldiers emerge from the vehicle and head for the bashed-in door.

Jacob couldn't resist a little humor. "If any of them go around back, I wish I could see their faces when they see those whopping big bird droppings!" The chuckles and bantering that followed helped relieve the tension while passing around a pair of binoculars. More armed troops poured out of the vehicles.

For several minutes a semicircle of soldiers considered the broken door. The watchers could only imagine their conversation. Were they wondering if another convoy had beat them to it? Perhaps they were speculating about rovers on the loose, hiding from the UA government. Watching various soldiers turn to peer around the shopping complex, the shoppers were glad for the distance.

After forcing the doors open with crowbars, the soldiers retrieved crates from the cargo beds of the trucks and hauled them inside the building.

When Gavin and Espirit took flight again, they patrolled east of the highway, so as not to be noticed. He peered through his binoculars. Soldiers were loading crates of goods onto the cargo beds. When the loading was complete, they closed the storefront doors, boarded them up, and returned to the truck cabs.

Meanwhile, in the dress shop, Jacob's running commentary provoked ripples of uneasy chuckles.

"Mm-hmm. Easier for us to break in next time, if there's anything left."

With a signal from the lead Jeep, the convoy headed toward Fry's.

With bated breath the group in the dress shop watched them slow to a stop. Guns ready the soldiers approached the front door. After a long pause for discussion, they returned to the vehicles. Sitting in the lead vehicle, the commanding officer gave the signal to move on.

The convoy turned left, moving at a crawl toward the strip mall. The hidden observers willed them not to notice the broken window. Unless someone looked closely, it would be hard to spot. For several minutes they listened to the engines of the convoy as the vehicles crawled past them toward the highway.

Suddenly, the soldier riding shotgun in the second Jeep craned his neck and shouted, "Another break-in!" The convoy halted.

"Oh crap. This is it," Jacob whispered. Swiftly, the men crabbed to positions behind a sales counter to ensure invisibility.

Marcus hastily switched off the radio as four of the soldiers approached.

"The scavengers wanted nice dresses for their wifeys," quipped one, evoking laughter from the other three.

The soldier who had spied the broken window walked around to it. Using the butt of his rifle, he jabbed a mannequin that fell to the floor with a loud clatter, taking part of the display with it.

A couple of men pressed their faces to the front plate glass to peer inside. The lieutenant held up a flashlight. The powerful beam zigzagged crazily around the room and came to rest on the racks at the rear.

The hidden observers prepared for the worst.

"Renegades are on the loose in this town," the officer barked as he clicked off the light. "But their days are numbered. The next mission will smoke them out and move the government in."

He turned, strode toward his vehicle, and jumped in yelling, "Move out!"

Inside the shop, no one moved until the convoy was well past and the lead jeep turned onto the highway.

As soon as Marcus clicked on the radio, Gavin's voice broke the silence. "You guys all right? Over."

"We're okay. Over." Marcus exhaled noisily.

"Meet at the RV repair shed? Over."

"We'll be glad to see the birds."

The crew was shaken and suddenly feeling drained, but they had one last task. They silently and swiftly broke into the music store to retrieve the requested guitar, violin, hammer dulcimer and drum and loaded the equipment on the wagons. With two men roped to each wagon, and two riding trail bikes, with a third bike loaded atop a wagon, they headed out.

As soon as Gavin gave them the all clear, the group crossed the highway for the challenging next five miles. Four men would haul an estimated four hundred pounds over hills with a continuous, gentle incline. The crew agreed to rotate between hauling and riding after every mile. A long, narrow asphalt road wound up and down through miscellaneous metal industrial buildings and stands of cedars. By the last mile, it seemed that they were trudging forward at a snail's pace.

At the end of the road, the crew turned onto a dirt driveway that led to a large steel building with one door wide open. Leaning wearily against the side of the front wall, the men gulped water and poured more over their heads.

"Birds approaching! Over." The welcome voice of Lori cheered them.

Jacob grabbed the radio from Marcus. "About time! Over."

"Roger that."

"Never have I seen a more beautiful sight." Mike feigned a melodramatic swoon as seven augurs that had been resting in a nearby field flew into view.

Within another half hour, with the weight and bulk distributed and enclosed in the packages, the loads were manageable for the birds.

As the flock flew northeast, the weary shoppers parked the wagons inside the building. Exhausted from the combined work and tension of the day, they spent the late afternoon and night in a nearby house.

They were twenty-five miles southwest of home as the crow flies. But the trek by foot added distance. The next morning they would begin an estimated thirty-five-mile trek northeast through the mountains.

Gavin helped Anaya carry produce to the science lab and then to Grandfather. He was impatient to hike back to the lab and to Leslie.

"Join us." A mischievous twinkle in the elder's eyes accompanied his invitation.

Reluctantly, Gavin delayed more appealing plans and helped fill squirrel skin herb packets. As he and Anaya stuffed the leather pouches, they sensed the elder's spirit traveled with the approaching one.

"So, the eagle still guides the young girl to Three Mountains," Anaya mused softly.

"Yes, she is important to our collaboration."

When a flock of noisy crows shattered the surrounding stillness, Matoskah reached under his leather vest to the breast pocket of his blue plaid shirt and with a wide sweep of his arm broadcast a handful of dried berries on the ground.

Disputing ownership with loud caws, the birds grabbed berries and threateningly chased one another away from claims with open beaks. Eying a berry that fell close to Grandfather's feet, a particularly bold bird approached, cocked its head to eye its benefactor, and grabbed the booty.

"My ancestors had great respect for crows," the old man announced as he reached into his shirt pocket to withdraw a leather pouch. He poured sunflower seeds into his palm and broadcast them to be devoured by the argumentative flock. "Wolves and crows are intelligent animals. They understand each other because they are both communal species. That's why we can communicate with them fairly easily."

"Go," the old man commanded with a dismissive sweep of his arm. The noisy visitors flew off, their loud caws fading in the distance.

As evening fell, Cosi's concern mounted, for there were surely cougars and bears on this mountain. Fearfully, she peered into the gathering gloom until she shined the flashlight inside the den. The light revealed that the one-foot high entrance opened to a roomy interior extending back about six feet. She shoved the length of her sleeping bag into the den before maneuvering her body inside.

The next morning Cosi awoke to find the baby creature snuggled against her bag. Her heart swelling with tenderness, the new wolf mother stroked the warm furry ball curled beside her, then wriggled out of the sleeping bag, awakening the pup. As she wrapped the bag around her body to ward off the early morning chill, the pup whined and licked her jaw. So she gave him a couple of wads of chewed meat and water.

A fleeting memory of her Russian grandmother's folktales of mythic heroes yielded a name for the pup. "You shall be called Valek for your bravery, little wolf." Cosi ruffled the thick silvery fur at the nape of his neck.

Feeling lost and alone, the girl trudged toward the unknown, with the wolf pup sleeping on her back. When despair threatened to overwhelm her, a glimpse of golden brown and the cry of an eagle encouraged her to keep going. By late afternoon, the mountains began to close in on her, casting long shadows in her path while the murmur of swaying pines warned of lurking danger. Even confinement in the youth home would have been preferable to being torn to bits by wild animals, which she imagined crouched behind boulders and tree trunks.

When Cosi began to sense she was being followed, she frequently looked over her shoulder and hastened her pace. At one point, while glancing behind, she tripped over a rock and fell facedown, allowing the pup to spill out of the backpack and scramble to the ground. With a cry she grabbed Valek and as he wriggled in protest, stuffed him back inside. Her erratic heartbeat drumming her exposed vulnerability, she grabbed a large rock, scavenged a thick branch to brandish, and strode on while shadowy patches of gray and brown paced her behind a screen of aspens.

Just ahead, half buried in soil and rocky rubble, a huge boulder jutted out of the mountainside. She scrambled to the top seeking a high vantage point to face her stalkers. Her arms raised threateningly with a rock in one hand and a tree branch in the other, Cosi faced her pursuers.

The first wolf to emerge into plain view stood perfectly still, panting as he eyed the human atop the boulder. Then another, followed by two others, trotted out of the forest to pace restlessly, milling around as though awaiting a signal from the alpha. None charged the boulder, but the suspense, the anticipation of an attack, squeezed Cosi's desperately racing heart.

What do you want? she asked mentally. *Is it me? Is it the wolf pup? I'm not going to let you have him. He's mine. I'm his mother now.*

A single tear rolled down her face as she stood poised for self-defense with the pup yelping and writhing to escape from the backpack.

At that moment a noisy flock of crows descended, squawking and flapping as they landed in raucous confusion. If she hadn't been so frightened, she would have found humor in the birds' outspread wings and open beaks as they boldly advanced upon the wolves. Lupine lunges challenged the birds' audacity, whereupon they protested, squawking indignantly, and franticly retreated to pine limbs.

As more crows crowded Cosi's stone bastion, the alpha wolf and his companions repeatedly charged and withdrew from the invaders. In the past, the pack had played meat tug-of-war games with crows, but never this annoying dance of advance and retreat. The wriggling in Cosi's pack escalated as the lupine-crow skirmish melted into the tree canopy. Behind the screen of pines, the shadows milled restlessly, as if inconvenienced by the troublesome flock, but loathe to succumbing to an undignified escape.

The confined passenger, excited beyond all restraint, risked the fall to the ground as he scrambled to free himself. Cosi screamed as he landed, righted himself, and bounded across the boulder and over the rubble to confront the noisy intruders.

Squawking more loudly than ever, the battalion of crows scattered and escaped to the limbs above, protesting the pup's assaults on their ranks with screeched retorts. Then, as if enjoying a spontaneously invented game, in groups of three or four at a time, the feathered warriors flew to the ground to taunt the baby animal. Daring him to bound after them in one direction, then another; each set of teasers retreated to the trees at the last second. Gradually, to Cosi's terror, the cacophonous game receded into the forest.

When Valek disappeared among the trees, her frantic cries for the pup abruptly ceased. Collapsing on the boulder, Cosi buried her face in folded arms and sobbed her despair. Like the dismal past, the frightening future loomed oppressively, indifferent to her bitter tears.

As Cosi's sobs yielded to sporadic dry heaves, the raucous protests abated. Bereaved silence prevailed until, with whimpering pants, a wet nose nudged her forehead, and the familiar tongue licked her tears. Breathing in jagged gulps of air, Cosi buried her face in Valek's soft fur, then reached into her pack to retrieve the last of the jerky. Although her stomach begged her to swallow the clump she chewed, she spit it into her hand for her only friend.

While the pup devoured the offering, something inside Cosi shifted. She no longer sensed a predatory presence among the trees. With Valek at her heels, she descended the rocky slope to follow the creek. For the next few hours, the brook gurgled the companionable message that they walked free of the lupine stalkers — safe in its guiding trajectory. As Cosi and the pup followed the stream bank, the cadenced murmur distracted her from gnawing hunger and, for a while, concern about lengthening shadows.

The deepening blue-tinged patches of sky above the ponderosa canopy nudged Cosi to find shelter. She scanned for a rock outcropping to shelter her and Valek, but to no avail. Descending into a shadowed valley, the girl began to gather branches for a meager lean-to as the brook tumbled toward its destined union with a welcoming river. The wider artery's grassy bank, padded with pale red sand, eased the trekker's progress as she balanced the bundle of sticks while keeping an eye on her rapidly tiring charge.

A bend in the river brought not only a broadened view of flat terrain for a camp, but also voices. The shouts of children hurled across the grass-covered expanse soon became clumped-together exclamations and uni-directional finger-pointing as all eyes targeted the furry animal that rode toward them in Cosi's arms.

When Grandfather stood up abruptly, Gavin flashed a look of alarm. "Everything okay?"

Mastoskah turned toward him, his boyish expression of happiness completely unlike the face of quiet dignity Gavin was accustomed to. "I must head down the mountain. My young apprentice has arrived."

With Gavin hurrying to keep pace with the medicine man's uncharacteristic speed, he nearly sprinted to the base of the mountain.

Gavin's thoughts were already with Leslie. He looked forward to being with her and telling her about the latest mission. Something inside had morphed since the expeditions with Eena and the shopping adventure in Durango. His view of himself had changed from being an observer of group dynamics to a participant with a growing sense of purpose. Besides, Leslie worked to further this collective vision, and his contribution as a patroller brought him closer to her.

Near the base of the mountain, the sounds of bantering around the pavilion grew louder. Gavin thought that the shoppers must have arrived, but when the pair reached the valley, Matoskah turned toward the excited shouts of children gathered around a young girl and a pup.

Protective tenderness beamed from Grandfather to the delicate sixteen-year-old. Light brown hair highlighted with gold cascaded over the shoulders of a body that couldn't weigh much more than one hundred pounds. After greeting the newcomer, Gavin drew back, sensing a singular bond being forged.

Matoskah smiled at the young medicine woman. "That wolf pup you hold will one day outweigh you."

The two intuitives walked companionably toward the pavilion. "I will call you by your full name, Cosima."

The tired walker smiled wanly. "Like my father."

"The voicing of your name will lend its resonance—*harmony*—to our village."

As a gentle gust stirred the overhead pines, their soft murmur whispered the closeness of two spirits.

Connections

17

The arrival of the shoppers was a festive occasion for the entire community. As radioed communications announced the arrival of the shoppers, people gathered from the surrounding valley. The shoppers stood beside fourteen large 'packages' lined up beside the pavilion—the largest payload to date. Men, women, youths, and children approached, eager to see what the shoppers returned with this time.

People continued to gather in a circle around the crew as they spread the tarps on the ground and began placing the goods on them.

When Eena spied Matoskah, she approached through the crowd, her voice conveying warm affection as she greeted him. "Grandfather, it's so good to see you again. It seems like forever."

The elder's eyes beamed a deep sense of connection with this warrior daughter.

The hush of the crowd was the opportune segue for George, a member of the team of shoppers, to speak up. "The goods are now ready for viewing. As you can see, on these first tarps are clothing and related items. We were happy to gather a fairly large supply of coats, gloves, scarves, and hats for next winter, as well as pants, blouses, shirts, underwear, and socks. We did our best to collect as much as we could for all sizes and ages."

"On the next tarp, you'll find kitchen utensils and sewing supplies." In his best sales pitch voice, George 'advertised' various tarps holding construction hardware, gardening tools, electronic equipment, bikes, radios, toys, and musical instruments. In a festive spirit the people murmured or cheered as various items were announced.

The science lab crew was noticeably elated to see the lab equipment, including two large screens for the room with the holograph projector.

The musicians, drawn to the new instruments, immediately began tuning them. A band member waved a violin over his head, shouting with exuberance, "Next up, music, dancing, and feasting!"

As the band began to play a rousing Irish jig, Chas approached Eena, who was animatedly sharing with friends. She felt a familiar little heart tremor as he stood quietly by her side, exuding solid, grounded strength.

Looking up, she saw in his expression, eyebrows raised, the invitation to dance. With a glint of humor in her eyes she quipped, "You mean I'm to dance an Irish jig with a Japanese man?"

"It doesn't look much like I'm dancing with an Irish woman either," he teased back.

After the dance the two strolled arm in arm into the rapidly cooling night air. Chas slipped out of his jacket and put it around Eena.

"How's the programming going?" she asked.

Chas sighed. "I put in my time at the technology lab every day, but you know where my heart is."

Eena laughed. "Oh yes, with cabbages, chickens and cows."

Chas playfully elbowed the woman who knew him so well. "And what about you, my beautiful bird jockey. How's your latest trainee coming along?"

Eena shook her head and smiled. "Without Grandfather's help, I'm not sure Gavin would have made it. But he's become a great asset as a patroller and scout."

"Congratulations! Now you have the team of four you need."

"With no time to lose," Eena replied.

The image of Eena as a handcuffed prisoner gripped Chas's stomach. "Eena, I can't help but worry about you flying around out there. It's so dangerous."

"No need to worry," she replied. "We're really quite well concealed. Besides, you know I'm doing the kind of work I love to do— have to do."

Chas wrapped his arm around her shoulder. "I do know that about you, Eena. It's just that, as happy as I am surrounded by cabbages, chickens and cows, one aspect is missing." He communicated his meaning with a quick squeeze.

Eena sighed. "You know I love to be with you, Chas. But it's just not practical to live together for now. Let's take it day by day."

Chas shrugged. "Okay. For now, let's head to my cabin. I'll light the fire."

"Great!" Eena replied. "I'd appreciate brainstorming with you."

Chas grinned in the dark, knowing that along with his feminine counterpart came a military strategist.

The musicians, who had taken a break to eat, retrieved their instruments and, once again, played as dancers gathered. Grandfather sat on the stump that people left for him by tacit agreement.

Gavin stood close by, a scowl on his face. Not much of a dancer, he felt a twinge of jealousy as he watched Leslie dance with Steve.

After pouring himself a glass of mint tea, he approached Grandfather, now seated on the stump. The elder noticed an unhappy frown shadowed the youth's eyes.

"You okay?" he asked.

Gavin's eyes automatically shifted toward Leslie and back.

Following Gavin's glance toward the perky girl with large brown eyes, Grandfather murmured, "I see."

Gavin glared at him. "What do you see?" he asked, not realizing that Grandfather had already assessed the situation.

"I see that you are fortunate," the elder replied.

Why does he always speak in riddles? Gavin furrowed his forehead as he looked at Grandfather with more than a little impatience.

Matoskah arranged his features in a thoughtful expression. "At least you don't have to brave blizzards, rushing rivers, and a demanding father — even though she would be worth it."

Gavin shook his head. "How do you do that?"

"Do what?"

A slight smile drew back one corner of Gavin's lip. He knew this game by now. "Grandfather, you know very well what I mean. Just answer the question."

"No special talent. Just age," Matoskah said with a smile. He gestured with his chin toward the dancers.

Gavin felt his face grow hot as Leslie made her way through the crowd, moving toward him.

"Gavin!" Her eyes shined her gladness to see him.

Momentarily tongue-tied, Gavin was furious with himself. He raised a hand in friendly greeting.

"Nice to see you, Grandfather." Leslie smiled, leaning down to give him a friendly peck on the cheek.

"You need to teach this young man to dance," he suggested by way of greeting.

The young woman smiled brightly at Gavin. "I'm so thirsty," she whispered as she fanned herself and headed toward an urn. By the time she returned, Gavin had collected himself, and Grandfather had moved on.

Leslie took a long swig of tea, followed by a refreshed sigh. "So, do you like being a patroller?"

Gavin nodded, experiencing an unanticipated sense of pride. "Riding the air currents on an augur is a feeling like no other."

Leslie's liquid brown eyes penetrated his. "I know that connection to chosen tasks."

As the band began to play again, they had difficulty hearing one another. Suggesting a walk along the river, Leslie grabbed her sweater from a chair, and they headed away from the pavilion.

"As much as I do like being a patroller, I dream of exploring the Earth one day," Gavin said falling into step with the vivacious brunette.

Leslie glanced sideways at him. "In a sense we're both explorers."

Gavin remained quiet, awaiting her explanation.

"You want to explore the physical world. I prefer the quantum reality."

"I never thought of it like that." His heart quickened with deepening identification with Leslie.

The pair walked in companionable silence for a minute or so. As their hands brushed, Gavin felt an electric charge. He wanted to hold Leslie's hand, but lacked the courage to take it.

"Hey, there's an extra sleeping bag at the technology crew bunkhouse," Leslie stated simply.

"Are you inviting me to sleep over?" Pleasure jolted Gavin.

"Sure, if you don't mind Ryan's snoring and Stephen getting up in the middle of the night to pee."

Gavin laughed. "I think I can take it."

Leslie guided their steps in a slight change of direction toward an outside light glowing in the distance.

When they reached the entrance to the technology lab, Leslie went in first and switched on the interior light.

Gavin followed her into the bunkhouse, where he recognized Steve's overflowing duffle bag to one side.

Leslie tossed Gavin a rolled-up sleeping bag. "How about we climb into our sleeping bags and talk?"

Recalling his chagrin during the dance, Gavin watched the ponytail shake down, and the glasses come off. He was more than happy with the way the night was ending — with talking or whatever.

After Cosima and Valek had spent two nights in the cabin of a kindly couple, Matoskah visited her. "We're invited to lunch."

He didn't tell her that he had plans for her that involved the friend she was about to meet. "Raiel adopted two children who lost their parents after Solar Flash and hosts the local school," was all he volunteered.

Raiel lived on Blue Lake Mountain just above the village. Like Matoskah, her place of residence included a large meadow bordered by a stream that flowed into the river. Expecting Raiel to be alone in the woods with the children, Cosima was astonished at the sight that greeted her. A collection of parents and children from the community were working and playing together on the grass and under the trees. Circling the open expanse were four shelters, open on three sides with pine boughs over the top. As she strolled with Grandfather, Cosima noticed the activities taking place under two of the awnings. They first passed three women, one at a spinning wheel with a collection of children who were carding wool. Under another shelter, two men, a woman and a couple of children were sawing and sanding wood as a man assembled a table. A soccer game, with players including a thirty-year age span, took place on the grass.

Raiel's eyes, focused squarely on the elder's face, widened with pleasure. "Matoskah!"

"Cosima, Raiel." Grandfather smiled, his gaze lingering on the youthful brow framed by a silvery halo of tendrils.

Her curly hair gathered at the crown, Raiel's hazel eyes reflected the sunlight as she smiled at Cosima and glanced at the tall elder. "I sense you have a scheme up your sleeve, Matoskah!"

The familiar undertones of their relationship warmed Grandfather's expression.

Raiel slipped her arm around Cosima's shoulders. "How about some lunch? We can talk since my kids are playing and picnicking outside with the others."

Raiel's two-room cabin, resting among the trees, included a main kitchen and living area, and a loft where Kevin and Ellen slept. Cosima was surprised to see shelves filled with books along two walls. Intrigued, she perused classic tales with compelling illustrations and books concerning enlightened guidance and education.

Enticing aromas and the scrape of a chair on the wood floor as Grandfather prepared to sit drew Cosima to the table where Raiel ladled soup into bowls. A wildflower centerpiece of purple columbines and yellow daisies interspersed with white Queen Anne's lace added charm to the place settings and steaming array of dishes. To Cosima's delight, the delicately flavored mushroom soup enlivened every taste bud, while the dandelion greens, creamed potatoes, and flat bread satisfied more than her ravenous hunger.

Sensing the deep friendship between Raiel and Matoskah, Cosima noticed how comfortable she felt with the two elders.

"So, old man, I'm glad you're still among us. You spend so much time with the eagles, I expect you to fly away one of these days," Raiel teased.

"No way, woman," Grandfather replied with a mischievous glance. "I wouldn't want to lose my opportunities to pester you."

The faint flush of pink on Raiel's cheeks contradicted her pursed lips. She held up a foot wearing a well-worn moccasin. "Then make me a new pair of moccasins to compensate for all I have to put up with."

Shouts from the ongoing ball game that now included Valek, echoed through the room.

Grandfather looked at Cosima. "Children—no, entire families—like to come to Raiel's place."

Following his train of thought, Raiel turned toward Cosima. "I could use the help of a gentle soul who likes children around here."

The face of the recently orphaned emigrant to Three Mountains glowed with a new radiance. She enjoyed the lively, happy activity of Raiel's school on this meadow. "I'd love to help."

Raiel refreshed Grandfather's glass with herbal tea and the fragrance wafted with his words to Cosima. "Daughter, a path connects Raiel's place and mine. Come to me as the spirit moves you. We have work to do together."

Raiel placed the pot on the table. "So, Matoskah, any ongoing special missions for the eagles?"

"None at the time," Grandfather replied. "I don't sense the eagle's participation in the next arrivals," he added mysteriously.

The
Arrival

18

On the nineteenth of June, after a day at the park helping the crew frame in the treehouse walls, Meyer told the children goodbye. A mixture of tears and accusations erupted from their sense of abandonment.

Hugging those who would let him, Meyer, their friend and mentor, bequeathed them the tools.

"They'll rust if you leave them out in the rain." As he walked away, heartache vied with gladness that he would never have to suppress their childhoods by oppressing them in classrooms.

Goodbyes to family and friends tugged on Meyer's heart while hopeful anticipation lifted his spirits as he packed books, curriculum and clothing. At five thirty on the morning of the twentieth of June, he hoisted a strap over one shoulder and closed the dorm door. Carrying a duffle bag in each hand, with a decided spring in his step, Meyer walked away from his old life. The creeping acknowledgment that he would never be a successful teacher in Transtopia spurred the hope of freeing creative imaginations in the township.

A twenty-year-old Chevy from the metro fleet of twenty cars, usually reserved for VIPs, had been secured to transport Meyer to the airport. The sun was up by the time he arrived and shook hands with the pilot, who introduced himself as Nathan.

Meyer had heard of ghost towns before, and he understood the UA was dotted with them post-Solar Flash. But the thought of a ghost airport had never occurred to him. Absolute stillness prevailed. Huge jets, their electrical systems fried, rested where they had been parked over three years ago—as if landed by novices that misjudged the distance to the gates.

Since there was no active control tower, there would be no radio communication during the flight. But the government had full trust in the experienced pilot, who had logged over five thousand hours of flight time.

Nathan Abelt looked forward to piloting the overhauled Cesna over the Rockies. This would be his first flight over the Continental Divide since Solar Flash. But he wasn't complaining. The Union of the Americas' Sector 10 Imperial Governor Charles Scholtz had allowed him to remain one of two official pilots, plus an extra designation as SEI spy. He was well paid to be their eyes and ears, on the alert for the slightest sign of rebellion among the citizens of Transtopia Metro. Nathan's disdain for dissenters was only matched by his loyalty to the government that had saved him, his wife and two children from starvation. Thanks to his diligence as a local snitch, he had the ear and the appreciation of Governor Scholtz and the social engineering team. Today's flight opportunity was one of many perks in his very satisfying life since Solar Flash.

After loading the gear, the pilot showed Meyer the parachute stashed behind him and how to put it on and open the chute. When they were settled in their seats, the initial hum of the engine turned to a roar and the plane coasted down the runway.

As pilot and passenger rose above the city, they gazed in shocked silence at the ruins of the northern two-thirds of the former Colorado Springs. On an unpredictable spree of destruction, fires from Solar Flash had blackened a swath several miles wide. As if this weren't enough, in portions of the ruins, a rampage of tornadic winds had tossed the charred remains about, leaving piles of rubble and wreckage. Word was that portions of cities and terrain across the planet had escaped the devastation that wreaked havoc elsewhere. The southern third of Colorado Springs was such an area.

Nathan grimaced at the sight of the wreckage. "We're among the lucky ones. We owe so much to the Emergency Government. Thanks to their leadership and organization, Transtopia Metro is recovering rapidly." The oft-repeated slogan "Like the phoenix from the ashes" rang in his head.

The engine hummed as they flew over similar scenes of nature's wanton destruction. Meyer noticed evidence of wreckage of two piper planes sprawled across grassy meadows within a few miles of each other. Viewed from above, they looked as though a child having a tantrum had thrown down his toy planes so hard that the tail sections broke off and wings flung around.

When they gained the desired altitude, Nathan relaxed. "We're in for a treat. Our southwest heading to Township 24 takes us over the Continental Divide."

As they continued west, millions of acres of undamaged forest made the scenes they had just passed seem like a bad dream. Yet soon enough they flew over a treeless swath several miles wide with downed trees strewn about like matchsticks. Just on the other side of that destruction, they flew over a small, perfectly intact town cut through by a highway. Although the town was relatively unscathed by Solar Flash, it was eerily devoid of life. The roads had become graveyards for cars permanently stalled at intersections and parked askew in traffic lanes. No eighteen-wheelers passed through, no pedestrians crossed neighborhood streets in this vacated reminder of daily life of a few years ago.

Nathan sighed. "My family and the surrounding neighborhood ran out of food a month after the solar disruptions subsided. During the final days of that ordeal, we were terrified of roving gangs. Our relief and joy were indescribable when military vehicles showed up to transport us to Transtopia."

Meyer nodded sympathetically. "I'll never forget the drawn, anxious faces of my parents under the control of rovers. The soldiers that mowed them down and distributed rations saved our lives."

"We'll be steadily gaining elevation now as we approach the Continental Divide," Nathan said. "The mountains up ahead average about fourteen thousand feet in elevation."

Again, the spectacular view of forested mountains was interrupted by the horrific site of a crash. Jagged stumps of sheered trees evidenced the airliner's helpless nosedive into the side of a mountain. Nathan shuddered to think of the terror of the passengers, their skeletal remains probably still seated in the plane.

Nathan glanced at his passenger. "You know, there are rumblings of a resistance movement in the Metro. I have no use for those upstart troublemakers. We should be carrying our weight shoulder to shoulder in support of the government that helped pull us through."

Meyer hesitated. "I've heard rumors of insurgents. But I confess, I've been too focused on my career to think much about politics. I have noticed the state of martial law is tiresomely frequent."

Nathan checked the gauges, which indicated the increase in elevation as the plane approached even taller mountains looming ahead. "Martial law is for our protection. To keep us response-ready so the government can do its job."

A half hour later the pilot turned the nose of the plane still higher. "We're crossing the Continental Divide."

The beauty of jagged stone peaks still hosting patches of winter snow was riveting. But Nathan was a city guy, glad to simply pass over this wilderness.

Meyer spoke over the hum of the engines. "As a child, I had great times on family camping trips. My brother and I had our own tent across the campfire from our parents. I loved waking up to the smells of breakfast cooking on the cook stove, the sound of the zipper as I opened the tent to the cool crisp air, and the early morning bicycle ride past campsites with my golden retriever, Rusty."

"Hey, look at that!"

Meyer craned his neck to focus on the flying object ahead. "Probably an eagle."

"Too big," Nathan replied.

"Vulture, maybe?"

"It's bluish green."

The two remained silent, unable to place the bird in any known classification.

Captivated by the oddity, which had turned and abruptly reversed direction, Nathan muttered, "Never seen a bird do that."

As the plane approached a triangle of high peaks, the bird changed direction again, but this time to circle back and pace the plane at a distance.

Something was strange about that bird. Nathan spoke his compounding befuddlement aloud. "Hey, look at the hump on its back." He craned his neck to get a better view. "Some type of rare species."

Suddenly a sputter from the engine stole attention from the strange bird's bizarre behavior. Nathan's alarm spiked when he looked at the control panel. "My gauges have gone haywire."

Again, the engine coughed and sputtered as they flew over the peak of the first of a triangle of mountains. Just ahead, on the next mountain, loomed a lake in an ancient crater near a summit.

"Parachutes," Nathan barked as he grabbed for his own.

Sheer panic hammered Nathan's rib cage as he slipped the straps over his shoulders and fastened the front of the parachute. His hands fumbled hurriedly and his alarm intensified as he glanced at the wildly gyrating gauges.

"Something's messing with my electrical system," he yelled.

The engine sputtered and cut out. Nathan desperately tried to restart it. Precious seconds were passing as the plane lost elevation. Nathan glanced at his passenger to ascertain that he had put on his parachute.

"Jump!" Nathan opened the cockpit door. It had been years since he had practiced parachute jumping. But he knew the sequence. "Hold your rip cord and pull when you're clear of the plane."

Nathan hunched over at the open door. For an instant, as he gazed below, his courage failed him. Then he closed his eyes and released his hold on the plane. He pulled the cord a moment later. Immense relief flooded his body as he felt the jerk of the opened chute.

Floating down toward the tops of the dense growth of trees, Nathan wondered how they'd ever reach land. It felt strangely like slow motion as he sped down toward a single pine. Limbs scratched his face as branches, assaulted by his descent, snapped until a stubbornly resistant branch held the chute captive. He jolted to a halt, his feet hanging ten feet from the ground. He bounced, pulled and twisted to force the offending limb to release its hold, but to no avail. He was stuck. The chute was securely snagged somewhere above his dangling body.

After hanging a few minutes, yelling repeatedly for Meyer, and receiving no response, Nathan gauged the distance to the ground. The drop was a sufficient distance to break bones. Again, he called for the passenger. Was he dead? An hour of alternating between energetic bouncing and yelling prompted the decision to jump. Unlatching the body halter and holding tight to the right shoulder strap, he slipped his arm out of the left one. His body swung downward, and he gripped the one remaining connection to the chute. When the reactive bounce lessened, he took a deep breath and let go. He felt a stab of pain when his right leg hit the ground, and then the snap of bone as the impact jolted his arm.

Mercifully, he blacked out.

The Pilot

19

Cosima had happily settled in with her mentor, whose overarching objective as an educator was children's bright-eyed involvement.

Raiel smiled. "We will feed the soul even as we teach the mind."

Suddenly, while reading to a child, a shiver convulsed Cosima's body, and she dropped the book.

Raiel's hazel eyes searched her face with alarm. "Are you ill?"

Cosima shook her head. "No." She didn't feel sick. It was something else she couldn't put her finger on.

Raiel gently took the child's hand, suggesting they go outside to join a group making beeswax candles.

When Raiel returned to the cabin, Cosima greeted her with wide-open blue eyes communicating alarm.

"Cosi, whatever is wrong?" Concern rang in the older woman's voice as she put her arm around the girl's shoulder.

Cosima shook her head. "Someone... something has happened. Someone is in pain."

"Who, Cosima?"

"I don't know. I just know it's urgent."

Raiel chewed her lip for a minute. "Let's go to Grandfather."

Surprisingly, Cosima shook her head. "No, that's the wrong way." Needing silent stillness, the girl held up her hand.

Raiel waited patiently until the girl spoke. "Above us, here on Blue Lake Mountain, someone is hurt."

"Can you lead us to him?"

"I don't know."

Raiel abruptly stood up, walked across the room, and picked up a radio.

"Eena, answer please. Over."

Eena's voice came over the radio. "There's a downed plane. Over."

"Cosi's aware. Over."

"Anaya's heading to him. Over."

"Where? Over."

"On Blue Lake Mountain. I'm resting Cesla, but will be ready to fly again in about ten minutes. Watch for the circling bird."

Raiel retrieved a compass and filled two canteens while Cosima charged the children with staying indoors with Valek. Once outside, the pair scanned the sky from the meadow.

Finally, Eena waved and turned Cesla northwest toward the mountain peak above.

Raiel checked the compass. "Must be higher on the mountain and northwest of this location." She and Cosima hurried into the dense canopy of trees.

Relying on the compass, Raiel pointed to a schism heading northwest. "Let's follow that ravine for a while," she suggested.

They continued at as fast a pace as possible over the uneven terrain, until Raiel tripped on a root. As she swayed out of control, the compass flew from her hand and plummeted over twenty feet into the stream.

Raiel recovered her balance and looked down. "I'm sure it's broken in several pieces." She sighed and shook her head. "Let's follow the ravine for now."

When the ravine turned sharply, alarms went off in Raiel's head. "Oh dear, we could end up going in circles."

Cosima stood absolutely still as if concentrating or listening. Raiel waited quietly, unwilling to interrupt whatever was occurring.

"I can feel him." The girl began to walk as if following an invisible trail.

Raiel followed, for now trusting Cosima's lead because they were continuing up the mountain. But as they hiked farther, Raiel grew uneasy. "I have no sense of direction among these trees."

Cosima was calm, paying close attention to an inward pull. "A sort of honing signal is leading us to him." Her voice was soft, remote.

They followed no apparent path, zigzagging among tree trunks. Raiel struggled to calmly follow Cosima.

When another half hour had passed, Cosima held up a hand to halt their progress. A sound. In response to a faint groan, she broke into a run. Just ahead a man lay moaning softly. The pair rushed to either side of him.

"My arm," he muttered, slurring his words. "Please, don't touch." His arm extended awkwardly from his body, a broken bone protruding beneath the skin of his forearm.

Cosima glanced at Raiel. "Help is coming."

Grandfather emerged from the trees.

Raiel made room for him beside the man's head. Grandfather surveyed the dangling parachute gear overhead.

"How did you land?"

"On my feet, then on this arm."

Grandfather nodded. "I am Matoskah."

"Nathan," the wounded man whispered. "Pilot."

"Nathan, show me how you can move your head."

Nathan obeyed.

"Your neck seems fine. I have something for you to drink to relax you and ease the pain."

Grandfather gently lifted Nathan's head just enough to slowly trickle a dark liquid into his mouth. Between grimaces, Nathan drank it all.

Minutes later his eyelids flickered. "M... M...."

Grandfather touched the man's unharmed shoulder, and put his ear close to Nathan's mouth. "What are you trying to say?"

"Meyer," he croaked, and lost consciousness.

"Meyer must be the passenger," Eena remarked, standing behind Grandfather with Anaya.

Anaya walked to the opposite side of the patient, opened the stretcher she carried, and placed it on the ground next to Nathan.

Eena suggested that all but Anaya and Grandfather fan outward to search for the passenger. She also radioed Gavin, although it would be difficult to spot Meyer through the dense canopy. The search lasted about fifteen minutes before Meyer responded to the calls of Cosima and Raiel.

Obviously grateful for the sight of them, he immediately asked, "Have you seen the pilot?"

Raiel nodded. "He's badly hurt. Two people remained with him."

By the time the searchers returned with Meyer, Grandfather and Anaya had shifted the patient to a stretcher. After introductions, they agreed Raiel's house was the nearest dwelling.

"Let's hope he remains unconscious." Grandfather shook his head. "This won't be easy."

Matoskah, Anaya, Eena and Cosima each took a corner of the stretcher. Carrying the compass and flashlight that Eena brought along, Raiel walked ahead to either find or clear the easiest path. Slowly, taking care to jostle the injured man as little as possible, the group navigated the rocky slopes as they inched down the mountain in darkening twilight until the flashlight shone on Raiel's log cabin.

When they shifted Nathan from the stretcher to Cosima's bed, he awakened and cried out with pain. Matoskah pulled the bowl and another small round bottle from his vest pocket. After he poured another dose of the dark amber liquid into the bowl, Anaya lifted Nathan's head, and he drank it.

As soon as his eyelids closed, Anaya and Grandfather looked at each other. Grandfather asked Raiel for a clean cloth, which she quickly retrieved. Then he rolled it and stuffed it into Nathan's mouth. Anaya deftly pulled his arm to force the dislodged bone to its correct position. Nathan's body convulsed and his head rolled side to side in response to the agonizing pain. Then, to everyone's relief, he lay still except for the slight rise and fall of his chest.

Early the next morning, people arose from sleeping pallets on the floor, stomachs alerted by the enticing smells of eggs and biscuits. While the rescuers gathered around Raiel's not so large dining table, Nathan ate in bed.

Mostoskah opened the door and entered, having already been to the top of the mountain and back. "Nathan, I'm sorry to tell you the plane has sunk to the bottom of a lake."

Feeling a mixture of despair at the loss of the plane and relief to be alive, Nathan looked around the cabin and at the gathered individuals. "So, where is this place anyway?"

The response was a charged, collective silence, with looks registering closed caution on some faces and outright distrust on others.

Nathan knew of no townships in the mountains. "This isn't a township, is it?"

Matoskah was the one with the presence of mind to respond with quiet simplicity. "We're just a handful of mountain folk."

Nathan sensed this was all the information he was going to get. But something in him knew there was more to the story, and the spy in him rallied to the challenge to find out what it was. He recalled Scholtz's words requesting that he be on the lookout for settlements and note coordinates, especially along the Continental Divide.

The crazy behavior of the big blue bird that had paced the plane popped into his head. He suspected he would have a good story to tell Imperial Governor Scholtz when he returned to Transtopia Metro.

The Storm

20

Darkening clouds approaching from the next peak warned Eena she should head down from the summit of Blue Lake Mountain. But as lightning flashed, warning of an encroaching storm, her depressed mood bound her feet. Defiantly facing the rumbling assault of disruptive forces, her gaze shifted toward the unperturbed surface of Blue Lake. With the airborne intruder secreted in its depths, the water serenely mirrored the cloudless azure above.

A plane. A single dive through the skies of Three Mountains had shattered her hope for the reprieve of a few years in which to marshal their forces.

Clouds spilled over the distant ridge as a surge of wind ruffled the placid waters, and an icy gust ripped through Eena's thin windbreaker.

Exposed. No means of self-defense against the inevitable invasion from air as well as land. Gaining allies in mountain settlements had proved challenging. Riveted by daily concerns and small pleasures, many negated the soon-to-encroach regulation of their lives.

Black curls hung in front of Eena's eyes, spiraling causeways for drops that spilled to her face. Like a flood of tears, the rivulets flowed down her cheeks.

Her father's intense blue eyes had bored into hers two weeks before the tornado took his life. An understanding of, and alliance with, natural forces empowered his naturopathic practice. "Eena, I teach my patients self-education and self-reliance—how to take charge of their health through healthful nutrition and habits."

Violent shivers shook Eena's body, and she backed up to huddle beneath a cluster of ancient pines. Ahead, the bombardment of hard rain pockmarked the surface of the lake.

Propaganda. She and her dad had watched money-is-the-bottom-line, corporation-driven television commercials. "Let's see what's really going on here," he had said, and drew her attention to evocative scripts and cinematography that triggered people to crave packaged foods that were colorful, sweet and salty. Dead fare with nutrition processed out—a setup for obesity and weakened immune systems. "The lies to entice you to give away your health and power are seductive." She felt the urgency in his voice.

Lightning struck a tree. Flames burst from a pine branch. Anticipation of the great tree becoming a charred lifeless post seared her heart. But the torrential downpour diminished the fire to wisps of smoke.

The landlords. She didn't know then that her father spoke as an insider to the puppeteers that managed the corporatized world stage. "The fabulously rich and powerful consider planet Earth to be *their* real estate—their *royal* estate, and humanity to be *their* work force."

Her reply was incisive. "Well, the vast majority would fight for our rights."

Her father grimaced. "The controllers are too wily to engage in overt aggression."

Eena hunkered down for warmth, pulling her windbreaker over her knees. The temperature plummeted as she recalled meeting her father's hard stare. "The landlords own the news syndicates. Scripted daily news turns the cogs of a usurious regime."

She stretched her jacket to her ankles and pulled her hood over her face.

"I don't understand."

"Daily doses keep humanity devitalized while generating fear and dependency."

Eena wanted to hurry down the mountain to escape the biting cold and disrupt unsettling recollections. A ten-minute descent from the summit to more comfortable temperatures would render the lake's ominous secret out of sight, out of mind. But the broad trunk at her back lent its strength to her huddled despair.

Sovereignty – the word both her parents used frequently. She had practically memorized its definition: "In alliance with natural forces we can birth our own; we can maintain a state of health; we can build our own houses; we can thrive independent of the control grid."

The great trees flanked Eena on an island of safety, as on either side water streamed, rushing toward the lake.

Her father had warned of a seductive march toward the next phase: bionic humans. "Now is the fork in the road, the deciding point for humanity's fate. Either to become robotic responders to a controlling AI, minus a heart, or awakened to collectively engage powers of co-creative intelligence driven by the heart."

She had buried her father's voice until the words of the doctor at Fort Carlson echoed the momentous portend of the royal defector's warning. Eena shouted her impotence into the storm. "But, Dad, no one wants to know. The corporations supply their livelihoods. The political regime, their safety."

An interior voice reverberated a reply. "Go deeper. Bypass the face of humanity to inspire a response from the deepest soul."

The sun's face asserted itself through broiling clouds, and the waves racing across the lake surface reflected a shaft of light. She felt the heat of her unseen father's incisive stare. "Those awakening are small in number, but great in might if you combine inherent forces. Find them."

The rifled waters of Blue Lake lapped the shore, its calm depths securing evidence of the controllers' penetration of this tiny mountain stronghold. As the rain slowed to a trickle, the turquoise skies clarified the next step.

Eena breathed deeply of the ozone-purified air. They, the runners from the townships, would return to penetrate the desert strongholds of the landlords.

Per prior agreement, Matoskah stayed with Nathan at Raiel's during the meeting called by Eena. Both chairs and standing room were filled as she introduced the topic. "The reach of the landlords is closing in on us. The plane that we hoped not to see for several years is now at the bottom of Blue Lake. Even worse, it has brought us a potential spy. In addition, the team of shoppers overheard an ominous statement by a UA military officer in Durango." She paused. The expectant tension in the room was palpable. "Top officials from Region 21 are moving into Durango, just thirty miles from us."

The alarm that shot across people's expressions segued into the plea that was the object of the presentation. "It's urgent that we establish networks with Techno City and the townships and, eventually, Transtopia."

Stepping to a flip chart, Eena opened it to the first page. "This plan calls for several categories of people to further our goals." She directed the pointer to the heading and sub-headings: *Community-Based Operatives*: *Connectors, Informers* and *Seeders*.

"Connectors will operate to actively promote our community's connection to the surrounding townships."

Using a pointer, she traced an invisible line beneath Informers and glanced toward Ansil.

Ansil rose to his feet, his countenance animated. "Some of you have read my essays on the new society. Drawing from these writings, I can create pamphlets to spread among the people in the townships."

Eena smiled and faced the audience. "In case you're not aware of it, Ansil is a talented and inspiring writer. He wholeheartedly carries the vision of equality and self-sufficiency held in common by our community."

Eena turned toward the chart and moved the pointer below Connectors. "Like every aspect of our mission, this operation involves risk. The connectors will establish direct, carefully concealed routes through the desert from strategic exit points to Techno City and the townships. The first phase of their task is to supply the routes with caches of water and other emergency essentials. The second phase includes resupplying the caches and providing a chain of communication. Using the radios, they will relay information between Techno City and the townships and Three Mountains Community."

She waited for the talk among people to die down before continuing. When Eena pointed to Seeders, Caellum signaled his desire to speak.

Caellum rose to his feet. "I've agreed to be a seeder. Basically, a seeder's job will be twofold. First, as undercover agents, we'll disseminate Ansil's pamphlets and start rumors about a free society thriving beyond the reach of the controllers. Second, per Eena's insistence, we don't get caught." Uneasy laughter broke the tension in the room. "Our first target is Techno City. Based on what we learn from my first mission, we'll establish a protocol for six more routes, one to go to each township."

Eena looked from Caellum to the circle of people. "Early on, the seeders will likely arouse scoffing in most, mild curiosity in a few, and piqued interest in rare individuals. Lighting the fires of a movement is likely to take time."

Caellum nodded. "For now, we may have to content ourselves with just sparking the tinder, so to speak."

The next page displayed the heading Techno City and Township-based Operatives. Three types of participants were listed below.

"Whereas Three Mountains is home base for the three groups we've discussed so far, the next three — the spreaders, infiltrators, and emigrants — will originate in Techno City and the townships."

Eena circled Spreaders with her pointer. "This group can interface with the seeders from Three Mountains Community and spread the word. We think colleges and universities may be the best source for our first recruits. These youths are likely to be receptive — no, more than that — enthusiastic to spread the word, based on the informers' and seeders' communiqués. The spreaders will develop strategies to discreetly gauge people's receptivity, so as not to arouse suspicion."

This new direction triggered an intense debate lasting another hour. The main protest was, "Completely unarmed?"

Eena shrugged. "What I'd give for our own arsenal."

Chas stood up and looked around the room awaiting calm. "It seems we are left with only one choice: to infiltrate the power hierarchy peacefully."

"Have you guys gone completely nuts?"

Chas continued unperturbed. "We're directing our attention to risk-takers to form groups and infiltrate the power structure."

Carla, a rosy-cheeked robust woman with gold-blonde hair, spoke up. "No chance."

Leslie pushed her glasses to the top of her head. "The divide and conquer strategy of the controlling hierarchy is only going to get worse. Now's the time for action."

Rigel stood up holding his toddler son. A tiny fist clasped his father's dreadlock as wide brown eyes stared at the circle. "Are we ready for that action to be turned back on us — with an armed military?"

Chas addressed his friend. "Our hope is for momentum from the growing numbers with switched on DNA." He smiled at Eena. "What Eena calls 'the activated sovereignty gene.' "

With quietly measured tones, she dove into the silence that followed Chas's words. "We can do nothing until the SEI tentacles of power reach us." Each word shot across the room with laser precision.

"I'm for taking action," Gavin said.

Eena smiled at him. How far he had come in two months.

After a long pause revealed no more comments were forthcoming, Eena continued to Infiltrators. To effectively increase our power base, agents will need to infiltrate positions of authority in cities and townships. Either rising from ranks of the spreaders, or being approached by them, the infiltrators are likely to include a very small number at first. This group also includes individuals, who, while already filling positions of authority, are unhappy with the subjugation of humanity. This tiny minority would genuinely like to restore power to the people."

"That's going to be problematic." The speaker's skepticism was palpable.

"The SEI hierarchy requires each member to sell his or her soul in exchange for status," said another doubtfully.

"Who's going to put their livelihood, their family, at risk?"

A buzz of agreement followed. The prevailing sentiment was that this was a very risky enterprise, which could easily turn against them.

But the plan's supporters were also vocal. "So, we just sit back and let the system strangle us to death?"

Eena moved the pointer to Emigrants. "Those who choose to emigrate to Three Mountains Community can join us in forming a model of self-governance."

Ansil broke in. "This working model is an essential element of peaceful insurgence."

After three hours of intense debate, those gathered consented to Eena's plan with reactions ranging from "I hope this doesn't bring disaster on our heads" to "How soon can Caellum begin his mission?"

Gavin was first out the door. He was glad the group had finally arrived at a consensus and even more glad to be free to go on patrol. Today he planned to explore farther north, beyond the routine Three Mountains perimeter flight. A hunch told him he would discover more people.

The Emigrants

21

Martha and Phil Seymour, the sole remaining residents in or around Lake City, faced one another across the kitchen table while their son, Chris, played in the scrubland around their home.

"Phil, we're not going to make it much longer. We need other people."

Phil glanced at his wife and then out the door toward the plot of land he loved.

Martha persisted. "Chris's shorts are too tight, his shoes don't fit, and he can't wear a single one of his T-shirts."

Phil didn't want to leave this plot of land that he had worked and tamed. "Any day now people will show up and want to stay."

Martha was growing impatient with her husband's desperate hope. "It's been three years, Phil."

At that moment, their thin cow, Mimi, plodded past the door, followed by Chris, nudging her toward the barn with a stick.

Martha pressed her point. "Chris needs other children. I worry about bears coming out of the forest and some serious accident needing medical help."

Phil sighed and rose from his chair. "I'm going to walk around for a bit."

Martha shook her head. *Most stubborn man I ever met.* She got up to make biscuits. *But I'm not giving up. Durango is not more than eighty miles southwest of us. We need to get there, and fast. Yesterday wouldn't have been too soon.* Opening the bin that held their last ten pounds of flour, she scooped up a cupful, including the weevils. In normal times, she would have been disgusted. Now she told herself they added protein.

The smell of oven-hot biscuits, green beans from the garden, and boiled eggs brought the ravenous appetite of a nine-year-old to the table. The remains of the meal were cold by the time Phil stepped through the front door and sat down. After filling his plate he placed his hands palms down on the table and looked from his wife to his son. "I brought the cart around. Let's load it this afternoon. Chris, you help me build crates for the chickens."

As though in a state of suspended animation, Phil's wife and son stared at him.

"In the morning we can hitch up Mimi and head out."

Martha stood up and busied herself washing dishes in the sink to hide the tears that overflowed her relief.

After pulling out the next morning, only Phil looked back as the family followed the southbound dirt road. After two days they passed an old mine, and the path became rocky ruts that tortured the wagon wheels until one came off. Phil's considerations leaped ahead as he unhitched Mimi. With no road, the cow wasn't going to be able to continue much farther. A sick knowing filled him with dread of what he had to do.

As the family gathered belongings from the toppled cart, Chris spied three men descending a grassy slope to the west.

Phil walked around to the opposite side of the cart to retrieve his rifle.

Chris, whose eyesight was the best, could see that two men supported one who was hobbling. "Looks like one of them's hurt," he exclaimed.

Phil wanted to keep walking, but muttered, "Whoever those characters are, they'll probably follow us if we move on."

Martha's first instinct was always to help. Nonetheless, fingers of warning clutched her chest.

Chris simply stared with the open vulnerability of a child.

When the three men reached the wagon, the supporting pair laid the third on the ground.

"Stepped in a gopher hole," said the spokesman for the trio. "Got anything for a sprain?"

Martha walked past Phil's restraining arm and kneeled by the reclining man.

An instant later, the downed man's arm gripped Martha's shoulder, a gun barrel thrust in her stomach. The other two, one with a rifle, the other a pistol, aimed their weapons at Phil and Chris. Phil's grip tightened, and then loosened on his now useless rifle.

Chris cried out and took a step to run to his mother.

"Don't come any closer," barked the man with the pistol, pointing it at Chris.

"No," his father yelled.

Chris stopped in his tracks.

The man on the ground stood up. Holding tight to Martha, he growled, "Hands in the air."

The family slept with their feet and hands tied that night. By morning they had figured out that the rovers' names were Jimmy, Marvin and Arnie. Jimmy was the swaggering leader; Arnie, the fidgety sidekick; and Marvin, the rifle-bearing one with a cold-blooded-killer look that sent shivers down Martha's spine.

Marvin took care of the issue of future rations for the group by shooting Mimi while Martha buried her traumatized son's face in her chest.

For two days and nights the rovers repelled wolves while the meat smoked. Then, with the meat packed on the family members' backs, along with whatever else they could carry, and chicken cages hanging from their arms, the rovers herded them through a ravine. Crows and buzzards descended behind them to pick clean the bovine bones.

As Gavin flew Espirit past the northern perimeter of Three Mountains, the cooler air in the heights blew back his hood and ruffled his hair. Leaning in close to the bird he had once shunned, he pushed his fingers through the densely layered feathers of her breast and pressed his face into the sparser softness of the tufts along her neck. Gavin never dreamed of this exquisite surrender to the rhythmic rise and fall of powerful wings. Navigating air currents, it was as though his very soul piloted the augur—captain and vessel merged as one in an aerial sea.

His thoughts soared ahead to tomorrow. Eena had okayed Leslie's request to visit Mu, and he relished anticipating Leslie's reaction when she first entered the mysterious land beyond the portal. The patroller looked forward to his human love meeting his augur bond-mate. He imagined her bright eyes and smiles of happiness when he showed her hundreds of augurs soaring over the savannah.

Approximately forty miles beyond the Three Mountains perimeter, he saw distant specks moving south through a gorge. Approaching closer to the small group of people, he circled slowly and pulled out his binoculars. As far as he could ascertain, there were four men, a woman, and a child. Suddenly, when they spotted Espirit, he noted to his horror that one was aiming a rifle. He quickly communicated to her to bank away. After a loud report, he heard a *zing* as the bullet ripped through the augur's long tail. Feathers spiraled to the ground as he turned the bird away, urging her to lower their altitude so the tree line could hide them from view.

A second shot rang out and the bullet penetrated the augur's flesh, miraculously missing Gavin. Suddenly, in a terrifying freefall, he and Espirit plummeted toward the trees. He desperately held onto her neck as inertia tore his body from hers. They crashed into a tree canopy and bumped through pine limbs, the ear-splitting cracks screaming protests against severed branches. Espirit's body bore the brunt of the hurtling assault on pine limbs that retaliated by slashing Gavin's face and arms with lethal spikes.

Ravaging forces tossed the rider aside to drape over a limb like a ragdoll while the mass of feathers, blood and flesh lurched and bumped through more hapless boughs to the final thud. Seconds later, a fresh shock of terror surged through Gavin as his temporary perch broke. Frantically, he grabbed a branch and managed to hold on with both hands as his body swung downward. Kicking his legs, he located a bough to support his feet as he grasped the upper limb and inched toward the trunk. As though he were a child and the tree, a parent offering solace, he wrapped his arms around the rough bark for support until his heart slowed its racing pulse, and his heaving gulps of air quieted to normal.

After several minutes, in dazed shock, Gavin removed the shredded remains of his flight suit and draped it over a limb. Secured by the tree's central source of strength, he began his final descent until, with a leap from the lowest branch, the welcome solidity of ground impacted his soles. He crumpled to his knees and fell forward, pressing his belly and face to a cushion of pine needles. Momentarily, covered by a merciful void, his torn and wracked body stretched across patches of soft grass, he breathed in the earthy scents as soothing warmth caressed his lacerated face.

Too soon an intruding nudge pushed Gavin to pick himself up and face what he dreaded, but must. With a jagged intake of air, wincing from pain, he turned toward the tangled mass of bloodied feathers and torn flesh heaped amid dismembered pine boughs. Sobs wracked him as he knelt beside Espirit's body. The hand that had once jerked away in fear tenderly stroked the memorized curvature of the beak, now wet with his tears. His finger lingered at the sharp tip that had brushed his palm while grasping fruit offerings. Moving his hand to the twisted neck, he recalled Espirit's responsive shiver when he first stroked her feathers, and the warm, soft down that blanketed his fingers in frigid heights. Lightly touching a crumpled wing, he recalled the powerful *phoom* of these air-sea oars and the unforgettable exhilaration of his first—and his last—flight. *We navigated the skies as one.* A sob wrenched his gut. *Espirit, I'm sorry. So very, very sorry.*"

After an interval lost in mourning, an insistent awareness intruded on Gavin's vigil. Though reluctant to leave Espirit's side, eminent danger bid him take action. The travelers, including the rifle-bearer, were headed in the general direction of Three Mountains Community. And now they might be searching for him. After radioing Eena, Gavin found a clearing where she would be able to see him.

Eena flew Cesla, leading a pack augur. Not being a bonded bird, Gavin might not be able to communicate with him, but thanks to the flocking instinct, the bird would follow Cesla. Flying north from the gorge, she spied the specks moving south through a mountain pass. The binoculars zoomed in on a family of three, obviously captives, and three armed rovers. After veering east and circling slowly for several minutes, the crop of blonde hair, as well as the bright red gashes that crisscrossed Gavin's face and body, came into view.

"I have a visual on you," she radioed. "Coming in with medical supplies and a second bird."

He turned toward the trees where Espirit's body lay. Eena landed the augurs, tethered them to trees, and followed. Rare tears streamed down her cheeks as she touched Espirit's ragged and stained feathers. She had known this creature as a young fledgling taking his first precarious flights from the rim of a nest. She had witnessed his first flight as Jarrod's bond-mate. She had been moved by Espirit's proud challenge toward Gavin to bond with her or release her. Touching her fingertips to her lips and then to the pierced breast, Eena sent a grief-stricken salute of wordless gratitude for the augur's faithful assistance.

Bandaged and cleaned up, Gavin returned with Eena to Three Mountains Community. Eena had called an emergency meeting with the words, "Rovers headed this direction. About three or four weeks out."

Leslie rushed into the pavilion as soon as she heard, compassion for Gavin moistening her eyes. When she threw her arms around his neck, his reddened eyes briefly met hers before, standing stiff and unresponsive, he pulled away.

"My fault," was all he could mumble, avoiding the stricken look on her face.

Chas hurried to Eena, hugged her long and tenderly, then stood with his arm around her shoulder.

The news spread quickly, and people crowded into the pavilion. Leaning on the cane lent by Anaya, Nathan arrived, his arm in a sling, and found a seat next to Matoskah. When those gathered saw him walk in and sit down as though he were a part of the community, there were barely disguised frowns and low-voiced warnings that those who had met Nathan didn't trust him.

The initial noise became hushed voices, until a quiet expectancy prevailed. The assemblage gazed toward Gavin. His face expressionless, voice monotone, he recounted the events of the day.

Listening to the noticeably beat-up youth, Nathan tried to piece together his account. *Espirit? Augur?* Suddenly, Nathan recalled the strange bird that had tracked the plane. The hump. *So, these people ride giant birds?* Nathan's close-set brown eyes darted around the room. Then and there he resolved to get to the bottom of this bizarre reality. Imperial Governor Scholtz would want to hear every detail about this place.

Gavin concluded his story. "...three armed and dangerous men."

Marcus, one of the shoppers, spoke up. "We need to head them off before they get here." His comment triggered a barrage of comments, if not solutions.

"And just how do we do that?"

Silence.

Nathan spoke the obvious. "We need to arm ourselves. Surely you guys have guns."

Rigel quietly replied. "Your—the government confiscated them."

"For our own good," Nathan retorted. At this moment he acutely missed the protection of the police force in Transtopia. Instead, he was an exposed and vulnerable part of a bunch of naïve peace-loving hippies.

Fear was palpable amid a barrage of comments.

"Not good odds."

"Well, we can't just let a band of rovers simply walk into our community."

"They're forty miles away."

"Actually, it's unlikely they'll find us."

"True. We're well hidden by the three mountains."

"If they do, they're well-armed."

"More than likely they'll bypass us to follow the ravine and reservoir to Highway 240."

"My concern is that poor family."

Noisy protests and arguing escalated.

Chas spoke up, calling on his knowledge of martial arts. "They'll reveal their weaknesses. The more we focus our own power, the more likely we'll find a way to disarm the enemy."

Eena smiled brightly. "Chas, I will keep in mind the wisdom of your words... while armed with my pistol."

Nathan's mental ears perked up at this. The existence of at least one gun among this renegade group was another important piece of information.

The meeting continued with people presenting various scenarios. Of foremost concern were the children, which they agreed to keep out of sight if the rovers arrived.

"But the mountains hide us well. Chances are slim to none that the travelers will find the community."

"Nonetheless, the patrollers can keep watch and let us know if and when they approach the outskirts of Three Mountains."

Lori and Chuck agreed to keep watch over the northern perimeter.

Looking increasingly gloomy, Gavin muttered to no one in particular. "I'm useless."

Though Leslie stood at Gavin's side, he held his body apart, she and any words of comfort rebuffed by an invisible wall.

The
Window

22

The topic of rovers moved the people to vent fear of both discovery and also word of the community getting out, referring covertly to Nathan. Several looked toward Matoskah, who rarely spoke at these gatherings. In his quiet way he offered an observation. "Our arrival at Three Mountains Community never guaranteed an isolated haven."

At that moment, a red bird flew in through an open window to zigzag frantically between the constricting walls. All remained quiet as the panicked bird flew around the room past the way to open air and with no place to land among an ocean of upturned faces. Finally, in desperation it flew upward to a high beam to land with a rapidly heaving breast. All eyes were drawn to the terrorized bird.

To Mastoskah this appearance from the animal kingdom was a sign. "High ground invites a broad view," the elder intoned softly. When a blur of red swooped down and out the window to freedom, some cheered. Only those closest to Grandfather heard him conclude with a hint of humor in his voice. "And clarity for decisive action."

The group quietly remained seated a few more minutes to process the sobering and frightening revelations of the day. Weighted with the knowledge of less than a month to devise a plan of action to save the captive family, they filed out of the room.

Having obtained a seat close to Matoskah, Nathan felt the power of his encoded, if not decoded, message. On the two occasions he had visited

Grandfather at his teepee, Nathan had decided that although Matoskah was simple-minded and superstitious, the old Native American was endearing. Besides, Grandfather was the only one in the community who was genuinely friendly. Everyone else was polite at best, treated him as a pariah at worst. He didn't know why, other than that they had guilty consciences for defying the Union of the Americas Imperial Government.

Nathan's espionage work was cut out for him. He hoped his stay at this primitive stronghold of renegades would be short, but in the meantime, he had three goals: to find out about those mysterious giant birds, to uncover some secret connected with the science lab, and to get Eena's gun.

Eena hugged Cesla's powerful neck as he banked south at Lemon Reservoir, the blue of the water sparkling her joy on this auspicious day in early August—the send-off of Caellum, first of the seeders to head out after weeks of planning. Considerable teamwork had gone into constructing the supply route across the desert. The six connectors had used steel landscaping wagons to haul shovels, a gallon of red paint and three twenty-gallon aluminum trash cans to hold three one-gallon jugs of water, packages of jerky, dehydrated fruit and veggies, and trail mix. They also carried a supply of matches, flashlights, binoculars, compasses, blankets and emergency medical supplies.

She had given Caellum final instructions as her finger traced the yellow line down on a map. "The three rest/refresh points along your route are a farmhouse with a green metal roof ten miles south of Lemon Reservoir Dam along Highway 502, the east shore of Lake Nighthorse twenty miles due west, and Cinder Gulch ten miles south of Lake Nighthorse and fifteen miles north of Techno City.

"By the last day of the twenty-one days allotted for your trip, connectors will position themselves at these locations. For two days they will form a radio relay team and will attempt to establish communication with you. Should you have left the city, but be in need of assistance, the three connectors will become a rescue team. If we cannot establish contact with you after two days, we will assume the controllers have captured you. But don't get caught. Working out plans for a rescue attempt could take weeks."

Caellum's bunkhouse mate, Rick, who had escaped Techno City the previous year, had given him the address of James, a trusted friend and sympathizer. Because of his ailing mother he hadn't joined Rick as a runner. This note introduced Caellum and asked that James allow him to sleep in his unit for a couple of weeks.

As Eena and Cesla approached the dam at the south end of Lemon Reservoir, she saw Caellum tie his bedroll to the bicycle ledge with a bungee cord and adjust his backpack. Perfect timing. "Sure you want to do this? Over."

Straddling his bike, the seeder unclipped his radio from his belt and grinned up at her. "Never more sure of anything. Over."

"Got the brochures?"

"Check."

"Letter?"

"Check."

"Map?"

"You're sounding like my mother."

"Okay, okay. See you in three weeks."

Caellum waved, reclipped the radio, and headed for Techno City.

Eena and Cesla circled for several minutes. She knew it was corny, but the phrase *May the force be with you* rose from the depths of her heart as she watched him cross the highway. Before she and Cesla headed back to Three Mountains, Caellum crossed the dam to follow Highway 243 south, with tall pines marshaling his trek.

The sturdy bike and tires easily managed the mildly bumpy terrain. Glancing at the eight o'clock sun, he estimated that averaging three miles an hour, he'd reach the tip of the east shore of Lake Nighthorse by late afternoon the following day.

On reflection, he could hardly believe that now he was headed away from the community. Next week he'd be spending his twenty-third birthday right back in a controller stronghold; a realm of lockdown that, a decade before Solar Flash, the citizens of his hometown, Pagosa Springs, would have insisted to be impossible.

As Caellum rode, he recalled climbing into an army cargo truck a couple of months after the Earth's changes subsided. Although he and his family were growing desperately hungry and wintry blasts tortured thin flesh, leaving his home tore at his heart. After a snail's pace trek into the desert, the military convoy unloaded the passengers into a bleak-looking tent city surrounded by a chain link fence with strands of barbed wire looped over the top. He had shared his parents' alarm that this felt more like a prison camp than a safe haven.

Building and food supplies had been stockpiled in a Quonset hut nearby. For several months, Caellum recalled the daily ride huddled against the cold in the bed of a cargo truck to and from the construction site at the edge of a forlorn-looking ghost town. For endless, mind-numbing hours that dragged on for months, a conscripted workforce of several hundred people erected cinder block walls and hauled wheelbarrow loads of concrete to complete the housing units for 800 families.

Caellum's dad, a visionary city manager in Pagosa Springs, was appointed as foreman to oversee the construction. His larger than life persona and status in the building project led to his friendship with Lieutenant Stone, likewise assigned to oversee the crews. Listening to their conversations, the twenty-year-old gleaned earfuls about the schemes played out before, during, and after Solar Flash.

Lieutenant Stone was glad to have someone to confide in, although he could have been court-martialed—or worse—if found out. "Like I told you, my battalion rode out Solar Flash a half-mile underground as part of a strategic plan. The government, having foreknowledge of the coming catastrophes, briefed us on post-Solar Flash strategies. They chose isolated small towns like this one with some infrastructure to support start-over populations." Lieutenant Stone raised one eyebrow. "The reasoning was that these townships are ideal to tightly manage populations of four thousand or less."

Caellum pulled himself back to the present, alert to possible traffic as he approached Highway 160, a major artery for convoys and retrievers. Crossing without mishap, he continued south, paralleling Highway 501 at a distance so as to remain unseen until he reached the farmhouse. The next morning he rode out early, the forlorn farms triggering more memories of Solar Flash.

Solar Flash had fried most power stations and electrical grids worldwide. But the following year, the Sector 10 engineering squad used electrical components that had been protected deep underground to rebuild the power grid at Township 26. A rebuilt power station and replacement wiring supplied sufficient electricity for the newly built housing units plus a few houses.

Five remodeled homes housed the town father and designated Directors of Social Engineering, the official umbrella for the Social

Engineering Initiative. Throughout the final decade leading to Solar Flash, the National Security Agency had profiled millions of people by means of cell phones, e-mails, social media, the Internet sites they visited, and finally, surveillance drones. This intel, which was provided to SEI, determined the assigned jobs of the workforce in Township 26.

Sector 10 lists had also red-flagged potential insurgents. The data indicated people least likely to question authority and most likely to obey rules and regulations. To this group, the DSE assigned positions of responsibility as bankers and heads of health, education and commerce. However, not among the chosen, Caellum's father was forced to become a warehouse clerk, and his mother, a cleaning woman for the five elite households.

Understandably, when people moved from tents to apartments, they were glad to have not only roofs over their heads, but also running water and electricity, even furnaces and ceiling fans. Most remained grateful to the government that had supplied both food and creature comforts. But in Caellum's family a pall of heavy gloom overshadowed dinner, and the food tasted like cardboard with only the clinking of forks to break the oppressive silence.

Caellum recalled the white knuckles of his father's clinched fists and his mother's tight lips as they sat in the old town hall listening to the town father. Arnold Wilkie faced the audience and grinned with paternalistic pride. "You are among the fortunate post-Solar Flash populations to benefit from the twenty-first century Social Engineering Initiative for the perfected citizenry of the future."

The DSE gave the molding of children and youth top priority. Having no choice but to hold a small Union of the Americas flag, Caellum had reluctantly marched with enthusiastic flag-waving teens to the drumbeat of "Corporate Candidates." His father's voice was terse when he explained that the DSE's core curriculum was engineering the next generation to become the ideal compliant workforce.

Caellum vividly recalled the harrowing trek from the township led by Eena. Even though he had relished the idea of an insurgents' political coup, he realized the unlikelihood of a takeover by the people occurring anytime soon. At least escape was one way to take action. Now, as a seeder, he had his long-awaited chance to sever the strangling tentacles of political control. By no means was this system of information distribution and infiltration the way he had envisioned fighting for freedom. Nor was he convinced that an armed group blasting their way through the offices of top officials wouldn't ultimately have to happen. But, for now, in the role of a seeder, he could work undercover for the cause.

Waves of heat shimmered off the sand. Caellum's muscles screamed their protest with each push of the bike pedals. His progress slowed considerably as an awareness of creeping weariness vied with his reflections. By the time he reached the lake, the sun was a huge orange ball nearing the horizon, and he was desperate to stop for the night.

He draped a towel over a bush to create meager shade from the relentless rays as he guzzled water. Suddenly ravenous, Caellum devoured a slice of apple pie given to him by Carla, a piece of deer jerky, and a couple of biscuits, in that order.

Scanning for the mountains to the northeast, Caellum felt a twinge of loss to see the distant peaks obscured by gray clouds. Relieved when the soft glow of sunset lit the western sky, he removed the bungee straps from the rolled bag. Seconds after throwing the sleeping bag on the ground, he flopped down, arms and legs spread eagle. Fleetingly, he felt exposed, and hoped a scorpion or rattlesnake wouldn't find him. But before he could complete the thought he was sound asleep.

Caellum awoke at dawn to see a hawk swoop down and swiftly ascend holding a small snake in its talons. After a handful of dried apricots and his last drops of water, he moved the stone with a red X painted on it, brushed away the sand, and lifted the lid of the buried trash can. A gallon jug of water was enough to refill his canteen and three empty water bottles, drench the hand towel around his neck, and trickle the last drops over his head.

Glad for the early morning cool of the desert, Caellum rolled up his sleeping bag and headed out. When he began pedaling again, he hadn't anticipated the pain in his thighs, but it eased after a mile or so as his muscles warmed up.

By the time he reached Cinder Gulch, thirty miles south of Durango, the sun was at about ten o'clock with the heat rising rapidly. When he climbed off the bike, he forced his legs to take one excruciating step after another, knowing his muscles would cramp up if he stopped. Limping and wincing, he resolved to suggest to Eena that the seeders ride bikes daily to build endurance.

Caellum topped off his water supply, grabbed a bag of trail mix, and returned the lid to the stash before brushing sand over it and replacing the sandstone. The sweltering rays seared his flesh with increasing intensity after he climbed back on the bike and rode, following the arroyo toward La Plata River.

When Caellum reached the trees that banked the river, the sun had reached its broiling zenith, and each push of the bike pedals was an exercise of sheer will. The backpack felt like a one hundred-pound heating pad and the soreness in his legs was an insistent ache. As he climbed off the bike, he knew his bike riding was over for this stint. He'd have to walk the remaining miles, which meant it would be the next morning before he would actually enter the city. The river valley offered the shade of an occasional cottonwood tree as he wearily trudged forward.

As the sun sank below the western horizon, Caellum saw the city skyline glowing in the distance. Judging he had about a mile to go, he unrolled his sleeping bag under a cottonwood, drank half the remaining water in the canteen, and ate deer jerky, hardly even aware he was chewing.

Through half-closed lids, he spied a vinegarroon—a creature that resembled an enormous scorpion with a whip-like tail—scurrying across the sand. He hurtled a stick and the creature changed direction. His nose twitched from the sudden smell of vinegar as he dropped the stick and shut his eyes.

It must have been the pungent scent that forced the arachnid into Caellum's dream. As the pincers loomed like huge claws, immobilizing him, he stared at it, noting something was very odd. The vinegarroon raised its thorax to an almost vertical position, sporting long black hair that sprouted from the top and fell on either side of its head. And stranger still, wispy strands veiled smiling blue eyes.

"Go away," Caellum muttered.

But the creature crawled even closer to probe the surface of the sleeping bag with an invasive pincer.

"I need rest," he insisted.

The vinegarroon crawled onto the bag and stroked his arm, its blue eyes shining brightly.

Irritated by the intrusion, Caellum knocked the creature away with a sweep of his arm. Mercifully, sleep cast a new set of more acceptable characters on its dreamscape stage and finally, sweet oblivion.

The next morning at dawn, Caellum followed the river south until he saw a highway up ahead. Backtracking, he found a well-hidden spot under a mesquite bush to secure his bike and sleeping bag. After shoving the radio inside the bedroll, he broke off a few branches from surrounding bushes to further camouflage his stash. Then he headed east toward the airport and into Techno City.

The dream of the vinegarroon was only a hazy impression as he walked, his thighs painfully stiff. A feeling of anticipation fueled his steps as he approached the airport, and he mentally prepared for the next and vitally important phase of his mission.

Communications 23

With their system of communication that needed no devices, Matoskah called his apprentice. When Cosima and Valek arrived, she felt an unusual urgency in Grandfather's demeanor.

"Danger approaches Three Mountains Community. Come. We will strengthen the heart's alliance with nature."

Cosima signaled Valek to her side and sat down near Grandfather with her hand on the scruff of the wolf's neck.

Grandfather spoke with his usual calm quietness. "The last gasp of the old ways threatens the birth pangs of the new Earth."

Grandfather's eyes twinkled as they gazed into Cosima's. "Let us see what Spirit has to teach us."

The elder and his apprentice closed their eyes and breathed deeply.

Before their inward gaze, a beating heart hovered in the midst of a vortex of light. They watched as tiny sparkling crystals rose one by one from Earth, ascending in a radiant spiral.

Suddenly, from the west, fierce winds roared their horrific power, hurling stones about, some as large as boulders that pummeled the lighted vortex.

No sooner had that storm moved off than a tornado approached from the east. Such was the force that it lifted houses and cars and tossed them about like toys before turning aside.

In its wake, a hurricane raged from the south, ripping up trees and flooding homes, only to veer away, repelled by the power of the vortex.

Finally, from the north the icy blast of the storm rained hail that demolished all life in its path as it headed straight for the vulnerable heart of the swirling light. And in the midst of that assault appeared an enormous grizzly with a magnificent coat of burnt umber. It paused for a moment and sniffed the air. *Ursus arctos* rose to its great height to stand on two legs, face the spectators, and emit a resounding roar, deflecting the last of the boulders as though they were mere pebbles.

Although within the last decade grizzlies had returned from the wilds further north to nearby mountains, the appearance of the Great Mato on Thunderbird Mountain was unexpected. After making its presence known, the grizzly dropped to four legs and loped past the spectators as if an important errand awaited its attention.

Eena met with the patrollers beside their bunkhouse to discuss strategy over the next weeks. While Gavin was out of commission, Chuck and Lori patrolled the perimeter and hunted for small game while Eena explored the forested world beyond and kept an eye on the rovers. But the full breadth of work required four augur pilots, especially since a military convoy of twenty-five vehicles, including huge moving vans, had been seen on Highway 160 heading to Durango.

"Gavin, it's vital that you return to the skies as soon as possible."

"I'm no longer a patroller." Gavin's voice was flat, emotionless.

"Gavin, ask Leiani to help you bond with an augur. Maybe it's possible with one that's nearly grown, perhaps an intended pack augur already bonded with Leiani."

His expression was closed. "Not gonna do it."

Gavin's intractable stubbornness was infuriating. Yet Eena chided herself. *Perhaps I'm rushing this.* She sighed.

She addressed the patrollers, returning to the imminent danger represented by the rovers. "We have two main concerns: not getting shot down and keeping track of where they are in relation to the community."

Nathan remained well-hidden while the patrollers adjourned. He'd learned a lot. He now understood about patrollers and the crazy behavior of the bird he had seen before the crash. But a major mystery remained. Where were those birds kept?

He hung around, unseen, for several days until he saw two unbelievable sights that shook the foundations of his life. The first was when he followed Lori until she simply disappeared between two trees. The second was when the gigantic creature emerged from the exact same spot to fly over his head. There was nothing in his life experience or logical brain to account for either.

At the conclusion of another patroller meeting, he stood in front of the vines where he had observed Lori's disappearance. Gathering his courage, he walked through to become captive to the land of everything giant. Dazed, unable to find his way back, he was paralyzed with fear by the time Eena appeared.

"How do I get out of here?" he blurted when he overcame his speechlessness.

Eena appeared nonplussed. "What are *you* doing here?"

He hesitated, sensing he was in territory the patroller would consider off limits to him. "The birds."

He watched her expression morph from shock, to recognition, followed by a slight smile. "Oh, I see."

"Can you just show me how to get back?"

A *phoom, phoom* overhead caused him to duck down. To his horror, enormous claws descended a hair's breadth from ripping his flesh. He moved and the tip of a giant wing knocked him off balance. Another creature landed on his other side and one more by his face. Terrified, he ducked additional landings, his escape blocked by a broiling sea of blue-green monsters.

When he cried out in abject terror, Eena approached, not toward him, but to feed and stroke the nearest monstrosity.

"Get me out of here." Desperation raised his tone to a whine.

In callous disregard of his fear, Eena mounted the creature she had petted. "Climb aboard one," she purred, blithely ignoring his plea. She mounted the bird and rose to soar over his head. "I suggest you follow me and Cesla."

His petrified fear darkened to sheer hatred as he realized he was the mouse in this feline game.

As Eena widened the flight circle, Nathan darted through an opening in the shifting mounds of feathers, razor-sharp beaks, and deadly claws. When the bird and rider disappeared through a stone wall, he stood paralyzed, his brain grappling with the impossibility he had just witnessed. Inching forward, one hand extended, he stepped into the realm of familiar pines and collapsed on the ground exhausted. In complete overload, he headed down Quartz Mountain, the despised image of Eena fueling a new and overriding goal — revenge.

In response to the radioed message from Chas about the science and technology meeting, Gavin mechanically trekked down the mountain with Eena. Feeling diminished as a person, for days he had shunned contact with Leslie until she ceased trying to break through his self-imposed barrier. Having cost Espirit her life and minus the prestige of being a patroller, he felt he didn't deserve her. With similar emotional distance he listened as Eena angrily described her encounter with Nathan on the Mu side of the portal. "Disgusting snoop" was how she described him. They walked the rest of the trek in silence.

When they reached the lab, Gavin was aware that Leslie's eyes sought his, but he rebuffed her glance. He knew the cold barrier of his self-imposed restraint was hurting her, but he couldn't summon an ounce of warmth.

Chas leaned his arms over the back of a chair as he acknowledged their arrival with a special look for Eena. Steve half stood with one buttock on a table, a remote control in hand, as Rigel, Meg and Ryan leaned back in computer chairs.

"We're close," Steve began. "Take a look at this computer-generated image of a forest."

The image of a dense pine forest appeared on the 4' × 6' screen. He zoomed in several times to demonstrate the quality of the pixilated image.

Ryan whistled his admiration. "For a computer-generated image, the fine-grained detail is astonishing."

Steve nodded. "We're working on an advanced level of holographic technology that top secret programs achieved prior to Solar Flash. The nanometer pixilation makes the projected image virtually indistinguishable from the real thing." Rotating the view ninety degrees to the tops of the trees, he simulated flying above the pine canopy. "We're close to being able to project the image of the top of a forest above this village so that it hides us from the view of aircraft passing overhead."

A buzz of comments followed this welcome information.

Eena's eyes were riveted to the screen, her strategic brain leaping to possibilities. She knew of military advances that would still put the community at risk. "But what about ground penetrating radar?"

Rigel sighed and nodded. "Once the controllers have that ability again, and if they are searching for us and know of our approximate location, we're sunk. And sooner or later this is likely to happen."

Steve shrugged. "We're simply buying time. I've called this meeting to discuss how to get the holograph emitter working."

All eyes were riveted on Steve.

"Several of you are aware that, as a soldier, I escaped a military convoy by simply driving a truck away and hiding it in the woods beside Lemon Reservoir. In the covered bed rests an essential part of the equipment for the holograph system that will protect Three Mountains Community from being discovered. The cargo bed holds two disks with concave mirrors, each in six sections, weighing about a hundred pounds each. The challenge is to transport them from there to here."

There was a rumble of voices as people discussed how to achieve this seemingly impossible feat.

"The only solution is an airlift," Gavin said decisively, bringing silence to the room. His suggestion gave everyone pause, though at first they were doubtful it could work.

After a couple of hours of brainstorming, the scientists and patrollers hit on the idea to rope together four pack augurs.

Feeling hungry and in need of a break, the group dispersed for fresh air, sunshine and lunch. Rigel headed home, the three holograph engineers walked across the grassy knoll toward a lunch invitation, and Eena strolled with Chas toward his cabin. Gavin noticed Chuck edge over to Leslie.

Steve interrupted Gavin's miserable fuming to ask him to help dig holes for the twenty-foot poles which would support the frames for the holograph mirrors.

Gavin nodded and volunteered to get the tools from the shed attached to the pavilion.

Fuming over his recent nightmarish experience, Nathan emerged from the bunkhouse. Eena's callous disregard of his terror fueled images of her being forced at gunpoint into a cell. Weary of this backwoods nineteenth century environment and smarting from his encounter with the augurs, he yearned to return to normalcy—to Transtopia and home.

Seeking a morsel of friendly companionship, he approached Gavin who was striding toward the shed on the north side of the pavilion.

"Hey, Gavin." Nathan fell into step with him.

After a momentary silence Gavin's tone was reserved. "I see you're walking without a cane."

Nathan nodded. "I'll be wearing this sling for a month."

When Gavin opened the shed door, Nathan mentally inventoried the array of mostly brand new tools.

"Whoa!"

Gavin shrugged. "Compliments of the latest Wal-Mart heist."

Nathan tried to hide his disapproving shock. He was more taken aback by Gavin's explanation than the sight of the tools. "The government declared all goods from stores in evacuated cities to be Union property." He deflected Gavin's barbed look, focusing, instead, on the youth's tight lips.

"Here, hold those, would you?" Gavin asked, handing Nathan two shovels. Culture shock stayed Nathan's tongue in the presence of the conscienceless thief.

Gavin retrieved a pickax and posthole digger. "We're sinking posts for a new piece of equipment," he explained.

Backing himself and Nathan out of the room, Gavin thanked the intruder, collected the tools, and turned to walk away. "Nice to see you, Nathan. Glad to see you're recovering well." Gavin shot his companion a farewell smile that looked forced.

Not to be dismissed so easily, Nathan hurried to catch up with the obviously irritated youth. Noting that Gavin's glumness consistently matched his own, Nathan gambled on the outside chance that he too was miserable living in this god-forsaken place. Having determined to find a fellow disgruntled person to trek to Transtopia Metro with him, he started with Gavin. "How do you like living in a place like this?"

"Like what?"

"I mean, like you've stepped back in time to backwoods, rural America."

"It's not so bad. More relaxed pace."

"But places like Transtopia are rebuilding the future. We're rapidly restoring the comforts and innovations of twenty-first century technology."

"Some prefer freedom to comfort," Gavin retorted, an edge sharpening his voice.

"There is no loss of freedom in the UA," Nathan replied defensively. "There are only well organized government agencies to help restore the rights and privileges of former days."

"Agencies with long tentacles," Gavin quipped.

As Nathan wondered how anyone could be so unappreciative, he spied the solar panels near the technology building. *These people have done some major burglarizing,* he mused as disgust joined his disdain. Following Gavin to Steve, who was in front of the complex, he wondered what the panels powered inside the building.

Steve nodded a greeting when Gavin introduced him to Nathan, then retrieved a shovel to start digging.

Nathan noticed the four poles lying on the ground. "So, what're you building?"

He waited, but the thuds of pickaxes and scrapes of shovels was their only reply.

Stubbornly, he stood his ground to force an answer. "What are you building?" he asked again.

"A stand for a large device," Steve replied.

No more was forthcoming. Nathan suspected some answers awaited his scrutiny inside the technology lab. As the mounds of dirt grew beside the diggers, Nathan casually slipped away, sauntering toward the solar array. When a sideways glance told him the two were completely focused on their work, he fast-walked toward the building, and slipped through the open door. Continuing from room to room, he grew more amazed and affronted with every step. The labs were filled with what had to be stolen equipment. When he reached the third room, the huge projector with Union of the Americas Army stenciled in bold white letters further offended his patriotism. These loathsome thugs were systematically stealing from the government.

Already restless to leave, he was suddenly beside himself to return to Transtopia. The government officials needed to know about this wholesale theft of UA property. As Nathan slipped out of the building, unnoticed by Steve and Gavin, he realized there was probably a lot of illegal activity he hadn't yet uncovered. Of one thing he was certain—this little smuggling ring must be stopped.

When Gavin looked up to see Nathan approach from the direction of the front door of the technology building, a sick feeling grabbed his gut. He felt as though he had just allowed a disaster right under his nose.

Nathan finally waved and walked away.

"To snoop somewhere else," Gavin said under his breath.

As though to completely thicken his gloom and underscore his loneliness, Chuck and Leslie strolled across Destiny River Bridge, her smile bright for the one at her side.

Two days later a team hauled over three hundred feet of strong rope to Promise Path and wove a strong net with four twenty-five-foot extensions. An array section would rest on the net, the extensions attached to the augurs' body halters.

Removing the array sections from the truck bed, they cleared a path through tangled underbrush, easing the heavy and unwieldy objects one by one to the rope net. With four augurs in a diamond configuration roped to one another and to the basket, the next hurdle to achieve was a simultaneous liftoff. After several failed attempts, crew members positioned themselves in front of the birds. In unison they shouted and waved their arms. Cesla lifted off and within milliseconds, with a slight jerk, the pack augurs followed suit. It took all day to fly the first three sections to the community. After four days, all the parts lay beside the ready posts.

The next day the shrieks of drills pierced the valley as a group assembled the sections of the disks. By the following day, using a rope system, twelve people flipped and hauled the lower disk until it rested on the floor of the tower with the concave reflector facing up. The crew built wooden staircases to walk the upper disk to a ledge attached to the posts and hoist it, mirror facing down, into place.

Nathan hung around for the week of assemblage and placement, frustrated that he couldn't get a straight answer about the use of the device under construction. Finally, when Steve called a second meeting of the science team behind the closed doors of the holography lab, Nathan got the bonanza of information he needed. His ear to the door, he listened for snatches of conversation until he heard enough to piece it together. They were planning to project a holographic image of a forest skyward to hide the community from overhead aircraft. Mystery solved. When he heard rustling chairs accompanied by quieted voices in the room, he scuttled away from the front door. Ecstatic that he now had crucial information to pass along, Nathan couldn't wait to see Imperial Governor George Scholtz's face.

Techno City

24

Caellum felt culture shock to be in the midst of a bustling city for the first time in over three years. Along with the busy sidewalks and shops, the fully operational trolley cars were a surprise to the newcomer.

Using the infrastructure of Farmington, New Mexico, the Emergency Government had established Techno City, with a population pushing thirty thousand. As the administrative capital of Sector 1, the city had jurisdiction over six townships, including Townships 21 and 22 to the east, Townships 23 and 24 to the west, and Townships 25 and 26, which were north of Township 24. Located in the desert at approximately forty- to fifty-mile intervals from one another, the townships each housed about one-fifth of the population of this busy capital of the sector.

Techno City was the ideal population center to seed with brochures because of the college. Although the townships offered some freshmen-level courses, high school graduates desiring a college degree had to request a transfer to the city, making Techno City the hub of youths from the entire sector.

Referring to the city map supplied by Eena, Caellum finally located James's apartment. He knocked at the door of apartment 109, hoping he had arrived before James had left for school or work.

An older woman with tousled pale reddish hair and wearing a bathrobe opened the door and registered a look of surprise when she saw the young stranger.

"Hello. My name is Caellum. I was hoping for a word with James, if he hasn't left yet." The smells of frying eggs and bacon that assailed his nostrils made him hope for more than an introduction.

"I'm Irma. Come in and have a seat." She smiled, gesturing toward the sofa. "Pardon me. I have breakfast on the stove." Calling for James, she walked toward the kitchen.

A man in his late twenties with strawberry blond hair, a crew cut, and a smattering of freckles across his nose walked into the living area. Like his mother, he was surprised to see a stranger, especially this time of the morning.

After Caellum introduced himself as having been sent by Rick, he handed James the envelope.

James quickly read the note and tore it up, saying with a lowered voice, "Listen man, I have to get to work. Yes, you can stay. You're a new citizen of the city temporarily bunking with me as far as my mother is concerned." Then more loudly he said, "Glad to meet you, Caellum."

He called to his mother. "Mom, Caellum's a friend of a friend needing a place to crash for a couple of weeks. Mind if he stays with us until he's assigned a dorm?"

She poked her head around the corner. "You're welcome to stay, Caellum. Would you like to have breakfast with me?"

Caellum's stomach growled a resounding *yes*! "Thanks."

With a friendly nod, James grabbed his lunch and headed out the door.

Caellum addressed Rick's mom. "Mind if I shower before breakfast?"

She pointed to the bathroom door and he relished washing away three days' worth of grime.

Dressed in one of three changes of clothes, he wolfed down eggs, bacon and pancakes as he got to know Rick's mom. Isabel was a sweet woman, sort of a typical mom, but the dark circles under her eyes indicated a tiredness that never abated, and after breakfast she returned to bed.

Too restless to remain confined in the small apartment, Caellum grabbed one of James's physics textbooks, slid a handful of brochures inside, and headed out the door. He had decided the best place to hang out was at the college.

Directions from passersby helped Caellum catch the trolley that would take him to the campus, and once there, students helped him find the Student Union Building. Using the money Phil had given him, he purchased a cup of tea, headed toward a table for two, and sat down.

Glancing around to make sure no one was looking, he discreetly dropped a pamphlet under the table and moved it with his foot until it rested in plain view on the floor beside the table.

He pretended to read James's mostly incomprehensible physics text until students began arriving in droves for the lunch hour. Within minutes, every chair in the place was filled, except for the one across from him.

A pretty girl with short blonde hair approached, carrying a tray. "Mind if I sit here?"

They made small talk for a few minutes, and she asked him how physics was going. He mumbled something about it being challenging. When she asked him if his instructor was Professor Tyson, he nodded.

"My boyfriend says he's really tough." She smiled. "I'm Jill, by the way."

"Hi. I'm Cal."

While they chatted, Jill ate a sandwich and fries.

"Hey, did you drop this?" she said, spotting the pamphlet. She leaned down to pick up the tri-fold titled "Community."

Caellum feigned surprise as Jill opened it. After reading through it for several seconds she rolled her eyes and looked up. "Looks like some propaganda from an insurgent. Listen to this:

> *"The forces of control use fear as their main tool of suppression. Deception, including staged propaganda events to generate alarmed dependency, is part of their suppressive toolkit. In a free and open society of people, whose hearts and minds operate in sync, self-governing individuals forgo scheming manipulations to, instead, collaborate, contribute and generate new ideas for the benefit of the whole."*

"Ungrateful!" Indignation was written on Jill's face. "The government has restored our lives, and foolish people want to replace our safe and secure existence with anarchy!"

Caellum adjusted his face in an *unbelievable, isn't it?* expression.

They exchanged small talk until Jill stood and disdainfully tossed the brochure on the table. "Time for my next class." As she slipped on her backpack, she cast a suspicious look at Caellum. "You're not one of those nut jobs fomenting trouble against the UA government, are you?"

Caellum looked affronted. "Are you kidding?"

"I thought not!" She smiled brightly. "See you around."

Inwardly shaking, he lost his nerve to try the dropped-brochure routine again. So he carefully and inconspicuously placed his book on it. Pretending to stretch, he slid the book, with the brochure underneath, back to reading position. Unable to sit any longer after the room emptied out, Caellum slipped the brochure inside the book to walk around campus. While he watched passing students, he wondered how typical Jill was.

Disappointed in his first seeding escapade, Caellum left the college to head for a cafe he had passed on the way. In line to order, he stood behind a man with graying wavy hair that curled over his ears and neck. A blousy white shirt, with folded, cuffed sleeves, hung down over faded jeans, which met worn leather sandals.

On a hunch, noting the book in the man's hand, Caellum addressed him casually.

"So, what's the best pastry?"

"I'm not one to ask. I usually just get croissants."

Noting the strength in the Mediterranean features as the man glanced over his shoulder, Caellum wanted to keep the conversation going. "I'm new around here."

"Best of luck to you, son. If you like being taken care of by the government, this is the place for you."

Code words. Caellum felt in his bones this encounter was going to be different than his first. After purchasing a tea and croissant, the man sat down, and minutes later, Caellum carried a tea and sweet roll to his table. "Mind if I join you?"

With a slight shrug the man gestured toward the chair on the opposite side of the table, and resumed reading his book.

"Hmm, Tolstoy." Feeling foolish for stating the obvious, Caellum felt his face grow hot. *Idiot.*

Caellum washed down a bite of his Danish with a swig of tea before he gathered the courage to speak again. "Matter of fact, I don't like being taken care of by the government."

Placing his hand on the still-open book, the man looked momentarily taken aback. Then, eyeing Gavin impassively, he sipped his tea. The slight clank of his mug on the table punctuated his nod for Caellum to continue.

"I just met a girl at the college who asked if I was one of those nut job insurgents."

During the long pause, the older man said nothing.

"I'm Caellum, by the way."

"Neil. So why would the girl say such a thing about you?"

"She found this on the floor at our table and thought I had dropped it." Caellum dug the brochure out of the physics book and placed it on the table.

Unlike the girl who had perused the brochure for less than a minute, Neil studied the contents at length. His expression was inscrutable, as if he were in a poker game playing for high stakes. After Neil methodically folded the brochure and returned it to the table, he asked coolly, "Well, did you?"

"Did I what?" Caellum asked, caught off guard.

The older man, his Greek profile facing a window, closed the Tolstoy, and moved to stand up.

Going on pure intuition, Caellum put out a restraining hand and spoke softly. "Yes. I wanted to get a response from whoever found it."

Neil picked up the book, its edges frayed from use. "Let's walk."

Caellum took another swig of tea. His mug thudded on the table as he grabbed the sweet roll and followed Neil out the door. They navigated the city sidewalks in silence, changing directions a couple of times until they came to a park.

Neil crossed his legs and leaned backward, his arms straddling the back of the park bench. "We can keep our distance from other people here."

Caellum nodded.

Genuine interest shone through Neil's hazel eyes. "So, this gathering of people that has formed a community is very intriguing. Freedom and equality are values that decades ago were frequently on people's lips. I like the term *sovereignty*."

Caellum relaxed into an open exchange with his older companion. "Yes. Plus connection—the sense that we're all connected to one another. The people of Three Mountains Community know that we have to reach out to the rest of humanity."

Caellum paused. The professor remained closed-mouthed, waiting to hear more.

"For starters, we realize it's only a matter of time before we're discovered. Secondly, we share a philosophy to collectively work for the greater good, while enjoying our current advantage of existing beyond the tentacles of the *corporatocracy*."

Neil nodded appreciatively. "Mm-hmm, the banking/industrial/military complex that has been engineering humanity's insidious slide to a population of automatons. And how does this tiny group of people plan to outmaneuver the global Goliath?"

"My being in Techno City is part of our strategy. I'm here for a short time to find people who are open to this information, and who will continue to spread the ideas after I've left. What about you? What kind of work do you do?"

"I teach American History at the college." Neil glanced behind and around them. "After what the people have suffered, they want to believe that all is well now. They're grateful for the tight grip of the perpetual *emergency* government, and feel assured it's really only temporary. The citizens of Techno City are glad to have schools for the kids and jobs that pay for food, clothing and a place to live. They basically just want safety, order and the small pleasures of normal life."

Caellum turned his head to look directly at Neil. "What you say is true of most, but not all. We need to find people who will listen to this information. People like you to tell them that there are those who reassert self-reliance, yet are allied through collaboration. Through you, we can encourage others to help spread the network of the 'awake and aware' to every township and city."

Quiet settled between them as they watched a couple of squirrels dart across the grass. The chase continued up the trunk of a tree and onto a limb, where a chattered disagreement erupted.

Neil continued looking straight ahead. "I'm a tenured college professor, but nonetheless, I have to teach fake history and government in order to keep my job. The course I teach discusses the elimination of the Constitution of the United States in favor of the *superior* Charter of the Union of the Americas. While the charter speaks in glowing terms of personal duty to the UA as a satellite of the World Federation, not one word concerns individual rights."

Harsh judgment of the professor broiled inside Caellum. "But, Professor Neil, of all the people in the city, aren't the young men and women who are your students most likely to be receptive to the truth?"

Neil thought for a moment before speaking. "Perhaps, but even among the collegiate population, those willing to question the system are a small minority."

"You're in the perfect position to reach them!" Caellum said heatedly.

The professor crossed his arms over crossed knees as if to shrug off the vehemence from his companion. "I would soon be out of a professorship. And my only legacy would be 'No matter how much you disagree with the creeping, invasive regulation of your life, keep your mouth shut'."

Caellum grew louder and more insistent. "Sooner or later, certain ones are going to become restless and begin to chafe at the restrictions, at the government files kept on the details of their lives, at the government-assigned tracks from early childhood through schools to jobs."

Neil sighed, glanced cautiously around the park, and looked directly at Caellum whose face was turning red with agitation. "I'm not necessarily disagreeing with you. I'm saying you need to be realistic about the enormity of our challenge."

Caellum realized he was getting out of hand, and glad to hear *our*, he took a deep breath.

Friendly humor lit Neil's eyes. "Occasionally, there's a hothead like you in one of my classes."

"I should hope so," Caellum said indignantly.

Neil continued, unperturbed. "Listen, your information about the free community has given me a kick in the pants."

Encouraged by a glimmer of hope, Caellum looked around for eavesdroppers. No one was close by.

In quiet, measured tones, Neil explained, "I can't confront my students in the classroom, but I can make note of the occasional questioning and rebellious ones. They can be approached outside of class."

Excitement warmed Caellum's response. "That's phase one of our strategy: to contact receptive people who agree to become designated spreaders to spread the word and meet regularly to strategize and collaborate. Eventually, from those will come infiltrators to connect with sympathizers in positions of authority."

"Count me in," Neil agreed decisively. "Now, if you will please give me the brochure, I have a class to teach in twenty minutes."

Caellum asked for the professor's address.

Neil waved his hand dismissively. "You can find me in the Humanities building. My office is on the second floor. Room 220."

Caellum handed the brochure to the professor. Happy they parted as friends, he felt an almost giddy sense of victory as he rode the trolley to James's apartment.

Searches 25

Nathan couldn't get his mind off the gun. The gun that was property of the police department of a township that was under the jurisdiction of Sector 10 of Region 21 of the Union of the Americas. The stolen gun, requiring a UA citizen, such as himself, to seize and return it to its rightful owners. Like all thorough, emotionally motivated rationalizations, this chain of thoughts allowed him to perform, with a clear conscience, the action he had already determined to take.

Nathan knew Eena lived on Quartz Mountain. Performing his duty as a government spy, he would locate her dwelling, break in, and confiscate the gun—the gun that would be essential for his return trek to Transtopia. First, he would follow her home.

He began to watch for Eena's emergence from the trail that led up Quartz Mountain. His opportunity came after she stayed overnight at Chas's cabin. Screened by pines he watched her kiss Chas goodbye, their long embrace accentuating his desire to return home and to Lydia. After waiting impatiently for her to head up the mountain, he followed several paces behind and watched her enter her cabin.

Gavin woke up feeling profoundly alone. Unable to endure being the object of pity, he had repeatedly shunned Leslie's overtures. When Chuck and Lori arose early to share breakfast over the fire and head out to hunt or patrol, he excluded himself from their camaraderie by rolling over in his bunk. It had been days since he had seen Eena. Suddenly realizing that his self-imposed isolationism and idleness were deepening his depression, he decided to approach her. She wouldn't be much comfort, but maybe the kick in the pants she'd give him was the jump-start he needed.

Since there was no answer when he knocked on Eena's door, Gavin walked to Anaya's "hobbit house" and peeked into the window. Anaya stood in the center of the room, wearing a necklace with a long silver chain and pendant resting at her breasts. He'd never noticed her with jewelry before, let alone something so conspicuous. Remaining perfectly still, she reached up and touched it. There was a flash of light, and she disappeared. Stunned, he stared into the empty room. It took several seconds to recover sufficiently from the shock to ruminate in amazement. *What just happened? Who was that exotic looking person with the odd accent who'd never lived in a township? Where did she go?*

With the return of the feeling of unrelieved loneliness, Gavin decided to head down the mountain. He wasn't ready to reconnect with Leslie, but maybe he'd stumble into someone needing help with an odd job. Anything was better than hanging around the bunkhouse, being useless another day.

Passing Eena's cabin, he was surprised to see the door, which was ajar, move slightly.

Deciding he had somehow missed her earlier, he approached and knocked.

"Eena?"

Silence.

"Hey, Eena."

Slight rustle.

The first thing he saw when he pushed open the door was the gun pointed at him. "Whoa! Nathan!"

"Don't come any closer."

"Hey, man, what're you doing?"

"Leaving."

Gavin's brain was racing. "So you're going to head out alone across the Continental Divide?"

Nathan motioned with the gun for him to move away from the door.

"Careful, man. Knowing Eena, that thing's loaded." Gavin detected a slight shaking in the hand that gripped the pistol.

"Just stay out of my way, and nothing will happen."

Gavin's brain began to clear. *A month-long trek with only a gun, no other supplies? Sure.* "Well, if you're determined to leave, I can lead you to a bridge."

"I don't need your help."

"Okay." *You didn't expect to get caught red-handed, did you?* Gavin continued to gaze at the thief.

Nathan's shoulders slumped slightly as he edged toward the door. He swung the muzzle of the gun toward the opening when a shadow suddenly blocked the light.

"How dare you!" Charging Nathan, Eena grabbed for the gun.

He jerked it away from her grasp to wave it desperately overhead, yelling, "Government issue. This doesn't belong to you!"

A head shorter she could only squeeze his wrist and shake it until his fingers released the weapon. The gun clattered to the floor, and Gavin dove for it, before chiding himself that with the impact, it could have gone off and shot him.

Eena was terrifying in her shouted outrage. "Lucky for you this thing wasn't loaded."

"I-I—"

"Get out, and don't *ever* set foot in my home again."

Red-faced and trembling, Eena stepped aside for Nathan's hasty exit. After she had cooled down and listened to Gavin's account, she said Chas was waiting for her. They parted company, agreeing something had to be done about Nathan.

Gavin headed on down the hill, suddenly anxious to apologize to Leslie for his attitude. Then he saw her: walking, talking and laughing with a tall, very good-looking, still-a-patroller Chuck who reached around and squeezed her shoulder. She looked up at him with the smiling brown eyes that would have been looking at Gavin if he weren't such a fool. With this third shock of the day, the gloom he had hoped would lift deepened. Through his own idiocy he'd lost both his bond-mate and his love.

Lori, conspicuously minus Chuck, returned with squirrels and a rabbit to be skinned and smoked. As Gavin worked with her, the urge to see Matoskah seeped in. Instead of a kick in the pants from Eena, he'd surely receive a rousing shake-up from the old medicine man.

Cosima had felt a wistful pull to see Matoskah for a couple of days. As the sun reached its zenith, she packed toiletries and a change of clothes.

Raiel handed her a compass and a radio. "I'll be along myself later this afternoon."

Valek tilted his head comically and perked up ears too big for his puppy face. Now, at the ungainly stage with legs too long and paws too large for his body, he was beside himself with excitement as they headed out for his kind of adventure. Everything that moved — butterfly, rabbit or squirrel — was in jeopardy, every scent excitedly explored by his lupine senses. Valek's inquisitive side excursions extended the hike to the bridge at the midpoint to well beyond an hour.

As they crossed the wooden expanse, Cosima paused to drink in the beauty. Sunlight sparkled through the trees while water gurgled a countermelody to the echoed song of an oriole. There it was — the profound sense of connectedness, the awareness of a presence that encompassed her, the trees, the brook and the birds. She inhaled deeply of a mixture of musty earth smells and pine resin before moving on.

"Valek," she called, waiting for him to return from whatever scent or object he was exploring. Her patience was rewarded when the pup bounded toward her, and together they crossed the bridge.

Close to another hour had passed when excited yips reached Cosima.

"Valek, come," Cosima commanded, assuming he had come upon a possum or skunk. Recently, they had endured the aftermath of a skunk encounter.

"Valek," she called again, but no pup was forthcoming.

Calling repeatedly, Cosima walked toward the direction of his excited yips, until she reached him whining and barking, circling something large and dark. In an all-absorbing frenzy the pup continued to ignore her frantic calls. Her dismay turned to terror as the bear stood up and bellowed a heart-stopping roar. Valek bounded to Cosima's open arms, and after a flood of momentary relief, she froze with the realization that she could become the target of the bear's rage. Holding Valek tightly to her breast in fear-gripped immobility, she considered her options. The black bear dropped to all fours. Cosima was sure that to run would be a mistake. The bear could surely outrun her.

"*Stay as you are.*" The voice was soft, then louder. "*Mato, we have no wish to harm your children.*"

Mato turned her large head toward Grandfather.

"*You know we are your relations.*" Matoskah remained absolutely still as the bear snorted and took several steps toward him.

"Now return to your children." Grandfather's tone was quiet but firm.

The bear pawed the ground protesting the human presence with *humphs* and *snorts*. While the two-legged human held his ground, Mato stiffened her front legs and stomped her paws for emphasis, her black coat rippling her power.

Grandfather stared at the ground so as not to challenge the angry bear, his fearless body language issuing a silent command.

As if to argue with the intruder who had dared to speak to her, the bear took a step closer and, lowering her head, waved it side to side.

Cosima wrapped her hand around Valek's muzzle, suppressing a small whimper.

Still, Grandfather faced the bear without looking into her eyes.

Abruptly, Mato raised her head and wriggled her nose before turning to amble toward the two small shadows suddenly visible among the trees. The protective mother touched noses with her offspring before melting into the forest as she led them out of harm's way.

Realizing she had stopped breathing, her energy momentarily depleted by the bear confrontation, Cosima gulped a deep inhalation. Awkwardly, she reached over her back to fumble for the pack's zipper with one hand as she held tightly to the wriggling wolf with the other.

Grandfather approached to unzip the pack.

She smiled gratefully. "The leash."

They continued forward several yards before she felt relaxed enough to return the leashed pup to the ground.

"That was amazing, Grandfather."

"I simply addressed the bear as a friend and relative with appreciation for her alarm."

"*Her* alarm!" Cosima laughed.

"Yes, and you can do the same."

"Grandfather, that wasn't the bear we saw in the vision."

"No. The grizzly, known as Great Mato, dwells farther north. Mato, a black bear, lives on Thunderbird Mountain with her cubs."

Nodding understanding, the girl wondered if she'd ever be able to face a large black bear with Grandfather's equanimity. She was glad when his teepee came into view.

After Matoskah went fishing and gathered wood for a fire, he suggested Cosi join him in meditation.

"We must prepare ourselves for a meeting."

The tap on the pendant transported Anaya to the ablution chamber, where, in preparation for the meeting with her people, the Erathans, she joined the purification ritual. Silently, one by one, the attendees appeared in the fragrant room of floor-to-ceiling polished marble. In the center, poised on a pale rose-colored pedestal, an alabaster maiden held a vessel from which poured a milky white liquid cascading over the fluted tiers of a fountain.

In the circular pool naked bathers sponged their bodies with the pearlescent liquid, which exuded essences of exotic flowers. As they emerged one by one from the fountain, attendants handed them towels, then folded clothing. Slipping into the proffered white robes, each tied a silken cord the color of burnt umber around his or her waist. Lastly, each donned a long chain bearing a large metallic pendant, its design specific to one of the seven races present. Solemnly, in hooded silence, the purified group filed into an adjoining conference room.

Anaya sat in a circle with forty-one men and women—in appearance like elegant relatives of Amerindian, Nordic, African, Caucasion, Oriental, Polynesian, and Arabic peoples. The Erathans were gathered to discuss their role in the challenges facing Three Mountains Community and, indeed, the world.

Anaya faced those gathered, glad to return to the vast subterranean cavern that was her home.

"Matoskah sends greetings." It was because of the powerful field that swirled around the elder and Three Mountains that the Erathans had supported Anaya's suggestion to leave them for the length of a human life span.

Anaya took a deep breath and stated her plea. "They are in grave danger, and may soon need our help."

The first speaker's appearance was distinctly Asian. "Our challenge is knowing how much to assist and how much to allow the birth pangs of transition from third to fourth density."

"Although we inhabit vast caverns deep in the crust, our fates are interwoven with those on the surface." The concerned voice was that of a Nordic-looking blond.

"Throughout the ages, after cyclic conflagrations and catastrophes, we have helped remnants of humanity restart civilization."

"Yet, despite technological advances, each age has descended into interpersonal and interracial barbarity." The speaker resembled a desert Bedouin.

There was an energetic stir as another, his lowered hood exposing shoulder-length hair that shone like obsidian, nodded. "In truth, the obstacles that now challenge evolving humans are the greatest in human history."

The nearly insurmountable forces that subjugated the masses loomed in Anaya's consciousness as she spoke. "The tiny minority gathered at Three Mountains represents the hope for humanity."

A resonant voice with African overtones countered her desperate plea. "So, do we want them to go from being the cannon fodder and labor force of despots to dependent wards of our benevolence?"

Again, Anaya spoke with measured passion. "It's in our best interest and the planet's for the people who live on the surface to end the reign of violence and oppression that has plagued humanity since the genetic manipulations."

"True. And it's also in our best interest for humanity to discover their vast and unexplored potential to save themselves." The speaker had features echoing those of Matoskah.

Anaya knew the truth of what they were saying, even as tears of frustration coursed her cheeks.

Waves of compassion caressed her from certain ones in the assembly.

The delegate next to her spoke gently. "Anaya, we are aware of the energetic intensification at Three Mountains Community. Certain ones are on the verge of gleaning the higher and exquisitely powerful energies originally encoded in their DNA."

A woman with Mayan features, Anaya's elder by several centuries, spoke with quiet finality. "Let us not deprive these awakening ones of a possible victory beyond the comprehension of most of humanity."

A man with skin the color of burnt umber looked into Anaya's eyes. "We have a rare and powerful backup. The cosmic stream that triggered the solar blasts continues to support the expansion of consciousness."

Anaya had forgotten about this still ongoing immersion of Earth in charged plasma—the field that interacted with the crystals on Quartz

Mountain to open the portal to the augurs; the magnetic charge that aligned with DNA fields, activating humanity to reclaim its sovereignty. "I am glad to be reminded of the galactic and solar boons to human genetics."

She returned the gaze of a man who could have passed for an Indian swami. "We can help, but graduation to fourth density must be humanity's attainment.

After a long and emotionally exhausting meeting, Anaya retired to a room that, at first glance, appeared to be a completely walled-in dome. She touched the wall, and a large window appeared, revealing a balcony just beyond. The transparent pane evaporated as she stepped through to sit in a chair and breathe in the fresh air. Her eyes followed the trailing indigo and yellow feathers of a distant bird that soared over the canopy of an emerald forest. Thousands of feet overhead and extending as far as her eyes could see, light escaped a vast cavernous ceiling. Above the tall white towers of the city, a glowing orb sparkled reflective light on the deep blue of a river. Its serene meandering under the granite and marble bridge to terraformed gardens beyond renewed her confidence in the eventual victory of humanity.

Anaya felt refreshed and recharged. In this serenity, away from the intensifying atmosphere of the people of Three Mountains, she regained a sense of equilibrium. Surely, the human experiment was intended for eventual triumph. She could assist them, but the discovery and activation of their innate power must be their own, whether that time was now, or a hundred or a thousand years from now.

Taking a long deep breath, she touched the pendant and disappeared in shards of light.

When Anaya reappeared in her cave living quarters, she removed the pendant, wrapped it in a silk cloth dyed with rainbow hues, and slipped the package into a rough burlap bag. Its resting place was a crevice between two veins of quartz in the stone wall of her sleeping quarters.

She walked into the healing room at the front of the cave to see Eena waiting impatiently, her green eyes flashing. "We need to meet with Grandfather."

Seeing Eena already had her backpack, Anaya returned to her quarters to change from the simple sheath she was wearing into a shirt and pants and fill her own pack.

Aikido

26

Meyer sat with Raiel as she gestured toward a group of children assembling a collection of interesting rocks. "The natural exuberance and creativity of children. The freeing of which offers humanity's greatest prospect for a more enlightened future."

Meyer nodded and smiled a hearty agreement—if these were the requirements of a teacher, he was up for it.

Raiel continued. "I feel like a visit to Matoskah this afternoon. Would you like to come along?"

No question there.

Just beyond the trailhead to Raiel's place, Chas felt the same pull to head up Thunderbird Mountain as he thumbed through a small, dog-eared book. Mulling over the fate of the community and the danger Nathan presented, he pondered whether the philosophy that had guided him personally for many years could apply to an entire group.

Admiring the self-discipline learned in martial arts, Chas's parents took their eight-year-old son to various dojos to ascertain which was most appealing to their family. The fifth demonstration they attended impressed both Chas and his parents with its distinguishing philosophy. Rather than aggressive opposition, Aikido's power derived from deflecting attack by adroitly orchestrating energy flows. The skilled practitioner allowed the opponent's momentum to carry him to his own fate—from directed attack to powerless imbalance. Chas was amazed when, at the moment the falling opponent was about to hit his head on the floor, the Aikido master actually cradled the skull to soften the impact. Like a series of compelling slides, that sequence of martial arts strategies sealed his fate, and he studied with Aikido masters until well into adulthood, earning his fifth belt just prior to Solar Flash.

Seeking inspiration from his bookshelf, he opened *The Art of Peace* to a random page, and instantly, Grandfather's wise old face appeared in his mind, triggering the impulse to talk with him. Knowing he might not make it back by nightfall, he slid the small book inside his breast pocket, collected his sleeping bag, stuffed a change of clothes and toiletries into a pack, and headed out the door. When he saw Rigel walking toward him, he asked him to come along.

"I want to seek Grandfather's counsel," Chas said simply.

Sharing the sense of urgency, Rigel took a few minutes to gather necessities for overnight and kiss his wife and son goodbye. Then with a quick scan for Nathan, who was nowhere around, he and Chas headed toward the path that led up Thunderbird Mountain.

When the men stepped into the clearing, they were surprised to see a small crowd had already gathered, most seated on stumps around Grandfather's fire.

"Who called the meeting?" Matoskah asked in his dry, deadpan way.

An eagle landed on the perch near the elder, but quickly flew away at the sight of the unanticipated crowd. Matoskah continued to tan the deer hide stretched on a frame.

Eena, her face flushed with intensity, spoke first with measured tones. "We're concerned about the danger Nathan poses to the community."

"To this movement," Rigel added.

"His loyalty to the government, which was the savior for him and his family may lead to our exposure." The cadence of Anaya's exotic accent measured the import of her words.

Gavin nodded agreement. "His suspicion of us is growing. He was obviously disgusted when he found out about the shoppers."

"I found him in my cabin making off with my gun." Eena's tone dripped her disgust. "The longer he remains here, the more he will learn our intent and our strategies."

"But to return him to Transtopia is unthinkable." Rigel's interjection rang with the resonant overtones in his voice.

Eena wasn't finished. "Also, he knows about the augurs." She feared Grandfather would minimize the danger. "Nathan is the first up close, serious threat to our mission."

"We have to think of something." Gavin spoke emphatically, having no suggestion as to what that something might be.

"We could make a little jail for him and imprison him in it for the rest of his life." Matoskah's voice was soft, his expression inscrutable.

Cosima looked at Grandfather with a quizzical expression as quiet expectancy filled the circle, displacing the turbid swirl of accusations and voiced fears.

"It sounds like we are a small group stuck with a big problem," Matoskah mused in a voice barely above a whisper. Silence met his words, as people considered their conundrum. "I suggest you speak softly and remain still," he added.

"Grandfather—" Gavin's voice died in his throat.

An instant hush fell over the crowd as a black bear lumbered into the clearing. Those facing the beast quietly signaled those whose backs were to her.

Cosima pressed her hand on Valek's neck firmly pinning him to the ground.

Frozen silence followed as Mato plodded straight toward Grandfather, who continued to rhythmically scrape the hide. At his back the bear stopped, raised her nose to sniff the air, and snuffled loudly. The low growl that rumbled from the wolf apparently didn't concern her as long as that pesky youngster kept his distance. After a heart-stopping pause, as if she had more important things to do than deal with puny humans and a wolf pup, the bear resumed her trajectory through the clearing.

When she disappeared in the forest, hands that had stopped mid-movement resumed action.

"Grandfather, aren't you concerned about that bear?" Astonishment was written on Meyer's face.

"No. Much like the rocks and trees and streams, my camp is simply one of the landmarks on Mato's path." After a long pause he added mysteriously, "Some unwelcome visitors pass on through. Others come to stay for a while."

Affection qualified Gavin's exasperated expression as the old Native American spoke another of his riddles.

Cosima looked at Mastoska with large, round eyes as though she sensed another impending intruder.

Taking a break from the discussion that was going nowhere, a few cooks began preparations for dinner. Grandfather had just caught some trout for the visitors he had known were coming, and Anaya had gathered vegetables from the garden. They decided to pan fry the fish and cut up the vegetables for a stew at the very moment the object of Grandfather's previous comment appeared — a visitor about as welcome as Mato.

All the color drained from Eena's face as Nathan stumbled into the clearing. A shocked pall settled over the group that was revved up for a *what-to-do-about-Nathan* debate. Mute stares registered frank rejection of the interloper.

Grandfather beamed a warm welcome. "Nathan, join us. Anaya probably knows what you can do to help prepare the meal."

Gavin scowled at Eena. "He never greets anyone else with such friendliness."

While the others overcame their dismay sufficiently to muster casual greetings, Anaya smiled at the newcomer, motioned for him to sit beside her, and handed him a knife. "If you don't mind slicing potatoes, I'll peel."

Eena glared as though Nathan, an intrusive threat to the community, to her plans and to the remote possibility of freeing humanity from its current bondage, had corrupted the circle.

Nonetheless, the serious tone of the gathering was set aside in the presence of the surprise guest. Companionable banter and small talk accompanied preparations and enticing smells until everyone was served.

When they were well into the meal, Matoskah directed his gaze toward Chas.

"Chas, did you study martial arts as a boy?"

Chas nodded at the wily elder. "Yes. As a matter of fact, I follow the path known as Aikido."

Eena looked pensive. "*The Way of the Peaceful Warrior* by Dan Millman was my first exposure to that philosophy. I remember when the teacher Socrates caught the hurled knife in midair. The state of *satori*, I believe it was called."

"I saw the movie," Nathan said. "Nice fantasy about gymnastics and an old guy that could leap on roofs."

Chas's smile was friendly and open. "On the surface, but it was really an account of self-mastery."

Gavin recalled his own childhood exposure to martial arts. "As a child, I participated in a Jujitsu dojo for a couple of years."

Chas nodded. "So did Morihei Ueshiba, the founder of Aikido. However, he had three visions in later life that led him to gradually eliminate all aggressive strikes from his techniques."

Nathan looked indignant. "I can't imagine how he could possibly defeat an opponent without fighting back."

"I know what you mean," Chas agreed. "Yet, to all accounts, as an old man of eighty, Morihei could disarm any foe, down any number of attackers, and pin an opponent with a single finger."

There was a break in the conversation as a table laden with pies and sweet breads beckoned those finished with their meals.

While attempting to be wholeheartedly involved in the conversation, Gavin's attention was diverted elsewhere, toward the opposite side of the circle. He peered resentfully at Chuck seated next to Leslie on a log. *Not wasting any time, are you?*

He desperately wanted to apologize for his behavior, to see that warm smile directed his way just one more time. When Chuck walked away to choose desserts, Gavin saw his chance to approach Leslie. A single means to entice her back into his world popped into his head.

"Leslie, I promised to take you to see the augurs."

She stared at him with wide eyes, apparently startled that he was suddenly in front of her.

Please, he inwardly pleaded, *just a glimmer of our old connection.* He sat down on the stump vacated by Chuck.

Leslie's lids lowered over her eyes.

"I... I know I've been distant—"

"Hey, Gavin." Chuck loomed over the two of them. As Gavin looked up, he felt the underlying pressure to return Chuck's seat.

Leslie's eyes remained hooded by dark lashes.

"I'm going to the portal tomorrow morning," he said spontaneously. He stood up to walk away after receiving no response. *Where did that come from?* Prior to this meeting, he had no intention of returning to Mu—*ever*.

Anaya asked about the meaning of the name Aikido.

"Morihei, who came to detest war, derived a non-violent path, which translates to *The Art of Peace.*"

"The art of peace is a well-armed military," declared Nathan.

"And a better armed populace," Eena quipped, her voice like acid.

Nathan eyed her suspiciously.

Raiel, used to working as a team with Matoskah, redirected the conversation. "So this martial art focuses on non-aggressive techniques?"

"That's all well and good when you don't have tanks or machine guns pointed at you," Eena commented.

"I've been pondering that very same thing," Chas agreed thoughtfully. "In his youth, Morihei did fight in WWII. However, he persisted in developing Aikido until as an unarmed, eighty-year-old, he avoided the cuts and thrusts of a high ranking swordsman and, without a single wound or wounding blow, defeated his opponent."

"Such an incredible feat would take years of dedicated discipline," Nathan said skeptically.

"You're right," agreed Grandfather. "How *does* a group that is faced with a dangerous opponent apply Aikido techniques?"

Apparently, having no idea that he himself was the most immediate "dangerous opponent" in question, Nathan spoke thoughtfully. "I suppose it depends on the skill level of the opponent as well as the group."

Dead silence met Nathan's comment.

Grandfather looked toward Chas. "Why don't you take that little yellow book from your pocket and read us something?"

Chas looked with surprise at the old intuitive who had his own arsenal of strategies. When he had retrieved the book it opened to the same page he had read in his home. After taking a sip from his mug, he read. "Opponents confront us continually, but actually there is no opponent there. Enter deeply into an attack and neutralize it as you draw that misdirected force into your own sphere."

Nathan looked disgusted. The tree shadows lengthening in the afternoon sun obscured the expressions on the others' faces. *Bunch of hippies. Harmless, but deluded.* He stood up, anxious to reach home before nightfall, but aware of the bear that roamed Thunderbird Mountain. "Matoskah, think I need to worry about that bear?"

"Mato has returned to her cubs for the night," the elder replied. "She keeps them higher on the mountain, away from the village."

Nathan looked around the group. *My life has been saved twice — first by the government and then by these ignorant, but good-hearted, people.* He raised a hand in friendly farewell and began the descent toward the valley. He was confident that after he helped the government locate this secluded group, they'd all be much better off — all except for Eena, who would hopefully be facing execution. Especially fond of that old Native American, Nathan would make sure he wouldn't have to live in a teepee and tan hides for the rest of his life.

As Nathan followed the path, the people gathered around the fire sipped their drinks in contemplative silence.

Raiel was the first to speak. "As I understand it, with each of Morihei's visions, Aikido became less about technique and more the discipline of a peaceful warrior."

"My teachers emphasized three main aspects of this path: self-victory, unflagging effort and to blend with the enemy," Chas agreed.

Rigel looked around the circle. "In regard to the quote from Morihei, exactly how do we draw Nathan's 'misdirected force' into our sphere?"

The group gathered around Matoskah's fire talked until late into the night about ways to draw Nathan into the community's sphere.

Taking the book from Chas, Eena leaned into the firelight and, chuckling, read aloud the page that randomly opened. "When an opponent comes forward, move in and greet him; if he wants to pull back, send him on his way."

The Unexpected 27

"There are six large movie screens in the city. One at the library, one at the college, and four at the old movie theater," James explained as he and Caellum headed toward the cinema on the college campus.

Having attended the movies often with his parents in Township 26, he was familiar with inserted newscasts which aroused strong patriotic feelings by means of two main thrusts: the pandering of fear and fanfare portraying political protection. Fear-gripped silence prevailed when that night's news clips featured rovers mowing people down; shots, confusion, people running on the streets; someone lying dead in a pool of blood.

Then the cameras captured the silence of the empty streets during a martial law lockdown. The audience waited with bated breath as the SWAT team stood in formation outside a building, ready to storm the door of a rover stronghold. The viewers cheered as the next scene revealed the criminals being apprehended.

For the next forty minutes, the moviegoers settled in to enjoy *Star Wars*.

The second news clip depicted the UA military on the front lines, fighting back an invasion. The succession of scenes included armed troops filing from a helicopter, battalions of marching soldiers, exploding missiles, people weeping and devastated coastal neighborhoods in ruins.

Evocative music transitioned the audience from the distressing scenes back to the movie.

After the next movie segment, cheery music signaled the next intermission introducing scenes of smiling government officials from the Union of the Americas. At a hand-shaking session with leaders of the World Federation, they recounted recent victories and jointly established new policies on the people's behalf.

The beaming government leaders appreciatively recognized the common citizens working behind the front lines to preserve the UA way of life. They expressed pride in the citizen army that was helping to build a huge block of power—the Union of the Americas. Rousing music faded into the concluding third of the movie.

Voicing terror of a foreign invasion on UA soil, the moviegoers poured out of the theater. Some sent fervent prayers for the protection of the troops. There were loud warnings that the plague of rovers terrorizing city after city would eventually infiltrate Techno City. But equally vehement voices reminded of the monthly drills on city streets, and stressed the importance of people cooperating to shorten response time. Statements of dependence on and gratitude for government protection interspersed the comments.

But Caellum wasn't buying it—any of it. He felt duped, as if his emotions were being played by dramatic performances.

James and Caellum headed to the local pub for a hamburger and fries. All the booths were taken, so they sat down at a table with four chairs. The tables were crowded close together to make room for the band and dance floor at the far end of the room.

Feeling relaxed in the noisy atmosphere, James and Caellum ordered burgers and beer and talked openly about their theater experience.

"Since we don't have Internet streaming capability, these disks arrive regularly from Transtopia," James remarked.

As the two leaned forward to be heard, they didn't notice the tall young woman with long black hair that sat down at a table near them.

"Yeah, those propaganda tools make the rounds through the townships as well, " Caellum commiserated.

James lowered his voice. "A member of the flight cargo crew has become a source of information for me."

Caellum listened intently, his eyes riveted to James's face.

"He is friendly with a guy who delivers the disks in Transtopia."

"And?"

"Apparently this person works at a studio."

"What kind of studio?"

"A movie studio for producing clips of rover invasions."

At that moment a passerby accidently bumped their table. James's beer toppled and spilled, splashing the young woman at the next table.

The apologies all around served as a conversation opener between tables as a waitress arrived with a mop and towels.

Still wiping her blouse with a napkin the young woman turned toward them. "I saw you guys at tonight's movie." She smiled, pushing a long, shining strand of black hair behind her ear. "Don't you just adore that *Stars Wars* trilogy?"

James and Caellum smiled at her, nodding agreement, not sure what to say.

She nodded toward James and smiled engagingly into Caellum's eyes. "I'm Dora. Those news clips are upsetting, aren't they?"

James provided their names, and then replied. "Yep, rovers and war... pretty alarming."

Dora scooted her chair sideways and leaned toward their table placing one elbow on it. A worried expression contorted her high forehead and full lips. "Do you ever have nightmares about those rover attacks?"

James dipped a fry in ketchup. "Not really," he muttered, looking down at his plate.

Caellum was more sympathetic. "I can understand that happening."

Dora's large blue eyes drew Caellum into their fathomless depths. "I do—have nightmares, I mean. It seems to me that any day now, a gang of rovers could take over our own city."

The warrior in Caellum was stirred to protectiveness. "I don't think you have anything to worry about in Techno City."

Dora smiled demurely and looked down at her fingers. "You seem to me like a pretty fearless person."

Caellum measured his words carefully. "True, I'm not afraid to confront the enemy, whoever they are."

James's cautionary expression passed completely unheeded as Caellum spoke.

Dora smiled and touched his arm, sending an electrical jolt through him. "You mean the rovers or foreign troops?"

Caellum had the presence of mind not to spew his theories. But he couldn't resist dropping a hint. "Strange," he said. "One of those rover scenes was so familiar."

Dora looked at him questioningly. "Familiar?"

Caellum nodded. "It reminded me of identical scenes of a terrorist incident a couple of years *before* Solar Flash."

Dora's forehead furrowed. "How is that possible?"

"It's possible if it's the same script," Caellum replied quietly.

Noting Dora's befuddled expression, James intruded aggressively, kicking Caellum under the table. "Caellum, while you're staring at this beautiful woman, your food's getting cold."

Caellum glanced at the burger he'd forgotten was there, a sheepish grin on his face.

Dora shook her head and placed her hand over her heart. "Please, forgive me. I'll scoot back to my table and let you eat your dinner."

"No," Caellum protested hastily. "We're glad to have you join us."

Gavin's heart pounded as he stood before the portal, the gateway to re-ignited memories of happy times with his deceased bond-mate and his probably lost love. His tension mounted as he waited, at first hopeful, then increasingly disappointed, as the sun distanced itself from the horizon. After an hour of chiding himself for being such an idiot, for rejecting the single brightest light in his life, he started up the path.

"Gavin." She stood behind him, unsmiling, her eyes veiled.

This was not the Leslie he knew. *I've lost her.* "Leslie, I—"

"Well, are you going to show me the home of the augurs?"

"Sure." His eyes sought hers to communicate his apologetic love. But she quickly averted her eyes.

Leslie's exclamations of amazement shattered the heavy silence between them as they passed through the portal and headed down the mountain.

Upon reaching the prairie, they watched with horror as a raptor dove for an augur, and then with amazement when, after an instant of talon-gripped flesh, the augur extricated itself from the predator. While the huge eagle, caught in the momentum of its downward swoop, struggled for equilibrium, the bird flew in a skewed arc toward a crash landing near the cypress trees lining the river. Standing motionless in momentary shock, they snapped to action at the sight of a figure emerging from the canopy. They ran to catch up with Leiani as she hurried to the bird which lay on his rapidly heaving breast with a bloodied forewing extended awkwardly from his body. As Leiani kneeled to examine his wound more closely, but out of reach of a possible beak lunge, she recognized him as a young bird barely two years old. He was noticeable among the flock because he was considerably larger than the others, and his feathers, a brighter aquamarine blue, shimmered in the sun with extraordinary beauty.

The augur's beak rested on the ground tucked under his head, his eyes lidded as though bound by excruciating pain where his torn right wing joined the bleeding torso.

Leslie knelt next to Leiani as Gavin stood a few feet away, the scene resurrecting his anguish beside Espirit's tangled remains. Then, suddenly, a powerful attraction pulled him to walk around the kneeling women toward the opposite side of the iridescent mound.

Leiani probed Gavin's eyes with hers. "Gavin, with the predators and scavengers that roam this place at night, there's no way this bird will make it through."

He placed his bow on the ground to kneel by the suffering creature. "I'm not going to let you die," he said quietly.

"Besides," Leiani continued, compassionate tones in contrast to her dispassionate expression, "this is a wild bird, well past the stage of bonding and training."

Stubbornly maintaining his stance, Gavin shifted his gaze beyond her earnest face.

Between the three, the augur remained motionless, except for his rapidly pulsing breast.

Gavin extended his hand to touch the shining wing feathers. Wild instinct shot a punishing jab from the wounded bird's beak, drawing blood from his forearm. He yelled, further alarming the bird so that the huge wings lifted for flight, knocking away the spectators. Sprawled on their backs, the three watched the creature straighten his legs and arch his wings over their heads. The magnificent specimen of *Avis gigantus* propelled his body up and forward, summoning reserves of panicked wildness. But the violated wing failed him, crippling his instinct to flee, and with claws still earthbound, the defiant bird slumped to a wretched thud.

Shocked silence met the collapse of the enormous creature. The trickle of blood on Gavin's arm propelled Leslie to his side.

"Anaya provided me with a salve," Leiani called, hurrying to her nest.

"I'm okay," Gavin assured Leslie as she examined his wound.

Gently, she held his jaw in her hands forcing him to look from the bird to her. "That's not Espirit," she said, compassion streaming from her eyes.

This first real contact with Leslie since Espirit's death jolted him as much as the sight of the plummeting augur.

"There's no connection between that wild creature and humans," she continued. Like Leiani, she wanted to pull him away quickly, to spare him the pain of seeing the bird die.

He wrapped her hands in his own to lower them from his face. Holding them tightly, he turned from her concerned gaze to the crumpled form beside them. Cords from his heart encircled the bird and locked in place. "Too late," he whispered. Whether or not this bird ever bonded with him, Gavin was already bonded with this *Avis gigantus*.

Leslie smiled her surprise, a glimmer of admiration vying with the concern in her eyes.

His tone intimated regret for his recent behavior. "I know... I know I detached myself from augurs and from... from you, but I can't leave this augur."

"And I won't leave you." Her voice was soft, but edged with determination.

Returning to the scene, Leiani sighed. "I see there's no stopping you." She held out a clean, damp cloth and a jar. "Anaya mixed this for me to help heal any scrapes or wounds." As she unscrewed the lid, fragrant herbal aromas escaped. Leslie glanced at Leiani and reached for the cloth and salve to gently dress Gavin's wound.

Leiani stepped toward the bird and hesitantly approached the wing with a damp cloth.

Gavin's stopped her, his tone firm. "I'll do it."

After taking the jar and towels from Leslie with a look of gratitude, he returned to the right side of the bird. The moment he touched the wing, a second punishing jab bloodied his hand at the base of his thumb as Leslie cried out.

Leiani left to return with two spears. Gavin's eyes widened with alarm.

Moving stealthily, Leiani blocked the bird's attack and speared the ground on either side of his head. Gavin nodded his thanks and resumed washing the wing and applying salve.

The orange sun's descent signaled fast approaching nightfall. Gavin grappled with conflicting concerns for Leslie, a half hour's climb from the portal, and his need to remain with the augur.

"Leiani, will you please walk Leslie to the portal?"

"I'm staying." Leslie's unwavering gaze met his.

Hearing the resoluteness in her voice, he also saw it in her slightly elevated chin. The momentary wash of gratitude yielded to an assessment of what must be done.

"We need wood to start fires."

Wordlessly, the two women walked into the grove of trees to collect branches, sticks, and twigs.

By twilight the three had cleared a perimeter twenty-five feet in diameter and piled wood for six fires.

Leiani handed Gavin a flint fire starter. "We have to move quickly. The scent of blood will attract nocturnal predators." Calling Leslie, she turned toward her nest. "We need supplies and weapons. Come with me."

As Gavin lit the fires, the women retrieved Leiani's canteen, a bow and arrows, an ax, a knife, a tree branch, a jar of chicken fat, and a sheet. They also brought flat bread, a bowl of bird eggs, a bag of papayas and utensils for the evening meal.

Gavin cut firewood while Leiani turned three branches into shafts and whittled a sharp point for each spear. Warning of a long night ahead, she handed each a spear. Next, she axed a branch that was heftier and shorter than the spears and told Leslie and Gavin to do the same. Then she notched the sheet and began tearing strips from it. "We need to wrap and tie these around the ends of these branches and soak them in the fat. When we light them in the fire, they'll become firebrands."

Overhead the velvet sky spread a jeweled array that had been invisible for a century to city dwellers on the other side of the portal. But, surrounding the compound, the augur guardians saw only inky blackness.

"Arrows may not be our best defense," Leiani said quietly.

Gavin, who was good with his bow, was counting on his skill to protect them. "Why is that?"

"The moon is only a sliver tonight. Notice how dark it is beyond the fires."

Gavin considered this a moment. "I see what you mean. We could lose our arrows out there."

Leiani wrapped a sheet around a branch and dipped it in fat. "And there's another reason as well. Even if we could see our attackers, should a pack of dogs, coyotes, or wolves attack, I'm not in favor of a wholesale slaughter."

Gavin picked up on her thought. "You're implying we can wound them without killing a whole pack."

"Exactly."

As Leslie and Gavin followed Leiani's example to make torches, he glanced protectively at the woman he was glad to have at his side again. "I imagine I'll just do what I think I have to in the heat of battle."

The three positioned themselves in a triangle with their backs to the augur in silent vigil, firebrands and spears ready. In still readiness they waited, hearing croaks, grunts, an occasional rush of wings, and the call of a bird repelling possible intruders to its tree residence. About an hour into their sightless vigil, snorting and grunting sounds approached.

"Wild boars," Leiani said quietly. "Like the other mega beasts in this land, these animals are huge, as large as ponies, with tusks as long as an arm."

"Definitely bow and arrow foes." Wearing his quiver of arrows Gavin retrieved his bow.

When the noisy snuffling ceased, the trio's expectant tension mounted. Wordlessly, Leiani switched positions with Leslie. She and Gavin notched their bows, their eyes riveted in the direction of the ceased sound, until the fires on either side of them cast light on lethal tusks that curved from a long snout. In defense of her herd, the sow faced the human threat, poised for instinct to signal either a charge or retreat.

Silence prevailed until Leiani's command. "Yell!" An instant cacophony of primal shouts, screams and roars broke out, even as arrows, notched against taut strings were aimed at the herd's leader. The overpowering onslaught of deafening bestial energy triggered the sow's instinct to turn her herd and flee. And behind them, as one roaring, intimidating beast, the three puny humans pursued the massive boars several yards before turning back.

Behind them, the augur lay still, perhaps mercifully removed from the immediacy of the throbbing wing, without the slightest response to the ear-splitting shrieks of his human guardians who had reverted to the instincts of aboriginal ancestors.

Hearts pounding from the exertion and the adrenaline that had shot through their extremities, the humans shared the exhilaration of their first victory with cheers and hops, shaking their raised weapons above their heads in an exultant dance.

Then, giddily registering the humor of three small humans terrorizing giant wild pigs, they laughed until their ribs could take no more.

Suddenly, Gaven was ravenous. "Let's eat," he said, voicing an emptiness felt by all three as they dove into the food.

Gavin scrambled the eggs, Leiani retrieved the papayas and passed them to Leslie, who sliced them. The warriors devoured eggs and pulpy sweetness until they were satiated. Leiani passed around the canteen as the three, seated in a triangle, with Gavin closest to the torn wing, faced outward toward the next potential challenge.

Soothing night sounds prevailed for the next few hours as the curved sliver crossed the sky, too insignificant to penetrate the encasing wall of black. Of the three watchers, Gavin resisted the powerful urge to doze, keenly feeling the warmth of the feathered body behind him as if it were an extension of his own. With every breath he willed the wing to heal and the creature to cling to life.

A chorus of bark-howls jolted the slumberers awake and Gavin to heightened alertness. He ran around the enclosure throwing wood on the fires, activating flames that leaped skyward and freed sparks from the cindered wood.

"Wild dogs," Leiani murmured.

Unions

28

Dora's smile was as bright as James's expression was dour when she accepted Caellum's invitation to join them. "I'll get my food, so we can eat while we talk."

When the newcomer's salad rested between the guys' burgers, James stirred a french fry in a pool of ketchup. "So what do you do for a living?"

"I'm a senior in college. Right now, I'm a physical therapist intern," she replied. "And you?"

"I'm majoring in electrical engineering. I also work at a nearby lab."

Dora nodded and looked at Caellum. "And you?"

Caellum swallowed a mouthful of burger. "I'm a student also."

"Majoring in?"

Caellum glanced at James. "Physics."

"Mm-hmm, one of those really smart guys."

Caellum winced at the admiration in her voice. He noticed a slight accent. "Where are you from, Dora?"

"I grew up in Canada."

Caellum was intrigued. "How did you end up this far south?"

"Dad's business. I was thirteen years old when we moved. Strange, the hand of fate. We were living in Colorado, while our old home was scorched by fires from the solar flare, as apparently that whole latitude was. Our family and friends perished."

Caellum nodded sympathetically. "Sorry to hear that." He was captivated by the play of expressions on Dora's face, the way her hands seemed to dance as she spoke. There was an air of innocence about her.

"To think our countries are one big union now," Dora added brightly.

"Yep, all the way from Canada to Argentina," James replied, a sardonic tinge in his voice. His eyes roved the noisy room restlessly.

Dancers strolled to the dance floor as the band returned from break. The singer crooned a love song, and the drums beat a seductive rhythm.

"Would you like to dance?" Caellum asked.

Dora's eye's lit up, and they walked to the dance floor.

After three consecutive dances, the couple returned to the table, glowing and laughing. James's face registered less-than-glowing boredom as he looked at Caellum.

"Class early in the morning."

"You go ahead."

"Remember the physics you asked me to help you with tonight?" James asked pointedly, his direct gaze locked onto Caellum's.

After a charged pause, Caellum turned regretfully to Dora. "May we walk you home?"

She smiled gratefully and walked ahead of Caellum toward the door.

Several minutes after they left Dora at the dorm, James broke the uneasy silence between them. "Watch out."

Caellum shrugged off this unwelcome intrusion into his private life. "Now you're acting like my older brother."

"I'm telling you—"

"When I want advice from you, I'll ask for it."

"There's more at stake here than your personal love life."

Caellum resented this insinuation—whether it was that he couldn't trust Dora, or that he didn't have the sense to watch his tongue. But he held his peace. "I know how to guard this mission," he said simply.

He spent the next two evenings with Dora. They met at the library to study a while. After he pretended to absorb physics for an excruciating hour, they walked to a nearby restaurant to eat and talk for two more hours. The next day they simply walked around town, holding hands and getting to know one another better. The next couple of evenings he didn't see her because she had physical therapy appointments and classes.

Caellum spent all four days dropping brochures around campus, in cafés and at the park. He stood or sat nearby to covertly watch people's reactions as they perused the literature. Some looked thoroughly disgusted; others dismissively dropped it in the nearest trash receptacle. On the first day, of twenty people who glanced at or read a copy of the brochure, only one person tucked it in among his belongings.

Caellum followed the youth two blocks toward a bench in the park. Retrieving the pamphlet, he read the contents, closed the tri-fold, turned it over in his hands thoughtfully, opened it again, and reread it.

Caellum's shadow fell over the section the youth was reading.

"You found it!"

The reader looked up at Caellum with steady brown eyes. "This is yours?"

Caellum nodded slowly.

"Who wrote this?"

"A guy named Ansil."

"How did you come by this?"

Caellum hesitated. "Whoa, you ask a lot of questions."

The youth's direct gaze was unwavering. "This pamphlet is important. Every word is carefully articulated."

"Sounds as though you like what's written there." Caellum was still hesitant to let down his guard.

The youth sighed before he plunged forward. "If you're a director of social engineering or government spy, so be it. I have to say that I dream of the world this author describes. Do you know him?"

Caellum was completely disarmed by the young man's candor. He even felt shamed by the courageous honesty. "I do know the author, and I'm a passionate advocate of the writings."

The intrigued supporter, who introduced himself as Barry, removed his pack from the bench to make room for Caellum. An intense conversation ensued—a nonstop two-hour exhilarating idea exchange.

Barry looked at his watch. "Well, I've missed my class. But this conversation was worth it."

"Then maybe you have time for me to introduce you to someone." Caellum grinned broadly, sensing that Barry shared his own feelings, the elation of two people discovering a special kinship.

They went to the second floor of the Humanities building, knocked on Neil's office door, and entered at his invitation. After introductions, Barry opened up to the professor, sharing both his frustrations and his desire to do something about them.

A half hour later, noting Barry's enthusiastic sincerity, Neil turned to Caellum. "So, it seems we have our first recruit."

Caellum responded to Barry's quizzical expression. "We believe there are freedom-seekers who are aware of the government deception. The brochures are a means to locate them."

Neil looked at the visitors on the opposite side of his desk. "I have contacted a student from last semester. We're going to meet Monday."

Caellum left Neil's office glad that the momentum, however small for now, was building.

The following evenings were spent with Dora. He realized, to his chagrin, that she was completely hoodwinked by the system. His point of view would be absurd to the extreme to her. A conflict was growing in him. The more he was with Dora, the more he wanted to be with her. But he didn't dare share with her the truth about his presence in Techno City, or that by the end of the following week he'd be leaving.

Leiani had seen the packs of wild dogs, the animals strongly resembling the dingoes of Australia, except the dogs of Mu were larger, closer to the size of wolves. She lit her firebrand, a grim tone in her voice. "This will not be as easy as the boar confrontation."

The others followed suit, and they faced the next threat, each with a flaming torch in one hand and spear poised in the other.

The specimens of *Canis lupis* that milled just beyond the fires and visibility panted their numerous and hungry presence. After hunting for hours without even bringing down a gazelle, this was their chance to fill their bellies. The smell of blood excited the very sinew of their powerful muscles, minimizing the instinctual fear of fire.

"Hold on to your spears," Leiani directed. "If we throw one into the darkness we will end up minus a weapon."

Nothing in Gavin's life had prepared him for this night. The Gavin who had escaped Township 23 four months before had fled in pursuit of an adventurer's dreams of a better life. Now, facing this invisible threat, a charged current rose from Earth through his soles to surge upward along his spine. A similar spiral, originating from the starry vault coursed downward through the human conduit. In the region of his heart, where the currents converged, he felt the power of the photonic flow that dispersed in every direction beyond his body. At that instant, his tensed muscles registered a marked increase in the warrior's strength. Sensing that Leiani was up to the fight, his protective urge encompassed both the augur and Leslie.

"Leslie, stay well inside the fires," he yelled.

His voice elicited growling responses from the dogs. The hunger of the circling predators made them fearless. The alpha paced just outside the milling pack of thirteen dogs, his nose targeting the bloodied wing, his eyes assessing the weak points in the defense. The predators spiraled inward, closing in on the perimeter, until one by one they charged the invisible ring between the fires.

Bared fangs gleamed in the firelight, and raised hackles came into view as the defenders lunged with their torches and jabbed with their lances. There were yelps and shrieks as sharp points pierced the dogs' flesh. Gavin's tension was double that of the women, for while repelling invasions at the head and right wing of the augur, he repeatedly glanced over his shoulder to ascertain Leslie's safety. Yet the powerful flow coursing through the youth lent the agility of a dancer and the precision of an accomplished warrior to his thrusts.

As the least muscular of the three, Leslie's lunges were relatively impotent, barely staving off the attacks in her direction. The cunning alpha calculated that this was the place to press his advantage. Larger than the others, one hundred pounds of muscle charged at Leslie with terrifying ferocity. Panic shot adrenaline through her body and, for an instant, multiplied her strength. Sheer will focused Amazonian power into the arm that drove the lance just above the shoulder blade of the alpha canine. Ripping the lance from Leslie's hold, the yelping dog and embedded spear disappeared into the night. Gavin looked over his shoulder to Leslie, who was weaponless, and the pall of her vulnerability gripped him with cold surges of fear for her life.

She waved the torch back and forth and then plunged the blazing end into the side of an emboldened dog. The acrid smells of burnt flesh and singed hair accompanied the loud whimpers of his retreat.

Then, with animal rage, unmatched to this point, bared fangs lunged toward Leslie's face as the alpha with the lance in his shoulder leaped forward. Leslie screamed as the horrifying assault knocked her to the ground. But the weight that fell on her was only a lifeless carcass sprawled across her body.

Gavin pulled his spear from the dog, and he and Leiani fought on with punishing jabs answered by yelps of pain, until every dog was wounded and growing increasingly weary from the drain of constant aggression. The knowledge that the alpha was down further weakened the pack. Gavin sensed the moment when the will to attack drained from the dogs. With a powerful surge that more than matched the dogs' waning energy, he chased the singed and battle-torn predators into the dark void from which they had come.

The silence that followed was total, unbroken by birdsong, croaks, or even the sound of crickets. Having extricated herself from the corpse, Leslie stood with her shoulders slumped and head down when the returning warrior gathered her in his arms. When Leiani approached, they folded her into their embrace. Leslie wept, burying her head in Gavin's shoulder, her grip tight around Leiani's waist.

Within minutes the last vestiges of the current that had choreographed Gavin's agility and multiplied his strength, drained from his body. When the three returned to their stations, he stepped over the head of the motionless bird, thrusting away the impression that the augur was dead and willing the creature to live. The moment Gavin folded to the ground, he drifted helplessly into a deep slumber, guarded by the women's wakeful vigil on an island of quiet amid a jostling sea of grunts, snuffles, cries and growls.

Synchronicity 29

Eena entered the portal at sunrise, anxious to see how Leiani's pack augur project was progressing. She had noticed Gavin's absence, and Steve had mentioned that Leslie was also missing. She wanted to ascertain that they were okay.

The hike down the mountain afforded a welcome chance to reflect on vying concerns, most immediate of which was Nathan's presence and what he knew. If he escaped to Transtopia Metro, he would put Three Mountains on the governor's radar. She knew that she would do whatever she needed to do to prevent that from happening. Period. Sitting around the fire reading Aikido passages was one thing. The reality was that Nathan, who would alert an opponent of epic proportions, must be dealt with accordingly. Besides, it wouldn't be that hard to shoot that weasely snitch.

The search for allies in the mountains had proved to be surprisingly fraught with dangers. She had hoped for hundreds of allies rather than handfuls of emigrants and a dead augur by now. In addition, the birds couldn't survive the frigid temperatures of Rocky Mountain winters. The approach of July left three months before winter and retiring the augurs until late May. They only had through September to infiltrate the townships.

Also, she was anxious for Caellum's return, to learn about the success of his mission. Would he come with news of spreaders or complete apathy?

Her greatest dread was that the now visible landlords, temporarily the political heads of Regions 1 through 21 of the UA, would again recede from public view. As before Solar Flash, from obscured Olympic heights, the self-proclaimed Titan kings would resume their power moves on chessboard Earth. With the thought of humanity as lowly pawns held firmly in the grasp of masterful maneuvers, an unanticipated weariness crept into her psyche.

As if these concerns were not enough, she felt the weight of the possibly approaching rovers and the family they held hostage. She knew that one way or another, the community must free that poor family. Yet a rescue mission would be very risky. She dreaded the thought of an innocent person being hurt or even killed in the attempt.

The sound of rushing water washed over her depressed mood, drawing her to a nearby grotto. Forming diminutive waterfalls, the convergence of trickles from the heights sprayed over jumbled boulders, which secured a portion of the flow to this secluded enclosure. Bird song heralded a magical world graced by a crystalline pool enclosed by orchids and exotic flowering vines trailing over granite walls. The musty scents of damp earth and perfumed flowers exuded a mystical ambience in the misty enclosure.

Feeling an irresistible pull, Eena clambered over a pile of rocks, peeled off her clothes, and eased into the cold snowmelt. Shivering violently at first, she kept her limbs moving vigorously to warm her goose-bumped flesh until the capillaries pulsed warm blood to penetrate her immersed skin. Ensconced in the pristine liquid, she could clearly see her toes and tiny fish darting in between the legs planted in their realm.

Sunlight glinted a thousand sparkles on the surface of the water, enveloping her in a glowing haze.

Suddenly, she became aware that her mother stood beside her, an ethereal, yet palpable presence.

"Ama´!" Emotion catapulted through her body.

"My warrior daughter, would you hear my story?"

Eena nodded, watching the fish nibble her toes, the closeness of her mother, familiar and comforting.

"When I was a toddler, my Hopi father came from the cornfield to dance the corn dance with me in his arms. Throughout my childhood, as I ate the delicious corn, I didn't know that it's practically impossible to grow corn in the desert. But my father scooped the sand into little mounds, placed the dried kernels inside, poured a little water on it, and prayed, calling on the collaboration of unseen hands."

"Ama´, why are you telling me this?"

"The power that helps farmers plant corn in deserts helped me midwife babies, and also supports the uplift of humanity."

"But, Ama´, my power must be a different kind, for an entrenched empire enslaves humanity."

"No more than scorching winds threaten crops or birth pangs accompany birth."

Mostly Eena thought her mother to be wise, but in this case she was naïve. "We live in a world of violent collisions, explosions and weaponized might."

"Nonetheless, the greatest power taps into a co-creative source that can green the desert."

"Ama´, I don't know how to use this power."

"Only seek it. Seeking propels the journey of life as depicted on the pendant made by your grandfather."

Eena touched the silver disc hanging over her chest.

"My daughter, this power is yours, though naysayers will tell you this is not so."

"We are so outnumbered, Ama´."

Her mother nodded, compassion shining from her liquid brown eyes. "At this juncture in the human journey, cosmic forces support the united alignment of the few. My daughter, you are midwife to the birth of a better world. When threats compound, remember my words."

A warm feeling, as though Ama´ had embraced her, enveloped Eena before her mother shimmered from view.

As a sensation on her big toe startled Eena out of her reverie, she watched a silvery fish nibble the exposed flesh. But on this side of the vision, she felt as though something had shifted. A sense of futility, which had vied for supremacy over her naturally indomitable spirit, had dissipated.

During the prolonged moments of stillness, the icy coldness of the water stippled her skin, and she vigorously paddled to shore. As she put on her shirt and pants, and adjusted the leather strap that held the quiver of arrows, she realized the sense of a futile struggle had lessened. The interlude had conjured a glimpse of the earthly home as a training ground to hone her physical skills and mental acuity in service to life. A renewed sense of power surged her stride forward.

Reaching the base of the mountain, she continued through the prairie canopy of seedpod-laden stalks, the *rumble-coo* of the augers growing louder with her approach. Yet, the calls that normally sounded notes of welcome, instead intoned a warning. When a slight movement in the grass grabbed her attention, she stopped, swiftly positioned her bow, and reached for an arrow. Notching it in the bowstring, she peered at a tawny coat about three yards ahead, barely visible through the screen of stalks.

Always prepared for predators in this ancient domain, she had observed a pair of red-maned wolves, a pack of wild dogs and huge eagles. But never a large cat. Knowing predatory felines must exist in this realm, part of a natural population control system, she would normally have skirted the scene to let nature take its course. But through the cloak of stems, she couldn't see what fixated the cat's stare, and an awful foreboding tightened her grip on the bow and string.

A powerful shoulder flexed as the large cat inched forward. Eena took aim. The arrow flew with a barely audible zing and thudded its impact with flesh, the obsidian point slicing through powerful muscles and into the beating heart. The instant the pulse ceased, the muscles, deprived of the living flow, lost their poised tension and crumpled lifelessly to the ground.

Eena lowered the bow, the barrier of hardened stalks protesting with creaks and groans as she pushed through. Expecting to see a large modern day lion, she was surprised to see the fangs of a saber tooth cat.

Agitated by another approach, the feathered grass pods released a spray of seeds clinging to Leiani's hair at her wide-eyed appearance. The two women's eyes locked, bound by the overwhelming closeness of Leiani's brush with death. Her legs buckled and, kneeling on the ground, her eyes roamed the fur of the collapsed predator. "You saved my life," she whispered.

Shared grief moistened their eyes as Eena worked the arrow free from its bloody lodging. "The timing," she murmured. She wiped the arrow clean on nearby stalks and hunkered down to stroke the coarse brown-gold coat. "Out of all the seconds in a day, how is it that I happened on this scene at this exact moment?"

The women exchanged looks of wonder and knowing. Something beyond their ken had orchestrated an event string that spared Leiani's life.

They remained silent for several minutes, offering reverent homage for the loss of a magnificent expression of predatory prowess.

Leiani got up first and, with a mysterious glint in her glance, offered Eena a flask of water. "Speaking of timing, this valley holds more evidence of synchronicity. "Gavin and Leslie are camped nearby with an unexpected companion."

When the late morning sun probed Gavin's eyes, he opened them to see pale green plumes as the augur drank water from a wooden bowl. Jubilant that the bird was alive, he nonetheless lay still. He wanted neither to startle the creature, nor to receive another punishing jab. Pressing his chin to his chest he inched backward until beyond range of attack. When he was several feet away, the alerted bird raised his head to eye the human's smoothly contrived shift to a seated position.

Arms slid around his shoulders, prelude to the kiss that Leslie planted on his cheek. "'Bout time," she teased, pressing her face against his. "Tea?"

He looked around to smile his thanks as he took the cup from Leiani. Then his eyes brightened with pleased surprise that Eena stood beside her.

Eena's gaze shifted toward the augur with astonished admiration. "Definitely an augur to stand out in a flock!" she quipped.

While sipping their tea the three described the events of the past night to Eena.

"I wish I had been here to help," she mused. "Yet, it seems I arrived just when I needed to." Eena looked thoughtfully toward Gavin. "You and Leslie were on the mountainside as this creature was struck down?"

Nodding, Gavin shared his happiness that the augur had lived through the noisy assaults of darkness. He sighed at the thought of more nights of the same as the bird healed. "Suppose we can erect an enclosure of cypress branches?"

Leiani agreed with his idea. "There's a savannah less than an hour's walk from here with a dead acacia tree that was struck by lightning."

The youth failed to make the connection and remained silent.

"The branches have four-inch thorns."

Her idea penetrated and gelled, generating an excited reply. "Four walls composed of a ground layer of cypress limbs topped with thorn-filled acacia branches."

Leslie's eyes lit up with her characteristic enthusiasm. "We can drag them here."

Leiani nodded. "For now, let's gather the cypress limbs for the base."

For the next hour, they cut scavenged limbs and erected the ground layer of the enclosure around the uneasy bird.

The first phase completed, Leiani headed away, calling over her shoulder, "Gavin, restart one of the fires. I'll be back with grub and a pan."

The smoldering charred wood responded to his probes with tiny flames that danced around the fresh wood. Friendly bantering continued as the friends breakfasted on scrambled bird eggs and kiwi. When their stomachs were filled, the women stood up.

Gavin didn't want to leave the augur exposed. "I—"

Leiani seemed to intuit his concern. "Don't worry. We can cut and drag while you guard." She handed Gavin the salve, gauze and more damp cloths. "Thought you might need these." She grinned. "By the way, when you decide to feed the bird by hand, you might want to wrap your hand in gauze."

Gavin smiled his thanks and looked over at the augur, head now resting on the ground. "He's probably hungry," he murmured.

Leslie presented Gavin with a bowl of exotic fruits. "While you snoozed, we were busy. But we didn't want to risk jabs from the bird or you, so we left the job of feeding him to you."

Gavin laughed his thanks and kissed his audacious girlfriend.

Leiani had rolled a large stump toward Gavin. "And one more thing. Occasionally large predators cross the plains during the day. You'll want to have your bow and arrow handy."

Anxious to get going on the first of possibly four trips, Leiani and Eena donned their own bows and arrows. The women headed toward the savannah as Gavin looked from the bowl of fruits to his wary companion.

He spoke in a low, mellow tone to the bird. "Now, I know you'd much rather take this fruit from the bowl than me." He slowly circled to just beyond reach of the hazardous beak. "But since this is the beginning of a relationship, it's going to have to be me." The head rose to alert mode following his movements. Gavin sat down and crossed his legs, the secured bowl resting between his crotch and folded legs. Carefully, he moved his arm to place tamarind pods within range of the beak, barely missing a lethal lunge.

"Yep," he mused conversationally as he reached for the gauze, "this stuff is going to come in handy."

The augur hungrily pecked the hard pods open to grab the fleshy fruit.

As he downed the last one, Gavin hastily placed a star fruit among the emptied pod shells.

When offerings of tamarillos, mangoes and passion fruit had been devoured, its eyelids began to close. Despite the nearness of the human, the satiated bird yielded to the irresistible urge to sleep and lowered its head to the ground.

Slowly, Gavin got up to retrieve his bow and arrows and sit on a stump with his back to the bird, scanning the grass for daytime predators. Two hours later he heard voices and stood up to watch Eena, Leslie and Leiani dragging branches behind them. As they approached, the augur raised his head and wings in alarm. Likely prompted by searing pain, he swiftly folded the torn appendage close to his body.

Careful to avoid the needle-like spines, the group worked to hoist the long thorny branches over the cypress layer.

"The augur's wing needs cleaning and a fresh application of salve," Leiani said before they headed out again.

Not wanting to hold the bird's head between spears again, Gavin wrapped the gathered folds of the still-intact portion of the sheet around the length of his arm, to extend from his gauze-wrapped hand. Forcing down his reluctance to brave the beak, he poured fresh water in the bowl, dipped the cloth into it, and dribbled the water on the wing.

Each time the augur's painful jabs penetrated the meager protection, Gavin cried out, though he had intended to bear the pain silently.

Holding his body out of the way as much as possible, he applied a new coat of salve as the bird extended its head for a renewed round of attacks.

Gavin winced from the blows, grimacing as he recalled his horror of being on the receiving end of such beak assaults. "Well, Grandfather, I've made another choice," he mused aloud. "One that would have seemed impossible a couple of months ago."

By dusk the group surrounded the augur, enclosed by a five-foot wall of thorns that promised to repel the most intimidating enemies.

Suddenly, Gavin instinctively drew back as the augur stood up, and a shiver cascaded over the layered feathers of the bird's torso and tail. Seeing the consternation stamped on Gavin's expression, laughter convulsed the women, standing near the tail feathers.

Steam arose from the huge bird dropping, forcing yet another series of strategic actions from the augur's protector as he poured sand on it and used large pieces of bark to shove it from the enclosure.

Gavin sighed, addressing his mirthful observers. "Well, I hope that big dump improves his disposition."

As Leiani walked away, Leslie sat down on the dirt, patting a place beside her. "We need to talk."

Gavin had dreaded those words, hoping he and Leslie could simply slide back into their former closeness. Reluctantly, he sat. His halted apology for his coldness led to a long discussion of disclosures of the woundedness that drove the mutual retreat.

"So, Chuck?" Gavin asked, mentally picturing Chuck's arm around Leslie and her eyes smiling into his.

Leslie's expression was wistfully thoughtful. "He's really attractive. Good-looking. Strong. Provider type. I could fall for him."

Gavin swallowed his jealousy.

Leslie picked up a stick to draw a squiggle in the dirt. "But, for some reason, a stubborn, sometimes morose, fellow explorer of worlds is more my type."

Gavin's sigh of relief was barely audible.

Leslie took his arm and snuggled against him. "I understand why you pushed me away. Next time, please don't take so long to let me back in."

At the moment Gavin thought there wouldn't be a next time because, like most twenty-year-olds, he didn't know himself that well yet.

The Opponent

30

The group that had gathered at Grandfather's three weeks before felt the meeting was inconclusive. So, in secret, minus Gavin and Leslie, they called for a second.

Eena eyed Grandfather. "I hope Nathan doesn't show up."

The elder addressed the group. "Has anyone informed Nathan of our meeting?"

Alarmed expressions greeted his query.

With a shrug he looked at Eena. "Seems unlikely."

Affection and frustration wrestled in Eena's expression. "Why do I sense there's something you're not telling us?"

As the group sipped tea around the campfire, Eena pulled *The Art of Peace* from Chas's pocket and opened to another random quote:

> "Do not stare into the eyes of your opponent: he may mesmerize you. Do not fix your gaze on his sword: he may intimidate you. Do not focus on your opponent at all: he may absorb your energy. The essence of training is to bring your opponent completely into your sphere. Then you can stand just where you like."

She looked around the circle. "With all due respect to Morihei Ueshiba, we need to assess everything about the enemy — the arms and troops at his disposal, his battle strategy, his location — everything. An overlooked detail can be fatal."

Chas, who had posed the very same concern to his teacher, nodded. "I know what you mean. In Aikido, it's a given to know the enemy as

- 215 -

intimately as a close friend. But beyond the ability to anticipate his moves when training or under attack, your power arises from tapping an interior source of *flow*. This power source knows when to bend, side step, whirl, make contact—whatever is needed to remain out of harm's way. It's an agile dance of energy."

The warrior in Eena was not attracted to the idea of a dance.

Chas smiled as though aware of her reaction. "According to Morihei, Aikido is precisely the *way of the warrior*—the invoking of an intuitive and creative flow to elude even the most skilled in cunning tactics."

Rigel was not convinced. "You mean we're to suggest that the people of the community draw Nathan into our own spheres of living?"

"Realistically, what other option do we have?" Raiel asked quietly.

Eena looked at her mentor suspiciously. "Grandfather, exactly how was it that Nathan just showed up at our gathering three weeks ago?"

When three people sprinkled more sage tea in emptied mugs, Grandfather took the pot of boiling water from the grill and filled the cups.

"He was invited," he said.

After slight gasps and knowing nods, the group waited for further explanation, but Matoskah had nothing more to say.

Word spread over the next few days about the "draw the opponent close" strategy—to invite Nathan into the people's spheres of sharing and activity. Amid collective refusals to hobnob with a spy, the same families who had helped him build his cabin now took him food and invited him for meals. He particularly liked to be invited to homes, playing with the children, enjoying the feeling of family, even as it evoked a painful longing for his own.

Often in the evening as Nathan sat with a gathering under the summer stars, the friends he could count on two hands related stories of their arrival at Three Mountains. One family even told of a band of rovers that stripped them of all food, clothing and supplies along with their horse-drawn wagon.

The recurring motif of a circling eagle that seemed to guide weary travelers to this destination triggered puzzled skepticism in the fireside guest. On the other hand, as he listened to the people recall their hunger, their fears and hardships, he felt moved to speak of his own family's similar trials. Despite his unwavering determination to get away, he had to admit a grudging kinship with people, who like himself, simply sought security and well-being for their families.

Thanks to the acacia thorn enclosure, the next nights on the savannah were minus the drama of the first, but the croaks, calls, howls, grunts and barks made sleep fitful as Gavin curled around Leslie's warm body. The savannah, which was relatively quiet during the day, except for augur calls, hosted a noisy cacophony under the cover of darkness. He worried about the fire that burned in the opening at the corner of the enclosure. Every hour he got up to feed wood to the flames and then returned to his and Leslie's hard bed. His sleeping partner sighed softly as he pulled the blanket over her shoulder, drew her close and buried his face in her hair.

Within a couple of days, he had received the last puncture wound and the following day fed the bird from his hand without wincing for the first time.

By the fifth night when the sky released a drenching downpour, the pair jumped from their tarp bed. They each grabbed a corner of the tarp and pulled it over the augur, and then huddled together under the blanket that was quickly soaked by the deluge. Soon, little rivulets flowed over the saturated ground and under their entwined bodies.

By dawn the rain had slowed to a dribble, but Leslie and Gavin were shivering from the cold and unable to start a fire. Offering welcome relief, Leiani approached with dry wood, plus a blanket and shirt for Leslie. After starting the fire, Gavin and Leslie peeled off their shirts, and she put on Leiani's.

"Sorry, Gavin." Leiani smiled. "I wish I had something large enough for you."

At that moment the tarp rose up and slid to the ground as the augur stood. He took a step toward Gavin, whose back was turned toward him, and stopped, his head and beak resting next to his benefactor's shoulder.

Gavin hardly dared move until an insistent push on his back made him stumble forward.

"He's probably asking for breakfast," Leiani offered. "Here."

Looping the handle over his arm, he reached into the proffered bag and held a mango below the augur's beak. As he held the fruit in both hands, the bird reduced the contents to a juicy pulp that soon disappeared. Leslie slipped Gavin a supply of kiwis, but quickly jerked her hand away. She'd learned the hard way that only Gavin had been granted the right to have any appendages in the augur's space. After an additional offering of cherry-like grumichamas, the bird turned his head signaling he was full.

Still standing, he flapped his wings, but it must have been the soreness in his right wing that immediately closed them.

For the next week Gavin still refused to leave the bird for more than a few minutes at a time. On currents of love, he began sending impressions of his hand touching the bird's neck. When the bird arched its neck suggestively, Gavin reached tentatively into the short tufted feathers to scratch the stippled flesh, and the fluffed feathers offered the hoped-for response.

By the third week they had a new problem. The augur was increasingly moving around, the thorns inside the enclosure threatening his huge body.

After conferring, the three dragged away one wall to form a sufficiently large opening for the bird to pass through. Their plan was to push the wall closed in the evening. Meanwhile, Gavin had fashioned a collar and lead rope of braided grass. After repeated trials he managed to slip it around the bird's neck. The following day, armed with his bow and arrows, Gavin and the augur took their first walk. He didn't attempt to guide, preferring instead to follow the bird's lead to a stand of mango trees. They roamed the savannah until sunset, when it seemed prudent to return to the enclosure. The huge creature followed the gentle coaxing of his companion willingly as though he sensed that safety lay within the thorny walls.

Gavin sensed Leslie's restlessness. "You want to return to the lab."

"There's pressing work to be done to make the hologram fully operational."

When the time came for Leiani to walk Leslie to the portal, Gavin held her close as understanding vied with his sense of loss. His lips brushed her earlobes. "Since we've guarded the augur, I've grown to want you next to me when we fall asleep and wake up. I like breathing in the scent of your hair. I love to crawl in our makeshift bed beside you, to pull you toward me and hear your soft sighs and to feel you curve into my embrace in the early morning cold."

Leslie pulled back from him, eyes sparkling, hands on his shoulders. "Did you honestly think you had to go to such lengths to get me to share a blanket with you?" she teased.

Leiani busied herself with her back to the lovebirds while the kisses continued as though they wouldn't see one another for a year.

Transportation

31

Martha thought of Durango, her family's destination, as she chopped the last pieces of smoked beef and dropped them into the pot of simmering pinto beans, sage and wild onions. While stirring, she looked up at the surrounding scene. According to the map, they were camped at the northern edge of a wide, flat ravine along a stream that flowed into a large reservoir about two miles south. Just beyond that was Highway 240, which would take them to Durango. She imagined a city brimming with life. A place to safely extricate themselves from the cruel enslavers.

Jimmy lounged with his back against a tree, holding his pistol in his lap and watching Phil chop enough firewood to last the night. Arnie was dozing, and Marvin appeared from the surrounding woods holding a freshly killed rabbit.

Chris was in his own world, following the path of a beetle. When he came too close to Marvin, the rover yelled, "Boy, git away from here before I knock you sideways!"

A renewed rush of outrage coursed through Martha. She turned her sight inward, appalled at the impressions flying through her brain. *Phil's ax... the large kitchen knife in her hands....*

For close to a three weeks the family had been herded south, stopping for short stays at remote cabins, where Jimmy added to his liquor supply—which the family was tasked to carry. Martha was filled with chagrin when they stopped again to camp along the river in the ravine. The rovers were content to walk for about half a day and stop the remaining part to hunt, fish, and nap. Martha estimated that the family could have reached this point more than two weeks before had they been alone.

Marvin tossed the rabbit toward Martha before turning to Jimmy. "I found something."

Chin down, Jimmy looked up at Marvin from under raised brows.

"Bikes are stashed 'bout two miles south of here along a lake."

Awakened by Marvin's voice, Arnie sat up. "Bikes?"

Marvin shot a sideways look of contempt at Arnie. "A dam and southbound road are just beyond that."

Jimmy chewed on this new information for a couple of minutes. "Bikes? What're bikes doin' in the middle of nowhere?"

While they ate their evening rabbit stew, Jimmy appeared to ruminate on this oddity.

With every day that passed Eena was more certain the rovers would bypass Three Mountains by way of the ravine and reservoir. Quartz and Thunderbird Mountains were just too imposing for them to suspect a settlement on the opposite side.

Wanting to ascertain just where they were in their journey, she took the western patrol over Promise Path to Lemon Reservoir and beyond. For a complete sweep Eena and Cesla headed northeast first. By now the travelers must be close to the wide ravine, the most obvious, and easy southbound route. Continuing along Promise Path she scanned the mountainsides to the left and right until the path narrowed along a river, and Cesla soared over the rickety bridge where Gavin had dangled above certain death. Eena shook her head, musing about the hair's breadth distance between the loss of life and the birth of a new one—for Gavin, a life far removed from the dismal existence he left behind.

Beyond the bridge, the ravine widened again. Ahead, the blue water of Lemon Reservoir sparkled in the midday light. And there were six people walking along beside it. For a heart stopping instant, she recalled the tragic day when Gavin had first spied this group.

She cut a wide swath beyond range of another bullet to peer through her binoculars.

Must be headed for Durango, she thought with initial relief, which was followed by concern for the captive family, then vehemence. *We have to figure out a way to free them.*

Expecting the group to follow the reservoir toward the dam, Eena lost sight of them behind a flank of the mountain. Surprise escalated to alarm as she guided Cesla for a better view.

They were gathered at the trailhead used by the connectors and Caellum. Then she saw the reason why. Five people stood around one who supported a bike. She calmed her reactive shock, reasoning that the three troublemakers would never associate the discovery with a current-day group close by. Challenging her logic, two of the rovers began moving around looking at the ground. Her heart pounded a fresh surge of alarm. *Oh no, fresh footprints left by the connectors or Caellum.*

Since the rovers were now facing the direction of Cesla, Eena and the bird banked away, hidden from view by the forest. She urged the augur southwest and circled out of sight for several minutes before heading back toward the ravine, hoping the group was continuing south toward the dam. But they weren't. They were following the trail that led between Thunderbird and Quartz Mountains. If the rovers and their captives kept to the obvious network of trails worn by shoppers and connectors, a new source of danger would arrive at Three Mountains Community in less than an hour.

The landlords, the SEI, Nathan and now rovers. Every fiber of her being screamed outrage at this approaching invasion. If it weren't for the family and the need to keep Cesla and herself out of view and range of the guns, she could have picked off the rovers one by one with arrows. But the continual shifting of positions would endanger the lives of the family members.

For a moment she slumped against Cesla for comfort, defeated by the compounding threats. Then, with Cesla's responsive arc toward the portal, she pulled out her radio. "Rovers approaching, an hour away."

For Caellum the days were breezing by heartlessly, as though leaving Dora after another ten days would be like parting from a favorite shirt. He wanted her to understand about the shadow of control and deception that loomed over mankind. But instead, the irascible shadow of his gloom squirmed between them as he helped her plant a flower garden in front of the dorm.

"Dora, you see the world through rose-colored lenses." Seated on the ground next to her, Caellum handed Dora an iris bulb as he spoke.

Mildly surprised, incomprehension in her glance, she placed the bulb in the prepared hole, covered it with soil, and poured water over it. Then she smiled at Caellum with disarming directness. Trowel poised in mid air, she replied, "We find what we look for in the world. If we focus on evil and deception, that's what we find. I see goodness in everyone."

She playfully shoved him out of the way so she could scoot over to plant the next bulb. But Caellum didn't feel playful. Yet, he didn't want to feel this growing impatience with her naïveté. He didn't want to push her away with his irritation. His heart's desire was to hold her close, to return with her to Three Mountains. With just over a week left, he could hardly bear the thought of parting with her. She was the opposite of everything he wanted to vanquish in the political and social hierarchy. She was his island of goodness in a usurious world.

Why was it inconceivable to Dora that there were powerful individuals so driven by self-love, that the masses of humanity were only a means to feed an insatiable appetite for power and wealth? He had been unable to penetrate the mind beneath that shining black hair.

"Caellum, you speak of self-generated phantoms."

With a sinking heart he realized he was dreaming of the impossible. The warrior in Caellum, not so protective now, wanted to shake her up. "The enemy is not invading continental shores or even roving the desert. It's hiding in plain sight."

She handed him the watering can. "Fill this, and while you're at it, pour some on that suspicious head of yours." She playfully shoved her somber gardening assistant.

When he returned, her large blue eyes invited him into their depths. "Caellum, let's not quarrel on this beautiful sunshiny day."

Taking the watering can from him, she spoke with the demureness that had first captured his heart. "I would like for you to meet my parents."

Startled by this turn in the conversation, he looked at her questioningly.

"I called them on the dorm phone. They've invited us to come for dinner tomorrow night."

Caellum groaned inwardly, grappling with this new step in the entwinement of their lives.

"Okay," he heard himself reply, helpless to do anything but comply and help her plant the flowerbed.

When the bulbs were in the dirt, Dora collected the tools and watering can and sighed. "I have to go to my room and write a physical therapy essay now."

Caellum left to make contact with more spreaders. It was a bonanza day in which he connected with Carissa and Sherry, who agreed to come to the Saturday meeting. If they became spreaders, the number would rise to six.

The following day, he approached James with a request, since they were about the same height and weight. "Got a nice shirt and pants I can borrow for a date?"

With a lighthearted feeling of accomplishment, Caellum dressed in anticipation of meeting Dora's parents later in the day. He inserted two dozen pamphlets between the pages of the physics book and walked toward the campus.

Walking into Neil's office, Caellum felt an upsurge of hope to see six youths crowded inside. The two latest added their zeal to the charged session for brainstorming spreader tactics, and each of them knew others that were desperately unhappy with the police state world.

Neil announced he had located a new place to meet, and led them downstairs to the basement. In the stark, windowless room painted pale tan, they pushed two tables together and gathered up the chairs scattered around the room. Comments flew around the table.

"I know a couple of people who are likely to jump at the chance to become spreaders."

"I think we all do."

"The greatest challenge lies in becoming infiltrators."

Neil nodded appreciatively. "I think infiltration will be the second phase of our mission." He looked around the room of eager spreaders. "Meanwhile, let's take note of possible supporters among individuals holding positions of responsibility in the city."

"Well, Neil, you represent an infiltration victory."

"I never considered the possibility of a bloodless coup."

"I still doubt its feasibility."

"What choice do we have?"

Caellum looked around the group. "I have to admit I've dreamed of incarcerating the controllers at gunpoint. But that's a pipe dream for now."

He offered the three aspects of self-empowerment gleaned from Chas: self-victory, unflagging effort and to blend with the enemy.

Discussion of the practical meaning of the three terms filled the next hour.

After the meeting, Caellum sauntered to his usual haunts for an afternoon of seeding. But it was what he called a dry day, with no one showing any interest. As he sat on the park bench under the five o'clock sun, he realized he would be late if he didn't go straight to Dora's, so he brought along the book with the remaining brochures tucked inside.

Caellum rang the doorbell and a roommate invited him to wait in the front room. With his heart in his throat, he watched Dora descend the stairs wearing a feminine dress of white cotton eyelet that softly accentuated her lithe body, blue eyes and silky black hair.

As he stood and turned to open the door for her, he anticipated they would either walk to a nearby apartment where her parents' lived, or catch the trolley at the corner to take them to a neighborhood on the outskirts of town.

Dora put her hand on his arm. "Let's sit here and wait. My father is sending a car."

Taken aback, Caellum looked at her. "A car? Who owns cars nowadays, not to mention has drivers to drive them?"

"My parents do," she said simply.

After a puzzled look, Callum sat in stunned silence, absorbing the implications of this information.

Five minutes later, Caellum found himself riding in a vehicle for the first time since riding in the cargo bed of the military truck. The car, a like-new, silver Subaru sported wood paneling and exuded the pungent scent of the tan leather upholstery.

"The hybrid engine's been converted to run with electricity and water," Dora offered.

They left the downtown hub that included the college campus, apartments, banks, retail stores and restaurants. After a couple of miles they came to a belt of homes, most of them the typical three-bedroom middle class houses that many had grown up in. The few with restored electricity and water had now been assigned to the directing and managing tier of the population. A half mile later the driver turned the car down a street lined with impressive two-story brick or stucco homes with Spanish tile roofs. By pre-Solar Flash standards, they were large custom homes of the wealthy upper class. By post-Solar Flash expectations, they were practically mansions — reserved for the highest-ranking members of the local hierarchy of control.

After the driver stopped at the third house on the left, which stood out among the rest as a magnificent mansion by comparison, the pair followed the stone walkway that wound through a manicured lawn toward a two-story brownstone with English ivy trailing up one section. Roses of crimson, gold, and salmon graced the beds below large bay windows on either side of the pillars that supported a spacious porch overhang.

A confusing knot of thoughts and emotions gripped Caellum. He put his hand on Dora's arm. "Dora, who *are* you?"

"This house must be a surprise to you. My father's the Governor General of Techno City and Sector 10."

Challenges 32

On Thunderbird Mountain as Grandfather prayed, immersed in the smoke of sweet grass, Chas received Eena's frantic call over the radio and, in turn, radioed everyone in possession of a radio to spread word of an emergency meeting at the trailhead leading to Lemon Reservoir. By the time the majority of the people were informed and had gathered, they calculated that the rovers were about forty-five minutes away.

With prior patroller reports that the group's south heading would bypass Three Mountains, it had appeared they would either continue south to a township or head west on Highway 240 to Durango. Occupied with multiple concerns, the community had not derived a contingency plan for a rover takeover attempt because discussions had shifted to how to rescue the captive family. Now, at a frantic pace those gathered could only plan how to initially meet the danger that approached.

First, the residents hid their children and made plans to keep them hidden at Raiel's place, their only safe play area. Henceforth, most traffic would take place behind the screen of houses and pines, with Grandfather's clearing designated their official meeting place.

A silence weighted with the pall of doom had fallen over the group by the time four men, a woman, and a child walked into the valley. A swarthy-looking man with his shirt open over his belly, which was covered by a leather belt for his holstered pistol, led the group along the river deeper into the community. Three of the men appeared to have been nowhere close to a razor, brush or soap for months.

Bold and grinning, the head of the group, who introduced himself as Jimmy, waved his gun toward the assembly. "Well, now, ain't this one fine reception committee? Which one's the leader I'm about to replace."

Chas spoke up. "We jointly share the leadership as well as responsibility for the welfare of this community. You can speak to all of us."

"Now ain't that just peachy." The lead rover grinned. "Well, meet your new gov'nor."

Jimmy's go-to man, Arnie, stared at the villagers with a deer-in-the-headlights expression, nervously fidgeting with his pistol. The wiry man's eyes darted furtively from one to another as though in an anxious assessment of his position in the group.

Marvin, who behaved like a menacing bodyguard, held his rifle with his left hand under the barrel and right hand trigger-ready while his cold brown eyes surveyed the crowd with cocky self-assurance.

The fourth man, obviously the husband and father, positioned himself protectively next to his family.

Jimmy put a hand on the boy's shoulder, pulling him away from his parents and in front of himself. "Well, now, how about a tour?"

Gavin had ached for Leslie's closeness after he watched the figures of the two women ascend the mountain. Dwarfed by the enormous redwoods, they soon disappeared among them, and he shifted his focus to the bird foraging close by.

For the next few days, the augur and his human guardian walked companionably toward groves of fruit trees for peaceful foraging sessions. Gradually, the relationship grew from allowing Gavin's touch to inviting affectionate exchanges. With fluffs and shivers, the augur placed his head against Gavin's chest, positioning his crown for pleasurable exposure to the hand he had savagely attacked weeks before.

Nonetheless, it was apparent to both Gavin and Leiani that a part of this *Avis gigantus* remained wild, and she dare not come too close for fear of swift lunges at exposed flesh.

The wing healed until only a thin line of scar tissue was visible in a section at the base of the forewing, which was still bare of feathers. Gavin knew it was time for the augur to fly again, so he removed the collar and ran before the grounded bird, flapping his arms to urge him to fly. The augur followed with hopping flights at first. But within a couple of days these became low soars over the grass. These lengthened through the following week to flights to tree limbs until the day when he lifted off and flew toward the horizon.

Gavin's heart skipped a beat when the startlingly beautiful bird took flight. But quick on the heels of his jubilation came a jolt of loss. He had both anticipated and dreaded this event, knowing it could mean the end of his relationship with the creature and a reversion to the augur's former wildness. Squinting into the late afternoon sun, the bereft youth searched the sky in the direction the bird had flown. He had decided not to psychically call the augur that might revert to wildness. The image shrank until a mere dot blinked out of sight, and feet dragging, he headed toward Leiani's nest.

Compassion shone through her eyes. "We knew this might happen."

He walked toward the acacia thorn walls to retrieve Leiani's gear.

She approached behind him. "There'll be others."

But Gavin wanted no others. The connection he felt with this bird would not simply go away.

Handing the folded blanket and utensils from his camp to Leiani, and feeling the vacuous closure on his stay in the savannah, not to mention his dreams, he suddenly felt a rush of air at his back and whirled to see the huge claws grab the ground. Forgetting the augur was still half wild, he impulsively threw his arms around the enormous neck. Wings flapping, the alarmed bird dragged the attached human several feet, then relaxed into the embrace of the now-familiar arms and hands.

With a wide grin, Gavin released his hold on this bird that offered consolation for the loss of Espirit. "You're like the phoenix, you know that? You represent the spirit of the augur resurrecting in my life." He ruffled the neck feathers. "In fact, that's what I'll call you — Phoenix."

The following morning the hungry bird pecked him awake with gentle nibbles on his hair.

"All right, all right." He laughed. "I just needed a little more shut-eye."

As he fed Phoenix, he spoke to him in a friendly offhand way. "I want you to think about something, about carrying me on our back."

Gavin pushed away the thorny wall, and the bird walked out only to lift off and disappear again, as if reveling in his newly recovered ability.

Still uneasy, Gavin watched the augurs of the surrounding plains lift off from the huge cypress trees, land in the grass near clusters of fruit trees, and rise from the grass to soar overhead. Mentally referring to them as the smaller augurs, he smiled inwardly, recalling how huge and terrifying Cesla looked the day Eena called him.

His musings shifted to the hundreds of miles of forest to be explored beyond Three Mountains. He felt the renewed intensity of the unmistakable urge that had pulled him northward on the fateful day that cost Espirit's life. How many runners from a dehumanizing system were hidden in secluded valleys on either side of the elevated terrain of the Continental Divide? His memory flashed to their earlier airlift of people from Highway 50. He was certain there were more such people, and he was determined to locate them, not merely as an explorer, but to establish alliances.

The image that flitted in the horizon of his dreams indicated the adventurer had traversed a far distance since the coyote intrusion in his sleep. Feeling drowsy he sat down to await the augur's return. As his lids grew heavy, the visage of Phoenix soared into his imagination. But he noticed something odd about the bird. Where the spread of aqua marine wings should be reflecting sunlight, a multi-colored mural interwove the scene of Espirit's death with his arrival that synced with Phoenix's escape from the eagle and a third event, less defined, in one great tapestry of connections. Somehow, beyond the bounds of time, synchronicity wove together prior events and the destiny he would choose.

Suddenly, the reverie receded and his eyes flew open, presented with a glaring new insight—Phoenix was an essential element of looming challenges. Gavin grasped that fact with certainty now. He stood up, poised for the dangers, losses and triumphs to come, and mentally called Phoenix. Illumined by a deepened, broadened sense of purpose, Gavin's interior vision focused with telescopic clarity on the mission that would propel the next phase of his explorations.

Grinning, he watched a speck in the distance become a turquoise jewel reflecting the sunlight. *"We are bonded, you and I,"* he communicated telepathically to the tamed creature. *"It's a done deal."* And as the wings that spanned fourteen feet came into focus, he sighed inwardly. *"And now, for the next bruising phase of our journey together."*

Phoenix glided to the ground, approached his human, and tucked his beak against Gavin's chest, positioning his neck for a vigorous rub.

Then, satisfied with what had become a shared ritual, Phoenix headed into the savannah with Gavin walking beside him.

This first day of Phoenix's flight training school, he couldn't do more than lean into the bird. Since even that small familiarity evoked sufficient flapping and shifting to get knocked to the ground, Gavin knew this next phase of Phoenix's training would be challenging, at best. And over the course of several days, each time Gavin picked up his sore and bruised body, he reminded himself, as a veteran of painful puncture wounds, that being ignominiously tossed to the ground was nowhere near as bad.

The day Phoenix first carried him skyward, he felt exhilaration reminiscent of his first flight. Suddenly, he "saw" the third part of the tapestry. It was him flying Phoenix over Three Mountains.

Over breakfast the next morning, Gavin shared his plan to fly Phoenix through the portal, and Leiani agreed it was time. "I'm still amazed at the bond that has developed between you two," she said between bites.

An hour later, holding binoculars and radio, he mounted Phoenix and they flew up the mountain. "*Through the portal,*" Gavin instructed. The wall of stone opened for their passage.

He looked for Eena, half expecting her to be walking on the path toward the portal. When he didn't see her, he flew toward the valley.

Thinking he'd wow the community with the sight of his magnificent new bond-mate, anticipating Eena's look of surprise and Leslie's admiration, he was totally unprepared for the sight that confronted him.

Headquarters 33

Eena's interior scream was unheard in the edgy silence that faced the rovers and their captives. Her eyes fixed on Phoenix and his rider, she hoped Gavin was looking through his binoculars and could see the "get out of sight" expression registered on her face. As Rigel stepped forward in response to Jimmy's demand for a tour, she was relieved to see the augur recede from view and locked eyes with Leslie in mute relief.

Rigel's resonant voice eased the collective tension. "I'll show you around."

Assuming the air of a tour guide, he showed Jimmy the greenhouses, gardens, beehives, households and science building.

"So, what's with the big outdoor structure?" Jimmy asked, pointing to the holographic mirrors.

Rigel decided to have a little fun by pulling out his best jargon. "It's a hologram emitter. The holographic image is an encoding of a light field as an interference pattern of seemingly random variations in the opacity, density or surface profile of a photographic medium. When suitably lit, the interference pattern diffracts the light into a reproduction of the original light field. The objects appear to be there, exhibiting visual depth cues, such as parallax and perspective that change realistically according to the relative position of the observer."

Jimmy cleared his throat, blinked and thrust out his chin as though he understood every word, while gesturing impatiently with the muzzle of his gun for the tour to move on.

His eyes widened with interest as they circled back to the pavilion. "What's this building?" he asked.

Rigel had a sinking feeling as he replied. "This is our center for meetings and other group activities."

The rover's eyes glittered as he stepped through the open door to scan the inside. Immediately, he saw this building and its location as an ideal base of operations. He'd even live in this space that housed a kitchen at one end and ample windows to watch the comings and goings of people from three directions.

"Well," he said, nodding approvingly, "your little town's about to have a real gov'nor now. Me and my crew are gonna plant ourselves right here. This here building's gonna be our headquarters. Anything needs to happen, starts right here with Gov'nor Jimmy."

Rigel thought fast. "This can be your temporary home while we build you a nice cabin."

Jimmy turned on him with condescending hostility. "I don't think you heard me, man." He gestured with his gun, waving the muzzle around the room. "I said this is where I'm gonna live and have my base of operations. Now, you run along and collect a crew to bring us some furniture to make this big empty room into a home and office. Marvin, you go with him, in case he needs any assistance gettin' our furnishings."

Marvin used this as an opportunity to show his own power by jabbing his rifle barrel in Rigel's ribs.

Rigel's brain raced as he and Marvin crossed the meadow, the communal hub that was usually filled with people coming and going, but was now overshadowed by a ghostly silence. Loath to place any families in danger, he headed first toward the nearest of two bunkhouses where he believed there were a couple of unused beds. But without remorse Marvin steered him to households to commandeer beds and furnishings from people's already sparsely furnished homes.

In the days following the unwelcome rover arrival, a pall hung over the normally friendly stir of life. Whenever Jimmy made a public appearance, either Martha, Phil or their child, Chris, well aware that a runaway attempt would mean being shot in the back, walked with him. Feeling bad for these personal slaves of the gang, the families felt they should do something, but what? An attempt to shoot the man with either bow or gun was just too risky. Besides, the retaliation of two enraged accomplices could mean bloodshed and even death to innocent people.

The days passed tainted with smoldering resentment and disgust, and the pervasive question: *What to do about the rovers?*

Jimmy stood in the doorway and scratched his belly under and around the leather belt that held the gun holster and munitions pouch. He smiled with the knowledge that he was owner of this green valley with a river running through it and three encapsulating mountains. He had never dreamed a takeover could be so easy, the people so compliant. Unfortunately, household searches had turned up no money, but food and clothing and other supplies were pouring in. The searches to confiscate weapons had revealed none. These spineless fools were not only penniless, they were unarmed.

Jimmy's house and headquarters staff included Martha as his cook and personal servant, Marvin as his personal bodyguard, Arnie as the perimeter guard, assigned the pavilion to keep an eye on the blind side where the shed was located, Phil as his go-fetch person, and Chris as his human shield.

After his initial gloating, Jimmy became bored with the ease of his takeover and abundance of food and supplies. He needed to increase his acquisitions in this little town.

People carefully hid their children away, concerned about the looks cast their way as they themselves passed within view of the three men. And, indeed, it was cunning calculations that arrested each look lasting more than a second on any passerby. Jimmy scanned for two main purposes: to acquire more hostages to serve him as part of his so-called staff and to find a wife to take care of him and all his personal needs. And not just any ole woman. He could've taken Martha whenever he wanted, but she was such a plain Jane, and he deserved better.

Jimmy recalled that pretty young thing he'd seen walking by while he was busy telling the moving crew where to put his bed. He'd put his hand on his gun, ready to shoot that wolf on sight if he showed any unfriendly traits. Momentarily diverted by furniture placement, the next time Jimmy scanned for the pretty teen with the wavy chestnut hair, she was several yards away headed into the trees between a gray-headed woman and an Injun. But he'd already decided she was to become his future wife.

Nathan observed the unfolding drama with disgust. These people were getting what they deserved. A rover takeover would never happen in Transtopia. Even if a gang of them gained a foothold in a small neighborhood, their reign would be brief. Martial law would be declared, and the entire police force would descend on the culprits in a speedy clean-up operation. From his point of view, Three Mountains Community, which prided itself on independent action, simply caved. They now lived in fear, hiding away their children, leaving the enslaved family to the mercy of this scoundrel and his accomplices.

Nathan's astute assessments included both the dangerous reactivity of Marvin and the furtive pliability of Arnie. Having failed to entice anyone at Three Mountains with a trek to Transtopia, Nathan had plans for Jimmy's more biddable sidekick.

The transplanted Transtopian's store of escape supplies was growing. Nathan now had a backpack, sleeping bag, dried fruit and berries, jerky, a bag of corn meal and a compass, which was his key to reaching home. Having piloted the plane to Quartz Mountain, he knew that he needed to head east, bearing about ten degrees north to reach Cyborg Highway at the now evacuated Pueblo, Colorado. He estimated the journey through the mountains would take about a month, but once he reached the heavily patrolled interstate, he could simply await a passing retriever car to hitch a ride home.

The third week of August nagged at Nathan that he'd better leave within three or four weeks to avoid traveling after the onset of winter. The one essential item he had failed to access was a gun, which would be a vital necessity for the trek home.

Nathan had taken the full measure of Arnie, who did have a gun, and, noting his cowering obeisance to Jimmy's brutal treatment, formulated a plan. His challenge was to befriend Arnie, to entice him with the prospect of living out from under Jimmy's thumb and being his own man in Transtopia. Then he'd draw Arnie into his escape plans. They'd have the gun for protection and killing small game. Then, somewhere along the trek home, he would wrest the gun from the rover.

Nathan was good at hanging around to wait for the right moment to achieve his ends. But in this case he instinctively knew he'd better stay clear of Jimmy's scrutiny, or he'd become one of Jimmy's personal slaves. He noticed that Arnie often sat on the corner of the porch that bordered the blind spot, the windowless end of the building that housed the shed at the end of the pavilion. That was the direction from which Nathan casually, albeit cautiously, approached the porch guard.

After guarded introductions, he asked, "So what's it like working for Jimmy?"

"What's it to you?"

"I was just wondering if this is a job you particularly like."

"It's okay sometimes. Not so good other times. When he gets riled, you better watch out."

"Ever flown in a plane?"

"No, and don't think I ever want to."

"Well, okay."

"So why'd you ask?"

"'Cause I'm looking for a co-pilot."

"Well, I certainly can't fly a plane."

"Of course not. But you can learn, can't you?"

"So, what's better about that job than mine?"

"Pilots make good money. And we're not anybody's puppet."

That jab angered Arnie. "I ain't nobody's puppet. I decided on my own to join this outfit."

"Okay. Just forget I said anything."

"Arnie, where are you, you lazy good-for-nothing?" Jimmy bellowed.

As Arnie jumped up to head for the front door, Nathan hurried out of sight behind the storage shed.

Jimmy boxed his assistant in the ear. "Took you long enough." Since Phil was busy scratching something on a piece of wood, the governor ordered Arnie, who was rubbing his sore ear, to go fetch a hammer from the toolshed. Jimmy had pulled down the sign with the name Pavilion on one side, and flipped it over to write his own name for the building. Arnie followed Jimmy's instructions to nail the new Headquarters sign onto the roofline.

The
Foyer

34

An upstairs curtain moved slightly as Dora's mother noted her daughter's arrival. Impeccably groomed, she took a last look in the full-length mirror and told her husband the kids had arrived.

Throughout her married life, Lila had focused her managerial abilities on the efficient running of the household, smoothing the way to success for her husband and daughter. She had enrolled Dora in exclusive schools to be taught by the best teachers, and to extend her daughter's accomplishments, she had faithfully taken her to ballet, singing, painting, tennis and horseback riding lessons.

Managing the serving staff and overseeing the planning and seamless operation of dinner parties and gala events, which included guest lists, invitations, décor, entertainment, delectable menus and the free flow of drinks, amounted to a full-time career. Prescription drugs assisted Lila through the strictly defined perimeters of her life.

Prior to Solar Flash, and well hidden from public view, Lila's husband, Peter d'Arc, chaired Nolan Pharmaceuticals, Global Financial, and d'Arc Industries. One of the wealthiest, most powerful families on Earth, they were among those who considered themselves to be the Landlords of the World.

Post-Solar Flash, with the elite families' numbers and circumstances reduced, along with the underlings, most of the remaining landlords had had been demoted to the reign of tiny segments of surviving population. Lila's new role, now that Peter was Governor General, was similar to the old, but on a much smaller scale.

Dora's mother approached the top of the landing to await her husband to join her so they could descend the stairs together.

The butler's manner was formal as he opened the front door, while his eyes twinkled affection for Dora. Caellum placed the incongruous physics book on the foyer table and the butler ushered the pair through massive double doors to the family room. As they walked across the shining hardwood floors, roses splaying from a Grecian urn at the hearth exuded a fragrant welcome. In the light streaming from the diamond-shaped panes of a bay window, the pair stood expectantly, fingers entwined. Feeling dwarfed by the paneled cathedral ceiling, Caellum stood on high alert, his gaze probing the spaces between massive oak beams.

Entering with the aplomb of a gala event, Dora's parents breezed into the room. After a peck on the cheek from her mother and a warm hug from her father, Dora introduced Caellum. Lila smiled a greeting and Peter shook Caellum's hand with friendly formality. Small talk filled the introductory space until the butler announced that dinner was served.

As soon as they were seated, a servant poured wine in crystal goblets, while another came behind ladling steaming asparagus soup into bowls, prelude to a wild greens salad with cranberries and pecans. During the main course, lobster bisque yielded to hungry assaults, and the diners loaded and reloaded forks with potatoes au gratin and mushrooms. Amid slight *clinks* of silver on china, talk boomeranged between the pre-Solar Flash conquests of d'Arc Enterprises and the present day Techno City college campus schools of physics and physical therapy.

Peter d'Arc forked tender lobster meat as he addressed Caellum. "Are professors still discussing the theory of the holographic universe?"

Caught off guard, Caellum cleared his throat, his mind racing. Aware that Dora was staring at him, his gaze crossed swords with that of her father. "Yes, sir. I'm convinced that the more we know about this world, the less anything is as it seems."

Peter's eyes widened momentarily, as though he sensed his daughter's date was dueling with him.

Adept at filling awkward moments, Lila rushed to steer the conversation in a new direction. "So, Dora, dear, is your latest patient progressing well?"

Neutralized conversation continued through the chocolate mousse dessert, after which Dora's mother suggested they retire to the family room. Anxious not to forget the physics book and what was inside, Gavin mentally noted its location on the table as they crossed the foyer to return to the family room.

Overstuffed sofas and chairs invited the group to relax around the fireplace. Dora's father poured himself a whiskey, joking about his need for a couple of these to unwind each evening, and settled in his favorite chair. Dora's mother, looking the most relaxed Caellum had seen her, sat ensconced by a sofa arm, facing the young lovers, who sat appropriately on the loveseat.

Listening to Dora's parents share humorous anecdotes about her childhood, it was obvious to Caellum that they had both lavished love and attention on her. Somehow, they had cocooned her from the despair and ugliness in the world, safeguarding not only her naïveté, but her innate sweetness as well.

Dora's parents also politely and thoroughly probed to obtain a complete inventory of Caellum's upbringing—especially lineage, education and likely career assignment. Not that he was a candidate for anything more than dating. The d'Arcs and the Scholtzses already had an agreement with regard to Dora and Shaun.

In anticipation of a parental interrogation, Caellum had prepared a fabricated and well-rehearsed version of his life, including the lie that he had been transferred from Township 26 to Techno City to earn a degree in physics.

When the grandfather clock struck nine o'clock Dora smiled gratefully at her parents. "We should go now."

Companionably, the group strolled into the atrium and the youths continued through the front door. As Caellum and Dora stood on the sidewalk saying their final goodbyes, a surge of alarm jolted Caellum.

"Oh, my physics book!" he exclaimed starting toward the door.

"I've got it," said Dora's father. As he reached for the book, his unsteady hand knocked it sideways and it fell, spewing a fan of brochures across the floor.

Peter picked up the book, but as his wife gathered the scattered pamphlets, his eyes were riveted to the tri-folds and he reached for one. After a quizzical glance, he placed it on the table. "Hope you don't mind," he grinned.

Caellum watched the whole scene in slow motion horror, smiling weakly as Dora's mother handed him the book and the neatly restacked pamphlets. Dora, assuming the brochures were from the college, didn't think to question that there were ten of them and watched the scene unconcerned.

As the Subaru sped away, Caellum muttered, "My goose is cooked."

Dora looked at Caellum in astonishment. "My parents really like you. I'm sure of it." She squeezed his hand. "You worry too much."

Mindful of the driver, Caellum stayed silent until they reached the dorm. Once they were out of the car, he asked Dora to join him at a park bench under a tree on the front lawn.

"I have a lot to tell you," he said. "But read this first."

She took the pamphlet and walked to the front porch to read it in the light, which spotlighted her facial contours. Caellum watched the upturned contours of her mouth, signifying an open invitation to understanding, tighten and morph into a downward arc that screamed broiling resentment. She walked toward him, the offending document gripped in one hand.

"Caellum, my father is implicated in these contrived inversions of the truth."

He stared at her, aware that the person who had sat beside him on the loveseat now stood across a chasm, trembling with outrage.

"Why are you carrying these things around?"

Caellum avoided her questions by asking one of his own. "Dora, when you were tested for a career path, what did the results show?"

She looked at him wide-eyed. "I've never been tested. It's simply assumed that in the future I will hold a position of responsibility in running this sector. In the meantime, because of my interest in physical therapy, an exception has been made for me."

"And is the plan for you to live in a housing unit?"

"Well, no. A house will be provided for me."

Caellum leveled a penetrating gaze at her. "Dora, how many people do you think obtain exceptions to assigned career paths, or have two-story houses promised to them? By what right do elite families like yours assume they will manage the rest of us?"

Incomprehension marbleized the patrician countenance.

Caellum continued. "In answer to your question, I was slotted to join the police force."

Caellum was aware of shattering his projected image into confusing shards.

Dora shook her head. "But I assumed you would either be assigned a career as an engineer or college professor."

"I'm not attending college, Dora. But I have mapped out my own career."

"And what career is that?"

"To defend the right of each and every person to have an equal opportunity to find their own way, to live their own passion. I stand by an egalitarian society of sovereign individuals and will fight for it 'til my dying breath."

"Egalitarian?"

"Putting it mildly, I don't support the idea of a ruling elite."

Dora looked at Caellum as if he were a complete stranger. "You aren't who I thought you to be. You have limited education and no definable goals. You refute everything my wise and loving father has taught me about myself and my role on behalf of humanity."

Through the dark void of silence, Caellum saw in Dora's face the beginning of the end. Lovingly, he pushed back a renegade strand of ebony hair. "Dora," he asked softly, "can it be that you see the people you want to help as inferiors? Can it be that I am now included in that group?"

Dora crumpled the brochure as with a look of numb exhaustion, she barely met his gaze across the chasm of their differences. "Goodbye, Caellum." She turned and walked through the front door of the dorm.

After sitting frozen in shock for several minutes, Caellum walked to James's apartment and fell on the couch fully dressed, hoping the oblivion of sleep would bring escape from the black hole that ravaged his heart.

Protectively, the men in Three Mountains insisted that the women remain out of sight of the rovers. This meant either staying indoors or sneaking out back doors to move about, screened by pine trees and cabins.

Jimmy, for his part, was perfectly aware of what was happening. The hiding away of the women accented his determination to attain one. But that was second to the foremost dream that soon consumed him. While the pavilion was the best headquarters the community offered, it didn't quite suit his needs.

Meats and garden produce flowed to his headquarters by way of hefty single males to keep the rovers from going door to door. But that suited Jimmy just fine and gave him plenty of time to think about how to improve his circumstances.

The problem with the pavilion was that he couldn't see all the way around the valley. That blind side of the building walled by the shed where the roof sloped to the ground was a source of frustration and suspicion. He figured that if he were in a two-story dwelling, with windows on all four walls, he would have a three hundred sixty-degree view of all the comings and goings of the inhabitants of the village. After all, since he was the boss, or governor, or whatever, he deserved to have a centrally located dwelling and center of operations that was more impressive than those of the ordinary citizens.

So, just as despots have done for countless centuries, he conscripted a workforce to build a new and more impressive abode. Arnie and Marvin set about collecting a work crew at gun point, herding them to the front of the pavilion for instructions from Jimmy. Soon, a crew of twelve men began sawing down young pines and hauling logs to the work site. Jimmy established Chas as the overseer of the construction and Marvin and Arnie as guards to keep the labor force in line. They alternated shifts standing guard at the workplace and patrolling the perimeter of the valley with a family member in tow.

Delays

35

Gavin was beside himself with concern for Leslie. He simply couldn't go back and forth through the portal and resume explorations beyond Three Mountains while she was endangered in the lab. Unlike the cabins, which were located among the pines, the science lab was out in the open, not more than a hundred yards from the pavilion. He imagined that any females would be at risk, but especially a petite, pretty one like Leslie. Besides, the others had husbands to protect them. Leslie had him.

He considered whisking her through the back door, but that meant a fifty-yard run up a grassy slope to the base of Thunderbird Mountain, and he knew that above the roofline of the lab, the slope was easily visible from the pavilion. And Augurs couldn't fly at night.

However, the construction proved a great boon to a possible rescue since the project consumed the bulk of the attention of two rovers. While either Arnie or Marvin guarded the perimeter of the valley, Jimmy barked loud commands, yelling expletives and ordering lazy good-for-nothings to get to work, as the second rover watched his back. A plan formed in Gavin's mind. The back door of the science lab opened to an attached yard, which was fenced-in on three and a half sides and served as a storage area for excess lab equipment. It was large enough to hold Phoenix for a few minutes.

Everything in Gavin rebelled at the thought of once again risking the life of an augur. However, as he continued to watch the proceedings of the rovers and work crew through his binoculars, he reasoned that if whoever was walking the perimeter was at the far side of the valley, and the other two were focused on the construction, he should have plenty enough time to fly in, collect Leslie, and fly away with her. He was certain that Phoenix was large and strong enough to hold the two of them, especially since Leslie didn't weigh much, and he was lightweight for a male.

When his idea had jelled, he radioed Steve and asked him to give the radio to Leslie. Forgoing the normal protocol his voice was forceful. "It's not safe for you there."

"Don't be silly. The rovers never come near this place."

"Nathan heard Jimmy talking."

"So what did he say?"

"He said Jimmy's other priority, besides the construction, is to get more women for his household."

"Well, he doesn't even know I'm here."

"Do you expect to imprison yourself in that building?"

Silence. "No."

"I'm taking you away from there."

"But I'm needed for the hologram work. We're so close to completion."

"You won't be able to help if, instead of me, a rover takes you away."

"They're not going to be interested in me."

"You're exactly what they'll be interested in. I'm flying you away on Phoenix."

"But—"

"We'll have a plan to get rid of them soon. Then you can return."

"I just need a little more time."

"I'm coming the first time there's an all-clear."

Three days later, as Gavin flew Phoenix around the perimeter, he saw his chance. Marvin was at the opposite end of the valley from the science building, while the construction absorbed the attention of the other two rovers.

Gavin radioed the lab. "Steve, tell Leslie I'm coming."

Silence. "Okay."

He flew Phoenix low over the trees and swooped down for a steep landing in the rear, fenced enclosure with a gateless opening on one side. Tethering the augur among piles of electrical cords and copper wiring, he ran into the lab and yelled for Leslie. When there was no response, he hurriedly looked into the bunkhouse, then turned toward her lab to look inside. Still no Leslie. He rushed through the main lab toward the one that housed the holograph equipment.

Steve and Leslie were hunched over a keyboard peering at a computer screen.

"Come on," Gavin shouted.

Leslie turned with an impatience he hadn't seen before. "Gavin, sit down. We have to finish this step in activation. We're at a vital threshold."

"There's no time," he insisted.

She put out her hand, pointer finger raised in a commanding *wait one moment* gesture.

Gavin collapsed onto a chair. As he sat with his elbows on his knees, chin on knuckles, he felt the successive minutes stretch into the time in which danger could be imminent.

Arnie could hardly believe his eyes.

"Hey, I just saw a giant bird fly down behind the science lab.

Jimmy looked disgusted. "You better not been drinkin' my whiskey."

Arnie fell silent. He knew what he saw, whether that fool believed it or not. He stood sullenly watching the work continue, periodically peering in the direction of the lab.

After a few minutes Chas suggested they delay construction to go cut down more trees.

Jimmy looked at Arnie. "You go with them."

As directed, Arnie followed the men into the forest. But as soon as they were occupied, he cut loose. He had to find out about that huge blue bird. If caught, he'd get a verbal and physical beating from Jimmy. Nonetheless, he had to see this thing. Hidden from Jimmy's sight by the row of community households and pines, he hurried toward the far end of the valley.

Finally, the scientists looked up. And they didn't look happy. "So close and yet so far," Steve murmured, shaking his head.

Leslie was obviously irritated at Gavin. "You're too much of a worrier. I'm needed here."

Gavin stood his ground, his eyes pleading. "I'm not leaving without you."

Leslie sighed with exasperation. "I have to gather some things."

"Please hurry."

For another eternity he waited for her to return from the bunkhouse.

Obviously still put out with Gavin, Leslie gestured with her chin.

Gavin bolted from the chair and headed out the back door.

Then dismay shook him to the core. "Oh no." Copper wire and cable were wrapped around Phoenix's neck in a tangled mesh.

"Oh, Phoenix, I should have known," he groaned. He attempted to gently remove a section of wire from the maze, but the movement tightened a copper noose around the bird's neck. Leslie started to giggle at the fix Phoenix was in, but a dark look from Gavin quickly squelched all mirth. She tried to help, but every time she came close to the augur, he attacked her, driving the wire farther into his neck.

"I have to do it," Gavin said forcefully.

Leslie sighed and sat down on her bedroll to wait.

Strand by strand, cable by cable, Gavin patiently freed the augur.

"Oh, Phoenix, I'm so sorry," he said when he spied a thin red line on the bird's neck.

Time and patience had changed his disposition. "I'm sorry for the way I treated you, Leslie. It's just that I love you so much."

"I know. It's just that the hologram problem won't let go of my brain."

As Gavin gingerly slipped the last bit of wire over Phoenix's head, he could tell she wished she were at the computer. "We'll be back soon. I'm sure of it." He strode to the corner where his bow and quiver leaned against the fence.

As Gavin reached the shadowed edge of the enclosure, a visitor showed up in the opening to the yard.

"Well, I'll be," Arnie declared, his eyes shifting from the bird to Leslie. "I ain't never seen nothin' like this in my life."

Speechless, Leslie eyed the intruder.

"Now, you know, sweet thing, I'm gonna have to take you with me to make my boss happy on two counts. First, 'cause he's been wantin' a pretty woman for our household. And second, 'cause I gotta prove I was right about big bird here." He pointed the gun at her. "Now, you jist—"

Arnie's sentence was interrupted with a loud cry as an arrow sliced through his forearm, the force sending the gun flying against a wall.

"Leslie," Gavin shouted, "get on now!"

Terrified to come within close range of the beak, she stood frozen.

Gavin pulled her to the rear of Phoenix. "Step over the tail."

Robotically, she followed his frantic command.

"Lean forward."

She froze, expecting one of Phoenix's lethal lunges.

Standing behind her, Gavin pushed her down and fell on top of her, communicating to Phoenix to lift off. "Grab her neck with me," he commanded.

At the same time, the rover, who had been screaming in pain, stumbled across the enclosure to get his pistol.

As the bird rose over the fence, he fired a shot with his left hand. The bullet tore through Gavin's shoulder. Unbearable pain from the arrow skewed the second shot. The rover dropped the gun to grip his right arm as the bird and riders flew out of sight.

Behind the screen of pines, alarmed by the sound of gunfire, people watched the moaning man with an arrow sticking through his arm stumble along the river toward the pavilion. When Jimmy broke the arrow and pulled the lodged portion through, agonized screams echoed through the valley until the relieved silence that ensued provided a hushed backdrop for murmured speculations in homes about what had just occurred.

By the time Martha was finished cleaning and wrapping Arnie's arm, Phoenix had landed near Leiani's nest.

"I can't believe I didn't get his gun," Gavin lamented, wincing as Leiani and Leslie removed his shirt. Fortunately, the bullet passed all the way through. After Leslie gently washed the entrance and exit wounds, Leiani applied her salve and gave him aspirin to dull the pain.

Nobility

36

"You what?" James shouted, alarm stamped on his features.

"After seeding I had no time to bring the book here, so I took it with me to Dora's."

"And?"

"Dora's father, who had been drinking, knocked the book from a table, and the brochures spilled out. He kept one."

James groaned. "Taking the brochures with you was a stupid move." Vehemence charged each word.

Shamefaced, Caellum agreed. "We—our mission is in serious jeopardy."

"And you." James shook his head. "You're dead in the water. You'd better get out of town tonight."

Caellum nodded. "Listen, James, we've got seven spreaders now. After I leave, can you start attending the meetings to lend them support?"

James nodded reflectively. "Okay, I'll do it."

"I'm taking twenty-five pamphlets to the campus with me today. I'll leave fifty with you."

James looked at him in disbelief. "You can't seed today. That would be suicide. And if this place gets raided...."

Caellum didn't say anything. He just looked steadily at his friend.

"All right." James sighed. "Help me find a good place to hide them."

They scoured the apartment, imagining a raid in which every drawer, cabinet and container would be emptied of its contents. Finally, James hit on an idea when he looked at his laundry hamper. He placed the bag of brochures in the bottom between the floor of the tall rectangular basket and the cloth laundry bag that served as a liner.

Later that morning Caellum left for a scheduled meeting with Neil. As he walked, the moan of a hot desert wind mocked the silent outcry of his heart. Its force held the building door closed to his entrance and retaliated against his defiant jerk on the handle by shoving him into the hall.

Neil's voice was friendly, his countenance welcoming with no sign of his initial reserve. Caellum dove for the nearest chair to regurgitate his revelation. "Peter d'Arc has seen the brochures."

As Neil listened, his quiet composure made Caellum ashamed of his initial impatient criticalness during their first encounter.

Neil stood up to peer at the campus sidewalks. "You must leave right away."

Inscribed on Caellum's face was a burning question.

Neil grabbed Caellum's shoulders. "Don't worry. We'll keep the momentum. I'll even print more brochures."

Closing the office door behind him, Caellum headed downstairs, the infamous physics book in hand and stuffed with brochures one last time. Pushing open the door, he lowered his head against the blast of hot wind shrieking into the hall. As he walked to a sidewalk intersection and looked at his watch, vengeful gusts hurled grains of sand that stung his face. Classes would be letting out in a couple of minutes, his opportunity for seeding.

As he turned to sit on a nearby bench, he was halted as someone roughly grabbed his forearm. "By order of the Governor General of Sector 10, you are under arrest for high treason against the Union of the Americas of the World Federation."

The book fell to the sidewalk. As though summoned by the click of the handcuffs, a capricious gust swirled around the pamphlets. Caellum watched in dismay as wayward mini-twisters scattered the brochures like dry leaves across the campus lawn.

Students spilling from classes stopped and stared as though wondering what crime the captive had committed. Some smirked their support of the police, while others silently stood apart as though repulsed by the sight of a captured human being. Several ran around the grounds chasing and grabbing brochures.

When Neil stepped onto the sidewalk the wind ballooned his blousy shirt and whipped hair in front of his eyes. Pushing aside the black and gray strands, he saw the police stuffing someone into a squad car, so he hurried forward, straining to see the profile behind the window as the car sped away. A sense of dread told him who that person was.

A woman turned a camera lens toward him. "Sir, what can you tell us about the alleged enemy operative? Was he one of your students?"

Her questions were directed at a palm firmly planted over the aperture.

The latest news clip of the recent apprehension of the dangerous insurgent Caellum Nichols, followed by Governor Scholtz's fatherly assurances of protection, smoothed the way for a segue into an additional warning. Assuming a pained expression, he advised the citizens, "According to the latest intelligence, a ring of insurgents may be hiding in your midst. Beware of treasonous operatives spreading propaganda against the Pan-American Union. We count on your loyalty in reporting literature and/or individuals attempting to incite rebellion against our sovereign nation."

Dora was appalled as she sat in the college theater and watched the media practically try to convict Caellum, portraying him as an alleged enemy operative who was a danger to the citizens of Techno City. She was equally shocked at her own defensive reaction. *Caellum, the champion of the people.*

Wanting to complain to someone in a position of authority, she went to her father, who feigned surprise.

Her own vehemence surprised her. "Who owns the media anyway?" she asked with an edge in her voice.

He looked her straight in the eye. "Basically, we do."

Dora stared at her father in disbelief.

"Over seventy years ago an assembly of pure bloods, of which we are a part, realized that media plays a vital role in managing the masses. Sensational news stories can fuel people's passions. They can either trigger resistance movements that complicate or even stymie our plans, or incite public loyalty. It was expedient to control the dissemination of information to the public, and thereby orchestrate the reactive masses."

"But how?" Dora assumed independent agencies released the latest news.

"Our corporate appendages absorbed hundreds of independent news syndicates. During the decades leading to Solar Flash, there were only six, all of which were directly under our control. Since then newscasters read only the scripts our editors cut, paste, slant and fabricate as instructed."

Dora stared out her Dad's office window. *Scripted.* She hid her disgust from her father's scrutiny. "Dad, Caellum is not 'an enemy of the people'."

"He is attempting to destroy our way of life. Do you want mobs of dissenters killing SEI officials in the streets? Can you imagine them gathering around our home, throwing rocks through our windows and capturing us, even killing us?"

Behind her father's stern expression Dora saw fear for the first time. "Caellum simply wants more rights for the common people."

"The only way for Caellum to get what he wants is to take away our rightful legacy as the ruling lineage."

"Maybe we control them too much."

"The workers are here to serve us. Nothing more."

"Because of our lineage?"

"Because of our *superior* lineage."

Dora recalled the strong feelings she had felt watching a movie about Queen Elizabeth I. The queen saw herself as a mother to the people of her realm, implying a caring and thoughtful intent behind her reign over their lives. This was the attitude that had absorbed Dora and tinged her dreams of the future when her father spoke of royal obligations.

Caellum had shaken that worldview. Dora stared at her larger-than-life parent as the revered image shrank, his diminished stature that of an alarmed defender of his turf, no different from the underlings he spurned. That fateful night she had been correct in her vehement accusation that Caellum was nothing like her father. The insurgent's image, suddenly superimposed over her dad's face, struck her with a startling realization. *Nobility and royalty are not synonymous.*

The conversation dead-ended with her father affectionately patronizing her. "Dora, one day you will pull the strings on the world stage. By all means, do so kindly, but wisely, or the herd will stampede itself right over a cliff."

The herd. Since childhood she had listened to condescending depictions without questioning them. Suddenly, she felt ashamed. Caellum was right. Until now she had viewed herself as assisting inferiors. Caellum risked his life to help those he viewed as equals. A noble, albeit foolish, quest.

The news clip that followed the announcement of the apprehension of the insurgent Caellum Nichols was addressed to a receptive public. Governor Charles Scholtz insisted on the need for stepped-up martial law drills, and he won the whole-hearted support of Region 21.

During the raids, the city streets became silent while citizens remained indoors for several hours. Police appeared on the streets and SWAT teams spilled out of vehicles to bang on household doors. Upon gaining entrance, squads rifled through shelves and drawers, contents spilling to floors, searching for materials disseminated by enemy operatives.

As Dora approached her dad's office, he was on the telephone. "Hello, Charles."

Imperial Governor Scholtz. Seized by dread, she stopped just beyond the doorframe.

"We've discovered an underground ring of insurgents...yes, yes... I agree."

Long silence. The volatile governor must be ranting.

"We've captured the ring leader... name's Caellum Nichols... absolutely... you and the ministers a week from today."

Nausea twisted Dora's gut. The coming meeting would seal Caellum's fate.

That night it must have been the phone conversation that caused the nightmare. In the dream, she followed Caellum down a flight of stairs into a musty basement, a ring of old keys rattling at his side. As cobwebs from the low ceiling attached themselves to her hair, she clutched the railing and frantically brushed away the sticky strands.

When they reached the floor, Caellum led her to a line of three doorways and handed her the keys. Fumbling for the right key she opened the first door. Rows of paintings of costumed royalty spanning countless generations and cultures leered at her. Some held diminutive adult humans on their laps, while others stretched out hands with blood dripping from their fingers. Repelled, she slammed that door, only to be irresistibly drawn to open the second.

Beyond the vault of the second door were bodies piled in front of people with animal-like expressions hacking one another to death. Yet oddly, atop a mountain backdrop to the struggle, a knight held a banner with a coat of arms high in one hand and a sword with a jewel bedecked gold crown resting on the hilt in the other.

Dora hastily closed the second door. As she peered through the third, chained skeletons sat up in their caskets, grinning at her. And in the midst of the rattling bones and clanking metal, the most repugnant giant scorpion she had ever seen raised up on six legs and reached toward her, waving its treacherous pincers. Repelled by the bizarre blue eyes that penetrated her own, she dropped the keys and fled up the stairs.

Beyond the basement door her father waited, the dim light accenting skeletal features, blood dripping from his fingers and splattering onto the floor. To his side a crowd of hollow-eyed people gripped the bars that held them prisoner. Caellum pushed past her holding the key that would free them, but at her father's command, uniformed men dragged him away.

After a night of inner torment Dora made a decision. She must dissuade Caellum from his reckless quest.

Eena could barely hear the connector for the high wind.

"...twen.... Over."

"Too much wind noise. Is the forty mile marker secured? Over."

"Forty... Saturday. Over."

Relieved, Eena wished the connectors luck and clicked off her radio.

With the first connector in position at the farmhouse south of Highway 160, the other two headed out Saturday morning. By early afternoon, the second connecter was in place at Lake Nighthorse. The third reached Cinder Gulch by Saturday evening.

Soon after sunrise Sunday morning, the closest connector began attempting to establish contact. "Caellum, Mike here ready and waiting at Cinder Gulch. Over. Caellum, do you read me? Over."

Wearing a simple powder blue shift, Dora brushed her hair until it shone and applied berry-tinted balm to her lips. Then she walked to the corner and caught the next trolley. She could hardly believe she was headed for the jail. But she had to see Caellum.

The guard pointed and Dora walked an open hallway lined with bars. For an unguarded instant when she locked eyes with Caellum, a stream of uncensored longing coursed between them.

After hesitant and halted greetings, she blurted the question she was burning to ask. "Would you like to hear the short version of a tale my father has told me since childhood?"

Startled, his curiosity piqued, Caellum nodded for her to speak.

"According to a legend handed down through our family for countless generations, over two hundred thousand years ago, our ancestor, Anu, conspired with other technologically-advanced races. Evidently, this led to a huge rebellion in our galaxy."

Caellum furrowed his brow, puzzled at this weird beginning.

"A group, our progenitors, escaped to this planet and settled here. They established gardens and gold mining operations, but the atmosphere was not hospitable to them, and the labor, unendurable. So, with Anu's consent, they engineered a hybrid race of workers suitable to tend the gardens and mine the gold. Anu's son, Enki, continued to genetically upgrade the race and teach them skills otherwise known only to the progenitors.

"In time, the progenitors began to sicken and die off. In order to prevent dying out completely, they created progenitor and human hybrids that could survive and manage the workers. It was decreed that these particular progeny not mate with the rest of the population to keep the ruling bloodline as pure as possible. Since then, those descendants, the royal bloods, have directed empires from Ancient Sumer to Egypt to Rome to Great Britain."

Caellum listened to her outlandish story with disgust.

Dora avoided his gaze. "My point is that as a destined leader I can do much to incrementally restore humanity's independence."

"Destined ruler, you mean. Benevolent or otherwise, I don't accede to the right of you or your kind to curtail my freedoms." The vehemence in Caellum's voice struck like steel darts.

"Can't you see how smoothly this city is running thanks to careful planning and oversight? People would be subject to tyrannical overlords without the resources and expertise my father commands."

"Social engineering," Caellum interjected.

Dora looked at Caellum blankly.

"The manipulation of people by appealing to their psychological desires and fears, using deception as needed, in order to ensure their acquiescence to the control of a ruling elite."

Dora looked at the floor, uncomfortably absorbing this echo of her new knowledge about the contrived media. With a change of tactics, she poured her feelings through her gaze. "Caellum, I'm here because I love you. I can't help myself. I want to see you free. If you will simply stop passing out those pamphlets and associating with insurgents, I'm sure I can persuade my father to order your release. I can even become a liaison between the royal bloods and you and other freedom-seekers."

Caellum returned her gaze, his own cold. "You just don't get it. There won't be liaisons. Only replacements."

"I... I understand now about your egalitarian goals. I want to help."

He turned his back to her and hardened his voice. "Just leave. Leave now."

"Caellum," she pleaded.

But he remained obdurate.

Wiping the unbidden tears from her eyes, she walked past the jailer and out the door.

Enticements

37

Carla couldn't believe her eyes. As the enormous grizzly emerged from the forest, she grabbed Rose, ran into their cabin and handed the child to her astonished husband. "Keep her inside."

As the huge paws padded silently across the grass, Carla saw a neighbor working in the garden, oblivious. Seeing that the bear's trajectory was several yards from the hunched-over figure harvesting radishes, Carla considered yelling but decided that could excite the animal and further endanger the gardener, so she watched in helpless suspense.

Ursus arctos had already progressed several feet ahead before the shocked gardener stood up and rushed toward his home. Carla's gaze shifted down the valley where figures gestured and suddenly darted away. As the grizzly continued its casual, even pace, more startled people melted into the forest, acceding the heart of the community to the steadily advancing intruder.

Approaching the pavilion, the grizzly stopped several feet from the door. As if disconcerted that the building was in his path, he swung his head and shook his trunk, sending waves of cinnamon sheen rippling across his coat. Then he rose up to his full eight-foot height and emitted a terrifying roar that rent the valley and ricocheted off the mountainsides. Even the birds stopped their songs in the shocked silence that filled the valley. As if satisfied with his challenge, the animal dropped to all fours and swerved right, toward Thunderbird Mountain at a quickened pace.

A particularly vehement string of profanity spewing from Jimmy was the only retort, heard only by the startled inhabitants of the pavilion. This was his rest day, when work was halted, and without distraction he could contemplate the next stage of his plans, which included Cosima. If she didn't come willingly, he'd capture her. And he wasn't going to have that wolf anywhere near, which was why he was going to shoot it.

Marvin stood at the window, his eyes glowing like black coals as he eyed the grizzly trotting across the bridge. Suddenly the swarthy man sprang into action.

"I'm gonna get me a bear," he bellowed with excitement unusual for his brooding nature.

Grabbing his rifle, he tore through the front door, ran across the deck, jumped to the ground and ran toward the bridge in pursuit of his enormous prey. When he reached the opposite side of the river, the bear was moving at a fast clip. The hunter stopped long enough to get the target in his gun site and fire. The echoing gun report sent shivers of dread through the spectators positioned on porches and behind windows.

The bullet grazed the retreating animal's hindquarters with a painful rip of flesh that caused him to break into a gallop. Determined not to let his trophy escape, Marvin quickened his pace in hot pursuit. Within seconds, the bear disappeared in the forest of Thunderbird Mountain followed by the hunter running as fast as his legs would carry him.

Unadulterated bloodlust drove the man to follow the receding patches of reddish-brown. Finally, the forest swallowed the bear in a cloak of invisibility, so that the hunter pursued him blind. But *Ursus arctos* couldn't elude an expert tracker that easily. Marvin's eyes caught tiny details missed by most: a broken twig, a tiny swipe of blood or a slight impression of a fresh paw print. The trail led straight up Thunderbird Mountain, or as straight as possible through the ponderosa sentinels that closed ranks behind the wounded animal.

Slowed by pain the grizzly limped through a clearing graced by a Lakota teepee. Just as he reached the far side, his heavily panting pursuer spotted him through a clump of young pines.

With renewed jubilance, Marvin quickened his pace. The ponderosas yielded to spruce trees that spread their pine needle skirts protectively behind the illustrious descendant of the grizzlies that had once roamed the Rockies this far south.

Tracking through the higher, rockier terrain became impossible, even for one as experienced as Marvin. But a hunch that the animal was continuing up the mountain drove him forward.

With increasing frequency the hunter stopped to gulp down air, his heart pounding violently against his chest, but driven by a merciless determination, he punished his protesting lungs until he had to stop. He stumbled toward a rocky ridge a few yards above and, gasping for air, collapsed.

The sun-warmed stone that cradled his cheek evoked the long buried memory of an embrace—one that was warm, but soft rather than hard. And in that long forgotten closeness, the comforting sound of a familiar heartbeat quieted the child's alarmed screams and soothed his rapidly beating heart. For a time the entrained hearts had merged as one into an ocean of calm. Ensconced in the bliss of a mother's love, he had rested until some brutal outside force ripped him from that comforting breast with a devastating finality. Ever since that moment the tender child buried in the hardened man had sought consolation for his loss.

Marvin's pulse slowed to normal, and he raised his head to look around. Confused by the descent into the mists of early childhood, he stood up, refocusing on his established trajectory: to hunt and kill his prey, to satisfy some unfulfilled lust to conquer. He searched the 360-degree perimeter, including the jagged seventy-foot drop on one side.

When eight-foot *Ursus* rose before him and emitted a shattering roar, he automatically fired his rifle. But as the bullet pierced nothing but air overhead, huge claws tore the weapon from his grasp. Blood spurted from a gaping wound as the powerful swipe ripped his arm from his body. Brutally assaulted by the enraged bear, the limp body flopped to the edge of the stone promontory. As the dismembered shell rolled over the cliff, oblivion cushioned the freefall of the retreating spirit called to the beckoning breast.

Exhausted by his flight and fight for survival, the grizzly slumped onto the vacated ledge, his right flank throbbing. For several days he lay still to bask in the ministry of the healing rays of the sun and stars, until the violated tissue mended, and the trees welcomed him into their midst again.

Matoskah informed the community of the fate of the rover the day before Nathan casually approached Arnie a second time. Escalating abuse from Jimmy had caused him to reflect on his role as submissive whipping boy.

A pilot. Now that would give him some deserved status. He reckoned he could be Nathan's co-pilot for a time and then knock him off and become the solo pilot.

When the pavilion guard, his arm bandaged and in a sling, saw Nathan sneaking up to the corner of the deck, he was ready for him.

"I'll go with you," he said simply. "But you better mind your Ps and Qs 'cause this gun's coming with me."

Feeling an edgy mixture of excitement and alarm, Nathan nodded assent, and the two agreed to meet just after sundown.

According to plan, as soon as the last light faded from the summit of Quartz Mountain to the west, Arnie ran across the grass. When he reached Nathan, he grabbed the bedroll and backpack, and they hurried through the trees. Nathan dimmed the flashlight and pointed it to the ground, so that the moving light wouldn't be visible from the valley.

When Jimmy yelled for Arnie, he expected him to come through the door in short order. Irate with the delayed response, he hurled an abusive string of expletives and unflattering titles at the damned good-for-nothing. When no response greeted his shouts, Jimmy banged the flask on the table and angrily jumped from his chair, which clattered loudly to the floor from its tilted-against-the-wall position. The family members instinctively moved closer together for protection from the blustering, banging and clattering.

Jimmy peered into the night. Fearing that he was now down two men, he turned his impotent rage on the huddled hostages. "Don't you try nothing," he warned, "or you'll get this."

He roughly yanked the child from his father's grasp and shoved him to the floor, pistol whipped the charging father and back-handed the defiant mother, all in short order. After another swig from his flask, the alcohol-addled "Governor of Three Mountains" headed for the door to shout a fresh string of warnings and curses at his long-gone sidekick.

The word projectiles hurtled through the village, ricocheting from household to household. In response, the lights that were on blinked out and mothers held their children close as men crept outside to confer in the dark.

Suddenly feeling vulnerable, Jimmy decided to take steps to ensure his captives wouldn't turn on him in his sleep. He grabbed Martha, pulling her away from her husband and the child she comforted. Holding the gun at Martha's head, he directed Phil to get a flashlight and lead the way to the shed to get some rope. With shaking hands the terrified husband did as he was told.

Then he followed Jimmy's instructions to tie Martha's hands behind her back. After checking to ascertain that the rope was secured, the rover motioned for Phil to sit his wife down on Jimmy's bed with her back against the wall.

As Jimmy waved Phil away from the bed, Rigel and Chas silently approached the pavilion. They crept along the wall to listen and peek over the window ledge to ascertain the locations of those inside. After a couple of minutes they were sure that Arnie was gone. He must have been the departing object of the shouted insults. They continued to watch as the interior drama switched direction.

Jimmy took the flashlight, propped a pillow against the wall and climbed into bed sitting next to Martha. Eying Phil menacingly, he removed his belt and slipped it between Martha's bound wrists to buckle it to his belt loop. "Now, I'm gonna sleep with this here gun in my hand, Martha tied to me. So you don't want to mess with me while I'm sleeping. Now you better shut up that bawling kid of yours and go on to bed yourselves."

Martha managed a weak smile at her husband and son. "I'll be fine. Now, Chris, you go on to bed with your dad."

Chris cried, struggling to pull away from his father's tight grip and run to his mother.

Martha nodded slightly. "I'm sending you a big hug, Chris. In the morning we'll share some eggs from Carla's chickens. Phil, why don't you tell Chris one of your bedtime stories?"

The vigilant spies listened and watched until Jimmy turned out the light beside the bed. Chas had retrieved bows and arrows, but it was too risky to shoot or even threaten the scoundrel when the light was on and impossible in the dark. So they simply remained below the window ledge for the night, silent guardians of the family trapped inside.

Requiring compensation for the loss, Jimmy demanded that the chestnut-haired teen be brought to him.

The largest number to ever meet on Thunderbird Mountain converged in front of Matoskah's teepee ten days after Jimmy's takeover. The meeting needed to remain quiet with no sounds of children at play echoing down the mountain. So, in households with children, one parent remained at home, while the other attended the meeting.

The gathering of seventy-five people in front of Mastoskah's teepee crackled with heat to match the blazing campfire. Arguing, brainstorming and debating continued with heated intensity well into the night.

"Let's draw Jimmy into our midst with a big celebration," Anaya suggested. "An inauguration for the new governor."

Momentarily, a stunned silence greeted this audacious idea. Instead of strategies of silent stealth to sneak up on the rover and disarm him, they'd surround, distract and confuse him. Then they'd swiftly remove whoever was being held as his bodyguard. From behind, strong men would grab Jimmy's arms, throw him to the ground, and wrest the gun from him. That was all that needed to happen to strip away the tyrant's power.

Eena spoke up. "I'll cozy up to him, then hold him at gunpoint as you guys get his weapon."

Chas immediately took issue. "No way."

Eena shot him a defiant look. "Do you honestly think there's any chance I'll become a damsel in distress?"

Contagious laughter broke the tension for all but Chas. Cold fingers of fear clutched his heart. But he knew the futility of arguing with her.

It was a risky scheme. They knew Jimmy would be drinking his whiskey. There was the idea of an alcoholic haze to help let down Jimmy's guard, but a single misstep could also precipitate a deadly shooting spree.

"I'll shoot him before that happens," Eena reminded them.

"Let's keep all the children at my place," Raiel suggested. "Meyer, Cosima and I can host a group sleepover with stargazing and storytelling."

Rigel agreed to be the one to welcome Jimmy to his inauguration. The next morning he hugged Jennifer and Andrew and headed toward the pavilion. The smells of breakfast wafted through the open door as he knocked on the frame. Startled by the unexpected visitor, Jimmy looked up from the table and put his hand on the gun next to his plate.

"What?" he demanded, swallowing a mouthful of scrambled eggs.

Rigel quickly took in the location of the family members before his eyes locked onto Jimmy's. "Good morning, sir. May I come in?"

"Come on. But don't take long. A man doesn't relish a cold breakfast."

Rigel came right to the point. "The people of the community would like to have a welcoming inauguration in your honor."

Jimmy's fork remained poised midair as he considered this surprising proposal.

"We figured that since you're our leader now, we should formally appoint you as such."

Jimmy eyed him suspiciously, as though calculating a host of possibilities. "This better not be a trick," he warned.

Rigel grinned broadly. "I have to admit, we have a selfish motive."

With a smug look, Jimmy shrugged. "Uh-huh."

Rigel quickly attached the next part. "We all just want to have a good time together. It's been a while since we had a party."

Ever the schemer, Jimmy had his own reason for liking this idea. "Only if that young, pretty little thing is there. Minus that wolf."

Cosima. Rigel fought down his revulsion at the thought of this man claiming Cosima.

Jimmy pressed the point. "You're gonna introduce me to her at the party, understand?"

Rigel forced a friendly grin. "Sure thing. How about we have the party Saturday night?"

Jimmy thrust out his chin and narrowed his eyes. "You better bring her so I can announce our engagement, or there ain't gonna be no party. Got that?"

Rigel nodded. "Mind if we start setting up a couple of hours before it starts? There will be a band and lots of baked goods and casseroles to get ready." He paused with a conspiratorial grin. "And bring your best whiskey."

This was sounding better and better to Jimmy. He stabbed his scrambled eggs. "My food's gettin' cold. Saturday night then. I'm putting you personally in charge of making sure my bride-to-be is there."

This new development suited Jimmy's plans perfectly. Besides, after making arrangements to bring his bride, Rigel was going to replace Arnie. Then he'd choose Marvin's replacement.

The Inauguration 38

Jimmy slicked down his graying hair and arranged his leather vest over the clean white shirt. The leather would be too hot in the summer heat, but it made him look more in charge. He wished he had a badge to pin on it. He recalled the vest and sheriff's badge his parents had bought him when he was five years old. He'd loved firing the caps in his pistol and riding his stick pony. He recalled his dad playing dead when he "shot" him and his mother calling him sheriff when he came to the supper table. After his evening bath, she'd carefully folded his vest at the foot of his bed before she read him a bedtime story and hugged him goodnight.

He'd sought that same gentle tenderness for many years since he was orphaned. The car accident that took away his parents that night landed him in a series of foster homes that ranged from uncaring to abusive. Now, at last, that sweet young woman with the shining hair would restore the love and care that was rightfully his.

The noise and activity level outside increased as people set up the folding tables and lined casseroles and desserts on them. Among the beverages available, his drink of choice would relax him and bring him the courage to propose marriage.

As the sun sank below the horizon, more people poured in, and the rousing music matched Jimmy's happiness, if not his anxiousness.

Martha had expected to be his hostage, but to her dismay, he grabbed Chris. This was especially alarming because she knew Jimmy was wearing a gun at his back. She saw him shove it in his belt, where it would be hidden next to his back under the vest. Hand firmly on Chris's shoulder, the self-designated governor went outside and sat on the stump that was usually reserved for Grandfather.

To Jimmy's surprise, he no sooner sat down than a beautiful woman with green-gold eyes placed a folding chair next to him.

"Mind if I sit by you? My name's Eena, by the way." She leaned toward him seductively displaying cleavage. She had left the peasant blouse unbelted to hide the pistol pushed underneath and into the waist of her skirt.

Jimmy appreciated the show behind the brightly colored embroidery of the low, gathered bodice as much as the next man. "Well, Eena, I must say you're as pretty a woman as I've ever laid eyes on." While he had to admit his attraction to her, she was definitely not his type. She exuded a strength that was almost masculine.

In eager expectation, he scanned the group for the one he had chosen to be his companion for this night—and always. Someone placed a chair under Chris as Carla brought Jimmy a plate of food. With bright pink cheeks, she informed him of his choice of desserts.

"I'll take the chocolate cake," he said, "and how about bringing me a table for a glass and this whiskey bottle here."

Carla soon returned with the folding tray table and glass, and Jimmy placed the bottle on it. At the same time, Chas brought a plate of food to Eena.

"Hey, git him," Jimmy said to Carla, gesturing toward Rigel.

Determined to capture his attention Eena flashed an engaging smile. "I hope you're enjoying this party. It's in your honor, sir."

Jimmy snorted. "I'll enjoy it more when it becomes my engagement party."

When Rigel stood before him, unaccompanied by Cosima, Jimmy narrowed his eyes.

Prepared to be met with impatient hostility, Rigel put on an apologetic face. "Sorry, sir. She's not here yet."

Jimmy's hard glare lent emphasis to his reply. "You better not break your word. Not if you know what's good for you."

Rigel grinned broadly. "Oh, she's coming, sir." He winked at Jimmy. "She's taking more time than usual to get ready. Wants to look real pretty for you."

Jimmy thrust his chin forward and squinted a warning look at the man that was going to take Marvin's place. "You know what I'm carrying. My fiancé better show up."

"Absolutely," Rigel beamed. "Excuse me, sir. I have to help with a hot tureen."

"Wait," Jimmy commanded. "What's her name anyway?"

Reluctance choked Rigel's reply. "Cosima."

Eena kept redirecting Jimmy's eyes to herself as he continued to drink his courage. As he increasingly felt the pull of the woman next to him, he had to admit he wouldn't mind a night in bed with this one.

But having started drinking with a clear intention, his brain repeatedly swung back to Cosima.

After an hour, anger set in when another scan didn't locate Cosima. He cursed loudly. "Rigel, you're a dead man."

He started to get up, swaying visibly, but Eena, with a firm grasp on his forearm, pulled him back down. Meanwhile, the boy he had held to his side was swiftly pulled away. Jimmy felt something hard press against his ribs.

"Don't move," Eena said, a steel edge in her voice. But his free arm was already under his vest. He whipped the gun out and fired. Chas grabbed Eena, blood spilling onto his fingers as she slumped forward. Within a split second, Jimmy fell to the ground, the handle of a large kitchen knife protruding from his back. Martha's husband held her shoulders while, white as a sheet and trembling, she stood behind the stump.

The sound of gunshot instantly silenced the music. People froze in the act of eating, drinking, talking and dancing, as if they were cast in a play, and some invisible director had called for curtains on a charged scene.

"Jimmy's dead," someone yelled.

But Eena was everyone's concern as soon as they learned that she, not Jimmy, had been shot. Anaya hurried toward her, Chas shouting for towels to staunch the flow of blood.

As Eena's pulse weakened, Anaya kneeled beside her. She looked around the crowd and then directly into Chas's eyes. "No need to be alarmed by what you're about to see. I'm taking Eena to get emergency help."

She leaned down to hold Eena tightly by the shoulder. On a hunch that morning she had donned the pendant that was her conveyance to her people. Pulling the pendant from under her blouse, she tapped on it. In a flash of white light, in full view of the stunned onlookers and before Chas could stop them, Anaya and Eena disappeared.

Nathan woke up the morning of the fifth day of the trek, buoyed by the fact that they had crossed the Continental Divide and were on the down side. He sat up, rubbed his face, and stretched. Since the harrowing escape in the dark, the farther they progressed away from Three Mountains, the more his spirits were lifted. Home. He could hardly wait to see Lydia and the twins, and he was beside himself with anticipation to return to civilization.

The evening before finishing up the beans and rice around the campfire, Arnie was still mulling over the piloting idea. "So what does happen if a plane goes down?" he asked. "I don't wanna be a dead man."

Patiently, Nathan explained about the parachutes and the way they work. "Saved mine and Meyer's lives," he added.

As silence greeted his final statement, Nathan climbed into his sleeping bag, assuming Arnie was placated with his answer.

But when Nathan looked around the camp that morning, Arnie was nowhere to be seen. At first Nathan thought his travel mate was already up and about, but he quickly realized something was wrong. Arnie's bedroll and backpack were gone. Nathan's eyes traveled to his own backpack, which lay crumpled a few feet away, the zipper open. With growing alarm, he jumped up and ran to it. Except for some underwear and the toiletries pouch, it had been emptied of its contents. Frantically, Nathan searched for the compass. Gone.

He sat down in dazed despair. Suddenly, home seemed a thousand miles away. Even at a lower, less mountainous elevation, it would be easy to lose his direction in the towering pines. And no food. He'd starve to death before reaching Cyborg Highway. He considered turning back toward Three Mountains. But that was equally risky. His heart sank as he realized he'd likely become lost and starve to death in either direction, unless an animal killed him first.

As Nathan ran his fingers through his hair, he noticed his cup and a drawstring pouch of tea lying near last night's fire. A steaming cup of morning tea would bring some small comfort, but when he looked around for matches or the flint fire starter, none was to be found.

When he thought things couldn't get any worse, a slight movement between two trees riveted his gaze to reveal a gray wolf facing him.

Nathan and the predator stared at one another for a full minute, before the wolf withdrew in the shadows. Frantically, Nathan grabbed a nearby branch and sat down on his sleeping bag, his back against the vertical rock face. As he sat holding his only means of defense across his legs, an interior nudge caused him to look up to see the wolf gazing at him from the ledge above. He jumped up, yelled, and shook his feeble attempt at self-protection at the creature. The head popped back behind the cliff.

"Got any tea?"

The voice to Nathan's right startled him. At first he thought Arnie was back, but then he realized it wasn't Arnie. His eyes followed the direction of the sound to see Matoskah walking toward him.

"Grandfather!"

"Thank you, brother."

"Thank you?" Nathan asked, confused.

Matoskah shook his head. "Not you. Brother Wolf. He led me to you."

Nathan just stared, not knowing what to say. He didn't believe that superstitious mumbo-jumbo.

"I can light a fire if you can spare some tea," Matoskah said.

Relieved that the old man carried a fire-starter, Nathan helped him gather wood.

Grandfather pulled out a small pan, poured water into it, and placed it over the fire. After they poured dried sage into the bottom of their cups, he reached into his pack and pulled out some cornbread and venison jerky.

Nathan gratefully took the offering. He hadn't realized how hungry he was.

A few bites into the cornbread, the import of Matoskah's explanation for the wolf hit Nathan. He peered at the old man. "You were looking for me?" he asked.

"I was."

"Why?"

"You're my friend. I sensed you'd come to no good with that scoundrel you chose to be your traveling partner."

Tears sprang to Nathan's eyes. Grandfather's generosity of spirit made him ashamed of his condescending view of the old man. Was there anything Matoskah didn't discern about the people around him?

The two sat in silence for a few minutes watching the excited dance of the water in the pot.

"I want to get back to my wife and children," Nathan said finally.

"I don't blame you," Matoskah assented.

Nathan couldn't help but unload his despair to his receptive listener who poured boiling water into his cup. "Without a gun for protection and hunting, and a compass to guide me, it's hopeless. I can't go home."

Grandfather stirred the sage tea with a stick. "I have a bow and arrow, a pack full of food, and a compass."

Nathan was puzzled. "Where are you headed?"

"Same direction as you."

The lump in Nathan's throat obstructed any words. He took a sip of tea instead.

After they finished breakfast, Nathan rolled up his sleeping bag. They shifted some of the food from Matoskah's overstuffed pack to Nathan's before heading out.

Momentarily, the instant after Anaya and Eena's disappearance, stunned silence surrounded the spot where Anaya had knelt beside the profusely bleeding victim. In shock, Chas clung to the words "to get emergency help" uttered by Anaya to quell the grip of his desperate fear.

"What just happened?" someone asked.

The dazed group recounted the events from varying points of view. Rigel comforted Chas, and Leslie helped Phil console his sobbing wife.

Two days later, Gavin radioed Chas, Rigel, Raiel and the lab, where Steve picked up the radio. "Anaya's back and wants to meet at the pavilion. Over."

Like an apparition, Anaya appeared at the base of Quartz Mountain. Chas saw her first and unable to bear the suspense, hurried toward her.

"Eena's out of danger," Anaya said.

The normally composed man crumpled into Anaya's embrace.

The two of them walked toward the pavilion as people gathered to hear the news. When everyone had breathed a sigh of relief about Eena, Leslie voiced the question to Anaya that was on everyone's mind. "So, exactly what happened?"

"That was like a scene from *Star Trek*." Gavin grinned.

"You must have been beamed somewhere," Steve remarked, intrigued by a possible scientific breakthrough.

Waiting for the barrage of questions to slow down, Anaya looked around the gathering. Then she held up a little glass dome that enclosed the scene of a house, a snowman and a deer. She turned it upside down, reversed it, and held it up for all to see the enclosed world of falling snow.

"This little dome represents the extent of humanity's current knowledge of their true history and the world that surrounds and permeates theirs. You and I, the spectators of this little dome world, represent the very present, but largely unknown, reality in which human existence on Earth's surface is immersed."

"You're speaking as if you aren't human," Carla said.

Anaya paused for a moment. "I am human, of a race that is related to yours, but far older."

"Where does your race live?" Meyer asked. "Are you an extraterrestrial?"

"I'm not an E.T.; however, I'm sworn to secrecy for now."

"Why? Why can't you tell us?" Lori asked.

The nods and murmurs confirmed this was the question on everyone's minds.

"A powerful cabal has held humanity in its grip for thousands of years. Their masters, outside your current realm of knowing, oppose us."

Raiel caught her meaning. "By cabal you mean the Landlords of the World."

"Yes. And beings unknown to you that manage them. While Three Mountains Community and others work toward taking the reins of power from this long entrenched group, we battle beings in another density."

Gavin slipped his arm around Leslie's waist as he imagined how Chas must be feeling. "So, how *did* you disappear with Eena?"

"We were transported, and yes, much like the *Star Trek* series portrayed."

"Your people's technology is that advanced?" Leslie asked.

"Even beyond." Anaya's eyes twinkled as she surveyed the befuddled expressions.

Chas had a single-minded intent—to make absolutely sure Eena would be returning to him. "When will Eena be back?"

Anaya smiled. "You would be amazed to see the extent of her healing even today. Her doctor tells me she'll likely return as good as new in a few days."

The mystery surrounding Anaya caused much speculation in homes and small gatherings for the rest of the day. As the community awaited Eena's return, they wasted no time to erase all evidence of the rovers. The group that had buried Jimmy's body vigorously dismantled the partially constructed walls of his intended home and cleared away all evidence of the rovers' presence from the pavilion and valley.

Terrains

39

Nathan and Matoskah made slow progress as they stumbled through rocky passes headed east. Experiencing the hottest part of their trip, they skirted the northern rim of Great Sand Dunes National Park. After silently surveying a swath of forest that had been devastated by three hundred-mile-per-hour winds, they were relieved when the ten-day trek landed them in hills covered with lush green grass. Seeking shelter as the sun touched the mountain peaks behind them, the pair spotted an abandoned farmhouse that had completely escaped the capricious ravages of hurricane force winds. After nightfall Nathan and Matoskah placed their sleeping bags on the porch.

As they sat companionably listening to evening bird calls, Nathan opened up to Matoskah. He wanted him to know his heart's intent to return the elder's kindness.

"Don't worry, old man, you won't always have to live in a teepee."

Mastoskah remained silent, glad for the shadowed porch to obscure the shocked look that must have flashed across his face. He had expected this soul-baring sooner or later.

"You're welcome to stay with my family until the housing authority finds a unit for you," the younger man continued.

"I'm grateful that you plan to open your home to me."

"Lydia will gladly take you in. And the twins will love you."

"Thank you, but I won't be going to your city."

Complete and utter incomprehension jolted Nathan. "But you wouldn't have to live in a primitive shelter near that defenseless community anymore."

"Many years ago, I chose that location to construct my home. Both remain my choice."

Nathan considered this surprising revelation for a moment. "I guess that's the way your people have always lived. You just don't appreciate the benefits of city life."

"My goal is to help you get to your home in the city and to return to mine in the mountains."

Two main categories of people populated Nathan's world—loyal citizens and renegades. Since he cared about Grandfather and wanted to think of him being in the first group, he pressed on. "The Union of the Americas offers protection, jobs and housing."

Grandfather nodded. "In Three Mountains we protect each other. We're self-employed and enjoy helping one another construct our houses and grow our own food."

"It's true you all look out for each other. But surely you don't like living in a house with animal skins for walls, exposed to the elements?"

"The home I designed and built for myself feels safe and friendly. As you implied, I'm a natural born teepee dweller. I believe others feel the same about their homes."

Nathan had to admit that his time at Three Mountains had opened a small window of appreciation for the proud self-reliance of the people, but the recent rover takeover accentuated their stupidity. Besides, they were on lands belonging to the Union. "But the fact remains—you're breaking the law of the land."

"I guess you'll have to tell your government."

"Tell them what?"

"About people like me, so they can make us obey their laws."

"Can't have lawlessness."

"You're right. I'll just have to trade governments."

Nathan looked at him blankly.

"Mine's in here." Grandfather tapped his heart. "Its Bill of Rights protects human freedoms. I guess your government has a Bill of Rights too."

Nathan was growing impatient. "Everything they do is to benefit the people."

"I see. They have a Bill of *In Your Best Interest*."

"They just decide what needs to be done."

"You trust them; therefore, you're loyal to them."

"The Union of the Americas has good reasons for the laws in place."

Grandfather nodded, assuming an agreeable expression and mild tone. "Sounds like you can count on those who control you to guarantee your freedom."

Indignation surged through Nathan. He was done with this conversation, done with this ignorant red skin.

Matoskah remained silent, allowing Nathan to stew in his resentment. When a cool wind swept through the porch, Nathan opened his bag and crawled inside. "Your presence is strong and grounding. But your words unsettle the foundations of my world."

The peevishness in Nathan's voice made the elder smile in the deepening shadows.

The unlikely pair of travelers reached Cyborg Highway a few days later. Waiting for a passing retriever vehicle, they camped among clumps of sage and dried grass near the outskirts of the ruins of Pueblo, Colorado. If necessary, the younger man intended to capture Matoskah to get him to the city and to safety. He himself would watch over this quirky elder whom he had come to love as a father.

When Nathan spotted the approaching car, he ran forward, waving his arms over his head. As the car slowed to a halt, he turned toward Grandfather with excitement.

But the old man had vanished.

Frantically, Nathan surveyed the surrounding scrubland. Still and empty.

Guns ready, the retrievers walked toward the hitchhiker. After one frisked Nathan, his partner questioned him at gunpoint. Nathan's explanation about the plane crash satisfied them.

With a final lingering scan for Matoskah, Nathan put his gear in the trunk, opened the car door and stepped inside. He had long imagined the joyful relief he would feel as the car sped toward Transtopia. But he hadn't anticipated the flood of memories of the past two weeks with the old Native American—or the accompanying ache in his heart.

Standing beside Anaya, Eena looked toward the glowing orb that simulated Earth's sun in the vast granite ceiling. A bell-like tone sounded as a section of the front wall of the room morphed into an arched opening for a masculine version of Anaya to walk through.

"Ealar!"

After a warm hug, Ealar looked into Anaya's eyes. "One hundred and thirty years old and still my little sister." He smiled.

Her eyes glistening, she smiled back at her brother, a mere one hundred years older, and then introduced him to Eena.

As the three gazed beyond the balcony, a silver disc materialized, moving at fantastic speed right through the cavern wall.

Speechless, Eena queried her companions with wide eyes.

Anaya placed her fingers over her lips, partially hiding a smile of amusement. "The Erathans have been around for millions of years — long enough to develop technologies that seem magical to you."

Eena watched the craft slow over the terraformed farmland beyond the surrounding forest. Suddenly, she realized the implications of the Erathans' technological advancement, thousands of years ahead of that of the surface population. A hint of accusation narrowed her eyes. "You could free humanity from the web of usury that imprisons our planet."

Friendly humor jostled the understanding in Ealar's response. "And deny you, our sisters and brothers, the adventure of proving your own power?"

Eena stared ahead, watching a flock of exotic birds, their blue and red plumage reminiscent of rainforest macaws.

"Those attempting to break free are hugely outnumbered when you include vast numbers of humanity that are duped by SEI indoctrination.

"Thousands of years ago we achieved a graduation from third density, such as you are now undergoing. By engaging every conceivable virtue of the heart/brain complex, with persistence and courage, we honed fourth density abilities."

Eena shook her head in amazement as she swept her hand in an arc encompassing the surrounding scene of serene beauty.

Anaya joined the conversation. "Despite the idyllic appearances, challenging confrontations between light and shadow continue in this realm. Like you, we stumble and pay for ill-advised decisions. However, our battle is more psychic than physical.

"I want to show you an artifact in our library, the Hall of Recorded Terra — Earth — Resonances." Holding Eena's arm, Anaya tapped on the pendant.

An instantaneous switch in location brought the three into an immense room of near white granite diffusely lit with pale yellow light. Anaya led the way through an assemblage of chairs shaped like open eggshells floating several inches above the floor. Some held people viewing and interacting with tiny moving images that looked as though they had stepped out of a screen. At the far end of the room they arrived at a glass divider, behind which a gigantic hexagonal crystal rested, mysteriously suspended above the floor and pointed at a thirty-degree angle.

Gasping at its size and beauty, Eena estimated the clear quartz object to be about sixty feet long and five feet in diameter.

Anaya's voice penetrated her stunned awe. "You are already aware of the power of quartz crystals. A portal has opened on Quartz Mountain due to the crystalline interface with the plasma bombardment." Anaya paused. "As for Nathan's plane. The huge deposits of quartz on the mountain interrupted its flight."

Eena silently acknowledged Anaya's words while waiting expectantly for those to follow.

"The crystal before us is a powerful resonance chamber containing an energetic record of a billion years of history on Terra."

"A billion years to grow to this size?" Eena was nonplused.

"This record, still incomplete in modern texts, includes occasions such as the seeding of life, devastating cataclysms that obliterated life waves of thousands of species, the insertion of upgraded gene pools for new ecosystems, and colonizations of humanoids from distant systems that have long since departed for other worlds, or to the interior crust of this world honeycombed with giant caverns."

Ealar gestured toward the people seated in the recliners. "By means of this crystal record, these researchers are tapping Terran knowledge and events, both current and historical — somewhat like you accessed via the Internet prior to Solar Flash."

With a light touch on the shoulder Anaya drew Eena's attention to the object behind the glass. "This crystal is a source of both joy and sadness to the Erathans. Its place of origin, located deep in Terra, is the Cave of Crystals, a planetary womb for crystals like this. You could say it's our central repository of knowledge. However, it has been commandeered by a race of galactic overlords."

Eena struggled to comprehend this barrage of information.

"Let's tap into a present-time viewing," Anaya said. "I warn you, it will seem strange, even shocking, so prepare yourself."

A faint ping and flash of light drew Eena into a fog that instantly cleared to reveal huge crystals, angularly attached to a cave floor and sparkling blue-green reflections of an inner Earth sea. Her breath caught as one of several beings milling around stopped and glared directly at her, apparently aware that he was being viewed. Although he walked upright like a human, his eyes were yellow with vertical slit pupils that bored into hers. His blunt snout and smooth scaled skin was that of a reptile. Entirely white, he loomed over her at about twice her height. Arms and legs with four clawed fingers and toes extended from a hard, muscular torso, He sported small vestigial wings, but no tail.

Unblinking, the intimidating reptilian stare shifted toward the image of Anaya at her side. "You pollute our territory with your presence, puny Erathan. You and your kind are the excrement of our planet."

Horrified, Eena watched as, with a swift sweep of his right hand, the clawed fingers grabbed for Anaya's torso.

The image went black. Eena blinked, shaken, and then refocused on the crystal in the Hall of Resonances. When she turned toward Anaya, she saw that her Erathan friend was trembling.

She squeezed Anaya's hand. "The sight of those beings with tiny wings reminds me of accounts of flying serpents among the ancient pyramid builders in South America."

Deep sadness veiled Anaya's eyes. "They are known as the Ophids. Our sacred treasure, the Cave of Crystal Records, has been commandeered by that race, which guards it ceaselessly. However, it's not the recorded resonances they value, but the trade value in a cosmic smuggling ring."

Eena turned toward Ealar. "So, you face your enemies just as we face ours."

"Yes. While, for the vast majority of surface humanity, the entire locus of activity is Terra and to a growing degree the solar system, ours is a galactic arena populated with a vast variety of hominids. The Ophids we witnessed are technically sophisticated galactic rovers of the fourth density."

Anaya tapped on the pendant. A loud roar emitted from the forest greeted their return to the balcony. "In a sense, although in different densities, the surface humans and the inner Earth humans are allies. You see, the Ophids claim ownership of this planet and humanity. They rule the landlords as part of a vast chain of command, a federation of enslavers."

"Are the Ophids technologically more sophisticated than the Erathans?

Ealar shook his head. "No. That's not our challenge. Our challenge is similar to yours in that we face graduation to the next density—the fifth. It's not crude force, but garnering all the wisdom we have gained in our present density that will achieve fifth density empowerment."

Barely comprehending Ealar's words, Eena turned toward Anaya. "So, beyond simply driving the Ophids from the Cave of Crystals, it matters how you get it back."

"Exactly. Thousands of painful lessons in fourth density have taught us that a violent battle, even when victorious, must be fought again after the Ophids regroup and return, perpetrating psychic warfare for another cycle. Our other choice, a shared inner victory of Erathan psychic coherence, will deflect the Ophid invasion. Watch this."

The Cave of Crystals appeared again in front of Eena. But this time, an invisible wall drove the invaders out and prevented access.

"Psychic coherence is like a laser light—focused and powerful for deflecting foes."

A light flickered on in Eena's head bringing new clarity. "Which may also disempower the landlords to some degree."

Anaya smiled. "That's why I have joined you in Three Mountains Community. Although from different densities, we are allied in our struggles."

Eena's voice was soft. "Thanks to your people, I have escaped death."

Ealar beamed. "The courageous determination to help the human family does draw support."

Anaya took Eena's hand. "We urge you to continue on your present trajectory to inform and assist others. With persistence, humanity's focused, co-creative power, your own lasered light source can disarm factions known to you by various names."

Eena listened respectfully, albeit dubiously, to the implication that a tiny number of unarmed insurgents could successfully oppose the grip of an entrenched regime. She was certain that seeding and infiltrating Techno City and the townships must ultimately necessitate accessing stockpiles of weapons. Talk of Aikido and density graduations was idealistic, failing to appreciate the weaponized power of the ruthless opposition.

Grounded in third density, realistic in her aims, Eena remained convinced that, in the end, only violent confrontation would destroy the stranglehold of the controllers. Nonetheless, she expressed her profound gratitude to her benefactors before requesting to return to Terra's surface.

Anaya nodded and after goodbyes to Ealar, she tapped her pendant.

Eena found herself in the valley a few yards from where Chas dropped hay in front of the mare while the foal, scampering and kicking, circled around them.

Sovereignty 40

Nathan's heart swelled to overflowing when the car stopped in front of his house. He ran inside — into the arms of Lydia and the four-year-old twins, Derrick and Kate — into his home with restored running water and electricity, thanks to his special status as pilot and spy.

Knowing the retriever division of the police department had sent word of his return to Imperial Governor Scholtz and the social engineering team, Nathan wrote up a detailed account of the crash and his stay at Three Mountains Community. At last he could satisfy the burning desire to disclose everything about the theft of UA property. It was therapeutic after swallowing his resentments for the entirety of that six-week exile.

The day after his arrival, the writing of his de-briefing narrative was severely hampered as martial law was declared, which meant keeping the twins indoors to constantly interrupt his work.

Lydia looked cross. "I'm sick of these things. They happen every weekend now like clockwork."

It was hard on the entire family to be closed in. Since Lydia had to work, both because the law mandated that both parents work, and because it was a financial necessity, they were all in separate buildings from early morning to evening every day except Sunday. "What's worse, it's always on our one day off."

The kids, who had been in day care since they were six weeks old, were frequently sick, and Lydia was convinced they needed the one day per week in sunshine.

Nathan stared at her. The rover problem must be worse than he thought.

After dark, fourteen hours after lock-down, as Lydia and Nathan lay in bed, the speaker attached to a retriever vehicle, cruising through the neighborhood, announced the rovers were caught, and the state of emergency was concluded.

The next day, Lydia left the children at the nearby day care and walked to her job as a secretary for the Social Engineering Department, while Nathan awaited his job assignment. In line with his detective tendencies he rode his bike for at least three miles in four directions, querying people to find out where the rover invasion had taken place, but no one knew. The driver of a retriever vehicle was closed-lipped, and a foot patrol policeman shrugged off the question impatiently. They either didn't know or didn't want him to know.

When the Social Engineering Department called him in a week later, he put the incriminating document in a briefcase and headed for the SED building, which had been a high school pre-Solar Flash.

Smiling from ear to ear, Deputy Governors Wayne Hendricks and Elma Stratford shook Nathan's hand and welcomed him back. Expecting to be queried about the period of time he was missing in action, he was surprised at their first remark.

"The Imperial Governor requests your help in a developing situation." Their expressions had become serious and direct.

Assuming the same air, Nathan sat up, spine straight, leaning slightly forward. An accomplished informant, he was more than ready for an assignment, both to get him out of the house and to win the favor of the UA government.

Hendricks spoke first. "Our intelligence has revealed a growing ring of insurgents. Thanks to expert detective work, we've hauled in three."

Nathan knew the long pause signified the SED representatives were reading his reaction.

"We have intel of several more causing a stir in the workers. We need our brightest and best SED spies to smoke them out."

"Count me in." Nathan was glad to be trusted to continue operating as a spy.

"Not a word of this to anyone, not even your wife."

Suddenly, the real reason for the drills clicked into place. "The martial law drills?"

"Raids to smoke out insurgents."

"You understand the need for secrecy."

Nathan nodded. "Certainly."

"The University of Transtopia Metro has apparently become a hotbed of rebellious youth."

Nathan looked from Hendricks to Stratford.

"All we need are names. With cross-references we can find the addresses."

"When do I start?"

"This afternoon."

Surprised, Nathan gulped. "I'm ready."

"Welcome back, Mr. Abelt."

As Nathan walked toward the campus, he realized he forgot to hand over the debriefing papers.

Grandfather radioed Rigel that he was a few hours away. The people prepared a feast beside the reclaimed pavilion, now emptied of all signs of the hostile takeover. Cosima positioned herself by the trail that led up Thunderbird Mountain to Grandfather's teepee. Awaiting her beloved mentor, she kept a sharp eye while Valek played with the children. She had trained him with great care to curb any wolfish roughness with his human pack.

That night, as the campfire crackled its cozy warmth, Grandfather listened with a series of nods and grunts as Chas related the story of Jimmy's would-be inauguration/engagement celebration. As toddlers fell asleep on their parents' laps, and older children played hide-and-seek just outside the circle, people told the elder of the shocking conclusion to Jimmy's party and Eena's unknown fate. Concern gripped Matoskah's heart momentarily, but he knew the Erathans' powers of healing far surpassed those of surface humans.

Pressed for information about his recent journey, Grandfather spoke of Arnie's ignominious departure, and with his peculiar style of dry humor that brought repeated peals of laughter, he described his meeting, journey and conversations with Nathan.

When Mastoskah concluded his tale, Gavin asked the question that was on everyone's minds. "Grandfather, as a pilot, Nathan knows our longitude and latitude. Do you think he'll reveal our location to the authorities in Transtopia?"

Grandfather picked up a long stick and stoked the fire. Red-gold sparks danced above the fire pit as, silently, the people awaited Grandfather's assessment of the possible fate of Three Mountains Community.

After a long pause he replied. "That remains to be seen. His loyalties are divided." The rising sparks blinked out in the surrounding darkness. "Who knows which direction the winds of life will blow his choice?"

It only took a week for Nathan to see a possible pattern. Twice, a group of five to seven youths had gathered around a table. Though their voices were somewhat muted, their expressions loudly proclaimed shared intensity. The next time they met, Nathan tried to look inconspicuous as he sat nearby, hiding behind a pile of textbooks.

The buzzwords now familiar from Three Mountains Community reached his ears. "Sovereignty," "oil and drug cartels," "free energy." It was puzzling to Nathan. As far as he knew, none of the Three Mountains runners were from Transtopia. But how was it they shared the same vernacular?

His next challenge was to get the names of the youths. It took a week to follow them all to classes, and by means of help from the instructors, he matched names on rosters to faces.

The following weekend Nathan was determined to get Lydia out of the house. By the time martial law was announced mid-morning the children were in the care of a neighbor and Nathan had whisked Lydia to the movie theater ten blocks away. They arrived early and after a two-hour wait, viewed *The Road* three times before the curfew was lifted. But it was worth it.

Nathan and Lydia were familiar with the sequence—the rousing news clips inserted in the beginning, middle and end that gripped the viewers with fear one moment and aroused patriotic exuberance, expressed with resounding applause, the next. At the conclusion of the movie, Governor Scholtz stood with President Estrada and his cabinet in Pan America Central. A child about six years old came forward and brought each of the leaders a bouquet of flowers. The president lifted the child into his arms as he waved to the viewers both on and off camera.

"Behold the child of the future, raised from birth under the protective care and scientific guidance of the Social Engineering Initiative."

The camera zoomed in for a close-up. Beaming a mixture of friendliness and proud dignity, President Estrada took the child's tiny hand in his. "Very soon, my friends, you will be privileged to view the new and improved race of the future. Transhuman bionic progeny, chip enhanced, and gestated from conception according to exacting scientific protocols."

Nathan joined in the enthusiastic applause of the audience, surprised that Lydia sat motionless, her hands clenched in her lap. As they walked out of the theater, he asked his pregnant wife what was wrong.

"I would give anything to be home with my children from birth. It's unbearable to think I can't even enjoy the first six weeks at home with our next child."

Nathan put his arm around Lydia's shoulder and pulled her close. Even though he knew government and science worked together for the benefit of society, he felt compassion for her longing.

"It's all for our own good, Lydia," he ventured softly.

Abruptly, his wife pulled away, and they walked to their house in silence, not even their hands touching during the charged disconnection.

Amid the charged flow of life around Raiel's house, Meyer and a group of children sanded a newly-constructed table. Cosima and two animated children shared the classic *Huckleberry Finn*, Raiel and four others mixed math and cooking, one group extracted honey from beehive combs under a cabana while five children ran in and out of the surrounding forest.

As Raiel approached, Meyer smiled wryly. "Apparently, fate deemed it necessary to crash a plane in the middle of the forest for me to get a real education degree."

Raiel glowed with contentment. Her staff was apparently growing.

When the large pot of stew was ready, people picnicked in small groups. Raiel and Meyer waved Cosima away, when looking more subdued than usual, so she called Valek, and the two followed the trail to Grandfather's camp.

A nagging question weighed on her heart as she reached his clearing. Grandfather sat near the fire in front of a stretched hide. Glancing over his shoulder, he touched the ground for her to sit next to him.

Cosima smiled tentatively. "Grandfather, over a month ago, you and I sat at the summit of this mountain together. When a dark force approached the village, we shared a vision."

Using knapped obsidian, Grandfather scraped the deer hide stretched over a frame. Next to him was a large pail containing a solution of brains and water that had been cooked and was now cooling. He handed Cosima a long stick to stir the mixture until it had cooled enough to receive the hide. The rhythmic cadences of the scrapping and stirring invited a companionable exchange of conversation as the old medicine man waited quietly for his apprentice to continue.

"I can't stop thinking about Marvin's horrible death. Did we cause that to happen?"

Grandfather considered the depth of her question for several seconds before answering with a question of his own. "Cosima, did we, even to the smallest degree, desire death or any awful fate for the rovers?"

Cosima's reply was swift. "No, Grandfather. We only invited a powerful force to protect the people."

Matoskah dipped a finger and then his entire hand into the mixture to ascertain that it was cool enough for the hide. Then he removed the stiff leather from the frame and used the wooden spoon to press the folds into the solution.

Cosima's next question emerged on the heels of the first. "Did you know that the rover was going to hunt down that grizzly, only for it to attack and kill him?"

Gnarled hands stuffed the hide into the brains mixture as Grandfather mused aloud. "I never know just how the forces of nature will adjust the possibilities. We both watched the grizzly present itself and walk by as we meditated. We knew it was likely Great Mato was to play an important role in the outcome."

A troubled look furrowed Cosima's brow. "By killing a man?"

Pulling and stretching the hide in the solution, Grandfather paused to look directly into Cosima's eyes. "Too many times I have seen the value of evoking the highest outcome for all concerned."

Firmly clasping a section at a time, he pulled and dipped to soften the leather. "Sometimes, the Great Spirit directs us to step aside to allow the outcome."

Cosima still felt unsettled. "The bear was sent?"

Grandfather swirled the hide in the solution as he ruminated. "More than likely, something deep inside Marvin attracted that bear."

Matoskah continued to push and swirl the immersed hide, then he put a lid on the bucket. "Now the hide will rest, and unseen forces will work it."

At that moment a tremor of comprehension offered the young seeker a vision. She saw an ephemeral Marvin rise from a battered corpse. And with a distinctly childlike expression of anticipation, his ascent brought him into a zone of scintillating light and to a smiling woman beckoning with open arms.

The pair sat for a while in reflective silence beside the bucket. Upon completion, the patient, time-honored steps of the "braining" process would render the whitened hide soft and supple. The old man imagined the deer hide would provide a lovely garment for the young medicine woman at his side.

"Grandfather, is Great Mato still on Thunderbird Mountain?"

Matoskah consulted the surrounding silence. "This mountain is too crowded for him. He has returned to his home farther north."

While the hide soaked in the warm mixture, the elder sat down to piece together Raiel's new pair of moccasins. Cosima got up and leaned over him for a cheek-to-cheek embrace. "Thank you. I understand now." Her heart buoyed by an indescribable lightness of being, she called Valek to her side and headed down the path to Raiel's house.

Crossings

41

Nathan felt the weight of Lydia's depression that seemed to lump him with the SEI's plans for their baby. He felt bad for her, but it wasn't his fault that she would be returning to work shortly after the birth. He was glad for his espionage assignment to take his mind off things at home.

The week after Nathan resumed his role as an operative of the UA, the cruising loudspeaker call for martial law was no surprise, but having their home raided was.

"Wait, I work as an attaché to the SED. You can't do this."

The officer simply pushed him aside. His sputtered protests had ceased long before the contents of drawers, including clothes, utensils and his briefcase were strewn on the floor. Ten minutes later, without having said a word, the two men and woman that had rifled through their belongings, as well as the armed policeman at the front door were gone. As Nathan stood beside his weeping wife and children and shifted his gaze from violation to violation, the impact of his helplessness ricocheted around the room.

A message came summoning Nathan to meet with Imperial Governor Scholtz two days later. In preparation for this impending visit, Nathan reviewed his detailed account of the crash and his stay at Three Mountains Community. He took particular care in writing about the holographic camouflage. At last he could satisfy the burning desire to disclose everything about the theft of UA property. It was therapeutic after a six-week exile, swallowing his resentments the whole time. Not to mention that he would be deemed a hero by Governor Scholtz.

When the vehicle arrived the following week to take Nathan to Imperial Governor Scholtz, he requested the driver wait in his living room for a few minutes while he put on a suit and tie. Grabbing the briefcase, he headed out the door.

After an hour wait in the foyer, a secretary ushered Nathan into Governor Scholtz's office. He stood a few feet from the desk for several seconds, before the governor looked up. Beaming his famous, friendly smile he motioned for Nathan to sit.

Anxious to share that he was back at work and already useful, Nathan was eager to inform the governor of the student suspects.

"Well, Nathan, are you glad to be home?"

"Yes!"

"You were gone for two months. You must have quite a story to tell."

Nathan nodded. "It all began with the plane crash."

"You're an experienced pilot; the maintenance of the plane up to date and thorough. How could this have happened?"

Uneasy concern for himself edged into Nathan's eagerness to show his loyalty as an informant.

His smile fading, Governor Scholtz waited silently for his response.

Nathan launched into the story, beginning with his crazily gyrating control panels and the bird.

"Let me get this straight. A giant blue bird?"

Nathan felt his face grow hot as the absurdity of his words echoed in his brain.

He continued, his account moving from the rescue to discoveries in the science lab.

The governor's stare was unsettling. "A holograph emitter in the mountains near the Continental Divide, the tallest mountains in Colorado."

As Governor Scholtz echoed his words, Nathan had to admit it sounded unbelievable. Disconcerted by the governor's derision, he quickly moved on.

The account of the shopping expedition received the respectful attention it deserved.

"That's going to end. As we speak, the military has likely restored electricity for the new SED employees soon to relocate in Durango."

Nathan stared at the governor in surprise. He knew how unwelcome this news would be to Three Mountains.

The account of the rovers drew chuckles, as though Nathan were relating a comedy.

When he arrived at his escape, emphasizing the daringness of it, the governor's loud belly laughter rankled. Nathan knew better than to mention the wolf that appeared just before Mastoskah's arrival to escort him to Cyborg Highway.

Governor Scholtz abruptly put up his hand to silence Nathan. He leaned forward. "You ready to fly again?"

Nathan stared at him, surprise and elation vying internally.

"Yes, sir."

"In your absence, our mechanics have rebuilt another Cesna engine. "Tomorrow, you're going to fly me to see this place."

Startled by the directive, eager for the chance to regain the governor's proud respect, Nathan tightly clasped the unopened briefcase. With an abrupt wave of his hand, Scholtz concluded the meeting.

Eena stood up to conclude the meeting with Gavin, Chuck and Lori. "I'll return as soon as I can," she said.

Gavin looked at her steadily. "Do return. The community needs you."

She smiled as she lifted the backpack to her shoulders. "Let's hope I'll be returning with Caellum." After a moment's hesitation she handed Gavin an envelope. "Please give this to Chas. He'll be upset that I've left. If he had learned that I was going on this mission, he would have wanted to come. It just wouldn't be practical."

As Eena began the descent toward Promise Path, she mentally inventoried everything in her backpack including the handgun.

The connectors met her at the base of the mountain. They were determined to camp at Lake Nighthorse while she was in Techno City.

She had opposed their leaving the community. Now she was very direct. "If you don't hear from me in two weeks, you must return to Three Mountains. There's no sense in them taking five of us." She was relentless in exacting a promise until they consented.

They reached Lake Nighthorse before nightfall on the second day. The following morning, Eena rode away at dawn, camped that night somewhere along the La Plata River and, the next day, walked into Techno City. Generally following Highway 64 east, she wound through the sidewalks to reach Main Street. Assuming James would be at work, she walked around the downtown area for a while to mentally map the area.

After a few hours of people-watching, she left a tea shop to head for James's apartment.

His surprised expression turned serious when she introduced herself. Hastily, he ushered her in and closed the door.

"Caellum's in jail."

"As I suspected. I want to know all of Caellum's close associations and where to find them."

Neil and Dora were the only ones James knew by name.

"Tell me about this Dora."

"Caellum was smitten with her. From my perspective, she's basically an airhead, a dangerous innocent, protected child of the upper crust—daughter of the Director General of the sector, as a matter of fact."

Eena gave a low whistle.

"She took him to meet her mom and dad at their mansion." James shared the after-dinner brochure fiasco that concluded the evening.

"Good one, Caellum," Eena said, shaking her head.

An hour later she met Dora at the dorm.

"Do you have a minute? I'm a friend of Caellum's."

Dora's eyes widened. "Let's walk outside."

They sat on the bench where Dora and Caellum had ended their relationship two weeks before.

"He's in jail."

"I know. I am asking you to take me to him."

"I've been to see him. He wants nothing to do with me."

Eena gauged Dora's attitude as she observed her. It was obvious she still cared about Caellum. She liked the disarming transparency in the young woman's demeanor.

"Dora, he needs our help."

"Well, yes. I'm meeting with an attorney tomorrow."

"Please come with me. You have connections. You can help get him out of jail."

"So can you. Why don't you just go alone?"

"You know this place better than I do."

A quizzical expression registered on Dora's face.

"Like Caellum, I haven't been here very long."

A glimmer of suspicion brightened the blue eyes that had captivated Caellum. "Who are you? Are you from that utopian place the brochure describes?"

"The 'utopian' place doesn't exist yet. I simply want to free my friend, and I would appreciate your help. That's all I can tell you."

Dora sighed. "I must admit I'm desperate to see him again."

Eena liked the open friendliness in Dora's gaze. "Okay, let's go."

When they reached the front of the jail, Dora froze as cold steel suddenly pressed into the middle of her back.

Eena spoke softly. "Look straight ahead and keep walking. As I said, I need your help."

"At the point of a gun?"

"As the daughter of the Director General you have clout. Does the jailer know who you are?"

"I don't know."

"Then tell him. I want you to ask the jailer to leave for a couple of hours. Assure him you'll take full responsibility. Where does he keep the keys?"

"Hanging on the wall behind his desk chair."

The pair walked up the concrete stairs.

"Good. Now tell him he needs to leave while you interrogate the prisoner."

Dora opened the heavy door and entered, smiling at the guard. An authoritative voice belied her engaging expression as she told him her identity.

"We need to speak with Caellum Nichols... alone."

After a few moments of confused discomfort, the jailor reluctantly stood to go. As soon as he was out the door, the two women headed for the hallway lined with barred cells. When Eena's eyes met Caellum's, surprised pleasure animated his expression.

"Eena, I can't believe you're here."

Eena turned toward Dora. "Get the keys." Then she faced Caellum. "We have to move quickly."

Consternation scrunched Dora's forehead as her eyes bored into Eena's. "This is suicide. They'll hunt you down until they find you. I told you I'd hire an attorney."

Eena gestured with the gun barrel toward the keys dangling from Dora's hand. "Unlock the door."

Dora approached the lock.

"Don't bother."

The heads of both women swiveled toward Caellum.

Again, Eena waved the gun toward the cell, her expression adamant. "Go ahead. Unlock it." Then, with urgency, she addressed Caellum. "We don't have a moment to lose."

There was a loud click and Dora swung open the door.

Intractability was written on Caellum's features, his posture a resolute statement. "I'm staying right where I am."

When the call reached Gavin over the radio, he heard the urgency in Leslie's voice.

"Patrollers, drop everything. You're needed for emergency patrol. Over."

"What's going on? Over."

"Unknown. Over."

"Who asked for this patrol? Over."

"Not sure. Over."

Silence. The patrollers jointly decided patrol sweeps. He wished Eena were back.

"Meet at the pavilion after perimeter loops. Over."

Gavin sighed. Apparently, there would be no cessation anytime soon of the tension and battles with the forces arrayed against them. Anxiety gnawed at his gut as he walked the familiar path to the portal with Lori and Chuck.

The two teal-colored birds arrived first, and their bond-mates suited up for patrol. Gavin scanned the sky expectantly until his eyes locked onto Phoenix's coppery underside. The wings extended for landing as great claws reached for earth. Admiring the shimmer of the bright blue-green plumage, fruit ready in his hand, he knew there was no rushing the greeting ritual that included vigorous head scratches with the augur's crown and beak pressed against his heart. Having no uniform of matching feathers, nor immediate need of the bridle and lead looped on his arm, he tucked the radio, compass and binoculars into the pouches and walked to Phoenix's tail feathers. When all three patrollers were mounted, Gavin met each one's gaze in a momentary salute before take-off.

As Phoenix carried his bond-mate above the Earth, psychic strands connected the bird and his rider, the only person allowed to touch him. They rose as one being, the pulsing of their hearts synched with the beat of the huge wings.

Gavin's memory flashed to his arrival at Three Mountains, his life dangling precariously between the slats of the rickety bridge—his sense of being the fool betrayed by destiny. He now realized that the bridge, Espirit, and the powerful wings that lifted him above the Earth were essential conveyances to a beckoning future. Humbled by the specter of death, his heart ignited by the searing pain of grief, he directed Phoenix to the portal. The young adventurer who had dreamed of exploring to observe humanity's fate had come of age, joining ranks with the small gathering of people at Three Mountains Community in a united quest.

Even amid the overwhelming odds arrayed against the community and its goals, the flight buoyed Gavin. He reveled in the feeling of freedom as Phoenix rode an air current, gliding effortlessly over Thunderbird Mountain. Soon, decreasing temperatures would prevent flights this side of the portal. The patroller knew he would miss these times through the long snowbound winter.

The
Hero

42

Piloting the imperial governor was the once-in-a-lifetime opportunity Nathan had yearned for. His chance to expose those renegades. His chance to get the notoriety he deserved. His chance to become a Union of the Americas of the World Federation hero. He followed the west–southwest coordinates he had charted two months ago to fly Meyer to Township 24.

At the exact coordinates he had flown over two months ago, the plane crossed the Continental Divide. It was like déjà vu when, through binoculars, he saw the speck in the distance, heading away from the plane. *Uh-huh, a big bird, all right. The blond hair must be Gavin's.* He wanted to get closer before directing the governor's attention to it.

Quartz Mountain, he was sure of it. Elation soared until the engine sputtered. He dropped the binoculars and looked at his wildly fluctuating gages.

"What's going on?" Alarm edged the governor's query.

"Dunno. Same thing as before."

"Damn! Do something!"

Nathan turned the plane sharply to the north. Within about a minute, the engine was humming; gauges, stable. He looked over at Governor Scholtz, whose shaking fingers wiped perspiration from his brow.

Nathan banked the plane west.

"Hey, what the hell are you doing?"

"Sir, I'm sure the community's close. We're skirting the area."

In a slow turn, continuing west, then south, they bypassed Quartz Mountain to cruise around the peak of Thunderbird Mountain. Nathan tightened the circle, relieved that the plane remained stable. This was his moment. Three Mountains Community would soon be in view. He glanced at the governor. "Watch below."

Governor Scholtz craned his neck and scanned the sea of pines through the passenger window. "This better not be a ruse."

The plane banked east. Nathan grabbed the binoculars. The river. But no valley. He turned the binoculars skyward and trained them on Gavin and augur, now close enough for a scan by Scholtz. He lifted the strap that held the binoculars over his head. Now his smug passenger would see the reality for himself.

Suddenly, pilot and bird dove, disappearing into the pines. Stunned, Nathan glanced at the passenger who was surveying the forest on the opposite slope of the mountain. The realization of what he was looking at dawned. They'd done it. The hologram was operational. This was the moment of disclosure—his moment of greatness. His brain presented a vision of the smiling governor awarding him a commendation medal before a filled auditorium. His status would be such that never again would a search crew rifle through his belongings, emptying contents of drawers on the floor. He'd have real status. Maybe become Scholtz's right-hand man. "What we're actually looking at is—"

Eena nudged Dora with the point of the gun, and she whirled around, knocking it from Eena's hand. "Lose that thing! If you only knew how this man has shaken my world; if you only knew that I would gladly free those arms just to have them around me; if you only knew that all that he is and all that he stands for has grabbed me and won't let me go; if you only knew *me*, you would know the deadliest weapon on Earth is nothing compared to the power of my love."

As Eena stared wide-eyed, a tumult of impressions collided. *Landlord's daughter.* She glanced at the gun lying several feet away.

"I—" *Not an airhead. She has a strength that matches my own.*

Dora's word's penetrated Eena's confusion. "Just lock me in here, as I'm sure you intended."

There is no opponent. As an interior barrier cracked, Eena's eyes shifted to Caellum. "Our time is short."

At that moment the connection that reached across the space between Caellum and Dora electrified all three. Dora's voice broke the charged silence. "Caellum, may I explain something to you?"

He stood still, attentive, his fixed gaze inviting Dora to speak.

"Since childhood my father's been my strong protector. I've always admired his strength. At first, I felt drawn to you because I perceived you to be like him."

Affront flashed across Caellum's face.

"I was disappointed when I learned about a very different you."

Caellum looked away.

"Now, I love you because, unlike my father, *you* are the protector of the people."

Eena stood mute, listening to words she never expected to hear from the royal bloodline. Caellum's expression softened as his gaze shifted from the cold steel to the warm caress of Dora's eyes.

When he turned his head to face Eena, his expression was resolute. "The spreaders will rally more if I'm in Techno City. I'm staying close to the movement and...." His gaze, locked on Dora's face, completed the sentence.

Yielding to the finality in Caellum's voice, Eena shrugged and walked toward the useless show of force. She stopped to stare at the discarded gun, then turned and walked away from it.

A flashback paraded recent events in Mu. The grotto. The sabertooth. Phoenix. Here it was again. Synchronicity — deep interior shifts. Today, hers paralleled those of Dora and Caellum. After passing the open door of Caellum's cell, she turned and grinned. "Caellum, we anticipated spreaders, but neither of us dreamed of an infiltration within the first two weeks — and certainly not the support of royal blood."

In intertwined closeness, the pair smiled at her.

Then to Dora. "You probably won't agree yet, but you have become important, not only to Caellum, but to our mission."

Eena continued to the end of the hall and turned again to smile at the pair. "I'll be returning. Dora, while you work to free Caellum, I'll work as the replacement seeder."

She left the reunited lovers to enjoy the remaining furtive minutes together. Besides, she relished her interior conversation with Chas, Grandfather, Anaya and Gavin. *A bloodless coup. Maybe not a pipe dream. Maybe a vision, an attainable reality.* As she began the return trek to Three Mountains, hope seeped into the widening crack in her armor and put a spring in her steps.

Within minutes of the radioed message, most of the community was gathered at the pavilion. All were abuzz about the unexpected call to come together. Were their sighs of relief over freedom from the rovers to be stifled so soon by yet another crisis?

Raiel, with her two adopted children, followed by Meyer, Cosima and Valek, emerged from Blue Lake Mountain.

Holding Andrew in his arm with Jennifer at his side, Rigel stood with regal dignity.

Standing slightly apart from the crowd, Chas scanned the trailheads for Eena's approach.

Carla pursued her little one, who beelined toward his approaching lupine playmate.

Raiel surveyed the perimeter of the valley.

"Grandfather said to tell you he'll be here soon. Had some work to finish," Cosima explained.

Nathan stopped mid-sentence when he saw the lake on Blue Lake Mountain. But it wasn't the sight of the water that choked the words rising in his throat. It was the person in plain view, standing by the lake — waving slowly at the plane, at him.

Grandfather. Got some tea? I sensed you'd come to no good with that scoundrel you chose to be your traveling partner. Echoes of his time with the old medicine man. *The home I designed and built for myself feels safe and friendly. I'm a natural-born teepee-dweller.*

The pivotal moment of Nathan's life was swept along in the wash of affection that drowned his eyes.

"Well?" Gruff impatience intruded on Nathan's reverie.

"...is a sea of pines. I thought the community was here."

"Sure it's not that holograph projection?"

"Too vast. I believe we're a couple of degrees off."

"Widen the search, you imbecile. But, for god sakes, avoid that danger area."

Nathan flew on, the valley hidden from view by the tall mountain sentinels. The pilot broadened the sweep.

Governor Scholtz's sputtered profanity and threats escalated until there was just enough fuel to return to Transtopia, which barely missed the emergence of a new hero.

Gavin rested his head on Phoenix's neck as they soared toward the community. But he immediately became confused. Was his compass broken?

Lori's voice came over the radio. "Hey, where's the valley?"

Circling the area where the valley should be, the alarmed patrollers saw nothing but a continuous expanse of pines with Destiny River running through it. In an unspoken agreement, they circled the area where the valley should be. A minute later, befuddling the air-born spectators even more, the scene changed. A dusting of snow covered the misplaced canopy of pines.

Steve's voice over the radio. "Fly in close, toward the bridge, and then bring the augurs down. It's safe."

A relieved chuckle escaped Gavin as the full realization of what was occurring dawned.

Seconds later, the augurs arced from three directions toward the central valley. Only Gavin spied the aircraft that was a speck in the distance.

Below them Leslie, Ryan and Steve sat in position in the science lab. Steve nodded and Leslie clicked the control for the third time. All at once the scene beneath the riders changed again. The green valley stretched below them where it should be—where the forest had just obscured their view. They saw the community gathered at the pavilion.

His heart swelled with love as Leslie emerged from the lab to wave.

As the birds spiraled to Earth, the group on the ground, which included Eena, who had just arrived, waited to hear why they had been called to the pavilion. Watching patiently as the three birds landed, all eyes were riveted on the gorgeous plumage of the largest augur they had ever seen. When the patrollers dismounted, Steve made eye contact with Eena and nodded slightly.

After Gavin announced that the patrollers had lost sight of the valley because of the holographic forest, spontaneous applause burst from the jubilant group.

Gavin put the seldom-used bridle on Phoenix and grabbed the lead to hold the head tightly in place, preventing a swiftly delivered beak attack as Leslie ran into his arms. For several minutes he enjoyed the bliss of connection with this woman he loved and the augur that was his bond-mate. Sandwiched between them, he spied Matoskah, the unassuming magnet for this unlikely convergence of futuristic science and portal to remote antiquity. Emerging at the base of Blue Lake Mountain, the old man approached the gathering.

Gavin gave him a probing look. "Grandfather, we spied a plane."

"I know. The pilot was Nathan."

Shocked reactions. The gravity of the situation slammed Gavin. "He was circling Three Mountains."

"Excellent pilot."

"You saw him?"

"Yes."

"How? Where were you?"

"On Blue Lake Mountain."

"He must have seen you too."

"He saw a friend waving."

"And...."

"And he flew away."

The impact of Matoskah's words sank into the thick silence.

"Then it wasn't the hologram that saved us?"

"The hologram was important." Matoskah walked toward Raiel, a pair of moccasins in hand. "Three Mountains wasn't all that disappeared today."

Eena and Gavin rolled their eyes.

"The opponent.... The opponent disappeared," Eena said softly.

Gavin surveyed the animated gathering, glad to share their happiness. Several months of immersion in this world had transformed the escapee into the activist, and he felt impatient to begin his next mission. But there was no way around the downtime of the coming winter. So, in the meantime, he'd seek the council of that quirky old medicine man and try to make sense of his crazy stories. Likewise, he looked forward to conferring with Eena about strategies to connect with other communities hidden in valleys like Three Mountains. The world beckoned, the hero's journey ahead.